WHAT COULD MISS CLEMENTINA BRADY SAY WHEN SHE FOUND OUT THAT:

—One of the men in her life enjoyed the favors of the most gorgeous courtesan in Paris.

—Another of her prospective mates had under his loving care a most lovely widow.

—And yet a third of her sophisticated suitors had a list of conquests that read like a Regency social directory.

What could Clementina say, especially with her own happiness and the very life of her reckless younger brother hanging in the balance—when she had to say yes to one of them. . . ?

The Incomparable Miss Brady

SIGNET Regency Romances You'll Enjoy

Sheila Walsh
The Incomparable
Miss Brady

A SIGNET BOOK

NEW AMERICAN LIBRARY

TIMES MIRROR

NAL BOOKS ARE AVAILABLE AT QUANTITY DISCOUNTS
WHEN USED TO PROMOTE PRODUCTS OR SERVICES. FOR
INFORMATION PLEASE WRITE TO PREMIUM MARKETING DIVISION,
THE NEW AMERICAN LIBRARY, INC., 1633 BROADWAY,
NEW YORK, NEW YORK 10019.

Published by arrangement with Hutchinson Publishing Group, Ltd.

SIGNET TRADEMARK REG. U.S. PAT. OFF. AND FOREIGN COUNTRIES
REGISTERED TRADEMARK—MARCA REGISTRADA
HECHO EN CHICAGO, U.S.A.

SIGNET, SIGNET CLASSICS, MENTOR, PLUME, MERIDIAN AND NAL BOOKS
are published by The New American Library, Inc.,
1633 Broadway, New York, New York 10019

First Printing, June, 1980

3 4 5 6 7 8 9

PRINTED IN THE UNITED STATES OF AMERICA

❧CHAPTER 1❧

"I wish to see Lord Cadogon," said the young lady very positively.

The footman at the door of Cadogon House sniffed. As a sound it was scarcely audible, but its implied criticism bespoke years of weighing people at a glance. Unaccompanied females were almost invariably trouble, not least when, like this one (she was standing now in cheerful expectation beneath the noble portico that was held aloft by a fine pair of Corinthian columns designed by Sir James Wyatt for the fourth Marquis in 1774), they came hung about with parcels and were so ill conditioned as to be waving off the driver of a shabby hired hack for all the world as though they was on intimate terms! Not genteel enough to be quality down on her luck, he suspected, covertly eyeing the dress of soft brown Merino that was well enough cut, but not of the first star; nor yet some up-from-the-country miss who knew no better. He'd say this one knew exactly what she was about—well up to snuff, in fact. Put him in mind of someone, though he couldn't just call the likeness to mind. Still—he became uncomfortably aware of her lively eye upon him—whosoever she might be, she wasn't rightly the kind you'd care to say no to!

He passed her to the second footman.

William was new to his job and therefore less inclined to be critical. He saw only bright, considering of a rich dark brown, fringed thickly with black lashes. Her eyebrows were straight and black, which surprised him, for beneath the demure bonnet trimmed with brown ribbons surely he caught a tantalizing glimpse of red hair. She smiled at him and he was immediately enslaved.

"The Marquis of Cadogon, if you please." She repeated the request in her light, pleasant voice very firmly, yet with a slight whimsical drawl, as though she viewed the proceedings with a kind of amused cordiality. "Oh, and I wonder if I

1

might set these parcels down here?" She moved toward a
Chinese Chippendale table with clustered legs, set against a
wall most intriguingly fashioned to resemble Italian marble,
and found William already taking the packages from her
clasp and passing them to yet another footman. "Thank you!
I've been shopping in the Pantheon Bazaar," she confided
amiably, "and have purchased a great many more things than
I had meant to! My name is Brady, by the way, Miss Clementina Brady—from Baltimore."

Peebles, His Lordship's butler, coming upon the scene in
time to hear this last, felt a vague pricking behind his collar.
Unlike the first footman, he encountered no difficulty in pin-
pointing the likeness; that oddly attractive combination of
black eyebrows and Titian hair, together with a certain ob-
stinate line to the chin, were so very reminiscent of the old
Marquis!

Peebles found himself carried back across the years to a
day when the whole house had been turned every which way
by that last and most violent of many violent quarrels, with
Lord Cadogon stomping about his room in a thundering rage,
bellowing that no skitterbrained, care-for-nothing daughter of
his was marrying one of those upstart colonials while he had
breath in his body! And the young Lady Melissa, who didn't
have the fine flaming hair of the Durrells for nothing, retort-
ing with equal fury that she for one had no intention of pan-
dering to his outworn, outdated prejudices! On which note,
she had stormed out of her father's room and out of his
house, never to return.

From that day His Lordship had refused to have her name
so much as mentioned in his hearing. Peebles heard later that
Lady Melissa had married her American gentleman and
taken ship the very next week. And here, if he did not mistake the matter, was her daughter—and a regular chip off the
old block!

The somewhat mournful features of the butler revealed
nothing of his inner turmoil, however, as he directed William
to show Miss Brady to the Crimson Salon, a courtesy not
readily accorded to strangers, as William was quick to note.
Mr. Burney, His Lordship's secretary, would be with her
directly, said Peebles, and he would himself apprise the Marquis of her coming.

She thanked him and followed William across a hallway of
noble proportions graced by four fluted columns from
whence an elegant stairway curved away out of view. A pair

of doors were presently being flung open to admit her to a room bathed in mellow sunshine where long curtains moving in a gentle breeze made shimmering patterns across a colorful Turkish rug. Panels of crimson silk lined the walls, setting off a pair of handsome Louis Quinze rosewood commodes standing on either side of the marble chimney piece.

"Oh, but this is quite delightful!" exclaimed Miss Brady enthusiastically.

"Yes, madam." William was loath to leave the object of his admiration, yet was uncertain in the face of his inexperience of the propriety of his staying. While he hesitated, she turned from a seemingly absorbed contemplation of a group of miniatures and met his earnest gaze. A single curl escaping the confines of her bonnet lay provocatively across a wide, unruffled brow, which, even as he watched, became troubled by a tiny furrow of doubt.

"What is he like?" she asked abruptly. "The Marquis, I mean." And seeing at once that he was acutely embarrassed, made a quick impatient gesture. "No, no—I'm sorry! I shouldn't have asked." A smile flickered briefly. "It's just that . . . well, it is quite ridiculous, but I am suddenly all nerves! Will he consent to see me, do you suppose? Should I perhaps have made an appointment?"

William, by now thoroughly intrigued, was anxious to reassure this most unusual young lady. "It's just that you've come at a . . . well, at an unfortunate moment, if you follow my meaning. It's not above ten minutes since as I saw Mr. Trumper coming from His Lordship's room, very red faced, with an armful of cravats."

Miss Brady's brows lifted enquiringly. "Mr. Trumper?"

"His Lordship's valet, madam."

"Ah," she said. "And the neckcloths?"

"No starch, madam. Not a one of them!" Seeing her continuing air of puzzlement, William confided further. "It's the Cadogon knot, madam. No use attempting it without starch, for it don't lie right."

"Good gracious! But a knot is a knot, surely?"

William tried to look shocked, but the absurdity of it struck him suddenly and he grinned.

"Oh, no, madam! The Cadogon is something quite out of the commonplace. Many have tried to master its folds, but nobody it seems has quite His Lordship's way of it."

"I see!" Miss Brady's eyes glinted with amusement and William, all at once aware that he was exceeding the bounds of his position, begged pardon and departed in some confusion.

Left to herself, Clementina Brady wandered about the room, pausing to admire a piece of porcelain here, a portrait there, whilst allowing her thoughts free rein. The vain old roué! So he was still not grown too old to play the dandy! Somehow the knowledge made her feel less nervous of meeting him; absurd, after all, to fear a man who set such store by the placement of his cravat!

Of course it was quite shameful of her to have tried to pump that nice young footman. So terribly crude—and un-English! But then, she wasn't English, and besides, it was as well to know what one must face.

The door opened and closed. She turned to see a gentleman in the uncluttered formality of morning coat and buff-colored unmentionables, one modest fob hanging from a gold chain at his waist, a quizzing glass, his only other adornment, raised in unsmiling scrutiny.

"Miss Brady?" he enquired at last. And then dryly, "Would you oblige me by setting that figurine down on the bureau before you drop it? It is, I believe, quite irreplaceable."

Clementina hastily returned the little French porcelain shepherdess she had been admiring to its place and clasped her hands behind her back in a manner reminiscent of a child caught out in some youthful misdemeanor. Feeling distinctly at a disadvantage without quite knowing why, she sought to retrieve her position.

"You have the advantage of me, sir," she said lightly, and when he made no answer, "I am here to see Lord Cadogon."

"So I was informed. Are you acquainted with His Lordship?"

"Not directly, no."

There was an uncomfortable little pause.

"And your business with Lord Cadogon?"

His interrogation was beginning to irk her; that it was his function to shield her grandfather from importunate strangers in no way excused behavior which, in her view, verged upon arrogance. Well, he should find that a Brady was not to be denied by a mere secretary who chose to give himself airs!

Drawing herself up a little straighter, she gave him back look for look. He would be about five and thirty, she judged; slim, a little above medium height, with light brown hair cropped and arranged in one of the prevailing fashions. The pale, severely classical features yielded nothing of his inner disposition, but the nostrils flaring slightly above a firm-set mouth boded ill, and the eyes, unfriendly as the storm-swept Atlantic of recent memory, were upon her still, awaiting an answer.

She resisted, quite nobly in her opinion, the temptation to give him a set-down. "It is vastly obliging of you to show so much interest, sir," she said pleasantly. "But I would much prefer to say what I have to say to Lord Cadogon personally."

He seemed to sigh and indicated a high-backed sofa upholstered in the same crimson silk as the wall panels. "Then you had best sit down, Miss Brady from Baltimore."

The mockery was so veiled as to be almost imperceptible and as such was impossible to counter without being made to appear foolish. Clementina swallowed her wrath and complied, sitting very straight and working off a little of her irritation by stripping off her gloves and arranging them neatly on her lap beside her reticule, smoothing them with restless fingers.

The secretary took his place on an identical sofa opposite, looking quite infernally at ease. In profile his fine patrician nose lost a little of its symmetry. I bet someone broke it for him, she mused pugnaciously.

"You are newly come to England, of course." He made it sound like an insult.

"Yes," she agreed, determined not to lose her temper.

The conversation languished. Again he sighed and prompted gently. "Well, Miss Brady? I am waiting."

Clementina stared at him, uncertain what he expected of her.

"You had something you wished to say to my head, I believe?"

"*Your* head?" All her good intentions melted away as exasperation set in. "No, indeed . . ." she began, and then something in his face stopped her. In her agitation she sprang to her feet, spilling gloves and reticule onto the floor. Unhurriedly he bent to retrieve them, setting them down on a spider-leg table nearby. After which he stood regarding her with a kind of patient irony.

"*You* are the Marquis of Cadogon?" The question was purely rhetorical and as such he deemed it worthy of no more than a slight inclination of the head. Now that she knew, it seemed absurd that she had not guessed from the first. "Oh, I should have known!" She aired her views with feeling. "You don't behave in the least like anyone's secretary!"

His brows lifted. "So I should hope," he drawled, well aware of her discomfiture. "Nor, as I am sure you will allow, can I convincingly assume the mantle of your grandparent, were I even wishful so to do!"

Her cheeks grew a little pinker. How mortifying to be placed in such a position. She said stiffly, "You must think me quite shatterbrained!"

"Not in the least," he said in a bored voice. "If you will be seated again, we may perhaps have an end to talking at cross purposes."

Clementina longed to set the blame for any confusion squarely at his door; only a strong conviction that he would demolish her accusation caused wiser counsels to prevail.

"You were, I collect, expecting to see the fifth Marquis? Regrettably, he expired more than a twelvemonth since; in the absence of any direct surviving male issue the title devolved upon me." He paused and then added softly, "I trust that clarifies the matter to your satisfaction?"

"I am obliged, sir," she was drawn to retort. "There would have been no misunderstanding, however, had you been more direct at the outset."

"Or had you been less secretive as to the purpose of your visit, perhaps? Ah, but I was forgetting—you took me for my secretary, did you not?"

"It was a perfectly reasonable mistake. Your butler said . . ."

"Quite so. I do not dispute your reasoning, Miss Brady. Mr. Burney does in general deal with unsolicited callers. However," the Marquis seemed quite unaware of her indignation as he fingered the plain black riband of his quizzing glass and fixed her with a pensive stare, "this being a family matter, so to speak, I preferred to deal with it myself."

"So you have known who I was from the very first?"

"Of course." He looked vaguely surprised. "Peebles assured me that you are Melissa's daughter, and I have always found him totally reliable in such matters."

Well, really! But curiosity got the better of indignation. "Did you know my mama?"

"Hardly at all. The relationship was not close and in any case, I was no more than a callow youth when she made her grand gesture of defiance." His glance rested consideringly on Clementina's face. "You are not very like her, I think?"

She had spent too many years in her mother's shadow for comparisons, even from such a quarter, to be odious now. "Not in the least," she said agreeably. And then, with a wry chuckle, "I don't believe Mama ever forgave me for favoring her father! She, of course, remained incredibly beautiful until the day she died!"

"Melissa is dead?" A fleeting frown troubled his brow.

"Yes. She and Papa, both. They drowned in a riverboat accident on the Mississippi during a freak storm, more than four years ago, now."

"I am sorry." Clementina felt his commiseration to be a conventional act of courtesy rather than any expression of real feeling. "A tragic end."

"Yes. But quite typical of them, you know. One could no more conceive of them dying in their beds like ordinary folk than fly to the moon!"

"It sounds as though you were less than heartbroken," observed the Marquis dryly.

This came so close to truth as to fill her again with the terrible sensation of guilt that used to assail her whenever people back home commiserated with her upon her losing both parents at a stroke, and positively weighed her down with coyly sympathetic references to her brave spirit.

"It is awfully hard to break one's heart over the loss of parents, however adorable, however charming, whom one has scarcely known," she now confided with disarming frankness. "They were like butterflies—forever off on some ploy, utterly selfish, utterly wrapped up in each other. The level of one's grief at their passing was, in consequence, less excessive than it might otherwise have been." Her chin lifted. "If that sounds unfilial, then I'm sorry for it."

"My dear Miss Brady, it sounds uncommonly sensible to me, but then I was never cursed with any strong ties of a caring relative! So." An odd note had entered his voice, but she was too preoccupied to hear it. "You were orphaned?"

"Oh, good heavens, no! Or at least only in one sense. The responsibility for our upbringing, such as it was, had always rested with Grandpa Brady," here her voice warmed with affection, "and with my Aunt Seraphina, who is a dear creature, but much too kind and gentle to be the ideal mentor for such wayward and incurably inquisitive young minds! She is just the kind of person, you know, who will never notice when the servants have skimped on the dusting—and if she did, she would not dream of mentioning the fact for fear of hurting their feelings! Matters improved greatly in that respect when I became old enough to take over the running of the household."

The Marquis looked quizzical. "Such ruthlessness! My heart goes out to the unfortunate lady!"

Clementina gave an unexpected gurgle of laughter. "Your sympathy is misplaced, believe me. My dear aunt could not have been happier to surrender her responsibilities!"

"You spoke of *our* upbringing. Do I then take it that there are more of you?"

"I have a brother, four years my junior." Clementina's voice was vibrant with pride. "Now, Patrick *has* inherited Mama's looks. He is just nineteen and *so* handsome, you wouldn't believe!" She saw Lord Cadogon's lip curl slightly. "No, truly. I do try not to be partial, though I must confess that this visit is largely for Patrick's benefit. Baltimore is a very friendly place, but it is a little insular in its attractions and I do think it *so* important for a young man to see as much of the world as he may before choosing his eventual path in life, don't you?"

Since no reply was immediately forthcoming, she took his silence to signify assent and continued. "London, of course, was an obvious choice. I had heard Mama speak of it, and of her father—she never bore him any lasting malice, you know. It was simply that her pride would not permit her to make the first move—or so Aunt Seraphina used to tell us."

"Oh, we Durrells are a selfish, stiff-necked brood, I'm told. Comes of being one of your back-to-the-Plantagenets families, no doubt. Nothing like a royal bastard or two in your lineage to stiffen the backbone and summon up the blood! The old man was every bit as obdurate as his daughter."

Clementina was fascinated by this unexpected insight into the workings of the aristocratic mind. "Yes, I know. But I didn't see why the embargo should extend to his grandchildren. Besides, I was curious to know him. I had always enjoyed the closest of relationships with Grandpa Brady. Indeed, I don't believe he would have managed his affairs without me after he suffered his stroke . . ."

She saw again that look of faint incredulity. No doubt she was confirming his opinion of her as a thoroughly managing female. Well, she cared nothing for his opinion, after all! It did not, however, prevent a note of defiance from creeping into her voice as she concluded, "When he died, we all felt his loss deeply and it occurred to me that the time had come when we should at least make a push to heal the breach with our maternal grandparent."

"How very enterprising of you!"

She ignored the sarcasm. "Also, Patrick is just at an age when the influence of someone older—a man of experience, for preference—would be most beneficial."

"I don't doubt it for one moment if he is at all like you," said His Lordship cuttingly. "However, you appear to have acted precipitately, as I would hazard is your wont. You would have done much better to seek your man of experience among your friends in Baltimore—or at the very least to have written before embarking upon what, in the event, has proved to be a wasted journey."

"Oh, not wasted, surely? It is a disappointment, of course—a small setback, if you like—but I believe all may yet work out splendidly. London is so much more elegant than Baltimore. We may very likely decide to stay for a while if only we can find a suitable house. The hotel is very comfortable, but my aunt misses the more homely touches. Perhaps you might advise me?"

The Marquis rose unhurriedly and stood looking down at her, a small frown furrowing his brow. Clementina met the look with interest; it was that nose, she decided, which gave him such an air of condescension! As though her frank appraisal unsettled him, he turned at last and strode across to the window, every inch the noble lord. A cluster of indiscriminating sunbeams came squeezing through the muslin curtains to play irreverently about his head.

Without looking round he said abruptly, "Is it money?"

A very real sense of outrage robbed Clementina momentarily of speech. And then, quite suddenly, the absurdity of the situation overcame her. There was no more than the slightest quiver in her drawled observation: "I'm not sure what that question is meant to imply, Marquis, but it sounds remarkably like an insult!"

He swung round, a tide of color running up under his skin. His deprecating glance, sweeping over the brown Merino dress, spoke volumes; his voice grated.

"Does it, indeed, ma'am? Simply, then—I am fully aware that you must have entertained expectations . . ."

"Expectations?" She allowed a small silence to elapse and then, as though comprehension had suddenly dawned: "Oh, you mean from my grandfather's estate? No, sir, we had no such expectations, I promise you. And if you should be imagining for one moment that we are like to prove an embarrassment to you, then you may be easy."

"You mistake the matter, ma-am . . ."

"Had my grandfather been alive," she swept on, disregarding his interpolation, "things might well have been otherwise. I had certainly meant to apply to him for that degree of patronage which I consider to be our just entitlement. However, I quite appreciate that it would be unfair to demand as much of you."

Recovering his aplomb, he inclined his head with sardonic precision. "Thank you. You overwhelm me."

"Though I'm bound to say," she concluded, "that it wouldn't hurt you to put yourself about—to at least take Patrick up—perhaps even introduce us into society a little."

"You are of course entitled to your opinion, Miss Brady, wrong-headed though it is. No," he lifted a staying hand, "pray allow me to continue. You asked me earlier to advise you. In general it is not a practice I favor, but for you I will make an exception. Have your holiday by all means, Miss Brady." Here his voice hardened. "But afterwards it will be much better if you go home."

"Better for whom, Marquis?" she enquired with a mildness that belied the martial gleam in her eye. "Better for you, perhaps?"

"Hardly, ma-am, since I go north next week and thereafter to Paris, where I shall make an indefinite stay."

"Paris!" she echoed, and her irritation gave way to an appreciation of his tactics. Being a very practical young woman, she saw little merit in hankering after lost causes, so she chuckled and said with gentle malice, "How very fortuitous that your removal will deny you the opportunity of lending us your support!"

His eyes glinted with answering mockery. "I doubt I should have done so in any case. I hold that, whenever possible, people should succeed by their own efforts."

"What an odiously selfish man you are," Clementina observed pleasantly.

"Of course. Did I not say earlier? It runs in the blood."

"So you did. How remiss of me." She eyed him consideringly. "So you hope we will go meekly home like sheep?"

"My dear Miss Brady, you credit me with too much interest in your affairs. I have made my views known to you; that, I think, discharges any obligation I might reasonably be expected to entertain in your behalf. How you choose to conduct your affairs from now on is a matter of complete indifference to me!"

"Good," she said briskly, pulling on her gloves. "Because some of this family's blood flows in my veins, too. Now, I will bid you good-day and trouble you no further." She stood up. "Thank you, Marquis, for giving me so much of your valuable time."

"Think nothing of it, Miss Brady. It has been an interesting encounter."

She grinned, unabashed. "Yes, hasn't it?" After which exchange of pleasantries she turned to pick up her reticule and in so doing her eye chanced upon his cravat. "Oh," she mused. "Is that the Cadogon knot?"

"It is." His eye narrowed. "But how does Miss Brady from Baltimore come to know of such things?"

It would not do to incriminate the sympathetic young footman. She said airily, "Oh, I guess I heard someone speak of it. It *is* much discussed, I believe."

Lord Cadogon's probing eyes raked her face and met only limpid innocence. "You sound disapproving."

"Not at all," she said. "I'm sure it's very nice."

"Nice!"

"Yes," she agreed demurely. "Though, of course, I know very little of such things."

He said no more, but she rather thought she had pricked his vanity. The thought gave her pleasure.

"You came in a hack, I believe." He pulled the bell rope. "My carriage will convey you back to your hotel."

"There is no need, sir. It is a beautiful day. If you will be so obliging as to direct me to Piccadilly, I mean to walk."

The door opened to admit Peebles.

"Tell Grimble to bring the town carriage round," said His Lordship as though she had not spoken.

"Very good, my lord." Peebles, in turning away, chanced to intercept a shaft of fury from the young lady. Definitely a chip off the old block!

"You are exceeding your obligation, sir," said Clementina stiffly. "I have no wish to avail myself of your patronage! I prefer to walk."

The Marquis waited until the door had closed behind Peebles. His voice was cutting. "And I prefer that you do not," said he. "I cannot claim to know the rules governing such behavior in Baltimore, Miss Brady, but here in London a young lady does not leave a gentleman's house on foot and unattended."

As he spoke the Marquis picked up the reticule, slipped the braided handle neatly over her wrist, and with an air of implacable determination escorted her into the hall. Clementina was uncomfortably aware that in one polite sentence he had somehow managed to damn her breeding *and* her want of social graces, along with the whole structure of American society. She felt the initiative slipping away from her, but was not about to concede.

"I am obliged to you for setting me right," she said with deceptive amiability. "Back home, of course, I am so well known that I may go about very much as I please without occasioning any comment. However, I would not wish to offend anyone's sensibilities! It will be a simple enough matter for Joshua to accompany me in future."

"Joshua?"

"Our young Black."

"A slave, Miss Brady?"

"Does that shock you, Marquis? It need not do so." They had reached the hall, where her eye was at once taken by the sight of several footmen standing like graven images, not betraying by so much as a flicker that they were alive; imagine having to live alongside so much rigid formality! Clementina felt a sudden wave of nostalgia for the friendly informality of home. "Joshua is quite as well off as any paid servant—better than most, in fact, for he was born into our family and is tied as much by bonds of affection as any notion of servitude."

"Then he is fortunate indeed." Politely. "And now, if you will be so good as to give me your direction," he said, "I will instruct Grimble where he is to take you."

"We are at the Pulteney Hotel. It is in Piccadilly, overlooking that charming park where the deer and cattle browse." She saw his eyebrows lift. "Oh, come now, you surely cannot object to our choice of hotel? We were specially recommended to it and it really does seem quite unexceptionable."

The footman, at that moment engaged in opening the front door, looked at William, who had reappeared carrying her parcels; they both seemed to be seized with a choking fit, immediately stifled upon meeting Lord Cadogon's steely gaze.

Not a quiver disturbed the beautifully shaped lower lip as His Lordship agreed blandly that the Pulteney was generally thought to be unexceptionable. It was, after all, where the

Czar of Russia's sister, the Grand Duchess of Oldenburg, chose to stay during the Peace Celebrations in 1814. She even persuaded her brother to join her there rather than take up his prepared staterooms in St. James's Palace, much to the embarrassment of the Regent, whom she disliked intensely. The Marquis did not quite know why he told her this anecdote, unless it was to hear again that infectious gurgle of laughter.

"Well, there you are then—it is obviously very respectable and you may wash your hands of us with a clear conscience, knowing we are safely housed!" She held out her hand, good humor restored. "Good-bye, Marquis."

He regarded the neatly gloved hand in silence, a slight frown between his brows. When he looked up, it was with a curious intentness. "Miss Brady, I do not believe . . . I cannot impress upon you too strongly that London is not in the least like Baltimore! It can be ruinously expensive and sets many traps for the uninitiated. Are you perfectly certain you know what you are about?"

Goodness! He was surely not beginning to display belated symptoms of humanity! Clementina withdrew her hand gently but firmly, and gave him her most confident smile. "Perfectly certain," she said. "And if I *should* come unstuck, I will engage not to involve you, sir."

As Cadogon House closed its doors upon her departure, she was quite unaware of the controversy raging belowstairs. Her looks precluded any suggestion that she was not related to the late Marquis; it was the nature of the relationship that absorbed their interest. Was she indeed Lady Melissa's daughter as Peebles had so stoutly maintained, or one of the old man's by-blows turned up to plague the new master?

Much the same question exercised the mind of Mr. Fabian Pengallan on the following day as he bore the Marquis company on one of his regular visits to Jackson's famous Boxing Saloon in Bond Street. Having long since established his own limitations in the execution of the various martial arts, Mr. Pengallan was more than content to watch his friend's strenuous workout without experiencing the smallest degree of envy.

Miss Brady would have owned herself astonished had she been privileged to observe how competently Lord Cadogon handled himself against the famous ex-pugilist.

"Displays well, don't he?" Mr. Pengallan was moved to remark in his lazy way when the bout was at an end. He grinned. "Tell you what, Jackson, damned if I've seen anyone pop one in over your guard quite so neatly!"

"His Lordship is always looking to take the lead, sir," acknowledged Jackson. "In fact, I disremember when I've seen a gentleman so uncommonly fast on his feet!" He shook his head regretfully. "If only matters had been otherwise, my lord, I'd have given a lot to've had the handling of you in the ring!"

"Reckon we'd clean out the Fancy, do you?" drawled Cadogon and reached for a towel. "Well, Fabian—do you care to stand up for a round or two with a might-have-been champion before I go and change?"

"Not on your life!" Mr. Pengallan looked visibly shaken. "I'd as lief face Jackson here any day of the week—liefer, in fact! He's one as 'ld make allowances for a fellow being bellows to mend after the first onslaught!"

The Marquis eyed his friend's yellow calf-clingers, his gleaming hessians, and the exquisite set of his coat and, meeting a hooded, half-wary grin, exclaimed, "Shame! He'd do better to run you into the ground. I would!"

He laughed as his remark drew from the acknowledged Corinthian a small shudder, and sauntered away, rubbing himself briskly with the towel.

"This American chit," ventured Mr. Pengallan, when they were presently strolling down Bond Street on their way to Whites. "Could be a touch awkward, Dominic—dirty dishes and all that! Not good ton, y'know! Anyhow, it all sounds dashed smokey to me—I mean, not coming on the scene until after old Jasper'd turned up his toes for good!"

Not receiving any answer, he turned aside to see the Marquis in frowning thought. "Not one to cast a blight, dear old fellow—daresay you've already considered the obvious?" He coughed delicately, apologetically. "Only they do say old Jasper's increase is scattered far and wide!"

The Marquis had a swift mental image of bright candid eyes set beneath uncompromisingly straight black brows; and of a single, flagrant red curl, which, for one moment just as she was leaving, had aroused in him a quite inexplicable urge to remove her bonnet in order to release its fellows. It was not the first time he had been prey to this fantasy since yesterday!

What, he hazarded now, would Miss Clementina Brady say to being passed off as one of her grandfather's side-slips?

Quite a lot, no doubt! He had a notion it would amuse her—she had at times, as he had discovered, a disconcerting turn of humor! He gave a sudden crack of laughter.

"Calm yourself, Fabian. Miss Brady is mettlesome, self-opinionated and brash, but she is no come-by-chance. That much I'd vouch for. Whether she will prove troublesome, however, remains to be seen."

❦CHAPTER 2❦

Clementina was amused to note the deference that her prestigious return to the Pulteney evoked in marked contrast to her departure earlier, when the pudding-faced porter had accorded her no more than a disdainful bow in answer to her cheerful "good morning." Now, as Lord Cadogon's town carriage bearing the distinctive Cadogon crest drew up before the hotel's impressive portico with its stone pillars and pretty bow windows and set her down at the steps, he was grown almost obsequious in his attentions.

Inside, she found all slumbering in deserted grandeur—everyone, with the exception of a few lackeys, presumably abed or out, or partaking of luncheon. In the wake of her recent confrontation, she found the hotel's aura of opulent respectability more than usually stifling and longed to shatter it by shouting "fire!" She reproved herself instantly, but the feeling of restiveness persisted and halfway up the second pair of stairs she fell prey to a lesser temptation. Picking up her skirts, she took the last few steps at an indecorous run, swung round exuberantly at the top, and cannoned into a gentleman making his way down.

There was a muttered curse; she was instantly seized in a merciless grip and looking up encountered blue eyes narrowed under hooded lids, which widened into enigmatic appraisal as the gentleman realized that he was not under attack. The fingers relaxed their grip and she was steadied and released.

"Mille pardons, madam," he said punctiliously. "Forgive my clumsiness. You are not injured?"

Clementina, endeavoring to collect her disordered wits and the use of her tongue, which had become most awkwardly tied, and feeling exceedingly foolish into the bargain, received a confused impression of a quite distractingly handsome face, curling black hair and a voice with a disturbing hint of *je ne sais quoi.*

"Oh, no!" she gasped, experiencing a breathlessness not entirely due to her exertions. "You are too generous, monsieur, when it is plain that the fault is entirely mine. I was not . . . paying attention to where I was going!"

The gentleman bowed. "Please! Let us not apportion blame." He was regarding her in a way that precipitated the tendency to blush that had assailed her from childhood. She knew herself for a level-headed young woman with few pretensions to being other than moderately well looking, yet now she found her mouth curving in pleasurable anticipation.

The blue eyes caressed her for a moment longer, lingered with something like regret over the brown Merino dress, and then, with another of those punctilious bows, he was gone.

Clementina watched him out of sight, relinquishing her daydream with reluctance. Then, laughing aloud at its very absurdity, she continued on her way. When she presently entered the spacious second-floor suite with its windows looking out over Green Park, she was humming cheerfully. In the sun-filled salon she stripped off her gloves and tossed them carelessly onto a walnut bureau, loosed the ribbons of her bonnet, removed it with a flourish, sent it after the gloves, and ran liberating fingers through a crop of tight red curls.

A towering young Negro, showing a wide, white-toothed grin, came soft footed to collect the discarded garments.

Two pairs of eyes watched Clementina with unconcealed interest.

"You are looking remarkably pleased with yourself," said Patrick. "I take it you were able to see our grandfather."

"No." For some inexplicable reason, she declined to mention her encounter with the fascinating Frenchman.

"He wouldn't meet you." Aunt Seraphina laid her tambour frame aside with a sigh—her movements, like her nature, gentle and somewhat indecisive. Seraphina Westbury had married for love at seventeen—a circumstance as unusual as it was romantic; at eighteen she was a widow; a blossoming so tragically brief that although initially distraught, she had emerged from her grief seemingly untouched, if a little vaguer than before. She had returned to the big, rambling house overlooking Baltimore harbor that was home, and with a kind of quiet thankfulness she had resumed an uncomplicated life with her father and her elder brother, Sean, as though she had never been away. When, after a visit to England, Sean had returned with his beautiful wayward English bride, she had stayed on to keep house for them in her haphazard fashion, and when the children came along to love them with as fierce an intensity as if they had been her own.

In consequence time had touched her but lightly. At five and forty, she looked too ridiculously young to be anyone's aunt. The sunlight, playing across the Hepplewhite sofa near the window where she sat, illumined an unlined face framed by hair that, though it lacked the guinea-gold brightness of youth, was still softly fair and quite untouched by gray beneath a fluted muslin cap. Her only concession to age was a pair of spectacles that she occasionally wore, having been short-sighted from her earliest days.

She now shook her head regretfully. "I feared it would be so. If you remember, dear, I told you . . ." It was the nearest she was ever likely to come to a reproof.

Patrick, however, was less inclined to be charitable. "You should have had me along with you," he said bluntly, rising from a confidante where he had been lounging in what he considered to be a languid, man-of-the-world fashion, idly flicking through the pages of the *Gentleman's Magazine.*

Clementina regarded him with a partiality born of pride and affection. He was as tall and straight as a young sapling, and every feature that in her scarcely rose above the commonplace in Patrick was perfection. They were of similar coloring, yet where her hair was an unequivocal red, his was of a rich dark auburn; where her eyes were brown, his were of a deep cerulean blue set in a face that might have been sculpted by Michelangelo. At this moment, however, the perfect features were marred by a scowl.

"This way you have of thinking yourself equal to any situation is all very well, but it don't always do," he drawled. "I may not have the advantage of your years, but I *am* a man. He wouldn't have denied me so easily, I can tell you!"

Clementina was obliged to hide a smile; in Mama's frequent absences, she far more than Seraphina had been responsible for guiding his early steps and had always encouraged him to think for himself, but she knew far better than he that, hampered by his present awkward transition from boyhood to manhood, he would have been reduced to incoherence by the Marquis in a trice.

"I did not see our grandfather," she said gently, "because he died last year."

"Oh dear!" said Aunt Seraphina. "How very unfortunate! And distressing, too, of course . . ." she added hastily, with her usual charity. Well, I mean . . . one didn't *know* him, except by repute. Still, on reflection, that was perhaps not entirely his fault, and one ought not to think ill of his shabby behavior in consequence . . ."

"I did, however, see the new Marquis," her niece continued ruthlessly. "Quite the most self-opinionated, condescending creature you can possibly imagine! You will be pleased to know that he neither feels it incumbent upon himself to in any way redress the shortcomings of his predecessor, nor has he the least desire to pursue our acquaintance!"

"Good gracious!"

"And I'll wager I know why." Patrick accused her with brotherly candor. "You flew up into the boughs—gave him one of your famous 'set-downs.' "

"Oh, my dear, you didn't!" Seraphina Westbury, being by nature a pliant creature, had never quite come to terms with her niece's more dominant spirit. "You can, on occasion, be a little more outspoken than may be thought seemly, you know . . ."

Patrick hooted.

"Stuff!" Clementina said airily. "I'm sure I made every effort to be conciliating, though His Lordship *did* have a few antiquated notions upon which I was obliged to set him right!" She ignored her aunt's look of reproach, her voice growing warm as she recalled fresh grievances. "He even had the temerity to suggest—more, I suspect, in his own interest than ours, for he very much dislikes giving advice—that we should return whence we came with all possible speed!"

"Really?" Just for an instant the image of their comfortable home back in Baltimore swam before Mrs. Westbury in a hazy cloud of recollection. She sighed. "He does sound a very disagreeable man, to be sure. You don't think, perhaps . . . in the circumstances . . . ?" And then she saw the two obstinately set chins and her dream faded.

"No!" cried brother and sister in unison.

"No crabby old lord's going to drive me away!" declared Patrick.

"Oh, Lord Cadogon isn't old—in fact, *you* would doubtless consider him to be the very paragon of perfection, though for my part I can think very little of a man who is so finicky about his cravats! I am persuaded that we shall manage very much better without him!"

Having thus disposed of the Marquis, Clementina felt considerably better and was able to apply herself with enthusiasm to the cold collation that Joshua at that moment announced. Never having been given to idleness when there were things to be done, she planned next to visit Hoare's Bank at Temple Bar. She asked Patrick if he would care to bear her company, but he declined, avowing a bank to be a paltry sort of place to spend one's time when there were so many more exciting places to visit. He rather thought he might step out on his own a little later. Her aunt also declined and so, with Lord Cadogon's strictures still fresh in her ear and determined that her behavior should not give rise to adverse comment, she took Joshua for chaperon.

At Temple Bar she spent a most satisfactory hour in the company of a genial, fatherly gentleman who proved immensely helpful in any number of ways. She parted from him on a most agreeable note with her business all in hand and knowing a great deal more about how to go on in London than when she had arrived.

She returned to the hotel in time for tea to find her aunt alone, Patrick having stepped out to see some of the sights of London.

"He spoke of going to Astley's Amphitheatre," said Mrs. Westbury, "and I don't suppose he can come to any harm there, do you, dear? To be honest, I was relieved when he suggested it, for the poor boy has had the fidgets all day."

Clementina smiled absently, sitting at the table and propping her elbows in a most unladylike fashion. Seraphina Westbury watched with a certain degree of apprehension as she began to rub the side of her nose with one finger in a thoughtful way, for the familiar mannerism usually preceded the announcement of some new and outlandish scheme designed to involve them all in considerable upheaval.

"I have been wondering," she said, "how you would feel if we were to cut short our stay here—go on to France, or maybe Italy?"

Mrs. Westbury managed to swallow her initial dismay. "But why, dear? We have hardly seen anything of London yet."

"Oh, I know—and I don't mean that we should leave immediately! But, well, you know how we were obliged to put back the date of our departure on account of poor Millie Trenchard's wedding . . ?"

"I don't know why you will keep calling Millie *poor!*" said her aunt. "I'm sure I never saw a more radiant bride!"

"I daresay." Clementina grinned. "But only imagine being tied for life to George Soames, who is a dead bore!"

Mrs. Westbury tried to look severe, but, remembering the very stolid young man, could only say gently, "The thing is, dear, Millie does not consider George in the least boring. *Love looks not with the eyes, but with the mind,* you know. I daresay you will find it so yourself when you come to fall in love . . ."

"Very likely, but as I have no plans to do so at present, we may safely abandon *that* argument! I only mentioned Millie's wedding because the delay made us much later arriving in London than we had intended, and that nice Mr. Beaver at the bank—extraordinary how like their names some people are!—explained to me that we must expect to find London very quiet, as the Season is over and everyone gone to the country or to Brighton with the Prince Regent. I do think it exceedingly shabby of Lord Cadogon not to have mentioned as much. No wonder he was looking smug!"

"But does it really matter, Clemmy? About London being quiet, I mean?"

"Perhaps not, though it might be a little dull, don't you think? Whereas, if we did all the other things we had intended first and then came back to London . . ."

Clementina saw her aunt's face and flew at once to sit beside her on the sofa, taking her hands. "Oh, dearest, we don't *have* to. Only you did say how wonderful it would be to visit Rome and Florence, and Paris, too. Remember how *green* you were when Millicent Bolton came back from Paris so full of having seen all the treasures that had been assembled by Napoleon in the Palace of the Louvre?" She smiled, not aware that there was in her eyes a beseeching look. "Do you now hate the idea so dreadfully?"

The older woman returned the smile, albeit a little weakly. "No, no, dear—not hate! It would be excessive to say *hate,* for I should indeed like to see all those beautiful things! It is just the constant traveling and not being acquainted with anyone. So strange! And with foreigners in particular, you see, I should not know how to go on."

The plaintiveness was quite unconscious and, as such, smote Clementina to the core. "Yes, I do see, indeed I do! And I see, too, that I am being quite appallingly selfish. You have been subjected to more than enough racketing around for the present. We will stay here, or perhaps take a little house by the sea. What do you say to that?"

It was a tempting prospect, if only Seraphina could be convinced that it was what Clemmy really wanted. She swallowed and said valiantly, "Dear Clemmy, you are too good, but I beg you won't heed my silly megrims. You and Patrick are everything to me . . . if to be in London, or Florence or wherever, is what you wish . . . then I daresay I shall contrive to adapt myself!"

"Well, we shall see." Clementina pressed an impulsive kiss on the petal-soft, unlined cheek, feeling as she almost always did, considerably older than her gentle aunt. "You are a darling and we don't deserve you. And I daresay Patrick will want to stay in London, you know. But whatever we decide, I promise I won't let you be teased. In the meantime, there are lots of ways to make you feel more the thing, for it's my belief that you have grown quite mopey, shut away in this stuffy room!"

Clementina stood up, brisk and businesslike again. "We begin this evening. I hope Patrick does not mean to be late back or he will overset all my plans." And as her aunt looked suitably puzzled, "I mean to take you both to the theatre."

"This evening?" The words came out on a kind of sigh, Aunt Seraphina looking for all the world like a child who has been offered the first choice in a box of sweetmeats.

"This very evening. I consulted Mr. Beaver, and upon his advice I have taken a box at Drury Lane, where Mr. Edmund Kean is playing in *Othello*. I am told he is very fine!"

"Oh, but . . ."

"No *buts*," said Clementina firmly. "All is arranged. I know it is one of the things you most wish to do, and if you mean to tell me that you have nothing suitable to wear for such an occasion, you will oblige me to call you absurd, which you are not! You can wear that pretty gray taffety gown with the matching silk turban you had for Mrs. Brandon's Sally's 'come-out' in Baltimore last summer. Remember how greatly it was admired?" She grinned. "You may even wear your spectacles!"

This was a concession, indeed! Mrs. Westbury needed no further convincing.

Patrick, too, coming in full of his afternoon's adventures, with which he regaled them without pause during dinner, thought the theatre a capital notion.

They must go to Astley's Royal Circus, too, he insisted—the most amazing combination of drama and spectacle, performing animals, clowns, and trick riding, such as they wouldn't believe! His account became somewhat garbled and incoherent from time to time, but they rather gathered that all else had paled into insignificance before the vision of an enchanting angel, a divinity, who had danced like some gauzy, roseate dream creature upon the back of a pure-white stallion!

He had also made the acquaintance of a very pleasant young man, Alfred Bennett, who was like to prove a most agreeable friend. "He's a famous fellow, I can tell you!" he confided with an eagerness that made Clementina smile. "Up to every rig in London! He's offered to show me all the sights—Madame Tussaud's Waxworks and the Royal Menagerie at the Tower, and there is a place called the White Horse Cellar where the coaches depart for Brighton!"

He neglected to mention Mr. Bennett's promise to take him also to Gentleman Jackson's Boxing Salon, and to the Daffy Club to blow a cloud with all the Corinthians, together with many less innocent pursuits. He had a notion that Clemmy might turn sticky if she knew. Females, said Mr. Bennett, by their very nature were apt to shrink from the merest allusion to such kick-ups! A remark that only served to show that he had never known anyone in the least like Clemmy! Still, for all that, it might be more prudent to keep her in ignorance.

Patrick's exuberance set the mood for the evening, although a successful outcome was never in doubt. The number of carriages converging upon Drury Lane, with all the accompanying hullabaloo of grinding wheels and arguments between postillions and coachmen as they maneuvered their vehicles into position, moved Clementina to remark dryly that if this was London out of season, it must be the saddest squeeze ever when the fashionable world was in residence!

But Seraphina Westbury accepted it all with the awed innocence of a child; from her first glimpse of the theatre's impressive portico until the moment she took her seat, she exclaimed in turn over the building's noble rotunda, its splendid foyers, and the unexpected magnificence of the audience, who thronged the many graceful stairways leading to the circular auditorium in a glittering, chattering array of color.

"Even if the play should prove a disappointment, I shall not feel in the least deprived," she confided happily.

The play, however, proved to be all and more than she had hoped for; by the end of the first act she was utterly under Mr. Kean's spell.

"Such an ugly little man!" She sighed. "But what passion—such a throbbing voice, such fierceness of eye and gesture!" She shivered deliciously. "One is scarcely able to tear one's gaze from those tragic black eyes!"

Clementina, both amused and pleased to see her aunt so obviously enjoying the drama, entered enthusiastically into the spirit of the occasion, agreeing solemnly that Mr. Kean's thundering voice was such as to reduce one to a fearful tremble. "And yet he may just as easily melt one's bones with devastating sweetness!"

Even Patrick allowed it to be a moving performance, although he seemed to be far more interested in scanning the auditorium, and from his occasional bursts of admiration Clementina deduced that he had far rather have been down in the pit among the ridiculous pinch-waisted, posturing dandies than sitting sedately in a box!

It was during the interlude between the second and third acts, when Mrs. Westbury was lost in admiration of the charming little Chinese canopies that adorned the first tier of dress boxes, that Patrick leaned forward suddenly.

"Good Lord! I say, Clemmy, look! In the box opposite, just to the left of that pillar . . ."

Clementina followed his direction and her cheeks grew unaccountably warm, for looking across at her with that enigmatic smile was her handsome Frenchman! He inclined his head in recognition.

"Who is it, dear?" asked her aunt, peering short-sightedly.

"Jefferson Pride!" snorted Patrick in disgust. "And what's more, he's seen us."

Clementina came to with a start and moved her gaze with reluctance to a man who sat nearby. Jefferson Pride! An insufferably smug, toadying young man who had traveled from Baltimore with them on the *Mary Rose*—a circumstance that he could be relied upon to make the most of now that he had seen them. But he redeemed himself almost immediately in her eyes by turning to address himself to the Frenchman; a moment more and both men rose, together with a third, and left their box.

"Mrs. Westbury, ma-am! Delighted! And Miss Brady—Patrick, too! Well, now—isn't this the most tremendous luck!" Jefferson Pride's bulk filled the doorway, his unctuous presence engulfing them; without the least abatement in his flow of commonplaces, he turned aside to admit the two other gentlemen. "Ladies, may I present to you Monsieur le Comte de Tourne and Sir James Barbarry."

The smug voice faded from Clementina's ears as the Comte carried her fingers reverently to his lips. She had never been greeted in quite that way before and found it a not unpleasing sensation.

"I am very pleased to meet you, Comte," she murmured, half-amused.

"And I, you, mademoiselle." The beautifully drawn features registered the extent of his pleasure, his curiously intense, hooded eyes said something more. She was surprised to find herself wishing desperately that she had found the time to purchase a new dress; perhaps it was the presence of so many exquisitely dressed women that made her suddenly feel a positive dowd, for until this moment she had always considered her blue silk more than becoming.

"You will recall, Comte, my telling you about these good people." Jefferson Pride was boring on. "Our journey across the Atlantic was a most enjoyable experience, was it not, Miss Brady?"

It was most unkind in her to wish to put him down, but she found his ingratiating manner quite nauseating. She flashed Patrick a quick, mischievous glance before saying cordially, "It was certainly memorable, but enjoyable, Mr. Pride? Surely you cannot so soon have forgotten that last week of squalls when you were, as I recall, extremely unwell?"

Patrick's eyes twinkled, the Comte looked quizzical, and Mr. Pride flushed with discomposure. He had not at all wished to be reminded of that week, culminating as it had in the humiliating moment when he had crawled out on deck at last, more dead than alive, to find Miss Brady and her brother in the highest good spirits and boasting, with what he could only consider a want of sensibility, that they had enjoyed the rough weather excessively!

Aunt Seraphina, reproachful of her niece's lack of charity, spoke to him with extra kindness, though she could not like him, and with the facility of the truly pompous he was immediately full of himself again. Clementina caught the Comte's eye and smiled ruefully. His shoulders lifted in an elegant little shrug of sympathy.

Her aunt was really looking very well this evening in her taffety gown and it soon became clear that Sir James Barbarry, a rather mannered, red-faced gentleman a little older than the other two, thought so, too. Clementina was amused to observe how his marked attentions brought a becoming flush to her aunt's cheek, though every now and then his glance returned to herself with a curious fixedness.

"I am giving a small soirée on Friday evening." Sir James cleared his throat self-consciously. "A lot of government people, y'know—but I believe you might enjoy it. It would give me very much pleasure to welcome you as my guests."

"Why, how very kind," said Clementina.

"You will consent to come, Miss Brady?" begged the Comte with flattering insistence. "My mother is in London with me and I should very much like to make her known to you."

Patrick almost choked.

"You will consent to come, Miss Brady?" he mimicked with devastating accuracy when they were back at the Pulteney. He snatched up his aunt's lace shawl from a chair arm and flourished it as a handkerchief, bowing and posturing before Clementina.

"Idiot!" But she blushed even as she shared his laughter.

"Lord, I nearly died! I tell you what, Clemmy—if you were on the catch for a husband, I reckon you could very quickly bring your so-handsome Comte up to scratch!"

"Patrick!" Mrs. Westbury was shocked. "Such a coarse expression!"

"Anyway, he is not my Comte, and I wish you would not talk such arrant nonsense," said Clementina dismissively.

But later that night, lying in bed with her hands clasped behind her head on the soft, downy pillow and sleep a long way off, she found her thoughts returning to the Comte with disturbing frequency. She had never been of a romantical disposition, her life having been much too full and busy to admit of any disruption. Falling in love—and out of love—seemed to be the most absorbing of preoccupations amongst her friends and had led her on more than one occasion to laughingly deplore the ease with which they, one by one, succumbed to the fatal lure of matrimony. But had she, perhaps, in consequence grown a little staid? Surely not.

The Comte had not looked at her as though he found her staid; it had been a surprisingly pleasant experience to find herself the object of such singular attention, though of course it was not to be taken seriously! Still, it more than made up for Lord Cadogon's scathing, if unspoken, denigration of her appearance, which had left her pride smarting. True, fashion had never exercised her mind to any great extent, but though she had always eschewed anything of a showy nature, her dresses had always been commissioned from the finest seamstress in Baltimore, and she was used to being considered very well, even elegantly, turned out, as befitted the granddaughter of Michael Brady.

But a very short time in London, the visit to the theatre, her meeting with the Comte—all these together had filled her quite inexplicably with the most frivolous notions. She was, after all, but four and twenty—not too late, surely, to cast her bonnet over the windmill? The idea, shocking at first, very quickly became a challenge, filling her with a heady exhilaration. She could never be a "Beauty" in the accepted sense, but it would be amusing to try to attain a certain distinction. The common-sense Clementina rose like a spectre to condemn what could only be accounted pure folly, but it was already too late. A few months, only, she promised herself recklessly; twelve at the most. And then I will be sensible again!

With the morning her resolve was undiminished and a few discreet enquiries were sufficient to set all in train. Patrick, upon hearing of her new resolve, was quick to voice his own dissatisfaction and, unwilling though she might be to admit of any flaw in her brother's appearance, her own observations had obliged her to acknowledge that his dress, though neat, lacked that degree of elegance that would set him apart.

Accordingly, Patrick was dispatched to Weston in Conduit Street in spite of Alfred Bennett's assurances that he knew a man who could turn him out in prime twig for a fraction of the great man's charges. Clementina, having met Alfred Bennett and found him enormously likeable, was nonetheless of the opinion that a young man whose collar points were so high as to impede the easy movement of his head, and who sported striped Cossack trousers, a waistcoat of lurid design, and a bright yellow coat, could not be accounted a reliable judge of a tailor. She was, however, unable to prevent Mr.

Bennett's accompanying Patrick and was obliged to put her trust in Mr. Weston.

She then bundled a rather bewildered Aunt Seraphina into bonnet and pelisse and carried her off in a hack to the show-rooms of one Madame Fanchon, who was, she had been assured, the best, the most fashionable, the most renowned of London's modistes. One glance at the richly carpeted room, with its little gilded chairs and profusion of long graceful mirrors, was sufficient to convince Clementina that she was also, in all probability, the most wickedly expensive! Still, if one were contemplating a radical change in one's image, one should not boggle at a little expense! So she dismissed Aunt Seraphina's faint gasp and her murmured: "Clemmy dear! Do you not think perhaps . . ." with an airy laugh and turned to greet the great Mme. Fanchon, who appeared at that moment, all smiles and graciousness.

Clementina explained her needs and Madame's graciousness expanded further; no doubt the prospect of a valued new client at a time when business was at its lowest ebb appeared as a gift from heaven, thought Clementina in some amusement, as Mme. Fanchon was kind enough (and shrewd enough) to compliment her upon her figure and the excellence of her carriage. Miss Brady had also, if she might venture to comment, a quality of assurance rare in so *young* a lady! For her, the most dashing styles were allowable—style was everything! They need not concern themselves with the insipid muslins and cambrics suited to the *jeune fille*—if Miss Brady would but trust to her judgment, she would not be disappointed.

All caution cast away, Clementina agreed, and Mrs. Westbury, rendered almost speechless by the extent of her niece's reckless and quite unaccountable extravagance, could only stare as Madame's assistants scurried back and forth with dresses for every occasion; the most gloriously colorful swatches of twilled silk and satins, of mousseline de soie and crepe, were pored over critically and the rival merits of French beading over spangles, silver fringing, and the like were discussed and displayed for her opinion.

Had Miss Brady ever considered this particular shade of rose pink? Madame wondered, slipping over her head a ravishing Chinese robe of embroidered silk. Miss Brady hadn't; a week ago—yesterday, even—she would have thrown up her hands in horror. "I'll take it," she said.

Mme. Fanchon's eyes glinted with triumph. It was rare

pleasure, she declared, to meet with such discernment in a client, as Clementina added to her immediate order three dresses for evening, a walking dress in pomana green crepe, a riding habit cut on severely military lines, an exceedingly modish redingote in Gros de Naples, ruched down the front and with an elegant little stand-up collar to show off her neck, and a braided pelisse in bronze green with a round cape.

Madame was horrified to learn that Miss Brady was without a lady's maid. So moved was she that Clementina thought it prudent not to confess that she had never felt the need for one! It just so happened, however, that she was able to put her in the way of an excellent woman who had been maid to the Lady Ariadne Westover until that poor lady's recent demise. And if she might also venture to mention—Miss Brady being a stranger to London—that Signor Franzoni was quite incomparable, should she require the services of a hairdresser. Clementina thanked her gravely.

Her aunt, by now convinced that she was temporarily deranged, scarcely demurred as Clementina ruthlessly cajoled her into purchasing a charming walking dress of blue twilled sarcenet and a pelisse in soft puce. But for the soirée she was determined to cling to the gray taffety, and resisted all attempts to interest her in a very pretty mauve silk, insisting that it was by far too fine for her needs. Clementina, knowing it to be her favorite color, was equally determined that she should have it, and quietly signed to Mme. Fanchon's assistant that it should be packed with the rest.

Mrs. Westbury was enjoying a restorative cup of tea when Patrick arrived back full of enthusiasm for his own purchases, which, aside from all manner of seals and fobs, included a pair of hessians complete with gold tassels and a pair of top-boots with white turn-down tops—"Alfred assures me they're all the crack. You don't mind, do you, Clemmy?" Mr. Weston was also to make him a greatcoat with several capes and a double row of buttons in Mother of Pearl. And his evening coat was to be of dark blue superfine, he told them importantly. And what did they think . . . ? The great man had particularly commented upon his fine breadth of shoulder—"He makes for Lord Cadogon, you know . . . observed that such deportment must run in the family . . ."

"Patrick!" Clementina exclaimed. "You didn't tell him that the Marquis was our relation?"

"Of course I did! Whyever should I not? It made quite a

difference I can tell you! Couldn't do enough, advised me on all manner of things. Alfred reckons I may expect to be rigged out for a trifling sum on account of its all being in the family, as it were!"

If he had hoped to please his sister with this intelligence, he was soon disabused. She turned quite miffy and declared in no uncertain terms that she neither expected, nor would she tolerate, any favors that might accrue directly or indirectly from His Lordship!

☙CHAPTER 3☙

For Sir James' soirée, Clementina had chosen one of her new dresses, or rather it had been chosen for her by Justine, the maid recommended by Madame Fanchon, who had arrived on the previous day, bright and sharp and French, with a quantity of red frizzed hair. Her restless eyes had sized Clementina up thoroughly throughout the brief interview; she had put a few quick questions of her own and, evidently satisfied with what she saw, had accepted the position there and then. As Clementina had later murmured to her aunt, "I would not have dared refuse it to her!"

The gown was deceptively simple. Of amber crepe worn over a slip of ivory satin, it had tiny puff sleeves, the bodice edged with seed pearls and the bell skirt ruched at the hem and caught up daringly at intervals with little clusters of pearl rosettes to show a tantalizing glimpse of ankle.

"Very becoming, dear," said Aunt Seraphina. "Only I don't recall it being quite so . . ." she blinked uncertainly and grew a little pink. "You don't feel, perhaps . . . a shawl . . . ?"

Clementina gave a gurgle of laughter as she quickly wound the rope of pearls inherited from her mother about her neck and stood back to inspect her image critically in the long glass. Justine had dressed her hair in a style she called *a la Tite;* and the pearls gave her skin a clear translucent quality. The overall effect was exactly what she had desired.

"Dear Aunt, the dress is perfectly proper, I promise you!"

"And you can't deny that Clemmy's figure displays to advantage in it!" said her brother with an irreverent grin. "I don't believe I ever saw her look half so well before. Cut quite a dash amongst the English nobility, I shouldn't wonder —to say nothing of the French!"

"Patrick!" Mrs. Westbury protested faintly. "Never say such things, I beg of you! And *do* mind your company manners this evening or your outspokenness is like to put us all to the blush!"

"Oh, pooh! What a fuss about a few paltry compliments!" He wagged a playful finger under her nose. "And such primness sits ill, let me tell you, when I have heard you protest a dozen or more times how Clemmy's figure was more than equal to Mama's if only she would exploit it a little more!"

"Well, I don't doubt that I might have said something of the kind—though not, I am sure in such a crude fashion—for it is very true . . ."

"Well, then?"

"Oh, do be quiet—wretched teasing boy!" admonished his sister, taking a pair of long French kid gloves from the table and beginning to pull them on. But, though her tone quelled him, her mouth still curved irrepressibly upward, for he really did look very fine! White satin knee breeches showed off his leg to perfection and though he had broken his aunt's heart by having all his curls cut away, his smart new crop did give him that slightly rakish air he so admired. He made every effort to appear nonchalant as she and Joshua, who was himself very proud and resplendent in a fine new livery, struggled to ease him into his coat; but when Clementina stood back at last and pronounced it to be worth every guinea of its seemingly astronomical cost, he had blushed as pink as any schoolboy.

Sir James Barbarry's house was in Hill Street, off Park Lane, an elegant house in an elegant situation. The salon was thronged with people—many more than Clementina had anticipated; she was conscious of many pairs of eyes on them, some returning more than once to linger upon her with more than common interest. She heard a tiny gasp from her aunt. And then Sir James was coming forward to greet them, apologizing for the fact that their acquaintance Mr. Pride had been inadvertently called away. He introduced his sister, a rather plain twittering woman, who presently took Mrs. Westbury away to set her at ease and make her known to one or two of her cronies. Patrick, seeing Alfred at the far end of the room, excused himself with obvious relief and went hurriedly to join him.

And Clementina, left alone with their host, found the Comte suddenly at her side, his hooded eyes glinting appreciatively as they took in her improved appearance.

"You came," he said. "I am overjoyed." He offered his arm. "Come—my mother wishes very much to meet you." And almost as an afterthought, remembering his host, "Sir James—you will permit?"

And Sir James, blustering, ruddy faced, and knowing, all but winked. "Oh, my dear Comte . . . delighted . . . by all means . . . just so!"

The Dowager Comtesse de Tourne received Clementina with an unnerving degree of hauteur. The meeting seemed to afford her little joy.

"Do not allow Maman's manner to upset you," Monsieur had murmured as he led her forward. "She likes very much to be 'Grande Dame' and refuses to converse in English though she is well able to do so. If you have difficulty in understanding, I will be happy to translate for you."

"Mademoiselle Brady." Cold fingers, limp under the weight of so many rings, touched briefly and, as though fearing contamination, withdrew. Cold eyes, as sharply brilliant as the collar of diamonds that encircled the scrawny throat, scrutinized every detail of Clementina's toilet and, it would seem, found little to please her, though they lingered speculatively over the simple rope of pearls.

"You are American, my son tells me. We have Americans in Paris, also." From her tone Clementina gathered that their presence was regarded as an intrusion. "You will know the Gallatins, perhaps?"

The Comte threw her a look of exasperation, but before he could intervene Clementina was replying with a commendable composure and fluency that she had not the pleasure of knowing the American Minister or his family. "But I do know Madame Patterson Bonaparte very slightly. Her father lives in Baltimore, you know."

It was obvious that she had said the wrong thing. The thin voice grew almost vicious.

"The wife of that creature Jerome Bonaparte . . ."

"Madame is very beautiful," the Comte interposed smoothly. "And a brilliant conversationalist. We see her occasionally, but she spends much of her time in Rome."

"I cannot like her." Very final. "Monsieur Gallatin is, of course, a Swiss by birth," the complaining voice continued. "One hardly considers him as other than a European. We are not always so blessed in those foreigners who frequent Paris these days."

"Maman!" The Comte's tone was decidedly brusque. "Miss Brady can hardly wish to hear your opinions . . ."

"I don't mind in the least," said Clementina, feeling for his embarrassment. "I trust that if we decide to visit your city, madame, you will count us a blessing rather than a curse!"

"At all events, you speak our tongue with reasonable competence, mademoiselle." It was a grudging enough compliment. "Is it that perhaps there is French blood in your family?"

"No, madame. None that I am aware of, at any rate."

"A pity." It seemed a curious thing to say, but the whole interview seemed a little curious, for though the Comtesse looked bored, her catechism was persistent. "And your visit to England at this time? You have connections here?"

Clementina hesitated, uncertain how to proceed; to say yes would entail revealing the nature of those connections. On the point of settling for an equivocal reply, she glanced up and was astonished to behold the Marquis not ten feet away! Their eyes met briefly; long enough, however, for her to receive the full force of his antagonism. For all the world as though she were deliberately putting herself in his path! Well, she could soon set his mind at ease on *that* score!

"No, madame," she said, sufficiently loudly that he must hear, adding distinctly, "we have no English connections worthy of mention."

A quick flaring of nostrils, the pulled-down mouth, the fractional tightening of an already rigid jawline, all betrayed that the shaft had gone home. Well, at least she could not be accused of trading on his name!

At that moment a new arrival claimed the Comtesse's attention and she relinquished Clementina, with scarcely disguised relief, into her son's care.

The Marquis watched Clementina move through the crowded room, attentively escorted by Monsieur de Tourne, and noted the number of heads that turned to follow their progress. His annoyance was well contained however, noticeable only to anyone looking closely into his eyes. He was presently joined by Mr. Pengallan, who had with him a young French acquaintance, Marc Drouet.

"So that is Henri's latest quarry," said Drouet, following the direction of Cadogon's gaze. He measured Clementina with the eye of a connoisseur. "She has a certain style admittedly, though from all one hears one would not have supposed her sufficiently *bien élève* to satisfy his mama's rigorous notions of what is due to the de Tournes! But then, her so charming son, though proud, is also a compulsive gambler." He shrugged and grinned, a little surprised to find that he suddenly had the Marquis's full attention. "And if *everything* they say of the American Miss Brady is indeed true, then the prize could well outweigh any small discrepancy of birth!"

"Brady?" Mr. Pengallan had turned to his friend with a frown. "I say, Dominic, ain't that the name . . . ?"

Lord Cadogon raised an admonitory finger. "Hush, Fabian! Don't interrupt. Monsieur Drouet is about to enlighten us." His glance shifted casually back to observe Clementina in animated conversation with the French ambassador, the Marquis d'Osmond, and his wife, the Marquise, his expression hardening as he saw her put back her head at that moment to laugh. "Do tell us, monsieur—what exactly does the world say of Miss Brady?"

Drouet's eyes twinkled. He tapped his nose knowingly and his voice sank to a confidential murmur. "A fortune from the grandfather, Marquis—a business empire worth—" he shrugged "—one half million American dollars, so I heard! Of course, the young brother will have his portion, no doubt, but even so! It gives one pause, does it not? Small wonder that the Comte is willing to overlook the unfortunate possibility that she is the natural daughter of an English nobleman!"

Clementina could hardly fail to be aware of Lord Cadogon's interest; at times it almost seemed that his eyes were boring into her back. But its only effect was to make her the more determined not to be deprived of an enjoyable evening; so that when they left the French ambassador, and Monsieur de Tourne announced his intention of finding a corner where they might be more private, she made little objection.

"I must make you my thanks, mademoiselle," he said as he guided her expertly between the groups of guests.

"Must you, monsieur? I cannot imagine why."

"You came this evening. Oh, I do not flatter myself that you came for my sake, but I take pleasure in your presence just the same. You cannot know how much I have wanted to see you again! You outshine every other woman in the room!"

There was something in his expression—a soft persuasiveness in his voice—that almost convinced her he meant it.

"You must not say such things to me, Comte," she said with a breathless laugh. "I am not used to such extravagant compliments. They will go straight to my head and I shall grow insufferably conceited!"

"This I do not believe, but I am yours to command." His eyes glinted down at her. "May I at least be permitted to applaud the way you handled Maman? She is not easy, but I knew I had not mistaken your qualities."

Again he seemed to invest the words with an extra meaning. Resolutely Clementina steered the conversation into safer channels. "Do you come to England often, monsieur?"

He shrugged. "Not often no. But my mother's sister lives here since the Terror. She is now quite old and ill and sent word that she wished to see Maman before she died . . ."

"Miss Brady!" Sir James had come upon them unnoticed, a familiar figure at his shoulder. She could have sworn that the Comte said something exceedingly rude beneath his breath. Drat Sir James! And drat the Marquis! Now what was she to do? She smiled.

There was an archness about Sir James's introductions, almost an air of suppressed excitement. Well aware of her betraying blush, she knew that there was nothing for it but to brazen her way through. She bobbed His Lordship a respectful curtsy.

"Lord Cadogon." She greeted him with due propriety.

"Miss Brady," he returned with extreme dryness.

"Monsieur le Comte, you and Lord Cadogon are acquainted, I think?" The two men exchanged curt bows.

"Indeed, yes. His Lordship honors us so often with his presence these last few years that we almost account him a Parisien!" Such a heavy vein of sarcasm ran beneath the words that Clementina was convinced that she had not mistaken Monsieur de Tourne's hostility. She wondered briefly at its cause.

Sir James, however, was too big with news to notice anything amiss. "My dear Miss Brady, you must know that Lord Cadogon asked most particularly to meet you! Such a coincidence! But there, I must not steal His Lordship's thunder. I daresay he will be wishing to tell you himself—" and as the Marquis lifted an expressive eyebrow "—you do not mind,

My Lord? Well, then—" Sir James pressed plump pink fingers together as though about to administer a blessing, and Clementina, knowing full well what was coming next, was obliged to suppress a giggle. "Miss Brady, you will be astonished, I daresay, to learn that you and His Lordship are almost certainly related. There! What do you say to that?"

She glanced at the Marquis and met a particularly sanguine look that caused her to bite her lip in half-amused vexation. "I don't quite know what to say, Sir James, except that from what little my mother told me, I had expected the Marquis to be a rather older man!"

He looked crestfallen. "You knew?"

"I knew that my grandfather was a Lord Cadogon . . ." She cast the Marquis a look of innocent enquiry.

"My late cousin and predecessor," he supplied suavely. "Your mother was, of course, his daughter, Lady Melissa Durrell. I am right, am I not, ma-am?" She inclined her head. "Then we share a great-grandfather, which probably makes us cousins, though I am not sure in what degree."

Sir James exclaimed, "Quite extraordinary!" and begged to be excused; from his demeanor it was evident that he was eager to spread the tidings.

"Extraordinary, indeed!" Clementina had momentarily forgotten the Comte. He, however, had been following the dialogue with interest. "It is true, this talk of relationships?"

"Oh, without a doubt, monsieur. However, the *connection* is so slight, it is entirely possible that Miss Brady may find it unworthy of consideration."

Clementina, being essentially a fair-minded young woman, could not but appreciate this thrust, though she had no intention of conceding the contest so tamely. So she smiled at him with limpid innocence, contrived a faint fluttering of the eyelashes, and gushed archly, "No, really, Marquis—you couldn't be more wrong! Why, I declare, I am utterly overwhelmed! If only it might prove to be true—just imagine how it must add to my consequence to be able to claim you for a relation!"

The swiftness of her retaliation was acknowledged with an ironically lifted eyebrow, which lifted even further as Monsieur de Tourne said, a faint edge to his voice, "You demean yourself unnecessarily, Miss Brady. Your consequence has no need of support."

"Why, thank you, Comte!" Really, she thought, darting a triumphant glance at Lord Cadogon, it was a little like hav-

ing a duel fought over one without all the more disagreeable
consequences. Nothing like this had ever happened in Baltimore! However, it would not do for them to come to blows.
Hoping to restore calm, she asked, "Please, gentlemen—can
either of you tell me how one goes about procuring horses
for riding in London? Does the hotel have its own stables or
must one hire them elsewhere?"

"My dear mademoiselle, nothing could be simpler. Whilst I
am here in London, the Embassy stables are at my disposal.
It needs but a word to Monsieur Osmond and I am sure they
will be only to happy to extend to you also their generosity."

"You are more than kind, de Tourne, but I believe it will
be preferable if Miss Brady and her brother avail themselves
of my cattle. I shall be away, but my secretary will be instructed that you are to be accommodated, ma-am."

The air was charged yet again. Clementina glanced from
one to the other; the Comte looked annoyed, Lord Cadogon
very much as he always did. Whatever had moved him to
make so surprising and uncharacteristic a gesture?

"I am overwhelmed by so much generosity," she said
lightly. "Thank you both." She bit her lip pensively as neither
spoke. "Of course, it might be better to buy my own horses,
but then one would be obliged to secure stabling for them
and engage grooms—and our plans are a little uncertain as
yet."

"Much better not to bother," said Cadogon ruthlessly.
"Horses, like wives, should never be chosen on impulse."

"Really, Marquis? What a very . . . illuminating dogma!"

It was perhaps fortunate that Monsieur de Tourne was at
that moment obliged to answer an urgent summons from his
mother. He left reluctantly, with assurances that he would return. Left alone with Clementina, the Marquis wasted little
time in further pleasantries.

"Now, my girl," he said abruptly, taking her arm and
propelling her with military precision across the room. his
manner precluding any but the briefest of greetings from
those of his friends who would have approached. "Just exactly what game are you playing?"

"Game?" She protested. "I don't understand."

"Oh, come now, Miss Brady—I am neither deaf nor a
fool! I had not been above ten minutes in this room before I
was being regaled upon all sides with rumor concerning the
Comte de Tourne's conquest—a young American heiress, no
no less!" He looked down at her. "Is it true?"

"That I am the Comte's *chere amie*, or that I am an heiress?" she enquired with deliberate flippancy.

His mouth thinned. "Miss Brady, your capacity for levity is, no doubt, an admirable quality in its place, but I believe we may do without it here. I would appreciate an intelligent answer."

She was not noticeably crushed. "But how am I to furnish you with a serious answer when I don't properly know what you have heard?"

"That you have inherited some quite ridiculous sum. One half million dollars was the amount mentioned, as I recall," he said without equivocation.

"Gracious! Mr. Pride has been busy to some purpose! But he really should learn not to exaggerate. Why, I daresay the whole estate is not valued much above that, and half will fall to Patrick when he comes of age!"

"Good God!" he ejaculated faintly. "Then it is true!" His fingers bit rather deeper into her arm and he bent upon her a most penetrating glance. "Why did you not tell me?"

Clementina remembered how derisively he had looked her over at their first meeting. She said quietly, "It was never my deliberate intention to mislead you, Marquis, but you had rather made up your mind about me, had you not? And I could hardly disabuse you of all those preconceived notions—and brag of my fortune into the bargain—without appearing vulgar as well as brash!"

His jaw snapped tight. "If I seemed hasty in my judgment, then I apologize. My opinion, however, remains unchanged."

"Why, so I would expect," she said lightly. "But I shall not regard it. Everything is going along splendidly as you can see."

"Do you say so?"

His excessive politeness irritated her slightly. "Lord Cadogon, it is ridiculous that I should be made to feel guilty about what is, after all, no more than an unfortunate coincidence. I had no possible way of knowing you would be here this evening, but in the event I had hoped I'd made it sufficiently plain to you that I would not seek to embarrass you by claiming kinship, and I think it very churlish of you in consequence to contrive to set the blame at my door because *you* chose to acknowledge me!"

"Did it never cross your mind that I might find it infinitely more distasteful to be drawn willy-nilly into the latest scandal broth?"

"Now you are talking in riddles!"

"And you, my dear Miss Brady, are being singularly obtuse for a young lady of more than ordinary acuteness!" The irony in his voice withered her. "There is nothing coincidental about our meeting—it was carefully contrived."

Clementina stared. "I don't understand."

"No? Well, I'm bound to say I didn't grasp it myself at the first, though it did strike me as deuced odd that Sir James should be suddenly so eager for my company—we have never been intimate. It was only when I saw you that everything became clear."

"But why?" She persisted.

"Because, my dear young lady, these out-of-season parties are without exception unconscionably dull affairs! What better way to enliven the proceedings, therefore, than to offer the spectacle of a peer of the realm—still relatively new and untried—brought face to face with one of his predecessor's side-slips!"

He said it quite calmly, as though he were commenting upon the weather, and it was several moments before the full import of his words sank in. When they did. Clementina turned pink with embarrassment, disbelief, and indignation in rapid succession.

"I don't believe such a farrago of nonsense!" she cried, looking around to find many an eye sliding away from them with elaborate unconcern. "These people can't possibly be imagining me to be a . . ." Her tongue boggled at the word.

"Why not? It was no secret that old Jasper lived a full and eventful life," said the Marquis imperturbably. "His increase, as I have been reminded so succinctly, is undoubtedly scattered far and wide—and you *are* very like him! It has afforded our fellow guests the delightful pastime of putting two and two together and coming up with anything but four!"

"Well, really!" Clementina's eye kindled. "And I had been thinking *so* well of Sir James!"

"Well, I shouldn't refine too much upon it." He shrugged. "Sir James is a shade pompous, but I doubt that any real malice was intended. Now he knows the truth he will be preening himself on being the first with the news that we are quite properly related. You are fortunate in that the sillier and more malicious tattlemongers are at present out of town. I did warn you, did I not, that London might prove to be riddled with pitfalls?"

"Yes, you did. And I daresay it pleases you no end to be vindicated!"

"Not in the least. It was fortunate, however, that I was on the spot and able to quash the rumor at once."

"And thus uphold the family honor? Is that why you were so quick to establish our relationship?" Clementina suddenly began to laugh. "Ah well, no great harm has been done, after all, as long as it doesn't reach Aunt Seraphina's ears. And if it does, she won't properly understand, for she mostly looks for the good in people and ignores the horrid!" He looked quizzical and she said, "It's true! She is the dearest creature—you had better meet her."

They began to walk back across the room. "She can even bring herself to be perfectly amiable to Jefferson Pride—and that takes some doing, I can tell you! No wonder he isn't here tonight; I guess he wouldn't dare face me! I have him to thank for introducing us to Sir James. They were at the theatre along with Monsieur de Tourne. At the time I thought the meeting quite providential!"

"It was certainly providential for Monsieur le Comte!" murmured the Marquis. "You are exactly what he has been looking for!"

"And what is that supposed to mean?" Clementina came to a halt, two bright spots of color flaming in her cheeks. "Well? No, you need not explain! Clearly you think that Monsieur de Tourne is only interested in me for my fortune!" When he did not immediately reply, she continued more quietly, "You don't suppose he might, just conceivably, find me attractive?"

"Oh, I'm sure he does! Monsieur's taste is always impeccable!" Lord Cadogon looked her over, his voice in her present sensitive state sounding almost patronizingly offhand. "And I daresay your forthright manner will constitute sufficient of a novelty when compared with the average pampered and protected French girl as to hold a certain eccentric appeal for him—though I doubt his mother will be so enchanted!"

"Sir, you are offensive!" Clementina turned on her heel and began walking again, rather too quickly. She was not to be rid of him so easily, however; in another moment his hand was on her arm, slowing her down, his voice maddeningly calm in her ear.

"Softly, Miss Brady. Your reputation is in the making tonight. Besides, you are allowing anger and vanity to cloud your judgment. You have but to make a few discreet enquiries and you will learn that the Comte is in the market for a wife. Of course he would prefer her to be attractive *and* well born, but—" here his voice hardened perceptibly "—most important of all, she must be immensely wealthy! Monsieur is in desperate need of money."

Clementina didn't want to believe him. She didn't want to believe that when Monsieur de Tourne smiled at her, as he did so charmingly, he was seeing her solely as a prospective bank balance. But considered rationally it made sense, and she was enough of a realist to admit the possibility. Her eyes lifted in search of him, as though seeking reassurance.

"He left about five minutes since with his mama," said the odiously complacent voice. "From Madame's demeanor I would hazard that she had just been regaled with the somewhat lurid account of your supposed unfortunate accident of birth and was not prepared to hear it refuted! A very high stickler, is Madame! Beware, Miss Brady—she would be the very deuce as a mother-in-law, always supposing her son can talk her round!"

And he had the impertinence to accuse *her* of misplaced levity! But she would not give him the satisfaction of quarreling further. She merely observed, in what she hoped was a convincingly offhand manner, "I don't hold with conjecture, sir, so we shall just have to wait and see, shan't we?"

Their steps had brought them to a sofa where Mrs. Westbury sat with a plump, comfortable lady. Close by, Patrick stood talking to Alfred and a pale, sleepy-eyed gentleman dressed in the very pink of perfection. As they approached, Patrick bent down to say something to his aunt that made her laugh. Clementina, seeing her as though for the first time, was struck anew by her prettiness and the lightness with which she carried her years. If the gossip had carried this far, it had not affected her.

"It's high time you met the rest of the family, Marquis," she said. "Aunt Seraphina, allow me to present our cousin, Lord Cadogon."

Lord Cadogon bowed over Mrs. Westbury's hand with a surprising degree of cordiality, and Clementina was amazed to see how quickly he put her at her ease.

"And this is my brother, Patrick," she said.

Somewhat to his astonishment, the Marquis found his hand being enthusiastically shaken. "I am *very* pleased to meet you, sir," Patrick said. "I must confess that Clemmy gave us totally the wrong impression of you . . ." He threw his sister a reproachful glance, which was returned in full measure. "It needed Mr. Bennett here to set me to rights. He tells me you are all the crack!"

"Patrick!" murmured his aunt in despair, but His Lordship appeared undismayed.

"I fear I do not merit Mr. Bennett's encomium," he murmured. "In my experience, such reputations are seldom merited. Now Mr. Pengallan here is to my mind far more worthy of your admiration."

The languid gentleman accepted Milord's tribute very much in the manner in which it was offered—with a gentle, satirical smile.

The plump lady was introduced as Alfred's mama and thereafter the conversation became general. Mr. Pengallan presently drew Clementina to one side, engaging her attention in a manner that went a long way toward restoring her ruffled feelings; she soon discovered that the two were particular friends. In the circumstances it was highly probable that they had discussed her—and that the M̶̶ ̶s would have left her very little character, yet she could determine nothing in Mr. Pengallan's manner beyond a kindly curiosity. It soon became apparent that his rather foppish appearance concealed a gentle, amiable nature

"Do you know Lord Cadogon well?" she asked, unable to equate the two personalities.

"Lord, yes! At school together, y'know. Dashed good friend, Dominic—always ready to stand up for a fellow." Mr. Pengallan gave her his sleepy smile. "I used to get roasted a lot—never one for the more energetic pursuits. Tell the truth, I was lazy—trifle on the stout side, too, in those days." He gazed down complacently, as far as the incredibly high starched folds of his cravat would permit, at the perfection of his now trim form. "Got me into trouble more than once, don't y'know, but there was Dominic, always ready and willing to pop someone's cork on my account."

"Fisticuffs! Lord Cadogon?" she exclaimed.

"By jove! I should just say so! Got a left that the incomparable Jackson himself don't disdain!"

"Good gracious!" Clementina glanced overtly at the restrained elegance of His Lordship's back, noticing for the first time that fine breadth of shoulder commended by Mr. Weston now displayed to full advantage by the unwrinkled perfection of a black swallow-tailed coat—one of Mr. Weston's masterpieces, no doubt. "Who would have thought it?"

"Ah! There's a lot more to Dominic than meets the eye."

Mr. Pengallan nodded sagely. "Take my word on't, ma-am. Wellington thought the world of him, y'know—and *he* ain't an easy man to satisfy."

"Lord Cadogon was in the army?" It was an evening of surprises.

"Lord, yes. Distinguished career. One of the Duke's most valued staff officers in Paris during the Occupation—speaks the lingo just like a frog—extraordinary! But invaluable, of course. Second home, very nearly, though since old Jasper got his notice to quit he's been kept pretty busy here setting all to rights . . . common knowledge the old man left his affairs in deuced queer stirrups . . ." He fell silent, rendered a little pink about the gills by a sudden recollection of the somewhat delicate situation existing between Clementina and the Marquis.

"Is it, indeed?" Clementina looked thoughtful, but when Mr. Pengallan muttered, abashed, "Shouldn't have said—curst loose tongue—beg you won't regard it . . ." she only smiled reassuringly. "I comprehend perfectly, sir. You have said nothing out of place, I promise you. The Marquis is fortunate to have so good a friend." Better than he deserves, she almost added, but he looked so gratified she hadn't the heart, and then Patrick took her attention.

He had been eyeing His Lordship's cravat with undisguised envy; before Clementina could stop him he was saying enthusiastically, "You won't mind my asking, I am sure, sir—but is that the Cadogon knot?"

She heard the familiar sigh of resignation. "It is. Do you also think it 'very nice'?"

"Nice?" Patrick echoed, mystified.

"*Nice!*" Mr. Pengallan was visibly shaken.

The Marquis smiled faintly, his eyes lifting to meet Clementina's.

"Yes, indeed. I have it on the best authority."

For once she didn't know where to look.

✳CHAPTER 4✳

Clementina was finishing a solitary breakfast on the following morning when word was sent up to her that Lord Cadogon had called. She at once despatched Joshua to bring him up, wondering what he could possibly want with her. To be sure they had parted cordially enough at the end of the evening, but she had formed the impression that he would not voluntarily seek her company.

"Alone, Miss Brady?"

He came briskly into the room, dressed for riding.

She rose from the little table by the window that framed so delightfully a view of Green Park which incorporated the white-stuccoed Ranger's hut just visible among the trees and Buckingham House's red brick facade in the distance backed by the misted Surrey hills.

"I persuaded Aunt Seraphina to take breakfast in bed," she explained. "She is unused to late nights; and Patrick, I imagine, is still sleeping like a sluggard. He left Sir James's house last evening with Alfred Bennett and I suspect they repaired to some horrid, disreputable club, for I didn't hear him return!" She chuckled. "But Alfred is a nice boy, so I cannot think he would lead Patrick too far astray!"

Lord Cadogon's eyebrows rose a little, but he offered no comment. If Miss Brady was unfamiliar with the kind of larks young men of that age kicked up, she had far better remain in ignorance.

"I'm glad to find that you, at any rate, are not a lie-abed," he said, coming to the object of his visit, "for I have horses waiting below." And, when she looked puzzled, "You did speak of wanting to ride?"

"Yes, I did."

"Well then?" he prompted. "You don't have a prior engagement?"

Since, if she had, it could only be with the Comte, Clementina regarded the question as provocative, but she resolved not to quarrel with him so early in the morning. Unquestionably Madame de Tourne's abrupt departure on the previous evening, taking her son with her, had been a disappointment, for the Comte would surely have returned later had his interest truly been engaged——or even, had he been a fortune hunter as the Marquis had intimated. That he had not done so must be a blow to her pride! However, it was not in her nature to be downcast for long.

"Thank you," she said. "A ride would be very pleasant. If you will allow me a few moments to change my dress and inform my aunt. Joshua, look after His Lordship."

Left alone with the young Negro, Lord Cadogon was half-amused to find himself being subjected to a frank and comprehensive scrutiny until, encountering the noble sardonic eye, the boy gave him a wide, abashed grin and recommended him to a chair. "Missus Westbury favors the sofa, but Miss Clemmy, she reckons this chair here by the fire is a sight more comfortable if you'd care to sit——" and as the Marquis took his ease, prepared for a lengthy wait, Joshua executed a quaint courtly bow, taking an obvious pride in his duties. "Can I offer you some refreshment, sir?"

The Marquis declined graciously.

"Only Miss Clemmy, she won't keep you longer'n a few minutes. She ain't one for a lot of fal-lals and fancy dressing——'cepting in the last few days, of course," he added with a high, pleased chuckle, remembering the goings-on of his young mistress, and his own fine new clothes. "Sech a time we've had!"

"You are enjoying your visit to London?" Lord Cadogon, unused to conversing with servants, found himself in the unexpected and somewhat novel predicament of feeling obliged to keep up his end of the conversation.

"*Yes, sir!*" His efforts were enthusiastically repaid. "Why, we've been just about everywhere! Such a fine big town, this is!"

Fortunately Clementina soon returned, dashingly attired in a habit of bronze-green cloth, close fitting, with epaulettes and braiding in black, which caused His Lordship's eyes to widen with something very like appreciation. Pulling on a pair of tan York gloves, she announced herself to be ready.

The park was almost deserted except for a few nursemaids with their charges, and they were soon able to put the horses to a comfortable canter. His Lordship had selected for

Clementina a very prettily behaved bay mare with sufficient spirit to tax her skill. She was warm in her praise.

"I guessed you'd not thank me for anything too placid!"

She could hardly fail to notice the way his glance returned more than once to survey the new habit with its accompanying black hat, very much *a la hussar,* perched with rakish optimism upon the red curls. Would he comment, she wondered. He did, but not quite as she had expected.

"Permit me to say how much I admire your taste, Miss Brady. If you aspire to true elegance, you can hardly do better than to patronize Madame Fanchon."

Clementina was much diverted. "What an . . . unexpected man you are, Marquis. Just as one has made up one's mind about you, you do or say something which upsets all one's calculations!" She chuckled. "I confess I am vastly intrigued to learn how you can so unerringly recognize where a lady does her shopping! I do hope you mean to gratify my curiosity?"

His manner grew more sardonic. "Certainly, my dear young lady, but I fear the explanation will prove nowhere near as fanciful as your fertile imagination is wont to devise! The truth is, I saw you, not many days since, leaving Madame's very exclusive establishment with more than enough bandboxes to fill the waiting hack! It crossed my mind at the time that you might well be in danger of outstripping your budget, but you had been so very positive of your ability to manage that I supposed you would not welcome any interference on my part. And in the event, you see, my instinct proved sound!"

Clementina wondered if this would be a good moment to broach a subject that had been disturbing her since the previous evening. It would require a certain delicacy of approach, which she was not sure that she possessed, but it had to be tackled for her own peace of mind, and he seemed in a reasonably good mood.

"Marquis, may I ask something?"

Something—a slight agitation in her manner—led him to consider the face turned toward him, a lively, intelligent face glowing from her recent exertions, but marred now by the faintest of frowns. He raised a questioning brow.

"It is quite providential your calling this morning," she began, speaking rather quickly as she tended to do when nervous, "for I had been wondering how I should approach you . . ." She paused. "Why did you, by the way?" Her bright eyes challenged him. "Put yourself to the trouble of riding with me, I mean, when I had no expectation of ever seeing you again?"

He had been asking himself the same question.

"It isn't every day one has an unknown cousin thrust upon one." He shrugged. "I believe I felt, on reflection, that I had been less than welcoming and that it behooved me to set matters straight, perhaps even to learn a little more about her."

"Very flattering, but I am not convinced. I can't imagine your being in the least interested in anything I might have to say."

"Then you would be wrong," he said calmly. "You wished to ask something?"

"Well, I daresay you may not quite like it, but I'd feel badly if I didn't at least make a push to find out . . ." Under his enigmatic eye, she faltered. Lord, she was making a mess of it! Wishing very much that she had never started, she stared straight ahead and said in a little rush, "Marquis—did my grandfather leave a lot of debts?"

There was a long pause—so long that she rushed again into speech. "It's simply that I heard a rumor last night that made me wonder . . ."

"You shouldn't heed rumor, ma-am." His voice had gone horribly distant and cold. "Your late grandfather's affairs are not your concern."

In her annoyance, her hand tightened on the rein, making the mare lose her rhythm and falter in her stride. Clementina laid a soothing hand along her neck. "I can't accept that! They are quite as much my concern as yours—more so, in fact. It seems to me quite idiotic that you should stand banker for any debts when I am well able to discharge them."

"The matter is closed. I don't wish to discuss it further, Miss Brady." His profile was distinctly unencouraging.

"Well, I do." Clementina persisted. "Oh, I daresay you think women don't understand matters of business, but I'm not so ninny brained, I assure you! I used to help Grandpa Brady considerably and have managed to keep things going very satisfactorily since his death, with a little help from our agent, Mr. Gourley." She saw that his look had changed to one of mild disbelief and was instantly put on the defensive. "I suppose you don't consider a woman capable of so much?"

"I didn't say so."

"No more you did!" Disarmed, she threw him a rueful

grin. "Patrick says I am by far too touchy upon that particular head!"

"True—but understandable," said Cadogon politely. "So what is happening to your vast enterprises whilst you are here in England?"

"I have left Mr. Gourley in complete charge. If I am honest, he is more than capable of managing without any help from me, but I mean to retain control until Patrick has age and experience enough to take over."

Clementina realized that she had been led very neatly away from the controversial question of the late Marquis's debts, but when she attempted to return to it, she met with the same blank wall of refusal to discuss any part of it and prudently abandoned the struggle. They spoke instead of her maternal grandparent, whom she had adored, of how he had become a legend in Baltimore and of how his greatest disappointment had been her father's total disinclination to follow him— "though Grandpa thought the world of him!"

"Such paragons are seldom easy to emulate. Perhaps your father suffered from a sense of inadequacy."

It was an intersting thought; Clementina, remembering her charming, feckless parent, gave it consideration, striving to be fair. "I don't think he did," she said at last. "It was simply that he was overindulged from an early age and work of any kind was anathema to him."

The Marquis gave her one of his more quizzical looks. "A deficiency that you sought to rectify?"

"Not consciously, no." She felt the remark to be a criticism and was about to refute it more positively when they were hailed from behind. Mr. Pengallan came abreast of them, doffing his hat to Clementina with impeccable courtesy.

"Good morning, Fabian," said the Marquis. "I don't usually look to find you abroad much before noon."

A faint look of pain crossed his friend's gentle features. "Gibson must have been deuced careless with the blinds last night—sun came streaming in on me at some ungodly hour—nothing for it but to rouse m'self." He sighed and turned his sleepy smile upon Clementina. "Worth it, though, Miss Brady—a sight to delight the eye, if you'll permit me the liberty of saying so! Ain't it a fact, Dominic?"

Lord Cadogon inclined his head in agreement and Clementina blushed.

"Why, thank you, sir. You are most kind."

"Not kind at all. Pleasure. By the by, just passed your brother, ma-am—tooling Alfred Bennett's tilbury."

"No, really? I hadn't expected to see him this side of luncheon."

"See him any minute now, I shouldn't wonder. Heading in this direction. Bang-up little rig! Displays well, ma-am— handles the ribbons very creditably."

"You may take that as praise, indeed!" drawled His Lordship. "Coming as it does from so distinguished a member of the Four in Hand Club."

Clementina smiled her pleasure and found Mr. Pengallan looking curiously at his friend's mount—a particularly fine chestnut with breeding in every line.

"Isn't that Castleton's hunter, Dominic?" The Marquis agreed that it was. "Thought as much. Didn't know it was on the market."

"Very few people did. Lord Castleton's pecuniary difficulties suddenly became pressing, I believe!"

Mr. Pengallan gave him a shrewd glance. "Heard Latham was after that animal."

"Yes," murmured His Lordship. "So did I."

Mr. Pengallan laughed. "Bless me if I know how you do it! You'd have to be up early to outwit Dominic, Miss Brady!"

"I should not attempt it, sir." Clementina's eyes twinkled. "Lord Cadogon does not, I think, approve of clever women! He would have us all at home with our tatting, a brood of babies about our feet!"

"You seem determined to invest me with opinions I have never knowingly expressed, Miss Brady," said he imperturbably. "In this instance, what you suggest would be highly improper since you are not married!"

"For that, you must blame Grandpa Brady." She laughed. "Like you, he was deeply suspicious of anyone he hadn't known from the cradle up, who had nerve enough to pay me court! The truth is, of course," she added with wry humor, "that he was by far too comfortable with things the way they were. He wasn't about to have his life upset and his granddaughter and helpmeet carried off by some pesky stranger!"

"I can't imagine that deterring you unduly," said the Marquis.

"Well, I don't suppose it would have done if my feelings had been sufficiently engaged," she acknowledged, "but they weren't. And as most of the local beaux had been known to me from early childhood, I soon discovered that it is almost impossible to feel romantical about someone who, however eligible in other respects, figures irrevocably in one's memory as a gangling boy spotted with measles or convulsed with croup!"

"A horrendous prospect," agreed Mr. Pengallan gravely.

"Or it would be," agreed the Marquis blandly, "were I not so certain that you are devilish hard to please!"

This wrung from her a little peal of laughter. "Perhaps. At any rate I don't feel in the least deprived. I have had a most full and interesting life to date and shall continue so to do until I meet a man capable of sweeping me off my feet."

There were more people about now; the time had passed surprisingly quickly and Clementina was about to suggest that they should turn for home when Mr. Pengallan looked round and announced that Patrick was in view. She looked back herself to see a tilbury coming toward them at a spanking pace, her brother, with Alfred beside him, very much in charge. "Oh, he does look well, does he not?" she exclaimed with pride, and then her heart missed a beat as she saw Monsieur de Tourne riding beside them.

Both parties stopped. Greetings were exchanged and while Mr. Pengallan and Lord Cadogon dutifully admired Alfred's most prized possession, the Comte managed to maneuver himself into a position where he was able to converse with Clementina with some degree of intimacy.

"I must make you my apologies, mademoiselle. It grieved me that I was obliged to leave with such suddenness last evening when I had so wished to have more time with you!"

"Yes, it was a pity, wasn't it?" She cursed Lord Cadogon heartily for his cold-blooded appraisal of the Comte's motives in seeking her out; as a result she now found herself weighing his words critically, wondering if they were not just a shade too fulsome. "Your mother was unwell, I believe?" She could not resist the temptation to give the words extra emphasis. "I hope she is now fully recovered?"

The Comte colored slightly, his handsome features stern. "I have not yet seen her this morning. Maman, I must explain, is afflicted with the most cruel migraines. It was so with her last evening. There was nothing but to take her home. At such a time and in a strange country she did not care for me to leave her. No other cause could have taken me from your side!"

Very convenient, thought Clementina, who did not believe that a migraine would have the impertinence to afflict

Madame without her previous connivance and approval! Did her son pay lip service to the fiction out of genuine concern or was he simply "mother-ridden"? Either way, such a relationship could prove troublesome, for she did not believe he could have remained unaware of the reasons that precipitated his mother's abrupt departure.

She said lightly, "You do not have to justify your absence to me, monsieur. In the circumstances you did everything that was proper."

"Ah, I knew you would understand! Such a generous nature, my dear mademoiselle!"

He had charm; she could not deny it, whatever might be his motives. Smiling slightly, she lifted her eyes and encountered a blistering shaft of irony from Lord Cadogon. She colored and set the little mare caracolling across the grass toward the tilbury. Determinedly the Comte kept pace with her and she was not altogether displeased, let Cadogon say what he would!

Alfred had climbed down to examine one of the carriage's brightly painted wheels where Mr. Pengallan had drawn his attention to the suspicion of a tiny scratch. Patrick, however, remained where he was, reluctant to relinquish his charge of the ribbons.

In her ear, Monsieur de Tourne's voice was apologetic. "Regrettably, nothing will content Maman now but to return home. We leave tomorrow . . ."

Clementina's head came up sharply in her disappointment; the mare shied at the unexpected movement and, almost in the same moment, the gelding between the shafts squealed, kicked out angrily, and set off in a confusion of flailing legs and dislodged earth. The equipage flashed past so close that the little mare barely escaped a scraped flank, and as Clementina fought to control her she had an agonizing glimpse of Patrick, who had been sitting with the ribbons loosely clasped between his knees, trying desperately to grapple for control. She saw Patrick's white-faced look of horror as the tilbury gathered momentum at an alarming rate and her cry rose above the terse-voiced instructions issuing from a strangely animated Mr. Pengallan, who leapt into his saddle and set off in pursuit.

The Marquis was already ahead of him, but quicker than either was the Comte, who was steadily gaining on the tilbury, now bucketing along helplessly behind the frantic horse, which had veered sharply from the tan and was coming dangerously close to a clump of trees. In a superb feat of horsemanship, the Comte brought his own mount parallel with the terrified runaway, so close as to risk severe injury, grabbed for the snaffle, and wrenched its head round, forcing it to change direction. As the horse lost impetus, the Marquis was at its other side and between them they brought it to a halt.

Clementina was there almost as soon as they stopped, kicking her foot free of the stirrup, slithering to the ground, and running across the grass in a fever of anxiety. Patrick was already being helped down, ashen faced and stiff, but apparently uninjured. She took his hands in a bruising clasp and, over the lump in her throat, upbraided him for his carelessness and gave thanks for his safe deliverance all in one breath and with something less than her usual air of calm.

"Don't fuss, Clemmy!" he implored in a very odd voice.

The Marquis, seeing his color, acted promptly. "Stand away—give the lad some air!" he said in peremptory tones. And then more gently, "Now boy—head between the knees—that's the ticket!" His leg was against Patrick, his arm supporting him.

In a relatively short space of time, however, Patrick was shaking off the supporting arm and insisting that he was as fine as fivepence.

"You don't look it!" insisted Clementina and received a quelling glance from her cousin.

A small crowd had collected and someone suggested brandy. Mr. Pengallan shook his head. "Don't advise it. Liable to case up his accounts on the spot! Would myself. Best leave well alone, I'd say."

Alfred, left stranded in all the commotion, came panting up at that moment, hatless and very much disheveled, his concern divided with almost equal impartiality between his friend's state of health and the condition of his beloved equipage. However, having reassured himself in a somewhat cursory manner of the former, he felt able to give his full attention to the tilbury, examining it anxiously for signs of damage, whilst the Marquis and Mr. Pengallan set themselves to soothing the frightened horse.

The Comte, his part played, stood self-effacingly aside, forgotten in all the ensuing fuss; but once Clementina had assured herself that Patrick, now sitting on the grass and expressing a wish to be left alone, was truly recovering, she went swiftly across to tender her thanks.

"But for your presence of mind, monsieur, Patrick might

at this moment be lying dead," she said, her voice choked with emotion. "I don't know how I am ever to thank you!"

For once, her ability to retain command of any situation had almost deserted her; the shock, the speed at which everything had happened, made her momentarily lightheaded. She swayed, and at once the Comte's hands came to steady her. For an instant she was pressed against him and was filled with the most curious sensations. Unsure whether it was these that made her tremble so, or the fright she had so recently sustained, she instantly drew back in confusion. He did not seek to prevent her, but retained a reassuring handclasp to steady her.

"I wish no thanks but your gratitude, *chere mademoiselle*," he murmured. "I was but the first to arrive. Monsieur le Marquis is to be equally commended, for I doubt I could have done so well, else."

Clementina shook her head wordlessly, much moved by his generosity.

He bent upon her a compelling glance. "This brother means a lot to you, I think? Then we must take good care of him."

"We?" She stared up at him, still not quite herself.

"But, yes. You do not suppose," he said softly, "that I mean to relinquish so easily that which I have just found!"

The Marquis, meanwhile, was engaged in running an exploratory hand over the chestnut gelding's side with meticulous thoroughness and was rewarded for his efforts when the animal presently flinched, whinneyed, and stamped a restive hoof. Mr. Pengallan, arrested by his friend's thoughtful expression, came to his side; together they examined an ugly-looking contusion, newly inflicted and fast swelling up.

"Nasty," observed Mr. Pengallan. "Devilish painful, too, I'd say."

"Yes," His Lordship agreed. "One is tempted to wonder how he came by it."

"Should have thought that was obvious, m'dear fellow. Happened when he bolted."

"How?" And perceiving that further simplification was required, "How did the animal come to injure itself in that precise spot?"

"How did . . . ?" Mr. Pengallan sighed. "Now look here, Dominic, if you're in one of your enigmatic moods, I'm off!" And then, giving the matter further thought, shook his head.

"You're right, dash it! Nowhere near the shaft—didn't crash into anything. It don't make any sense!"

"No. Unless it was the infliction of the wound that caused the horse to bolt. I wonder?" The Marquis's gaze rested pensively on Clementina and de Tourne standing at that moment in an attitude of intimacy. As he watched, she raised her head and smiled at the Comte.

Mr. Pengallan followed his gaze, but did not immediately perceive the trend of his thoughts. "Make a handsome couple, don't they?" And then, suddenly struck: "Good Gad, Dominic! You ain't suggesting . . . not our gallant rescuer? I know you don't care for the fellow . . . not sure that I do myself, but . . . no, that's coming it a bit strong!"

"Is it? Think about it—a swift jab with a sharp implement, easy enough to accomplish unseen. He was close enough to do it, and he *was* quite fortuitously quick off the mark when the horse bolted, wouldn't you say? Almost as though he had been expecting something of the sort!"

The logic of this moved Mr. Pengallan to remark forcibly, "But in God's name, why? Why would he attempt such a cork-brained trick?"

There was little mirth in Cadogon's laugh. "My dear Fabian, use your eyes. I would hazard that his object is already achieved."

"Eh?" Mr. Pengallan saw that the young couple had turned and were walking slowly toward them over the grass, the Comte's arm most considerately supporting his companion. There was already in his attitude more than a hint of possessiveness. "Ah, yes. I take your point. So that's to be the way of it!" A fresh thought occurred to him. "But, dash it, Dominic, that boy might have been killed!" His sleepy eyes opened with a snap. "Lord! You don't suppose . . . ?"

"In this instance, I think not, though the possibility must have been conceived. After all, a tragic accident would have served equally well. Miss Brady must still have been sensible of his efforts to save Patrick. Furthermore," the Marquis added slowly, "she would be the richer by the better part of one quarter of a million dollars!"

"Thunder an' turf! It don't bear thinking about!" Mr. Pengallan looked again at the approaching couple. Miss Brady *did* appear uncommonly taken with the Frenchman. "Shall you tell her?"

"That her precious Comte is blackhearted enough to put her brother's life at risk for his own ends? Oh, I think not,"

said the Marquis softly. "You see, I have already been so unwise as to infer that he has designs on her fortune. I doubt
she would pay much heed to any further attempts on my part
to denigrate Monsieur le Comte."

"But then . . ."

"My dear Fabian, we can only hope that Monsieur over-
plays his hand before any real damage is done, and leave the
rest to Miss Brady's good sense."

"No one's fool, that young lady," Mr. Pengallan offered
hopefully. "Not had much dealing, y'know, but remarkably
sensible, I would have said."

Lord Cadogon was slow to answer. "In the general way I
would agree," he said at last, his eyes fixed in a curious manner upon Clementina. "But in affairs of the heart, I fear my
new-found cousin is as green as they come!"

Lord Cadogon might have been less sanguine concerning
his cousin's good sense had he been privileged to overhear a
conversation two days later.

Clementina had accompanied her aunt on a visit to Mrs.
Bennett's. Hardly were they seated when it became clear that
their hostess was laboring under the strongest desire to impart
news of a most exciting nature. It came rushing forth in the
form of an invitation that both she and Mr. Bennett were
most pleased to extend to Mrs. Westbury, and her niece and
nephew, to visit with them in Paris when they returned there,
as they must shortly do.

Clementina, very much attracted by the idea, held her
breath as Mrs. Bennett warmed to her theme, outlining her
hopes and enthusiastically regaling them with the many delights awaiting them should they but consider such a visit.
Would her aunt care for it, she wondered, and blushed as the
good lady hinted coyly of "a certain French gentleman of *our
acquaintance*" who had let it be known that he very much
wished to pursue his all too brief intercourse with Miss
Brady!

And then there was Patrick, Mrs. Bennett reminded them.
"He and Alfred are such good friends already. I am persuaded that he would like Paris excessively! And you need
not feel yourself in the least cast among foreigners, my dear
Mrs. Westbury," she assured a wavering Aunt Seraphina.
"Why, I dare swear we number as many Americans as English amongst our friends—the Gallatins, your own minister,
you know—a most charming, refined family! They have two

sons, I believe, one very close in age to Alfred and your Patrick, and a girl, younger, a most delightful child; and then we have the Courtneys . . ."

As she rattled on, Clementina watched her aunt's face and saw it light up at the mention of her fellow-countrymen. She knew that the day had been won. Mrs. Westbury, fast becoming resigned to her niece's determination to cut a dash, gave in without a struggle and even managed to sound pleased as she accepted Mrs. Bennett's kind invitation.

Mrs. Bennett clapped her hands with delight. "We leave London ourselves within the week . . . only give me a day or two to prepare, my dears, and you shall be as comfortable as we can make you, and you may stay as long as you please!"

And so it was arranged.

At the end of that same week, Lord Cadogon honored them with a brief visit; he had called once during the intervening days to enquire if Patrick was fully recovered, and had taken Clementina driving in the Park. Neither of them mentioned the Comte's departure and the afternoon passed in unexpected harmony, disturbed only momentarily when Clementina had eyed the splendid fast lines of his curricle and confessed to a long-standing, though secret, yearning to possess just such an equipage, together with its splendid pair of matched bays. The one-horse chaise she was used to drive back in Baltimore, fine though it was, seemed very tame by comparison. If, said the Marquis dampeningly, he interpreted her affectingly wistful comments aright as a devious ploy to be allowed to take the ribbons, she was doomed to disappointment; he had a particular dislike of being driven. He did not add "by females," but it was implicit in his tone. Clementina shrugged and laughed, but did not press the matter.

On the occasion of this second visit he found only the two ladies at home, Patrick having been carried off by Alfred Bennett to witness a mill.

He came hard on the heels of Sir James Barbarry, who seemed to have set himself the pleasant duty of entertaining them. Ever since he had discovered the true worth of their acquaintance he had taken to calling upon them frequently at the Pulteney—"just to make you feel quite at home, you know"—and prosing on in the most boring fashion imaginable about his travels through India several years since.

It was not difficult to divine his purpose, since most of his discourse was directed at Mrs. Westbury, who owned that her spirits were apt to sink at the merest knock upon the door—a state of mind that Patrick's irreverent teasing did little to alleviate. She was therefore delighted to welcome Lord Cadogon, who seemed, she thought, a little withdrawn and reluctant to converse. Clementina, too, watched him curiously; his manner toward her and her aunt was everything it should be, but when Sir James was so unwise as to enquire whether His Lordship had ever visited India, he received so short an answer as made him blink nervously. He soon recovered, however, beamed upon them all, and said that he quite saw how it was—Lord Cadogon wished to be private with his relations . . . no, no, Miss Brady must not disturb herself. . . . Joshua came forward with Sir James's hat and stick, and the door soon closed behind him.

The two ladies relaxed visibly with his going; only the Marquis still seemed ill at ease. Mrs. Westbury asked hesitantly if he would take tea with them, but he declined.

"I cannot stay, ma-am. I came only to make my adieux. I go north tomorrow, and since I plan to leave for Paris almost immediately upon my return, it is possible that we may not meet again."

"Oh! Well . . . as a matter of fact . . ." Aunt Seraphina began. Clementina, perched beside her on the arm of the sofa, gave her a swift, warning prod that caused her to relapse into incoherence. It was quite unforgivable, Clementina knew, but a sudden imp of mischief had prompted her to withhold from Lord Cadogon the intelligence that they, too, were to visit Paris. It would be so much more amusing—and, she fancied, marginally less contentious—to present him with a *fait accompli!*

"We are very glad you did decide to call," she said, returning his quick, frowning look with one of limpid innocence. "For we shall almost certainly be gone by the time you return. And I daresay you will be equally glad to be rid of us," she added, walking with him to the door.

"You are trying to put words into my mouth again, Miss Brady. In fact, I had not thought to say so, but I have enjoyed our brief acquaintance, though I believe you are right to reconsider your decision to stay."

Guilt suffused her; she stifled it by convincing herself that neither of them would wish to part on a quarrelsome note. As if to give point to this conviction, she saw that he was smiling a little, studying her face as though he would commit it to memory; and she knew that the future would lose a little of its savor were she not so sure of meeting this cousin of hers again very soon.

The humor lurking in his eyes found an answering echo in her own as she put her head a little on one side to say, "Well, cousin? Will you know me again, if we meet, do you think?"

"My dear Miss Brady," he returned equably, "I cannot conceive of anyone, having once made your acquaintance, ever forgetting you!"

❊CHAPTER 5❊

It was love at first sight. By comparison with Baltimore, Clementina had thought London a prodigiously fine city, with its harmoniously proportioned houses set in secluded squares, its superbly ordered parks and gardens, and the wealth and variety of its shops. But it was Paris, serene in the mellow sunshine—Paris, by turn magnificent and squalid, quaint and unbelievably beautiful, which had claimed her heart from the very first moment of their arrival. Looking down from the Place de L'Etoile as their carriage emerged at last from the cramped and dingy suburbs, she had seen the road descending through a mass of autumn foliage to where the Tuileries lay in a distant golden haze, and there and then she had known that this was where she belonged.

Sunlight had glittered on everything that first day; on the beautiful marble sculptures; on Napoleon's splendid arch; on the endless ribbon of carriages moving along the Champs Elysées, their lamps and harness and windows winking and shimmering amidst the continuously flowing and ebbing tide of color provided by the pedestrians who strolled along the wide pavements beneath the trees; it even picked out the occasional leaf that fluttered to the ground, turning each one to a sliver of pure gold.

News of their arrival, much heralded by Mrs. Bennett, was soon rippling through the fashionable salons of those ladies for whom gossip was the *raison d'etre*. It reached the Russian Embassy, where Prince Metlin—unrepentant philanderer, in-

corrigible flirt, and sometime Colonel in the Czar's Imperial
Guard—had it from the ambassador, Count Pozzo di Borgo.
The Prince, whose official duties sat very lightly upon him,
grinned with pure pleasure and gave his luxuriant red-gold
whiskers a special tweak of anticipation. The news even penetrated the august edifice of the Elysée Palace, where it came
to the ear of the king's nephew, the Duc de Berry, whose reputation for dalliance far exceeded Prince Metlin's.

And in the heavily mortgaged mansion farther along the
prestigious Faubourg St. Honoré, Monsieur de Tourne smiled
confidently and prepared to complete his conquest of the
young lady who had so obligingly responded to his skillfully
cast lures. He lost no time in calling upon the Bennetts,
scarcely giving their guests time to collect themselves after
the rigors of their journey.

He remained no longer than was proper, but managed during his brief stay to charm the two older ladies and, taking
Clementina aside for a few moments, to assure her of the
surprise and pleasure that her coming evoked in him.

For answer her eyes laughed at him, so that he was not to
know how wildly her blood pulsed at the sight of him, or
how gratified she was to find him so quickly upon the door-
step.

"But surely, monsieur, you were expecting us?" she said,
her mouth prim. "For was it not at your instigation that Mrs.
Bennett issued her invitation?"

Clementina saw that he was annoyed and instantly regretted that the playfulness of her tongue had betrayed Mrs. Bennett's indiscretion. She would have to remember that he did
not care to be teased. "I'm sorry," she said. "That sounded
ungracious and I didn't mean it to be so."

The Comte managed a stiff smile. "Not at all, mademoiselle, it is I who must apologize that my scheming proved
so inept. But time was pressing and there was no place for
subtlety." His eyes grew warmer. "However, since you were
aware of my clumsy contriving and still came, it must give
one to hope, perhaps?"

Her breath caught on a laugh, but deep inside she felt
vaguely troubled. She had forgotten how persuasive he could
be. If they did not have matters quite clear from the start,
there was a danger that her very real sense of gratitude, together with what was at present no more than a disturbing at-
traction, might precipitate her into something for which she
was not ready. She said firmly but lightly, "I came to Paris

for many reasons, monsieur, but certainly I would wish us to be friends."

This was not what the Comte had envisioned; his momentary irritation subsided, however, as he discovered that her resistance but added a certain piquancy to the situation. He said softly, "Friends only, mademoiselle?"

"Friends only," she reaffirmed hastily.

His shrug was fatalistic, his smile veiled, for he had seen the confusion in her eyes, the panic swiftly stifled that sent her glance winging toward the two older ladies as though willing them to deliver her. Almost, he regretted the exigencies of his situation, which would not permit him to prolong his courtship—to play like a fish this woman who thought she could manage her life so well that she did not need a man! But his creditors were pressing uncomfortably close, and there would be time enough later when they were safely married. That she might refuse him never entered his head; that moment of revelation had betrayed her. With a very little persuasion, she was ripe for fulfilment!

For now, he was all gentle reassurance. "But you will permit me to be your escort—to show to you the beauties of my city?" His eyes crinkled into a persuasive smile. "And soon, perhaps, you will feel that we are friends enough to call me Henri?"

It was enough; Clementina returned his smile and accepted his offer with pleasure, finding in him a most agreeable and attentive companion. Nor did he confine his attentions solely to her, but endeared himself further to her by taking Patrick very much under his wing and introducing him to a number of his friends.

The Bennetts, too, were extraordinarily hospitable, sparing no effort to make their guests' stay a memorable one. A small reception given in that first week had ensured them an unremitting stream of visitors, and thereafter the knocker was seldom still. The invitations upon Mrs. Bennett's mantelshelf mounted until its rococo absurdities all but vanished beneath a sea of pasteboard.

Soon, Monsieur de Tourne found himself having to compete with a great many other people for the favor of Clementina's company, but though the circumstance galled him, he took comfort from the fact that she appeared to favor no one gentleman as she favored him. Prince Metlin must be accounted his most likely rival, but *his* extravagances seemed to rouse her to laughter rather than passion. He consoled himself that no one but a fool would take the Prince seriously, and whatever Clementina was, she was not a fool!

Indeed, she was not, but, thrown into a totally new way of life, she was in serious danger of behaving foolishly. It had taken her but a short time to recognize that in this Paris she already loved, society's values were shallow, flirtation was an all absorbing pastime amounting almost to a way of life, and passion was a highly negotiable commodity. Hardly anyone, it seemed to her, was immune, from the lowest to the highest. The only noticeable difference being that amongst the latter, affairs were conducted with rather more panache. And she was not a little shocked to find that people she liked very well not only indulged themselves, but regarded it all with a kind of amused cynicism.

Perhaps this was why she found Prince Metlin so endearing; he flirted like all the rest, but for him, life was so obviously a joy that one could not possibly accuse him of being anything other than delightfully, but harmlessly frivolous. It occurred to her that if she were to remain in Paris for any length of time—and with every day that passed the prospect became more tempting—she would have to come to terms with this constant pursuit of pleasure.

It was in this atmosphere that Henri de Tourne subtly, skillfully resumed his courtship, in such a way that she could not but be aware of him. She told herself resolutely that such attentions cost him little, though his eyes said otherwise; that he undoubtedly kept a mistress like all the rest—he was by far too attractive and too *experienced* for it to be otherwise, even she could see *that* much; and that her fortune must weigh with him, for she suspected that all was not well in that direction. But if he truly cared . . . And if it were not for his mama . . .

The Marquis would say unequivocally that her wits had gone a'begging. Indeed, she thought so herself in her saner moments, but there was a headiness in the Paris air that mocked at sanity, and the more she ridiculed her own foolishness in paying so much heed to a word—a touch—a glance, like any silly schoolroom miss, the more did she look for him when he was not there!

Clementina had thought she might have to coax her aunt into staying, but rather to her surprise, she discovered that Aunt Seraphina had also taken Paris to her heart. Clementina attributed this very largely to the kind offices of Monsieur Gallatin, who had conceived the happy inspiration of throwing a small dinner party in their honor at which the guests were drawn entirely from amongst the more agreeable American families at present residing in Paris. Nothing could have pleased her aunt so well, or been more calculated to set her at ease. She took at once to Mrs. Gallatin. "Such a pleasant, unassuming lady, Clemmy dear—and so kind! And, oh, it is so agreeable to meet someone to whom one can talk of home without sounding ungracious!" From which Clementina deduced that Aunt Seraphina would not be averse to a considerably longer stay. And Patrick, already having a famous time, was only too happy to fall in with her wishes.

So it was that one afternoon—as Mrs. Bennett sank into her favorite chair, pink from her exertions, having closed the door upon Monsieur Guillard, a plump, obsequious and exceedingly tedious gentleman who had condescended to make Clementina the object of his admiration and was forever haunting her steps—Clementina brought the conversation round, as tactfully as she was able, to the matter most on her mind.

"A house?" The good lady flew into a fluster. "Oh, but my dear Miss Brady, you must not be imagining that you are the least trouble . . ."

Clementina's eyes twinkled. "No, of course not, dear maam, how could you possibly be other than delighted to have so many callers forever tramping in and out, wearing out your carpets!"

The look of guilt was quickly stifled, but not quickly enough. Clementina exchanged a speaking glance with her aunt, who nodded, thus confirming her in her resolve. She said, "I fancy, however, that you might grow weary of it before the winter is out!"

"You have decided to stay!" Mrs. Bennett clapped her hands together. "Oh, that is famous news! But I knew it must be so if only we could tempt you to come." One hand wandered unerringly in the direction of a dish of comfits, strategically placed upon a little satinwood pedestal table at her elbow. "As to a house, I know for a fact that there is a delightful one standing empty at this very moment in the Rue de Varenne, for the Maslovs returned to St. Petersburg not two weeks since." A comfit was popped into the waiting mouth and consumed with relish. "Not that you must be imagining that we are not happy to have you with us for as long as you should wish," she puffed amiably, safe in the knowledge that she was in no danger of being obliged to make good so rashly generous an offer. "Why I am sure we have all been as cozy together as we could wish for, have we not?"

They assured her that it was so.

"But, there, I know how it is with you. There is nothing quite like one's own home . . ." She beamed on Aunt Seraphina and Clementina in turn. ". . . and so, if you think the house will suit, I am sure Mr. Bennett will be only too happy to negotiate on your behalf. You have but to say the word and he will speak to Monsieur Marais, his man of business."

"You are more than kind, ma-am, but if Mr. Bennett will be so kind as to introduce me to Monsieur Marais, I would very much prefer to deal with him direct." Clementina gave the bewildered lady her warmest smile. "I daresay you will think it a little odd in me, but I have always been in the habit of ordering my own affairs."

For reasons she was reluctant to fathom, Clementina was loath to tell the Comte of her decision regarding the house until all was settled; perhaps in her heart she knew how he would interpret such a move. Yet it was hardly to be expected that such a piece of news would remain secret for long in Paris, so the revelation could not be put off forever. It was rank cowardice—and she knew it—and was well served when her scheming misfired.

On a cold, sunny afternoon in the Bois de Boulogne a small party made its way along the Allée de la Reine-Marguerite, voices echoing, laughter floating out on the clear air. Clementina led the way on a bay, with Henri at her side astride a raking black hunter. A little way behind them came the younger members of the Courtney family, recently arrived from Boston to take up residence in Paris. Miss Dora, a budding beauty of almost eighteen, and Kate, two years her junior, rode in the family barouche while their older brother, Eugene, rode alongside them.

Prince Metlin was also riding in the Bois that afternoon, in the company of an older man, straight backed and distinguished looking. The Prince, resplendent in his Colonel's uniform, recognized the approaching figures and a light came into his eye. He leaned across to say something to his companion.

At almost the same moment, Henri, too, exclaimed, "Uncle Etienne! *Dieu!* I did not know that he was back in town." As Clementina looked puzzled, "Maman's brother—he is younger than her by two years, but they see little of one another. In general they do not agree." He shrugged.

The two groups met, greetings were exchanged, and the Duc de Menton introduced. The Comtesse de Tourne's younger brother was everything that his sister was not—courteous, charming, and with an excellent command of the English tongue, his years of exile during the Terror, as he explained, having been spent largely in England. It seemed to Clementina that he was regarding her with more than a passing interest as Prince Metlin said in his droll way, "So, my dear Miss Brady, you find our company so irresistible that you are to make your home amongst us?"

All eyes turned upon her. She bit her lip ruefully and felt her cheeks growing warm.

"Why? How is this?" Henri's voice sounded sharp. Oh, dear, now he would be annoyed that she had not told him; the more so, since Prince Metlin was before him with the news! "Clementina, is this true?"

"Of course it is true!" The Prince looked from one to the other and an expression of comical dismay crossed his curiously beautiful, crooked features, yet Clementina would have taken an oath that he was deriving a puckish delight from placing Henri at such a disadvantage. "Oh, la-la! I am indiscreet, I think? But it *is* true, is it not, Miss Brady, that you have taken up the lease on the Maslovs' hotel?"

She shot him a reproachful glance, only too aware of the lively interest he had provoked. The Courtneys clamored with questions, the Duc looked on in quizzical amusement, and Henri said nothing, but looked as though he awaited only the opportunity. She took refuge in laughter.

"Oh, heavens! What a fuss!" she cried. "Yes, Prince, I have, as you have so obligingly revealed, taken a house in the Rue de Varenne, though how you found out when the formalities are barely completed, I cannot imagine! I had no idea my affairs were of so much interest!" Her tone was brisk, her manner, outwardly at least, perfectly amiable and easy. A certain irritation betrayed itself, however, in the restless way she wheeled her horse as the questions persisted. "No, I don't want to talk about it anymore now. Gentlemen, Monsieur le Comte was about to show us where the Parisians skate in the winter. Will you not join us?"

She set off at a canter, scarcely waiting for their consent, hearing with acute clarity the crunching of wheels as the barouche began moving, the laughter of the two girls in response to some sally of the Prince's—and the thud of hooves coming closer.

"Why did you not tell me, Clementina?" Henri de Tourne's voice was accusing in her ear.

She drew a steadying breath and faced him frankly. "I think because I didn't want you to . . . to attribute more to the move than a simple desire on my part to remain in Paris."

She blushed, and his blue eyes raked her face; to her dismay he laughed softly, a glint of something like triumph in his regard. "Ah, cherie, if that were your sole object you had no reason to be secretive." He leaned closer, a note of indulgence, almost of complacency, entering his voice. "Shall I tell you what *I* think? It is that perhaps you do not understand your own feelings as well as you would wish to believe!"

He had a point; the turmoil of her emotions exasperated and confused her, but there was no time to explore them now, for the party had arrived at the Petit Lac and reined in. It was difficult to give the whole of her mind to what was being said as Henri and the Prince explained how fires were lit at intervals along the lakeside to keep the spectators warm . . .

". . . and sometimes we hold a *Fete de nuit*—a gala of the most spectacular kind imaginable—and then the trees are all hung with Chinese lanterns."

"It sounds marvelous!" sighed Miss Dora.

"Marvelous!" echoed Miss Kate, and fell silent, blushing at the sound of her own voice; a paler, lumpier version of her sister, she had always longed to be pretty and assured like Dora. But lately Dora had quite paled into insignificance beside Miss Brady; more than anything else now, she dreamed of emulating her new idol, who had simply *everything!* And yet was *so* kind!

The Duc was kind, too; he was smiling at her and wondering if he was to have the pleasure of seeing the young Misses Courtney performing on the ice when the winter came. Kate was too tongue tied to reply, but her brother hooted with laughter and a vigorous shake of the head set Dora's fair curls dancing beneath a charming chip hat as she confessed that she had never mastered the art and that Kate had been too terrified even to try.

"Do not despair, young ladies!" Prince Metlin's bold tawny eyes were alight with merriment, his whiskers quivering, creasing into a smile. "In France, as I have often remarked, only the married ladies appear to skate—and very badly at that! So for you I shall provide a sledge of the most sumptuous comfort in which you may take to the ice with the utmost safety." Amidst laughter, he enquired gallantly, "And what of Miss Brady? Will you also ride in my sledge?"

Clementina came out of her absorbed contemplation of Henri's profile to meet the Prince's amused gaze. Did he guess that she had not been attending? She made an effort and pulled her thoughts together.

"I will do so with the greatest pleasure, Prince," she said gaily. "But I feel bound to confess that it will not be from necessity. I took to the ice with a quite shocking lack of sensibility almost as soon as I could walk. I look forward to being able to skate in these idyllic surroundings."

"You should have seen our beautiful forest before the Allied soldiers decimated it, Miss Brady." The Duc's voice took on an unexpected note of bitterness.

"You have touched a sore place, cherie," said Henri with a sardonic grin. "My uncle longs for the Paris that is no more."

"Not entirely, my boy. I am not against change, only wanton destruction. These trees were hacked down to no good purpose."

The party rode on, and Clementina found herself beside the Duc. A fine, distinguished profile, she thought and was a little disconcerted when he turned his quizzical glance upon her.

"So you mean to make your home in Paris, Miss Brady?"

Clementina felt her cheeks growing warm. He might just as well have said, "Do you mean to marry my nephew?"

One could not entirely blame him; Henri's partiality was sufficiently marked to preclude its being mere politeness, and the Duc *was* Henri's uncle. On further reflection, however, she decided that it was nonsensical to read so much into what was probably a perfectly innocent remark.

So she met the Duc's heavy-lidded smile with equanimity. "How can one possibly say what the future holds, monsieur? We had not planned to stay so long, but I have quite fallen under the spell of your beautiful Paris. Even my aunt, who views everything foreign with deep suspicion, is content to remain for a while." And she told him about the lovely old house in the Rue de Varennes, and of its air of tranquility, which extended beyond the house into the enclosed courtyard and gardens. "We hope to move in by the end of the week if I am able to secure sufficient servants by then. Madame de

Tourne has very kindly put me in the way of an excellent chef, and I am to interview for the rest tomorrow."

A droll lift of the eyebrow indicated more clearly than words that he could not conceive of his sister's being *kind* to anyone! "Well, I can see that you are a young lady of splendid capabilities," he said. "I shall give myself the pleasure of calling upon you when you are comfortably settled."

"Please do. You will be most welcome."

"And now, my dear Miss Brady, I have monopolized you for long enough. My nephew, I see, is giving me the blackest of looks! Perhaps we shall meet again before too long. Do you go to the Ball at the Elysée?"

"Yes. The Duc and Duchesse de Berry have been kind enough to invite us. I must confess to a certain nervousness at the prospect, and Aunt Seraphina is frankly petrified!"

"Then you must reassure your aunt. Our young Royals these days do not practice any great degree of formality." She thought he sounded vaguely disapproving.

❊CHAPTER 6❊

The chef de cuisine, Monsieur Clichet, was black browed, extrovert, and authoritative, and brought with him an impressive entourage. Any misgivings Clementina might have harbored due to his being recommended to her by Madame de Tourne were quickly dispelled. He ruled his domain with a despotic zeal equal to anything the Comtesse might display, but as a result the kitchen functioned with superb efficiency and produced confections of a quality she had not seen bettered anywhere. It remained only to engage the requisite number of footmen, housemaids, and outside staff. She also acquired a housekeeper of Russian origins and fearsome appearance, who came with unimpeachable references.

"I dare swear she's as bald as a billiard ball under that monstrous cap!" Patrick murmured wickedly when encountering her for the first time. "Wherever did you find her, Clemmy—in a circus sideshow?" He executed an imaginary drum roll on a nearby table and struck a dramatic attitude. "Ladies and gentlemen! Come up and see the ugliest woman in the world! Observe how the hair grows out of an extraordinary mole on madame's chin? That is no ordinary mole, ladies and gentlemen—madame was frightened at birth by a billy goat!"

"Hush, horrible boy!" Clementina hissed, trying not to laugh. "The poor woman can't help her looks! And she'll hear you."

"No matter. She don't speak a word of English." He made her an exaggerated leg. "Do you, gruesome old Madame Rubal?"

"Monsieur?" A stiffly bobbed curtsy was accompanied by a blank, beady-eyed glare. Clementina dismissed her in considerable haste before mirth got the better of them.

"You see?" Patrick crowed as she waddled from the room.

"Oh, but I am assured she is a superb housekeeper," gasped Clementina.

"You are naughty, teasing children," said Mrs. Westbury, but there was a twinkle lurking in her eye. She was fast coming to terms with her new way of life, so that even the prospect of a pack of foreign servants no longer had the power to dismay her. And at least Maurice spoke English.

Maurice was undoubtedly Clementina's most inspired acquisition; a dapper man, thin to the point of emaciation, he had a definite presence. In repose his ugly face was doleful, yet it needed only a smile from the darting, button-black eyes and it was transformed. He was, he assured Miss Brady, a major-domo without equal—an artiste supreme in the management of a household—without whom she could not hope to advance her reputation as hostess to the Beau Monde! Indeed, his references were so commendatory as to persuade her that he had composed them himself! Clementina found his impudence irresistible and engaged him on the spot.

He shook his head over the appointment of Madame Rubal, while she in turn viewed him with a vigorous and undisguised contempt that augured ill. For a time it seemed inevitable that one of them must go, until it became apparent to all that both protagonists were more than content to live in a state of armed truce.

Patrick had taken their latest move very much in his stride. He had enjoyed being at the Bennetts and couldn't quite see why Clemmy had this maggot in her head about having their own place, but it was all one to him. As the days passed, he was less and less at home; he was able to go about with Alfred much as before, and with Alfred's circle of friends who had so good-naturedly widened their ranks to admit him.

He was gradually acquiring other friends, too—friends older than himself and altogether more sophisticated, friends such as Gaston Rivas, with whom he had become acquainted through the good offices of Clemmy's comte, who seemed to be devoting a deal of his time to making Patrick feel at home, prompting him to observe that Monsieur was only turning him up sweet to keep in her good books, a suggestion she roundly denied.

It was Gaston Rivas who told him about the curricle, a splendid racing model with huge bright blue wheels. Of course he had to talk Clemmy into letting him have it— "Honestly, Clemmy, it's an absolute gift! This friend of Gaston's . . . run himself into the ground . . . has to sell the whole equipage to pay his gambling debts!"

The whole equipage, when presented for Clementina's inspection, proved to include a mettlesome black horse with a tendency to show the whites of its eyes when fresh, and a small, swarthy groom as quick and nimble as a monkey—not an endearing character, but one who certainly looked as though he knew what he was about.

"Joshua will be disappointed," she prevaricated.

"Stuff! Joshua's my valet. If he wants to play at groom, well, you'll surely be having your own gig or somesuch. He'll look very fine standing up behind you—set a fashion for it, I shouldn't wonder!" He saw her wavering and pressed his point with all the charm and cajolery of which he was capable. "Oh, come on, Clemmy, I'll never get another chance like this! You wouldn't throw a damper when it's just exactly what I have always wanted!"

Of course she'd succumbed, as he had known she must. It would be a poor day when he couldn't bring her round! The trouble was, she was still very much inclined to treat him as a child. She'd have a blue fit if she saw some of the places he was frequenting! Places where he was made to feel like a regular man of the town! For Patrick was fast discovering yet another Paris—a Paris that was a veritable paradise for a young man, full of pretty girls who were not in the least like the girls he danced with so decorously at the balls he attended with Clemmy and returned politely to their mothers when the dance was ended. At first it was not easy to quiet his conscience, but he quickly became adept at leading a double life, escorting Clemmy and Aunt Seraphina home when required to do so, and slipping out again when they were safely abed to sample the exhilarating, fascinating and delightfully dubious extravagances to be found in that "other world" nightlife of the boulevard cafés.

It was some time before Clementina noticed anything amiss. Preoccupied with their move to the Rue de Varenne, with visits, with balls, and the endless succession of invitations, she merely assumed, as Patrick took to rising later and later in the morning, that he was finding the pace rather more than he was used to. When she suggested, as tactfully as she was able lest his sensibilities be outraged, that he might be the better for a few early nights, Patrick's capacity for deception was stretched to the limit. He blushed bright red as he muttered that she might be right and perhaps he wouldn't attend Madame Recamier's musical soirée on the following evening. Since he had been heard to complain more than once that it was like to be a dead bore, Clementina could not feel that such a forfeiture would occasion him any real distress. However, she agreed gravely that he was very wise and no doubt he would wish her to convey his regrets to Madame. Patrick grinned.

Had he been less of a novice in the art of duplicity, this dual existence might have gone unchallenged for much longer. Had he been content to forgo his pleasures on the following evening he would not have become involved in a particularly riotous party at the Maison Dorée, given by the Duc de Berry for his friends in the *coulisse* of the Opera. He had been almost speechless when the Duc extended to him and to his friends a cordial invitation to join his party. And what a party! With so much wine flowing, so much dancing and feasting and so many enchanting coquettes to bedazzle him, time ceased to exist. At about three in the morning he found himself sitting in the lap of a woman of ample charms who had called him her "bébé" and when he finally stumbled home, supported by Gaston Rivas on the one side and Alfred on the other, both in little better case than himself, the little chiming clock in the upper hall was striking six.

He was handed over to Joshua, ever faithful Joshua, who had paced the foyer through the misery of the long night, trembling anew as every quarter chime of the clock convinced him that his young master was lying somewhere in a pool of blood and trying to nerve himself to go and wake Miss Clemmy. At least now that particular tragedy was averted, and there remained only the problem of getting the uproariously incoherent and uncomprehending reveler up two pairs of stairs to his room without discovery.

"Oh, hush your mouth, Mars' Patrick, do! Or we're goin' wake the whole house, for sure!" he pleaded vainly as Patrick waved him aside and lurched toward the staircase.

Clementina also heard the clock strike. She lay half awake, going over the events of Madame Recamier's party and the news imparted to her there with malicious relish by a lady quite obviously eaten up with jealousy. ". . . so you have not met Desirée St. Denis yet, Miss Brady? She is beautiful . . ." The eyes had swept her consideringly. "Oh, yes, quite incredibly beautiful, of such a fairness—the perfect foil for Monsieur de Tourne's dark good looks!" A tinkling laugh. "With such a one, mademoiselle, how can we poor creatures hope to compete?"

With several pairs of eyes on her, Clementina had managed an answering laugh. "How, indeed, madame!" But the thought had depressed her a little.

She tucked her hands under her head on the pillow and sighed. Had Henri deliberately kept his mistress out of her way? Ah, well, it was no more than she had suspected, after all. She told herself that it didn't matter . . . but it was not easy to be philosophical so early in the day. Perhaps she would rise soon and take an early morning ride.

Gradually she became aware of sounds—extraordinary sounds—bawdy singing and much uneven thumping and banging and muttered oaths as someone blundered along the passage beyond the door. Her immediate thought was that the servants had been at the brandy and were holding an orgy! Wide awake now, she pulled on her dressing gown and marched across the room, stubbing her toe painfully in the darkness on the protruding foot of a small Louis Quinze table most inopportunely placed in her path. She made a mental note to move it first thing in the morning, and realized it *was* morning!

She flung open the door to discover a faint flickering of light at the end of the passage. There was some scuffling and giggling, which turned to panic as she approached and, unbelievably, she saw Patrick being pushed unceremoniously, and to the accompaniment of loud protests, into his room by Joshua, who then stood with his back to the door.

The candle quivered uncontrollably in the black boy's

hand, the flame showing the whites of his eyes, luminous with fear as he barred her way.

"Let me past, Joshua."

"You don't want for to go in there, Miss Clemmy," he pleaded. "Young Mars' Patrick—he's goan be sleeping like a babe, for sure!"

"You are lying, Joshua."

"No, ma-am!" The candle was shaking so much now that it almost guttered, but Clementina was in no mood to give quarter.

"What did the Reverend Turner teach you about people who tell lies?" she demanded ruthlessly.

Joshua moaned, torn between his lifelong devotion to Patrick and the fast beckoning flames of eternal damnation. There had never been any doubt in Clementina's mind as to which would win, and any treacherous sensations of guilt she might have entertained concerning her tactics were stifled, for only Patrick was important to her.

She had never seen anyone really drunk, so she was totally unprepared for the sight of Patrick, her beloved Patrick, sprawled across the bed insensible—his face red and blotchy, a horrible, stentorious snoring sound coming from his open mouth.

"Oh, lordy, lordy, Miss Clemmy! He ain't never been as bad as this!"

Clementina rounded on the unfortunate boy. "You mean this is not the first time Patrick has . . . ?" The words she wanted wouldn't come and she returned, angry and frightened, to her inert brother, shaking him, begging him to wake.

"You will do no good, mademoiselle."

Unheard, Maurice had come into the room. At any other time Clementina would have been highly entertained by the spectacle of her major-domo exquisitely attired in gold brocade dressing gown and matching tasseled cap, his dignity not one whit impaired! How Patrick would appreciate him! She uttered a little sob and clasped his clammy, limp hand in both of hers.

The major-domo cleared his throat. "You will permit me to advise?"

"Oh, please, Maurice! He looks so ill!"

"You will return to your bed and leave the young gentleman to my ministrations. I shall make him comfortable with

Joshua's aid. And when he wakes, I shall prepare for him a draught."

"But should I not stay with him?"

Maurice was adamant; the gold tassels on the bed cap bounded. "Believe me, mademoiselle, it is for the best that you go. When your brother awakes he will feel extremely unwell . . . and perhaps a little ashamed. He would not wish to know that you had seen him thus . . ."

"No, perhaps not." She turned to the door with dragging step, all thought of riding now forgotten. "Thank you, Maurice . . . I don't know what to think!"

"It is nothing, mademoiselle! You must not distress yourself," he assured her with great kindness. "Me, I have seen it all *many* times—it is but a part of growing up." He shrugged, his eyes twinkling suddenly. "In your brother's case, I can almost guarantee that the experience will have no repetition."

"You think not?" She seized upon his words, eager to be convinced. "I do hope you may be found to be right." At the door she looked back, returning his smile, albeit a little weakly. "We won't mention this to my aunt, I think."

The gold tassels were emphatic.

It was not the most propitious moment for Lord Cadogon to arrive, but arrive he did while the ladies were still at breakfast. Maurice received him with ceremony, and ushered him across the black and white lozenge-tiled hall toward the Petit Salon, the doors of which a footman already held open in readiness.

"Be pleased to step in here, Monsieur le Marquis," he said importantly, "and I will discover if mademoiselle, my mistress, will give you audience."

Cadogon looked at him. "She will see me."

"Eh, bien! Then it is but a formality." Maurice, well used to sizing people up at a glance, recognized in His Lordship a gentleman accustomed to being obeyed without question—and one, he suspected, who would be intolerant of fools. It would perhaps be prudent to humor such a one!

"A moment, only, monsieur." He strutted to the rear of the hall and up a short, curving pair of stairs embellished with a delicately wrought ironwork rail, to a painted black and white door that he threw open with a flourish. "Mademoiselle Brady," he announced impressively. "I have the honor to inform you that the Marquis of Cadogon is called."

In the pleasant, south-facing breakfast room both ladies looked up from the table.

"How nice!" said Mrs. Westbury.

"Oh no!" exclaimed Clementina faintly, a teacup halfway to her mouth. And then bracingly, "Well, I suppose you had better show him in here."

"He *is* in," said Cadogon, following on the major-domo's heels, a voluminous driving coat flapping about his heels. Slightly disconcerted to find them at table, he bowed to Mrs. Westbury, who was rendered temporarily speechless, and then turned to her niece.

"Miss Brady." There was such hostility in the curt greeting that Clementina, still clutching her teacup, took a recruiting sip before setting the cup down carefully. Hastily she assembled her disordered thoughts. How very disobliging of him to arrive this morning of all mornings! And at breakfast-time, when one was seldom at one's best! She had meant to be prepared so that she might enjoy the task of persuading him to accept their presence here in Paris with a good grace. But life these past few days had spun past like a whirligig, expunging from her mind all memory of his imminent arrival. And now he was here, glowering down his nose at her in that censorious fashion, and all desire to conciliate him fled.

"Why, Marquis, what a surprise!" she managed at last with studied brightness. "Do you know, it had quite slipped my mind that you, also, were proposing to visit Paris!"

"Then you must suffer from a chronic inability to remember!" His voice was soft, clipped with anger. "Or would it be nearer the mark to conclude that you possess a convenient facility for forgetting that which you don't choose to remember!"

Clementina saw her aunt's bewildered face and rushed in before she could speak. "I'm sure I don't know what you mean."

"Yes, you do, so don't try that kind of flummery on me! You don't know me all that well as yet, but well enough, I am confident, to not take me for the kind of gudgeon who can't see through a very pretty piece of plotting!"

"Oh, I don't take you for any kind of gudgeon, Marquis! But nor do I consider that my affairs are any of your business!" And as she heard a faint gasp from Aunt Seraphina, she concluded with deceptive sweetness, "May we offer you some breakfast? You seem to make a point of coming at breakfast-time."

"Thank you, no," he said stiffly.

Clementina saw that Maurice still hovered, an enthralled spectator, his black eyes darting from one to the other, showing clearly that his sharp wits had picked up the undeniable undercurrents. She nodded her dismissal, which he accepted with reluctance, endeavoring to convey by means of a pugnacious thrust of the chin as he left that he would be close at hand should she have need of him.

Cadogon frowned as the door closed. "Where did you find that oddity?"

"Maurice? Oh, he comes highly recommended, and indeed we are already finding him invaluable!" Clementina considered his ever impressive figure and added deliberately, "Though I must have a word with him about admitting callers when we are at meals."

"Clementina!" gasped Mrs. Westbury, immeasurably shocked by her niece's lack of manners. It made her feel more sympathetic than she would otherwise have been toward the Marquis, who had gone a curious shade of red. "Lord Cadogon, do come along in and sit down. We are very pleased to see you!" Clementina's eyes were kindling in a way that made her nervous. She added hurriedly, "You mustn't mind dear Clemmy . . . her natural inclination toward levity occasionally betrays her into going beyond what may be thought seemly, but it is only within the family, you know . . . why, she and Patrick are forever sparring together . . . she doesn't mean anything by it . . ."

"Thank you, Aunt!" said her ungrateful niece. "I am well able to answer for my own behavior."

"Don't distress yourself, ma-am," said the Marquis as though Clementina hadn't spoken. "I know exactly what Miss Brady *meant!*" He turned to her. "Perhaps, however, you would be good enough to accord me a few minutes of your time?"

"Certainly!" she replied defiantly. "You may have as many as you please! Only I would as lief you *did* sit down. I shall certainly sustain a cricked neck if I am obliged to go on peering up at you!"

In her agitation Mrs. Westbury pushed her plate away too violently, jarred her cup, and spilled tea into the saucer. "Oh, dear! Forgive me . . . so clumsy . . ."

"On the other hand," Clementina said, scraping her chair back with an impatient sigh, "I think we had best repair to another room. You are obviously set on being disagreeable, and Aunt Seraphina scares very easily!"

"Then I suggest you might try giving a little more thought to your aunt's feelings," he said evenly.

"And I suggest you might refrain from interfering. It may feed your vanity to consider yourself in the guise of head of the family, but you have no authority here!" She swept past him and left the room, slamming the door behind her. Cadogon stood briefly staring after her before turning to take his leave of Mrs. Westbury. He found her regarding him with a respectful, if troubled, gaze.

"Your pardon, ma-am; I have ruined your breakfast."

"No, no—not at all, My Lord!" And then with a tiny, head-shaking frown, "But I do not understand what has made dear Clemmy so out-of-reason cross! She has not been herself at all this morning and it is so unlike her . . . she is such a good-natured child in the general way of things . . ."

"Really?" He sounded politely disbelieving.

"Indeed, yes. She takes such good care of me that I really don't know how I should go on without her!" Mrs. Westbury's manner portrayed a certain diffidence. "Forgive me, but you must not refine too much upon Clemmy's outspoken ways."

Then, with an outburst of candor that seemed to take her by surprise: "You know, I sometimes wish that my father . . . great man though he undoubtedly was, and of course one would not seek to detract from that greatness in any way or heap calumny upon one who is departed and to whom one owes so much . . . but such men are often incredibly selfish, don't you think? If only he had not made Clemmy a substitute for my brother . . . though of course she was so very much more like Papa than Sean ever was or wanted to be . . . and so you see Papa encouraged her undoubted capabilities at the expense of . . . indeed, with a quite appalling disregard of any of the more homely, womanly aspirations that should occupy a young girl's thoughts . . . and that would in consequence have led her to be much less critical of those attentions . . ." Here, a certain embarrassment combined with the complexities of her peroration brought her to a temporary halt. Lord Cadogon, though mildly amused, found time to sympathize momentarily with his cousin.

"Well, you know how it is, Marquis," she finished in some confusion. "Gentlemen don't very much like women who are sharper-witted than they are themselves, and I guess, too, that it just isn't in Clemmy's nature to settle for second best! Which is such a pity, for a better, dearer, more capable creature I'm sure one couldn't wish for!"

"Perhaps, but that is largely, I would hazard, because she has always been allowed to go on very much as she pleases," he observed dryly. "It is patently obvious that she doesn't like to be taken to task!"

❧CHAPTER 7❧

In the hall Maurice lurked, the very embodiment of polite belligerence.

"Your mistress?" barked the Marquis. It was the indisputable voice of authority.

Two pairs of eyes met and locked. At last Maurice lifted his shoulders in an elegant little Gallic shrug. Family quarrels! *Dieu me sauve!* So much for the English plegm! He bustled forward without further ado and opened the doors to the Petit Salon to admit the Marquis, closing them again with infinite care.

Lord Cadogon found himself in a room of great charm; in each corner fluted pedestals supported plump cherubs who balanced on tiptoe, their chubby arms extended to scatter white plaster roses with happy abandon across the blue compartmented ceiling.

Clementina was standing in one of the window embrasures looking out, her fingers drumming unsteadily on the sill. She did not immediately look round, and Cadogon made no move to speak.

At last she said jerkily, "Well—will you not say it and have done?"

"Does it need to be said?" he returned.

Her fingers stilled; her shoulders moved as she drew a deep breath. "No." The word was forced out on a half-angry sigh. "I was insufferably rude to you, and I distressed Aunt Seraphina, who will heap coals of fire on my head by forgiving me with a much greater measure of generosity than I deserve!" She turned suddenly, and he saw that her over-bright eyes still held the lingering traces of defiance. "I daresay I cannot expect as much of you?"

When he was slow to answer, she rushed on. "Well, why should you be forgiving, after all?" And then, with a brittle laugh, "The devil of it is, I had fully resolved to be conciliating when next we met. It seems to me quite absurd that we cannot be above five minutes in the same room but we are brought to a bout of verbal fisticuffs!" For an instant her spontaneous smile flashed forth. "And in that department, sir, I am reliably informed that you hold superior skills!"

His stern resolve wavered in the face of that smile. "Fabian tends to be oversanguine in his praise, I fear!"

"Oh, well, that's what friends are for," she quipped, and fell silent.

"Miss Brady—Clementina . . . it gives me no pleasure to be constantly at odds with you. I admit that your presence in Paris has angered me, but will you believe that I have only your well-being in mind?"

"Yes, if you, for your part, will believe that my little deception arose out of nothing more sinister than a spontaneous, if misplaced, desire to tease." She wasn't sure if he was wholly convinced; well, that couldn't be helped. "For my behavior this morning," she added, grimly determined to see the thing through to the end, "I can only crave your pardon and plead in mitigation a disturbed night, which has left me shockingly blue deviled!"

"Your aunt said that you were not yourself." He looked at her keenly. "Is something wrong?"

"No, of course not." It was too quickly said. She began to pace about the room. It would be comforting to tell someone, and Aunt Seraphina would never understand.

Clementina stole a glance at Lord Cadogon and found his calmly considering gaze disconcerting. She was sorely tempted to confide in him . . . he was a man, after all, well versed in the ways of the world . . . and for all that he could be so disagreeable on occasion, she knew instinctively that his judgment would be sound.

"You had much better tell me, you know," he said with surprising mildness. "Are you regretting your impetuosity? Does the prospect of becoming the Comtesse de Tourne begin to pall?"

"Certainly not!" She bit her lip. "I wish you would not persist in that nonsense. There is no such thought in the Comte's

mind, I am sure." She recalled Henri's warm glances, his pro-
prietary air, and she blushed.

Cadogon didn't argue, and in a moment she was pouring it
all out to him—her worry about Patrick, his practiced deceits, his all-night revels. In her preoccupation she scarcely
noticed how keenly he listened. In fact, in her present sensitive state his reaction seemed offhand.

"Oh, if that is all . . ."

"No, it is not all!" she was driven to retort. "He was stumbling along the passage and . . . and singing fit to wake the
house! Ditties that would have put Aunt Seraphina to the
blush had she but heard and understood the half of them!"

"In other words the silly young cawker was badly disguised. Well, it was bound to happen sooner or later."

This was not at all the attitude she had expected. Righteous
indignation welled up in her as she relived the hours of
misery she had endured. It had been a mistake to confide in
the Marquis, she could see that now, but having committed
herself this far, she was determined to make him understand
that she was not one to make a fuss about nothing. She explained with great insistence that Patrick wasn't simply
drunk, but insensible. "And he remained so for most of yesterday! It was quite mortifying, being obliged to conspire
with the servants to tell Aunt Seraphina the most shocking
bouncers so that she wouldn't go to his room!"

A great, unfeeling shout of laughter rang in her ears.

"I'm glad you find it so amusing," she said stiffly. "I had
hoped—quite mistakenly as I can now see—that you would
advise me, for even this morning I have been able to get very
little out of Patrick. He just sulks and will not say where he
was or with whom—or even how he came to be in such a
condition . . ."

"You astonish me! One would have supposed your brother
to be in exactly the humor to sustain such an interrogation!"
His Lordship's gentle derision made her squirm with fury.
"My dear girl—how would you like someone ringing a peal
over you when you had a mouth like the bottom of the
kitchen grate and all the hammers of hell pounding in your
head?"

She felt the question to be totally irrelevant. "Oh, it's easy
to see where *your* sympathies lie! Perhaps you would be less
sanguine if Patrick were your brother!"

"Not at all," he declared with odious superiority. "If Patrick had been my brother, I should have known what was

likely to happen. There are certain places in Paris—or Balti-more, for that matter—ready and waiting to draw young men like iron to a lodestone; cafés like the Maison Dorée where there are plenty of little opera dancers to be wined and dined and dallied with!"

His calm acceptance appalled her. "And it doesn't trouble you that Patrick is being so corrupted?"

"Have you any reason to believe that he is being corrupt-ed?" The question was casual.

"Well, what else would you call it? He's only nine-teen . . ."

Cadogon took her by the shoulders and propelled her willy-nilly in the direction of a tête-a-tête, prettily uphol-stered in pale blue striped satin. "Now you just sit down there and listen to me for a minute." She sat, too astonished to do otherwise. "I know nothing of your life in Baltimore," he said, "but I strongly suspect that Patrick has been, from his earliest days, protected by you and spoiled by his aunt . . ."

Clementina opened her mouth to protest, but wasn't given a chance.

". . . You will hardly deny that the boy means everything to you? It is in your eyes, in your voice whenever you speak of him!"

"Is that such a crime?" she cried.

"No, of course not! It is apparent that you have always been very close—and that as yours is the stronger personality, he has, until recently, been willing to let you order his life." Cadogon's voice took on a little more emphasis. "But Patrick isn't a boy any longer, Clementina—he is a young man, ripe and ready to cut the leading reins, and you'll have to let him go with a good grace or suffer the consequences."

"But he's so inexperienced! He could get hurt . . ."

"Quite possibly. He will certainly make mistakes, and do a lot of things he would be ashamed for you to know about."

"Maurice said something very similar."

"Then the man has more sense than I gave him credit for." The wretchedness in her eyes made him speak more roughly than he had intended. *"My dear, green girl!* What did you ex-pect? You take him from the safe, and probably rather dull, confines of Baltimore society and set him down in Paris, of all places! Good God! Any lad of nineteen with an ounce of spirit—and I suspect your brother has plenty—would find the temptation irresistible!"

"Do you suppose I am not aware of that?" she cried. "And that if he comes to grief, the blame must be mine."

"Nonsense!"

"It isn't nonsense. It was my idea to visit London, my idea to come to Paris! Patrick was quite content with Baltimore until I filled his head with talk of travel."

"True. But what has happened would still have happened there. At your brother's age, one town is very much like another."

Clementina blinked up at him through a sheen of tears. "You seem very sure. Do you speak from experience?"

A smile flickered in his eyes. "When I was nineteen, I was a very raw subaltern, still grass-green! And although I can remember nowhere to compare with Paris, every town of note had its 'Maison Dorée.' I sampled most of them until I finally became satiated. I know very little of your brother as yet, but I daresay it will be the same with him. In fact, I suspect he has been much too well brought up to seek after more than a few vicarious thrills! However, if you are really troubled, I will engage to keep a discreet eye on him."

The magnanimity of his offer was so unexpected—so totally out of keeping with his character as she knew it, or thought she knew it—that she stammered, "But . . . helping people is, of all things, what you most dislike . . . I remember most distinctly your telling me so!"

"I know. I shall probably regret the offer tomorrow, but no matter." The smile had faded to a brooding, considering gaze that brought a faint blush to Clementina's cheeks. To cover her embarrassment she said lightly, "May I get up now?"

He reached out and brought her easily to her feet. For a moment they stood close, not speaking, hands still clasped, and for the first time Clementina became aware of him not just as her cousin, but as a man. His eyes were really more blue than gray, she discovered, and thickly lashed. And they weren't cold at all! She knew a momentary inexplicable impulse to rest her head on the inviting expanse of his shoulder, still clad in the voluminous folds of his drab driving coat. It put her in such a panic that she tugged furiously at her hands. He released them at once and this time it was his turn to flush.

"There must be more to family ties than I had thought," he said slowly. "I find it increasingly difficult to rid myself of the notion that I have in some way become responsible for you!"

"Oh dear! How very disconcerting for you!" Her sudden uprush of emotion found relief in laughter. "Never mind, cousin—if you do not regard it, I daresay the feeling will go away."

Her rallying tones found a faint answering echo in his eyes. "Possibly. On the other hand, you don't suppose I might grow to like the idea?"

"Good gracious, I do hope not! It wouldn't suit me in the least to be obliged to conform to someone else's notion of what might be good for me!"

"It would do you a power of good," he declared with a sudden frown.

"Quite possibly, Marquis. But, like you, I am a monstrously selfish creature; I cannot bear interference! And besides," she said, mocking him, "what of your high-flown principles . . . your avowed policy of noninvolvement? I could never come between a man and his principles!" She saw that the smile had returned and deepened, and ended kindly, "No, no,—you had much better wash your hands of me now before I do something outrageous that will remind you how cordially you dislike me and oblige you to cut the connection!"

He laughed aloud and then said slowly, as though the thought had taken him by surprise, "I have never said that I dislike you."

"No more you have," she said lightly. "I really must stop putting words into your mouth. But you cannot pretend that it would please you to be made answerable for a parcel of brash American relations who are no more than mere cousins umpteen times removed?"

"Miss Brady, you talk a great deal too much—and most of it is nonsense!"

"And you, sir," she returned accusingly, "are aping the coward, which I know that you are *not*, by evading the question! Furthermore—when you were being kind to me earlier, you addressed me as Clementina."

"Very well, Clementina—to show that I am capable of true magnanimity I shall consider it an honor if you will consent to take a drive with me."

"Now?" she asked, staring up at him, wide eyed.

"Now," he said. "You may have . . ." he glanced at the clock, ". . . ten minutes to get ready."

Within seven minutes she was back, dressed charmingly in a frogged pelisse of her favorite soft brown with a matching toque tied enchantingly under one ear with jonquil ribbons. She found Lord Cadogon, having shed his driving coat, stretched out in the salon's most comfortable chair. He rose to his feet, one eyebrow lifted in surprised, grudging approval.

As she was pulling on a pair of yellow kid gloves, the door opened to admit the major-domo, who advanced bearing a card on a small silver salver. This he presented to Clementina with an air of scarcely suppressed triumph.

"Prince Metlin!" she exclaimed with pleasure. "Oh, do show him in at once, Maurice."

"It will be my pleasure, mademoiselle." Maurice's chest swelled visibly as he left the room; first a Marquis and now a Russian Prince—and all in the space of one morning! Not forgetting Mademoiselle's Comte, also, together with a veritable mountain of calling cards that had been left—almost everyone of importance in Paris! Assuredly, he had chosen well when he had chosen this position with Miss Brady. There were those among his contemporaries who considered that he demeaned himself to work for an American lady— even so wealthy an American lady—but he had trusted to his instincts, which were never wrong. He would enjoy to see them eat their words!

Clementina turned to Lord Cadogon. "Are you acquainted with Prince Metlin?"

"I am." He looked quizzical. "So, it seems, are you. At the risk of being accused of interference, perhaps I should warn you that he is a shocking flirt."

"Yes, I know." She chuckled.

Prince Metlin came across the room with eyes only for Clementina, bowed formally, and carried her proferred hand to his lips, as she smiled her welcome.

"Miss Brady, I have been impatient to come until finally I could wait no longer! Tell me that I do not incommode you?"

"Certainly not, Prince. I am very pleased to see you."

"Ah, but I am to be disappointed." His quick, appreciative glance took in her dress. "You are going out?"

"Yes, but only with Lord Cadogon, and I'm sure he won't mind a little delay," said Clementina, ruthlessly sabotaging her cousin's plans. "You already know one another, I believe?"

Prince Metlin exclaimed and strode forward to envelop the Marquis in a bearlike embrace that astonished Clementina almost as much by its warmth as by the obvious pleasure with which it was returned, for, although His Lordship's greeting was caustic, there was a light in his eye that belied it. The Prince grinned pugnaciously.

"But how is it that I find you here attempting to steal a march on the rest of us? I appeal to your British fair play—is it permitted that a late-comer lays siege to Paris's newest, most enchanting prize in so cavalier a fashion?"

Clementina didn't know where to look. Cadogon's voice was heavy with irony. "Not only permitted, but perfectly proper, my dear Alexei, for the *prize* happens to be this particular late-comer's cousin—and I'm not at all sure I approve the company she's keeping."

"*Ah, mon Dieu!*" The Prince winced in mock dismay. "*My reputation, Iago, my reputation!*"

"Won't bear investigation, that's for sure!" retorted the Marquis unfeelingly.

"But, no, I am a frippery fellow—quite harmless. Everybody knows this. Miss Brady, I appeal to you—am I not harmless?"

Clementina was hard put to it not to laugh, but she entered enthusiastically into the spirit of the charade, saying gravely, "Harmless? Oh, I really couldn't say. I fear I hardly know Your Highness well enough as yet to venture an opinion."

"Mademoiselle—you wound me! And I thought you my friend!"

With his moustache drooping mournfully and one hand clasped dramatically over his heart, he looked so comical that she could not remain serious a moment longer. Her peal of laughter brought the light instantly back to his eyes.

"It is well," he said, beaming on them both. And then, "Ah, Dominic, it is indeed good to have you back. Paris has missed your most refreshing brand of sanity —and so have your friends. Tell me, have you seen Elyse yet—and the little one? How she is grown, that one!"

For a moment Clementina wondered if she had misheard, but no, for the Marquis was saying, as though it were the greatest commonplace, that no, he hadn't seen them as yet, but would be doing so very soon, and then he passed on to speak of matters Parisian, leaving her consumed with curiosity. She determined to quiz Prince Metlin at the very first opportunity and continued to ponder the question while the Prince brought Lord Cadogon up to date with all the latest "on dits," including the latest attempt to unseat poor old King Louis . . .

"Of course, on the surface all is gaiety, but it becomes clearer every day that many, including members of the Royal Family, would like to pluck out 'fat Louis' and put Monsieur, his brother, in his place! Of course, Monsieur is categorically denying complicity in this latest conspiracy, but it is inconceivable that he did not know! Several of his supporters were involved, including young de Tourne, and everyone knows how, urged on by his mama, he aspires to his father's dream of becoming right hand to Louis's successor . . ."

In his enthusiastic desire to impart the latest scandals to his friend, the Prince had momentarily forgotten Clementina. She, on the other hand, was suddenly giving him her full attention.

". . . but in order to achieve such eminence he needs money. He has already squandered one fortune and is now desperately seeking another. His best hope, of course, lies in procuring for himself a rich wife . . ."

Something in Cadogon's expression arrested the Prince in midsentence; in the ensuing silence horror flooded his face as he realized the enormity of what he had said. Clementina watched in mounting anger as he turned, red faced, toward the Marquis as though appealing for help, only to find his friend strangely uncooperative.

"Don't look at me, Alexei—I am already damned for speaking my mind on *that* head!"

The Prince's mouth dropped open in even more ludicrous dismay. He looked from Cadogon's tight-lipped inflexibility to meet the full force of Clementina's blazing indignation. There was more here that he could divine, but he was too miserable to succumb to more than a passing curiosity.

"Miss Brady, what can I say, except to beg your forgiveness? My tongue—my accursed passion for gossip! But no, there can be no excuse!"

"I should think you had rather apologize to the Comte de Tourne," she retorted, angry out of all proportion with the nature of his offence. "That of which you accuse him far outweighs any slight against me."

The Prince looked more unhappy than ever.

"Don't be a fool, Clementina." Cadogon, shrugging himself into his driving coat, was brusque. "You know nothing of affairs here."

Clementina had removed her gloves and stood dragging

them through her hands, her anger directed almost entirely against the Marquis, for it was now abundantly clear to her that he had come this morning with the avowed intention of lecturing her yet again about her friendship with de Tourne. For a while she had been almost in charity with him. Now she remembered only how terse he had been on his arrival and saw the notion of a drive simply as a ploy meant to sweeten her.

"I am sorry, gentlemen," she said. "I feel a headache coming on. Marquis." She turned a smouldering glance on him. "I regret that I must decline your offer of a drive."

"As you wish." He was coldly formal.

She turned to Prince Metlin and held out her hand. He took it and carried it to his lips. "Prince, forgive me. I am abominable company when I am out of sorts. Perhaps you will call again when I am more the thing."

"Miss Brady," said the Prince, his eyes gently concerned. "You are more kind than I deserve."

Clementina, feeling an absurd and quite uncharacteristic desire to succumb to tears, walked quickly to the door, but he was before her, waiting to open it.

Outside, so close that she was convinced he had been listening, stood her major-domo. She stared at him coldly. "Maurice, His Highness and Lord Cadogon are leaving."

"As you say, mademoiselle," said Maurice with great dignity. There was a hint of reproof in the words and he looked very much as though he, too, would burst into tears.

❧CHAPTER 8❧

In the courtyard where the Marquis's curricle and the Prince's cabriolet waited side by side, Alexei spread his hands in rueful disbelief. "How could I do it, Dominic? Of all people, for me to make a blunder like a . . . a simpleton, an unbreeched, mindless whelp! *Dieu!*" He smote his forehead in a gesture of pure melodrama. "What is your cousin to make of such a clod!"

The histrionics were wasted on the Marquis, who only murmured absently, "She will probably deplore your lack of finesse," a look of pain passed briefly over the Prince's mobile features, "but by now she will have succeeded in convincing herself that you were primed by me."

"You think it? Ah, but no . . . never shall I live down the shame!"

"Gammon!" said His Lordship with a glimmer of a smile. "Your conceit is a trifle bruised, but you will come about—and so will she. I doubt my cousin Clementina's the kind to nurse grudges. Take her some flowers or whatever you usually do . . . turn upon her the full extent of your charm!"

"If that is what you really advise . . ."

"Oh, I never advise," said the Marquis softly. "It is but a suggestion." He considered the matter closed and resumed his preoccupation. "Alexei, have you run across the young brother in those dens of pleasure you frequent?"

The Prince chuckled. "He is so young, that one! So naive! At the Maison Dorée he is like an innocent set down in a seraglio; he knows there is much pleasure to be derived, but is unsure how to make a beginning!"

Lord Cadogon's smile was fleeting. "But is he mixing in bad company?"

"How does one define *bad?* Most often he is with the Bennett boy or young Gallatin. He will take little harm there, I think." Alexei shrugged. "Perhaps he is too much with de Tourne's more wild followers than is for his good, but . . ."

His words were seized on with surprising swiftness. "These friends of the Comte? Would they be likely to exploit that naiveté you spoke of?" The Marquis gave Alexei a brief account of what had occurred in London. The Prince listened attentively, punctuating the narrative with lively comment.

"So!" he said at the end of it. "You are sure of this, Dominic? You think the boy's life to be at risk?"

"That's the very devil of it! I am sure of nothing!" said the Marquis with feeling. "I simply have an uncomfortable notion that young Patrick is ripe to be used—as a weapon, if nothing worse. And, little as I relish playing the nursemaid, I cannot ignore the situation."

"You wish me to keep my eye open?"

"Would you do that? It would certainly occasion less comment, since you are more like to patronize the same disreputable haunts!" He ignored his friend's indignant protest, climbed into his curricle, and took up the reins. "Perhaps, between us, we may steer him away from trouble. And Alexei—I would prefer that no word of this comes to Miss Brady's ears, if you please!"

Oblivious of the concern being generated on his behalf, Patrick faced the day ahead of him with something less than enthusiasm. The haziest of recollections, allied to a faint nauseous throbbing at the temples, were sufficient to bring him low, though Maurice had proved a regular trump. His imperturbable manner had gone a long way to restoring Patrick's self-induced notion that he was truly a man of the world and might have carried him through, had not a visit from Clemmy and a positive rain of questions that he had felt ill equipped to answer soon reduced him again to the level of the schoolroom, a condition that the silent, but equally telling reproaches of Joshua did little to alleviate.

He was therefore astonished, and not a little relieved, when, on finally swaggering downstairs, with his newest spotted cravat arranged in a style much favored by his friend Gaston, prepared to brazen his way through the renewed onslaught of his sister's wrathful interrogation, he found her so wrapped in contemplation of her own shortcomings as to grant him an unexpected reprieve. Aunt Seraphina, too, seemed a trifle distraught; to be sure, she peered at him through her spectacles and pronounced him to be looking a little peaky, but before she was able to press on him one of her inevitable James Powders, he had made good his escape.

With the resilience of youth, his spirits soon revived. He resolved never to be caught in such a sorry state again and, deeming it prudent to keep out of the way of his womenfolk for the remainder of the day, he ordered his curricle and went in search of Alfred Bennett. Together the two young men spent a pleasant, uneventful day until Alfred was obliged to return home to fulfil his filial duty at some stuffy Embassy function.

Once more at a loose end, Patrick decided that he too would return home and play the penitent. He had never yet failed to coax Clemmy round after one of their quarrels—she never could sustain her rages—and he was confident of his ability to insinuate himself back into her good graces again. His plans received a severe setback, however. In the Rue de Varennes he discerned an atmosphere. Maurice, aloof to the point of moroseness, pronounced that Miss Brady was gone out and Mrs. Westbury had prostrated herself with the headache. On being pressed further, he became suddenly voluble, but cryptic, his dialogue punctuated with many gloomy animadversions upon the folly of committing social suicide, which seemed to be tied in somehow with the possibility that he had made a terrible mistake.

Unable to make sense of it all, Patrick shrugged off the mystery, changed his clothes, and ventured forth yet again, but with his recent overindulgence still painfully fresh in his mind, he resisted the lure of the Maison Dorée and went instead to the Opera.

There he met Rosa, a petite, deliciously curvaceous charmer. Her eyes, as blue as harebells in summer, promised untold delights; her hair was a riot of dusky curls. She responded to his eager, stumbling overtures with a flattering degree of warmth and invited him to take supper with her.

Her apartment in the Rue de la Paix was a revelation—too luxurious by far for one so young. The probability that there must be a wealthy patron in the background caused him a moment's unease, but it was quickly stifled as she beckoned him to the candlelit table before the fire that was already laid with covers for two. Beyond a door left tantalizingly ajar, he caught a glimpse of the boudoir beyond. Rich cerise hangings draped about the most enormous, most opulent bed he had ever seen, its canopy held aloft by a pair of voluptuous, heavily gilded nude figures.

A hot flood of embarrassment rushed up under his collar and he was glad of the subdued lighting to hide his blushes. His blood began to race—his very first intrigue! He hoped Rosa would not notice how his hand shook as he set down his wineglass and stretched tentative fingers across the board to meet hers. Their tips had scarcely touched, however, when the sound of a door opening and closing in the hall tore them apart.

"*Mon Dieu!*" gasped Rosa, springing to her feet. "*Je suis perdu! Cachez-vous . . . cachez-vous! Vitement!* Oh, quickly, please hide!"

Patrick, his newly acquired manhood shattered by this unexpected display of panic, allowed himself to be bundled ignominiously into a cupboard, where he was obliged to cower in acute discomfort, his heart thumping, his ears straining to catch what was going on.

A voice, vaguely familiar, said softly, "Well, my little Rosa! What is this?"

He heard Rosa falteringly expressing surprise—she had not expected her Monseigneur this evening . . . he had said he would be away . . .

"And so?" the voice pressed with gentle insistence. "You are entertaining a secret *amant*, perhaps?"

Patrick's mouth went suddenly dry, for he had recognized the voice; it was Monsieur de Tourne! Oh, the devil take it! Now what was he to do? The embarrassment if he should be thus discovered!

"*Ah, non!*" Rosa's denial came to him, sharp with fear. "Nothing of the kind, I promise you! It was . . . my sister. *Yes, that is it* . . . my sister! She was so overwhelmed at the prospect of meeting my Monseigneur that she ran away the moment she heard you arrive!"

"I see! I did not know that you had a sister. How unfortunate that she left so . . . suddenly! I should have enjoyed meeting her."

The Comte sounded politely disbelieving, and Patrick was not surprised. Even in his own ears, the shakily delivered lies sounded feeble and riddled with guilt. Poor Rosa! He discovered a large crack in the door of the cupboard through which it was possible to see part of the room, and at once his heart plummeted, for on a chair, clearly visible if the Comte should but glance in that direction, was his hat! Any hope that it might remain unnoticed fled as a figure blotted it from view; and a moment later it reappeared, held up as though for inspection.

"So, little one!" The endearment fell upon the air like a chill caress, and Patrick's stomach lurched uncomfortably. "It would seem that this sister of yours, who so shyly effaces herself rather than meet me, has some very curious habits! Can it be that she wears a gentleman's hat?"

Rosa's terrified gasp decided Patrick; he could bear the suspense no longer. Honor demanded that he should discover himself and take the consequences, however unpleasant.

He burst from the cupboard with more speed than grace, and blurted out, "I am Rosa's sister, Comte! That hat is mine!"

There was a ghastly silence, broken by a sudden outburst of hysterical sobbing. It was like some macabre tableau, thought Patrick in despair—the girl in passionate supplication at the Comte's feet, whence she had flung herself, himself hot, crumpled, totally disadvantaged, and not a little nervous, and Monsieur de Tourne, the very epitome of grace and ele-

gance, his greatcoat falling open to reveal the perfection
beneath. He let the hat drop and rested one hand negligently
upon the intricate gold knob of his cane, the other being
raised, quizzing glass in long white fingers as he surveyed the
scene. He seemed to be in no hurry to speak.

Patrick rushed in blindly, stumbling over the words. "Forgive me, Monsieur le Comte, it seems I am . . . I should not
be here! I did not know . . ."

The words dried up under that stare. The Comte seemed to
see beyond his disheveled auburn hair, his finely rounded
boy's face; beyond the bright blue eyes where fear now
lurked, and deep into his soul. Only when he seemed satisfied
did the Comte's gaze shift to take in the table set for two, the
meal scarcely touched, and finally to rest upon Rosa's heav-
ing shoulders.

"Quite so."

The statement was devoid of expression.

Again Patrick launched himself quickly, too quickly, into
Rosa's defence, one hand clasping the edge of his coat as
though it were a sword hilt. "I insisted upon escorting Mademoiselle Rosa home from the Opera," he said, dry mouthed.
"In recompence she invited me to sup with her. Any blame
must therefore attach to me. I am at your disposal."

One corner of the Comte's mouth lifted in a sardonic
smile. "You think I would stoop to fight—over this trash?" A
toe, shod in the finest leather, fastidiously stirred the girl so
that her sobs grew afresh. "My dear Patrick, one does not
chastise a young, untrained dog for going after a bitch in
heat. It is the way of nature! One simply guards the bitch
more closely, and if it becomes a nuisance, one deals with it!"

It was so casually said that for a moment Patrick didn't
grasp the full import of his words. When they finally sank in,
his voice shook.

"In God's name, you go too far, sir! Mademoiselle Rosa,
do not cry so, I beg of you! If Monsieur has no further need
of you, you may come with me. My sister will not refuse you
shelter!" He moved forward as he spoke, attempting to urge
the distressed girl to her feet.

Henri de Tourne watched with narrowed eyes before
shedding his greatcoat. He threw it over a chair and, fingering the riband of his quizzing glass thoughtfully, forced a
lighter note into his voice.

"Come now, Patrick, this all grows much too serious! The
situation is an embarrassing one, *bien sur,* but between

gentlemen of the world such as ourselves the solution is simple enough, would you not agree?"

Patrick hesitated, torn between his initial instincts, which told him that all was not well, and the irresistible notion of being deferred to as an experienced man of the world. While he still hesitated, the Comte pressed home his advantage. "It but requires you to depart and forget that you were ever here, and we will do likewise." His voice, still verging on the jovial, took on a little more emphasis. "Get up, Rosa. Can you not see that your guest is on the point of leaving? If you do not cease that appalling caterwauling and make him your thanks, Patrick will think you ungrateful as well as inhospitable!"

Rosa uttered one brief, shuddering moan and scrambled to her feet, a truly pathetic figure; devoid now of her earlier charms, she looked young and very vulnerable. As she muttered her thanks, Patrick was prompted to a spontaneous outburst of chivalry.

"Mademoiselle!" he cried. "Are you perfectly certain that you wouldn't rather come with me?"

"I doubt your sister would welcome such a one as Rosa." Henri's affability was fast becoming ragged at the edges.

"Clemmy would understand!"

"Furthermore, you are being a little insulting to me, I think. Really Patrick, I took you for a sensible young man, eager to be accepted into our world. But it is a world where there are rules, *mon ami,* by which you must abide. Oh, take a mistress by all means . . . choose wisely, discreetly, and she will be accepted almost everywhere." He smiled faintly. "Your reputation may even advance!" His passionless glance flicked over Rosa. "Pleasures of an earthy, more transient nature, however, are quite another matter and have *no* place in that world!" His voice was softly insistent. "I hope I make myself plain? And now——" with finality "——I believe we have detained you long enough."

It was an unmistakable dismissal; but it was Rosa who made up Patrick's mind for him. There was resignation in her voice and a curious dignity in the way she drew herself up straight. "Go, monsieur," she said. "You will do no good—— for me or for yourself—by remaining."

And so Patrick went, but all the way home the girl's image was before him, her painted face all smudged and blotchy with tears. She could not be any age—certainly she was younger than himself. Would the Comte be harsh with her? It seemed likely that he would. Clemmy ought to know how things were, but even without Henri's warning, it went against the grain to turn tale-bearer . . .

He entered the house just as Clementina was mounting the stairs. She turned to see the footman relieving him of his hat. At once her despondently drooping shoulders straightened and her expression lightened. "Well, little brother?" she said. "Are you resolved upon an early night, too?" And then, chiding him, "Oh, Patrick! No greatcoat? My dear boy, you will take a chill!"

He realized that he had left the coat at Rosa's and the memory jarred, like a wound unwittingly prodded. He muttered something incoherent about "not fussing" and sounded churlish. Standing beneath the great Venetian chandelier at the foot of the stairs, he looked up at her and his misery was plain to see.

Clementina, misinterpreting its cause, came running down the stairs to cup his face in a quick, impulsive gesture.

"Oh, my dear! Don't look like that! I won't tease you any more about last night, I promise!" She sighed. "It hasn't been a good day for either of us. Let us forget it and be friends!"

What Patrick wanted to do more than anything at that moment was to throw his arms around Clemmy and pour out the whole wretched tale! She had always been fair, had always listened patiently to his childish outpourings, ready to laugh him out of his fears, or patch up his hurts. But now the words wouldn't come; and it wasn't fear of the Comte that held him silent, or shame or even his overriding sense of guilt, but a sudden need to prove to himself that he was no longer a child; that he could stand without Clemmy.

So he drew himself up and forced a smile to stiff lips.

"Friends," he agreed.

Clementina studied him a moment longer, then a smile curved her mouth. She linked her arm through his, and together they mounted the stairs.

Patrick found his sleep that night much troubled by laughing blue eyes grown dark with terror; concern lay like an unbearable weight within his chest throughout the following day. He didn't leave his room until well after midday, and then he ordered his curricle to be brought round.

The apartment in the Rue de la Paix was ominously silent; it yielded not a movement in answer to his repeated knocking. The concierge, when roused, was taciturn and incurious. Yes, he believed the young person had left with Monseigneur late on the previous evening. No, he had not actually seen her, just the two figures passing his window. No, he did not know if she would return. He shrugged. It was all one to him. He was but the caretaker.

❧CHAPTER 9❧

Clementina was not given to repining over what was past and done with, but the light of a new day found her puzzled and deeply regretting her recent behavior. Her temper had been known to flare suddenly, but she hoped she was never rancorous—and *never* petty! Yet here she was, at odds with everyone—Patrick, her aunt, the Marquis—especially the Marquis! Even poor, inoffensive Prince Metlin had not escaped her displeasure!

Well, it wouldn't do. She didn't at all like the picture of herself conjured up by her thoughts and must do what she could to mend matters. A sharp dose of humility would be a salutary physic for her pride! But her path was not to be made easy. Maurice, when encountered, was the very acme of politeness, but she was left in little doubt that she had fallen from grace and would have her work cut out to regain his approbation. Drat it, she decided with a flash of spirit that boded ill for her resolve, I will not apologize to my majordomo!

A solitary breakfast depressed her still further. Patrick seldom put in an appearance so early, and anyway she had made her peace with him, but it was unusual for Aunt Seraphina to sleep so late. She came at last, the dark circles under her eyes reproaching Clementina more deeply than words. She proceeded to treat her niece with such gentle solicitude, very much as though she were an invalid to be humored, as to drive Clementina almost to despair.

In consequence, when Prince Metlin called late in the morning resplendent in his colonel's uniform, full of contrition and exuberance and bearing the most enormous bouquet of flowers she had ever seen, she was more than ready to fall upon his neck.

The most amiable of arguments ensued, and by the time that each had steadfastly refused to allow that apologies were in any way due to the other from any cause, either real or imagined, all her earlier opinions were confirmed and they were well on the way to becoming fast friends. Indeed, Clementina had seldom known anyone half so amusing, or with whom she had felt so readily at ease, and her spirits were well on the way to being fully restored.

Aunt Seraphina had lost her heart to the Prince from the first. To be sure, he was not so handsome as the Comte, or so authoritative as the Marquis, but he had such kind eyes! And besides, there was nothing quite so guaranteed to stir her heart as a fine set of regimentals!

"Since I was largely responsible for depriving you of your drive yesterday," Alexei pleaded, "permit me, dear Miss Brady, to put myself and my carriage at your disposal this morning."

"Why, thank you. But you mustn't feel that you have to . . ."

"Please! I would count it an honor. Mrs. Westbury," he turned gallantly to Aunt Seraphina. "You will take a drive with us?"

She gave him her gentle smile. "My dear Prince, I am persuaded you can't want me along. But take Clementina by all means and see if you can contrive to put the sparkle back in her eyes. She has been quite out of sorts this past day or two."

Clementina, in a fitted redingote of sea-green twilled silk and a modish hat whose deep brim of ruched silk becomingly shaded her eyes, was presently handed up into a smart little cabriolet and wrapped in furs. When the Prince came to sit beside her, she was amused to note that there was just room comfortably for the two of them, and wondered how he would have contrived if Aunt Seraphina had insisted upon playing propriety! The result would have been a sad squeeze! The thought continued to divert her as her escort negotiated the courtyard and emerged onto the road.

"And now, Miss Brady," he said. "We must decide how best to restore your bruised spirits."

"My bad temper." She corrected him. "I am heartily ashamed, I promise you." He would have spoken, but she said on a laugh, "Yes, yes, I know, Prince, we agreed to be done with self-recrimination . . ."

"*Alexei*, please, if we are to be friends."

"Very well. Alexei. I should like that above all things. And you must call me Clementina. Oh, I am so glad that you came this morning!" She gave a sudden gurgle of laughter. "And so, I vow, is Maurice. Did you see his face as he announced you?"

"Your major-domo?" The Prince was intrigued. "Why should my coming give him pleasure?"

"Oh, Maurice aspires to the very pinnacle of his calling," Clementina declared blithely. "I believe he intends that my salon shall become a venue for the whole of fashionable Paris, and when I was so disobliging as to quarrel with you and my cousin yesterday, he was quite desperately cast down!"

"I see." He smiled.

There followed a companionable silence. Clementina snuggled back among the rugs feeling warm and cherished, until they came at last to the wide sweep of the Champs Elysées; as always, Clementina gave voice to her pleasure.

"Ah, but spring is the time when Paris comes so superbly into her own." Alexei glanced at her. "Will you be here in the spring, do you suppose?"

"Oh, heavens, I haven't any idea."

He said casually, "Dominic has told me a little of your history. Just the barest facts, you understand . . . and those I had to drag from him!" His eyes twinkled. "Poor Dominic! You have unsettled him quite considerably! Did you know?"

There was a silence, then Clementina said in a small, tight voice, "Alexei, tell me truly—do you find me brash and overbearing?"

"Ah, no! Never that!" Alexei spoke quickly, impulsively. "You have liveliness of spirit—a vivacity—to excite the imagination, and you speak your mind with complete honesty. It is one of the things I instantly admired in you. And you do not simper. *Mon Dieu*, you can have no idea how refreshing you are!"

She was at once mollified and amused by his impetuous outburst.

"And you must not mind about Dominic," he continued, "it will be good for him to be shaken out of his complacency. When he was first in Paris with the army he was quite a fellow, I can tell you! But now, since Elyse, he grows too staid!"

There was that name again. She confessed her curiosity.
"Do tell me, Alexei—who is she?"

"Elyse Robart? You do not know? *Eh, bien,* then I will tell
you." He diverted the carriage from the busy thoroughfare
into a quiet, tree-lined boulevard and brought it to a halt.
The sounds of traffic faded to a distant rumble. "When Dominic first came to Paris with the Allied Armies the Robarts
were good friends to him. For a while he lodged with them
and he and Paul were as brothers. And then, it must be almost
three years ago that it happened . . ." Alexei's face took on a
brooding look. "There was some trouble—the circumstances
were never clear—and Paul Robart died. He was known to
be a radical and as such he clashed many times, as others
did, with the returning Royalists who wanted all to be as it
was before.

"At that time Dominic was charged by Wellington with the
task of maintaining order and fostering good relations between the two factions." A shrug. "He took Paul's death
hard. It was as though he held himself responsible for what
happened and from that day he has taken Elyse and her
daughter, who was but a babe at the time, under his
protection."

"I see," said Clementina slowly. Here was yet another facet
of Lord Cadogon's character to conflict with what she already
knew of him. "Is she his . . ." she began and found that her
outspokenness had suddenly deserted her, though her meaning was clear enough.

Prince Metlin looked amused. "Did you imagine him to be
less of a man than the rest of us?"

"No, of course not!" She was astonished by the violence of
her reaction and blushing, forced a quick laugh. "I suppose I
just wondered why they had never married, but I should be
used by now to the way people in Paris flaunt their affairs before the world!"

"And that troubles you?"

The directness of the question, the touch of whimsy in his
voice, made her feel even more harrassed. She thought of
Henri, who had a mistress, and told herself that she didn't
mind in the least. "I guess I don't really understand," she
confessed. "You see, I am not in the least romantical myself."

Alexei was much diverted. "Were you never in love?"

Clementina took refuge in flippancy. "Yes, once—when I
was fourteen. I fell passionately in love with Mr. Ball, our local curate. At the time I thought him a truly romantic fig-

ure. In retrospect, of course, I realize that he was quite dreadfully thin, with an already pronounced stoop, but at fourteen, you know, such trifling imperfections only served to confirm to me how much he was in need of my ministrations!"

Alexei chuckled. "What happened?"

"He married the Widow Hamilton and they moved to Virginia. I nursed my secret grief for all of two weeks and resolved that I would never love again."

"Poor little Clementina!" He commiserated. "But later? Were there no young men in Baltimore with initiative enough to make you change your mind?"

"Not really. Grandpa Brady had a way of discouraging strangers, and besides, romance does not flourish easily when common sense leads one to suspect that one is desired mostly for one's fortune!"

"My dear foolish girl!" The Prince's eyebrow described a wildly quizzical arc. "That is patently a nonsense! Why, have I not desired you from the very first? And I do not have the least regard for your fortune!"

Clementina colored up delightfully. She knew that pretty speeches came as naturally to Alexei as breathing, but she also fancied that he was probably remembering his remarks about Henri, though his name had not been mentioned, and this was his kindly way of making amends.

So she laughed to find her heart beating a little faster. "Thank you, dear Prince. You have all my gratitude, even if I can't quite believe you!"

"That is a dangerous statement to make, *moya dorogoya,* for you will oblige me to prove it to you. But later," he added, his eyes brimming with laughter as her confusion grew. He raised her hand to his lips and released it. "For now, I mean to show you the Paris you do not often see." But just before he set the little mare in motion, his manner grew serious. "We have spoken lightly of love, dear mademoiselle," he said cryptically. "But do not, I beg of you, give your heart too readily to any man. I would not have you hurt!"

Clementina knew that this time he was undoubtedly referring to the Comte. She would have liked to ask his advice, but she hesitated and then the moment was gone. Anyway, she was surely capable of making up her own mind on an issue that affected her so vitally.

"Don't prejudge people, Clemmy," Grandpa Brady was

used to say. "And don't pay too much heed to other folks' opinions. Your own opinion's the only important one for you!" Well, Grandpa ought to know! And it would be absurd to think the worst of Monsieur de Tourne simply because of gossip, or because her cousin Dominic disliked him.

Alexei was an entertaining guide, taking her where Henri would never have thought to take her, let alone have approved of. There were boulevards gay with cafés, which on sunny days, as now, disgorged clusters of tables outside onto the pavement so that the gentlemen might gather there to inspect the demimonde who tripped past, displaying their wares with an insouciance only the Parisienne can boast. At Tortoni's he stopped the carriage and procured for her one of their famous ices, a most glorious and extravagant confection! In buoyant mood by this time, they went on from there to Les Halles, a noisy, jostling, exhilarating collection of market stalls, where the lusty, well-endowed fishwives were disposed to sell their bodies with as much good nature as they did their wares.

Here it required all of the Prince's skill with the ribbons to negotiate a passage for his carriage between the crush of carts, but he still found time to respond to the blatant camaraderie of the posturing women with a gallantry that sent them into whoops of laughter. He turned to grin at Clementina.

"Forgive me!" His voice rose jovially above the clamor. "This is not, perhaps, the place to bring a lady, but if one would know a city such as Paris, one must experience all her moods!"

"I don't mind!" Clementina shouted in answer. "I love the feeling of life about it all!"

"It is said that Napoleon once drew up a plan to regularize this area into one vast, covered market—the mess, the lack of discipline affronted him—but, praise be, like many of the Emperor's schemes, it came to nothing!"

With the market left behind, they bowled on through a labyrinth of streets that became quieter and meaner as they progressed. On a corner a little way ahead of them an altercation was taking place. As they drew nearer, Clementina saw that a frail-looking child was resisting with much kicking and screaming the attempts of a well-built, dandified creature to drag her into the gloomy abyss of a cobbled street where the overhanging houses crouched eye to eye, shutting out all light and kindness.

The struggle was plainly an unequal one and it did not need a particularly vivid imagination to divine the man's purpose, yet, though several people passed by, none showed more than a cursory interest in the girl's plight.

"Oh, Alexei, please!" she implored. "Do stop!"

Puzzled, but ever obliging, the Prince did as he was bid. He was astonished, and more than a little apprehensive, however, when she at once leapt from the carriage and marched across the road and into the thick of the fight. Without hesitation she prodded the *maquereau*, for that was assuredly his function, in the back with her parasol—for all the world, as he later told the Marquis with great delight, as though the creature were some vile excrement upon the road.

"Monsieur!" she demanded in clear, ringing tones. "Do you hold any authority that permits you to molest this child?"

The girl's screams died in midflight as she fell to gaping, open mouthed. The man, caught unawares, swore viciously and, keeping a one-handed grip on his victim, swung round on his assailant, who nimbly side-stepped the flailing hand. Prince Metlin, busy securing the reins, sprang down to go to her aid, throwing a coin to a small boy who stood nearby, an interested spectator, with orders to stand guard over the carriage.

He arrived on the scene to find Clementina managing very well without him and the man, his eyes unpleasantly narrowed, weighing his chances of success faced with not one, but two, aggressive females.

"Look to your own business, madame," growled the villain in a most threatening manner, "and leave me to mine!"

Clementina was not noticeably impressed. "I shall be very pleased to do so," she returned with spirit. "If you can furnish me with proof that *your business is with this child*, which I take serious leave to doubt!"

The girl found her voice, her quick Parisian wits recognizing possible salvation in the shape of this extraordinary lady.

"You speak truly, madame . . . I have never laid eyes upon this . . ." She spat a crude, but pungently descriptive word at him, "until he this moment accosted me!"

"Be quiet, you!" A blow aimed at the girl earned him a sharp rap across the knuckles from Miss Brady's parasol, the force of which almost caused him to loose his victim and drew a spontaneous "bravo!" from Alexei. With a distinct air of persecution the man uttered an exceedingly rude expletive, thrust the injured member under his oxter, and muttered an aggrieved: "And who might you be, madame, to doubt or not to doubt?"

"I am Miss Clementina Brady," she said with a fine martial glint in her eye. "And I have with me Prince Alexei Metlin; besides being a Colonel in the army of the Czar, the Prince is a very important man. If you do not release this poor child at once, he will be obliged to deal with you!"

Alexei, who had been vastly entertained and who had not until this moment felt the least necessity to intervene, looked now at the well-developed muscles easily discernible through the villain's close-fitting coat—and blenched.

But the man had had enough. He loosed a stream of vituperation, most of which fell dismally short of its mark, being well outside the scope of Clementina's otherwise excellent command of the French tongue. Then he thrust the girl at her and slunk away, swearing revenge.

"You have made an enemy there, I think," Alexei observed in his droll way, and then faintly, as the enormity of what had transpired sank in, "Diabolical girl! Do you hold the lives of all your friends so cheap? I? To deal with such a brute as that? *Dieu!* He might have broken me into little pieces without the least effort!"

"Stuff! I knew he wouldn't stay to fight you! He was patently a bully, and bullies are invariably cowards at heart!"

"I am naturally relieved to learn this!" he said with mock solemnity, and then overcome with sudden mirth, he seized her hand and raised it to his lips in salutation. "Ah, Miss Clementina Brady, you are incomparable! I only hope that you permit me to live long enough to be glad that you have come to Paris!"

She joined in his laughter. "Well, but what else was I to do?" she demanded reasonably. "Allow him to carry the girl off to an obvious fate?"

"Most people would, *moya dorogoya*, but not you! Though what you are to do with her now . . . ?" Alexei shrugged, wiped his eyes, and turned his attention to the girl, amazed at the resilience she had shown in the face of her ordeal. It came as something of a shock to discover that she was not quite the child they had taken her for. Incredible violet eyes, large and round, that had watched their behavior with undisguised interest, rather as though she thought them a little mad, now settled speculatively upon Alexei; and as she stooped to pick up an inadequate bundle that lay discarded against the railings, there was an awareness, an unmistakable allure in every movement of the thin body, in the way she straightened up and tossed back the riotous mane of her golden hair.

"Come here, child." Clementina was beckoning. "What is your name?"

"Clothilde, if you please, madame." There was a likeable pertness about her.

"And how old are you, Clothilde?"

"Please madame, about sixteen years."

"Only sixteen! *Mon Dieu!*" murmured the Prince.

"Be quiet, Alexei! Well now, Prince Metlin here asks what I am to do with you, child. Do you have a home? Parents, perhaps?"

"No, madame. No one. I was sent from my grandmother's home two years since to go as a kitchen maid. Now she is dead."

Demure. Eyes downcast. Very prettily done!

"So you do have a place?"

"No, madame, I have been turned off. That is why I was walking the streets."

The words struck just the right note of despondency, but Alexei, watching her, was at that moment treated to a look from under sweeping lashes that made him chuckle inwardly. The girl was undoubtedly a coquette! He wondered if he should enlighten Clementina.

But Clementina needed no such enlightenment. Everyone would think she was mad, of course, but she too had been studying her protégée and had decided that she might repay a little trouble—a good wash and some more becoming clothes . . . She really did have the loveliest eyes. She swallowed her qualms.

"Do you think you would like to be a lady's maid?" she asked.

Clothilde's face was instantly transformed. "Oh, yes, madame!"

"I suppose you do know what you are doing?" murmured Alexei good-humouredly. "Should you not at least ask why she was turned off from her last place of employment?"

Clementina grinned at him. "If you like. But I'm not quite stupid. I expect it was a man . . . it most often is." She turned to Clothilde. "Am I right, child?"

Clothilde nodded at her with an air of limpid innocence. "It was the younger son, madame. His mother accused me of encouraging his attentions!"

"And, of course, you did no such thing!" finished Clementina dryly. "Well, I give you fair warning, Clothilde—I have a young brother, and if I catch you so much as attempting to flirt with him, I shall wallop you so hard, you won't sit down for a week!"

The journey home was not achieved without a certain amount of discomfort, but Clothilde, her quick wits busy assessing this unexpected turn in her fortune, was more than content to curl up on the floor at their feet hugging her few possessions, and treating Alexei to the occasional lingering, surreptitiously inviting glance from under those preposterous lashes.

Halfway across the Pont-neuf they were hailed by a familiar voice.

"Oh, no!" groaned Clementina.

Alexei chuckled. "Courage, *mon ange!*" he murmured, and as they reached the far side of the bridge he pulled up to allow the Marquis to come abreast of them. He was riding a young black stallion with a bright, nervy eye. "Good day to you, Dominic. A new acquisition?"

"Yes. I've only had him a few days. Brought him from England—good stock, but he's a bit fidgety, yet." The young horse threw up its head in emphatic agreement.

Clementina, who was feeling distinctly fidgety herself, sympathized. "Then you won't wish to keep him standing about, will you?" she urged and earned for herself a particularly inquisitorial stare that made her very conscious of the terms on which they had parted yesterday. She supposed he might be expecting her to make some gesture of appeasement, but decided in quick succession that she could not be forever apologizing to him and that in any case this was definitely not the moment to encourage the least hint of intimacy!

So far, Clothilde had remained out of his view and if only he might be persuaded to leave, or if Alexei would have the wit to drive on, they might yet avoid the need for embarrassing explanations. But maddeningly neither showed the least inclination to move, and as her fingers itched to seize the ribbons, the Marquis, keeping the stallion on a tight rein, rode in closer. At the same moment Clothilde, her curiosity aroused by the unknown masculine voice, rose to her knees with the grace of a young Aphrodite to peep over the rim of the carriage, so that he received the full impact of those incredible eyes. He swore, the horse shied and kicked out at the carriage, and for a few moments pandemonium reigned.

Of course, when order was restored, the whole story had to come out. Alexei told it most amusingly—far too amusingly to Clementina's way of thinking, for he invested the whole incident with a much greater degree of drama than it merited. And of course Dominic lapped up every word.

"Oh, good God!" He passed a smoothing, gauntleted hand over a face grown rigid with disbelief. "But Alexei, could you not have intervened?" He looked into his friend's twinkling eyes. "No, of course not, you are as incorrigible as Clementina!" His glance slid onto the girl and he seemed to wince. "But *surely* you could see what she . . ." He hesitated, then stopped.

Clementina said on a sudden gurgle of laughter, "You may speak your mind freely, cousin! Clothilde doesn't understand English—though she may, of course, be able to interpret expressions, and yours, if I may say so, is excessively revealing!" He jerked on the rein and the stallion showed its mettle. She said with contentious affability, "You know, I'm sure it isn't kind to keep that poor animal standing. You should take it to the Bois where it may have a good long run."

The Marquis dragged the horse's head round, his eyes kindling, but whether with laughter or annoyance she wasn't sure. "Thank you, cousin. I will do just that, for I am plainly quite out in trying to bring either of you to your senses! I can only hope that you don't have cause to rue this day's work!"

"Oh, stuff!" she called after his retreating back.

As might have been expected, Clementina's proposed addition to her household met with a certain amount of opposition in other quarters, also. Even Maurice, who was swiftly adjusting to the discovery that his mistress could be a creature of unpredictable whims, had misgivings; one could not but fear for the outcome when his young lackeys were exposed to the undoubted (though perhaps not immediately obvious to the inexperienced eye) charms of such a one! However the uncontained hostility of Madame Rubal toward the girl made of him her instant champion. A violent argument ensued that required all of Clementina's skill to resolve.

"A trial period, madame," she promised. "A month, perhaps. Clothilde deserves that much of a chance to prove herself. And I do not expect you to hold yourself responsible for her; my maid, Justine, is willing to take her in strict charge and train her. If the experiment fails, I will reconsider and make other arrangements for the child."

Madame Rubal waddled off, muttering of disasters, and
Maurice, catching Clementina's eye, gave his elegant little
shrug.

It was not to be expected that such a story could be kept
secret for long, but Clementina had not expected it to leak
out so quickly. That same evening at the Ballet news of it
came to Henri's ears. Assured that there must be some mistake, he related what he had heard to Clementina—and
found that it was no more than the truth, embellished a little,
to be sure, but the truth for all that. Caught off guard, he
took her to task.

"But surely you can see that it will not do! A girl like
that . . ."

"A girl like what, Henri?" She was determined to remain
calm, to make him see how it really was. "You haven't seen
her, I think?"

"I do not have to see her! *Mon Dieu!* A common street
girl and you take her under your roof! No wonder there is
talk!"

The orchestra was tuning up; Henri's hissed words were
lost in the hub of conversation, but from all parts of the auditorium the Comte and Clementina were under veiled observation, interested parties noting her animation, the way his
hand resting on the padded rail of their opera box clenched
from time to time, striking the crimson velvet as though
making his point with some force.

"Oh, heavens! What a fuss about one small, insignificant
human being!" Clementina had a swift mental vision of
Clothilde's entrancing velvety eyes, the fluid young body, now
becomingly clothed under Justine's expert supervision, already showing a disturbing tendency to wiggle! She swallowed a tiny qualm and rushed into a brief explanation of
what had caused her to act as she had done. "Would you
have had me leave her to that man's mercies? She is little
more than a child!"

The Comte remembered what was at stake and drew a
deep breath, then he said with patient indulgence of one who
knew better, "You are an innocent, *cherie!* Believe me, these
girls are professionals from the cradle and are well able to
account for themselves. Give her a few sous and a pretty
dress and she will be more than content to return to her old
haunts!"

The growing conviction that he could well be right did
nothing to soothe nerves already stretched by being obliged to

justify her action on all sides, but the music had begun and the curtains were parting, so she contented herself with a brusque "Don't patronize me, Henri!"

❧CHAPTER 10❧

Seraphina Westbury, with Prince Metlin's fingers reassuringly at her elbow, moved among the grand assembly of guests thronging the glittering ballroom of the Elysée Palace, totally obscured by magnificence and profoundly grateful to be so.

She had made her first curtsies to royalty, presented by kind Monsieur Gallatin, in an atmosphere more cordial and informal than she could have hoped for, neither the King nor his brother being present. Indeed, she had found the rigid punctiliousness of the Comtesse de Tourne far more unnerving than either the Duc or Duchesse de Berry or the Duc and Duchesse d'Orleans, all of whom had been most gracious in their greeting.

Such a curiously animated creature, the Duchesse de Berry—all nerves. Italian, of course, which might account for it, and very possessive of her handsome husband, running to hang upon his arm when he was conversing with friends. Mrs. Westbury had been a little shocked to learn that the Duc had formed a liaison with a Miss Brown during his time of exile in England and that he had fathered two daughters by her. Did his wife know, she wondered, and supposed that she must.

Mrs. Westbury tried not to let the story influence her opinion of him, but she had not quite liked the way he'd looked at Clemmy. So bold! Taking in every detail of her dress and figure . . . though to be sure, one could not dispute that Clemmy looked as fine as any duchesse tonight in her gown of palest apricot silk, embroidered with tiny silver acorns, which set off her lovely neck and shoulders to such advantage and made her waist seem incredibly small. Still, that did not excuse the familiarity with which the Duc had taken her

hands in both of his to raise her from her curtsy, holding on
to them and smiling in such a way!

"Ah, yes! The incomparable young American lady who res-
cues little scullery maids from their undoubted fate!" he had
said, which set everyone close by to staring. But though *she'd*
felt ready to sink, Clemmy was more than equal to the occasion, protesting laughingly that it was only one scullery maid
and a very young one at that! At which the Duc, too, had
laughed and begged the favor of a dance a little later—a
waltz, perhaps? Which, her aunt supposed, must have put her
in high feather!

It was the Duchesse d'Angouleme, however, who interested
Mrs. Westbury the most among the royals—a sad but superbly regal figure. Her dress was of the most exquisite lace with
a stomacher fashioned entirely of diamonds and emeralds;
her train was white velvet thickly encrusted with silver fleur-
de-lys, and on her head she wore a diadem all of four inches
high, again made up of diamonds and emeralds. She looked
every inch what she was—Madame Royale, the daughter of a
king—the only survivor of that dreadful revolutionary holo-
caust! (Though to be sure, they *had* met a lady in Baltimore
only last year who had been out West and swore she had seen
the boy who should have been Louis XVII; said he had been
brought up by a tribe of Indians!)

It had distressed Mrs. Westbury to learn that the dress
worn by the Duchesse had belonged to her mother, poor
Marie Antoinette. It was a very beautiful dress, of course—
too beautiful to be entirely discarded, perhaps—yet strongly
though she felt the tragedy of the Duchesse's life, to be wearing her poor dead mother's clothes seemed the outside of
enough, more than a trifle morbid, in fact. She confided her
thoughts to Clementina, who wrinkled her nose in distaste.
"Positively goulish, dear aunt!"

The formalities over, Monsieur de Tourne had carried Clementina off to dance, and Mrs. Westbury faced the prospect
of sitting a while with Henri's mama—indeed, the invitation
had been more in the nature of a command. The thought
oppressed her and when the press of people separated her for
a moment from her escort, she allowed herself to be carried
along in its train. It was thus that Prince Metlin found her
some minutes later, looking rather lost. His ease of manner
lead her to confess her crime and she found in him an instant
ally.

"Say no more, madame! I know exactly how it must be with you!"

"Do you?" She sighed. "Well, I cannot but own myself to be a shocking coward . . . and indeed, I do mean to return to the Comtesse as soon as I have gained but a short respite."

"Take what time you will, Madame. Enjoy yourself." He leaned forward with the air of a conspirator. "I shall be happy to assist you to remain undiscovered for as long as you please."

There was certainly much to take the eye; if only she might have been permitted to wear her spectacles! Without them, all but that which was in her immediate vicinity was a confused mass of color. The chandeliers swam in a kind of blurred brilliance as if to rival the myriad jewels that hung about most of the guests with—dare she even think it—vulgar opulence?

She recalled Clementina's absurd, but no doubt well-intentioned assurances before they set out, that she looked exactly as she ought and that not another lady present would come anywhere near her for elegance, which was patently a nonsense! She smoothed the new lavender silk with loving fingers; it was very fine, of course . . . and the pretty lace cap complemented her fairness. But elegance! She chuckled at the thought, and Alexei glanced down at her inquiringly.

"Ridiculous of me to have been in such a taking," she confided happily. "Why, with so many people here and so many fine jewels to dazzle the eye, no one will even notice me!"

"And is that what you wish?" Alexei's eyebrow quirked upward, his superbly burnished side-whiskers twitching in amused astonishment. "Then I must tell you that I noticed you at once, sweet lady."

"That is because you are a good, kind boy," she assured him, patting his hand, and growing a little pink with the discovery that she was not yet beyond being most agreeably moved by such a pretty speech, nonsensical though it might be! She observed mistily that the Prince tonight, in his dress uniform rich with gold braiding and orders, was every bit as handsome as the Comte, and oh my—he had a way with him!

Realizing the direction her thoughts were taking, she took herself sternly to task, saying with a firmness that was totally at odds with her dimpling cheek, "However, you must not suppose that you are obliged to stay here and entertain me,

Prince. I am sure there must be more than one young lady in all this throng languishing for a sight of you."

"Many, madame." Alexei grinned impudently. "But it does no harm for them to languish a little. They will be the more compliant when I deign to smile on them!"

"For shame!"

"Not at all! It is what they expect. Ah, dear lady, it is all a game! You do not believe? Then you have but to observe how ridiculous we all make ourselves! Take Madame de Duras, for example, who is presently causing much amusement with her open jealousy of Madame Recamier, who has stolen Monsieur de Chateaubriand from her . . . no, no, it is true, I promise you!" His voice dropped to a confidential murmur. "And there is more. Do you see that extraordinary, coarse-looking woman dressed like a cook . . . the one with the strange eruption on her face? That, madame, is the Queen of Sweden, though she is not received as such at Court. I believe the King receives her privately as Madame Bernadotte. A most odd woman! She has conceived a violent passion for Richelieu and follows him everywhere!"

"Ah, how sad. The poor woman!"

"No, no, madame! Say rather, poor Richelieu. The Duc is the most simple of men, the whole affair causes him acute embarrassment!"

There was no malice in the Prince's whimsicality; Mrs. Westbury knew it was but a ploy meant for her entertainment, and so she was smiling a little as she turned sympathetically in the direction he had indicated, with the vulnerable, searching gaze of the short-sighted.

And that is how the Duc de Menton first saw her—a shy, unspoiled violet lifting its head among a sea of exotic, overblown blooms. He swore softly beneath his breath and at once cleaved a path through the crowd until he stood before her.

"Alexei," he demanded without preamble, "present me, if you please."

Prince Metlin obliged with the greatest good will. Clearly the Duc was laboring in the grip of some quite uncharacteristic emotion and with his own undoubted propensity for romantic intrigue, Alexei immediately recognized in him the spectacle of a man in the first exquisite throes of love.

For the second time in the space of an evening, Seraphina Westbury found herself the object of a gentleman's regard, but whereas she had little difficulty in discerning the first to be a kindly display of gallantry on the part of a young man toward an older woman, this present situation was quite unlike anything she had previously experienced, except perhaps once, a long, long time ago. . . . The inevitable conclusion of this line of reasoning left her pink and breathless, and with a strong inclination to tremble.

Alexei's introductions scarcely registered, and though she conversed, she was oblivious of what the Duc or she said in those first moments. Her mind, her whole spirit, was filled with his physical presence. She took in every detail of his erect, distinguished figure, the strong-boned face, and the white hair springing from a noble brow. She was acutely conscious of her hand in his, his lips lightly brushing her fingers. Through it all, it seemed, her eyes never left his, for in their depths she experienced a curiously gratifying feeling of contentment, as though she were coming home after a long journey.

For Etienne de Menton, watching the shy, flowerlike face turned up to him in a kind of half-smiling expectancy, the years fell away. He caught his breath on a sudden surge of emotion and wondered in a bemused fashion if it were possible for a man to fall in love so suddenly, so irrevocably, at his age. *Mon Dieu!* He must tread warily or he would make himself an object of ridicule! The thought troubled him briefly, then faded before her diffident smile.

Alexei, seeing the way things were, left them together, and his departure went unnoticed.

The Duc sought the right words and finally took refuge in the banal. "Are you enjoying the ball, madame?" he enquired with the gaucheness of a stripling.

She appeared to give the matter thought before answering with a sweet gravity, "It is certainly very grand . . . and beautiful, of course! But a trifle overwhelming. I have to pinch myself occasionally to assure myself that it is not a dream."

He abandoned discretion. "I know exactly what you mean," he said softly. "For when I first saw you, I could not believe that *you* were real. I felt that I must speak with you, touch you, without delay, lest you vanish like *Cendrillion* on the stroke of midnight! And now that I am here with you, I am still plagued by uncertainty."

She did not simper or feign embarrassment, though her eyes widened a little more and her heart was beating suffocatingly fast. But he must not look at her so—it would not do! He must be made to see her as she really was.

"Alas, Duc—I have no glass slipper," she confessed and resolutely exposed for his perusal her pumps, their lilac sateen stretched with unbecoming tightness across uncomfortably bunched toes. "You see?"

His reaction was not in the least what she had hoped for; indeed, his tender mirth was almost her undoing, but she held fast to her resolve. "And it grieves me to own that these shoes have been pinching abominably for the past hour or more," she declared. "So much so, in fact, that it is all I can do not to think of home and my comfortable fireside chair with its little padded footstool . . . and perhaps, a nice cup of tea."

There was a wistfulness in this last which drew from him a soft laugh.

"Madame! You are clearly very miserable! Would you then prefer that I escort you home immediately so that you may rest your poor feet?"

"Oh, no! It would be quite improper for me to leave! The children would wonder . . . and besides . . ." She sighed. "I must go to sit with the Comtesse de Tourne, who will by now be wondering where I am." She remembered too late that the Duc was her brother, but he seemed undismayed by her obvious lack of enthusiasm.

"Let her wonder. To be obliged to sit with my sister at any time must be accounted a penance! I have a much better idea. Will you trust yourself to me?"

He offered her his arm and she laid her hand upon it, puzzled but confident. He led her purposefully through the crowd, acknowledging here and there the greetings of friends who eyed them curiously. She listened, even more intrigued, as he gave crisp authoritative instructions to a white-wigged lackey who bowed and said *"Oui, Monseigneur!"* and turned to bark equally incomprehensible instructions at another, lesser lackey, who ushered them along corridors that were more like massive apartments, of such beauty and grandeur that she was beyond speech. Now and again through a window came iridescent splashes of color from the illuminated gardens. All sound was soon left behind, save for their footsteps and the soft *hush-hush* of her silk skirts.

At last, when it seemed they would walk forever, the lackey threw open a pair of doors and they were in a salon, unexpectedly small and comfortable after all that magnificence. Soft light from a candelabrum placed on a table near the fire cast a welcoming glow over striped rose satin furnishings. Mrs. Westbury, lost in admiration, needed no urging to try the merits of a wing chair, which received her with such unbelievable comfort that she uttered a little involuntary sigh of contentment.

Almost immediately the doors opened again and their lackey reappeared, soft footed and bearing a massive silver salver, which he set down upon a pretty inlaid walnut table at her side. The lackey asked something of the Duc, who shook his head and dismissed him.

"I said we would manage for ourselves. Is it to your liking, Madame?"

Seraphina gazed entranced at the exquisite silverware, the charmingly fashioned kettle, and the delicately embossed, paper-thin Japanese cups.

"Tea!" She sighed, dimpling. "Oh, Duc, how very clever of you! But however did you manage to procure it?"

Monsieur's smile held a trace of smugness. "I am not quite without influence." And then, his voice deepening, "Ah, my dear madame, you have but to command me and anything it is within my power to bestow upon you is yours!"

"You dance the waltz with an enviable fluency, Miss Brady," said the Duc de Berry as they circled the floor. "But then, I am told you are a young lady of many accomplishments."

She looked up into his bold, handsome face. "I can't imagine who told you so, Your Highness. I only wish it were true!"

He smiled. "And full of modest humility, also. Very proper! In point of fact, my informant was your brother."

"Patrick said that? I had no idea he thought so well of me!" Mention of Patrick reminded Clementina of where they had most likely met—in some disreputable café.

She knew she ought to disapprove strongly of this ultraroyal nephew to the King of France. Many of the ideals he nurtured—ideals that had already been the cause of so much bloodshed—were anathema to her. He was by repute intemperate, hedonistic and dissolute, with at times an ungovernable temper. Paradoxically, he could also be, as she was rapidly discovering, generous and witty and was so richly endowed with Gallic charm as to make one forget all the rest. She decided to follow Grandpa Brady's advice once more, and thus found herself able to respond to the Duc's provocative flattery with an ease she had not possessed a month since, even venturing a little tentative raillery herself. "As for dancing, sir—I have always understood that a lady can only perform as well as her partner's accomplishment will allow!"

His response was disconcerting; obviously delighted by her remark, he said, "That is a fact, Miss Brady? Let us examine it further!" And, despite her laughing protests, with his eyes twinkling down at her, he commenced to swirl her around the room with a precision, an expertise, and indeed an abandon that appeared to require that he hold her very much closer than was seemly! At times she could distinctly feel the hard line of his thigh against hers and, very much aware that she had brought it upon herself, she wondered dizzily, breathlessly, what would be the punishment for rebuking a member of the French royal family in the middle of his own ballroom floor. With laughter bubbling up inside her, she decided that it couldn't be done and gave herself up instead to the insidiously sensual lilt of the music, succumbing without a struggle to sensations that, if not entirely proper, were not wholly unpleasurable either!

"That is much better!" He approved softly in her ear. "Now, you dance with your soul, also!"

It was true! For those few moments decorum was forgotten; she didn't care that eyes might be on her. Her head was filled with music. Its rhythm beat in her brain, spinning her round as it was spinning the crystal chandeliers above her until their candles shivered into a thousand splinters of light. She was floating, dipping, swirling as though in a trance until the Duc's soft laugh brought her back to the realization that the dance was at an end.

"That was a good experience, yes, Miss Brady?"

"Oh, yes!" She had little breath left to speak, but the answer was writ in her glowing cheeks and the way her eyes sparkled. Then a degree of common sense returned. "But it was quite outrageous of you to use me so!" she chided as they left the floor.

"Was it? It pleases me to shock people now and then. That way they do not grow complacent."

She stopped in her tracks, the careless words jarred. The royal profile at that moment mirrored such disdain for the sensibilities of others as to dismay her. The change was so abrupt. It was not only the sentiments expressed that caused her disquiet, but the brief glimpse it had afforded her of that "other self"of his.

She could find no words and thus remained silent. Presently she could feel his eyes on her and looked up to find the handsome, rather florid features wrapped in frowning concentration.

"I have shocked *you*, perhaps?"

Clementina chewed her lip furiously. Common sense told her that it would be prudent to conciliate him—smooth the moment over—but she wasn't feeling sensible at all.

"Yes," she said. "I rather think you have."

His frown deepened. "Well! That is frankness! Do you presume to rebuke royalty?"

"I'm sorry, Highness—but you did ask."

"I did, indeed!" He gave a sudden short bark of laughter. *"Dieu!* You are right!"

"But I should not have said . . ."

"No, no!" Quickly, impatiently. "No, the fault is mine. So. We must endeavor to change your opinion of us." A pause. "You appreciate music?"

Once more his mood switched. She was relieved to see him restored to good humor.

"Very much, monsieur. But I do not perform well. My family will vouch for the fact that I both sing and play the pianoforte abominably."

"Then you shall go with us to the Opera," he said magnanimously. "Your aunt also." He smiled. "And how do you feel about the flute?"

Uncertain where the seemingly innocent question might lead, she was moved to prevaricate. "The flute, monsieur?"

"It is a wind instrument." Ebullient again, teasing, he mimed an imaginary obligato. "One blows it, so—very pretty!"

Clementina gave an involuntary trill of laughter. "Yes, of course, I *do* know what a flute is, but . . ."

"The instrument is a particular passion of mine. I have a small regular gathering of friends who share my appreciation. Together, we learn to make music." A significant pause. "I would very much like you to become one of our number."

Was that *all* he wanted her to become? Color flooded her face at the thought of anything else. Even her—what was it Alexei had called it?—liveliness of spirit and complete honesty boggled at the prospect of attempting to explain to so exalted a gentleman that she had no intention of becoming his mistress! Or was she being oversensitive, even arrogant, to assume that such was his intention? Perhaps she could defer the decision until some more suitable occasion. She drew a deep breath.

"I don't really think . . ."

One eyebrow lifted in amusement. "You will be quite safe, my dear Miss Brady!" he drawled, divining her thoughts with mortifying accuracy. "My wife and one or two of her friends are invariably present. You will permit me to arrange that she asks you?"

Clementina was obliged to agree; she really could not do otherwise.

"That is splendid. And now, my dear young lady, I must not monopolize your time. I see Henri de Tourne's mama gesticulating in this direction and I think it is not me she wishes to command!"

The Duc led her up to the Comtesse, with whom he exchanged a few words of polite conversation before taking Clementina's hand and carrying it to his lips. "I shall not forget," he said. *"A bientot, mademoiselle."*

She looked past him as he turned away and saw Henri standing a few yards away, watching tight-lipped.

❊CHAPTER 11❊

"Sit here beside me, Miss Brady," said the Comtesse, her words stabbing the air, her furled fan stabbing at the frail-looking spindle-legged chair. She was looking more regal than her hosts tonight in deepest black, having worn no other, as she had been heard to declaim on numerous occasions, since the passing of her beloved Auguste almost nine years ago—a singularly inappropriate degree of mourning, malicious tongues were not slow to point out, for a man who had flaunted his paramours quite blatantly under his wife's nose for a good twenty years prior to his demise! But then, the gossips concluded, betraying their sympathies, the Comtesse was enough to send the best of husbands hotfoot in pursuit of more congenial pleasures!

It seemed to Clementina that madame was more liberally sprinkled with diamonds than usual. They adorned her bosom in the form of an elaborate collar; they hung glittering from her ears; and more nestled in the snow-white coiffure, holding in place the black ostrich feathers that swayed majestically each time she inclined her head with an exaggerated air of condescension to passing acquaintances. At her other side, perched with an air of desperate uncertainty upon a chair similar to Clementina's, was Madame Grover, the Comtesse's pallid companion, looking ready to spring into action at the least of her mistress's commands.

Clementina took her place with reluctance—still restless, still half-exhilarated, half-unsettled by what had passed. She supposed she might guess what the Comtesse wished to speak of, but she had no intention of discussing Clothilde with her. Her eyes sought Henri, but he had disappeared. She felt a stab of annoyance, recalling how studiously he had kept her from his mother's side earlier, and just now the look on his face as she had been with the Duc. Was it jealousy or cowardice that kept him from her side? Either way, she could not count upon him for support.

A contre-danse was forming; she had promised to partner the odious Monsieur Guillard and little as the prospect pleased her, it would be preferable to facing Madame de Tourne's inquisition. But Monsieur Guillard was nowhere to be seen. She saw that Patrick was already standing up with Dora Courtney, who was fast falling in love with him—and he enjoying every minute! Next to them, Alfred Bennett was partnering Princess Galitzin, a pretty Russian girl. Patrick was laughing, showing off, and the two girls—Dora overtly adoring—were giving him every encouragement.

Clementina was bewildered by the rush of conflicting emotions that filled her breast. Pride! Oh, yes, she was proud, for there wasn't, she dared swear, a handsomer young man in the whole room. But, surprisingly, there was jealousy, too—and fear. He was growing away from her; yet it was stupid to blame poor Dora for simply highlighting the extent of Patrick's emancipation. A feeling of desolation engulfed her. Once, such a short time ago, *she* had been his audience, the sole recipient of his confidences. Now, he flirted outrageously with Dora and Katinka Galitzin, and probably countless others—opera dancers, even—who smiled encouragement!

The figures before her blurred slightly; she blinked and pulled herself together. She would *not* become like Henri's mama, a doting female clinging pathetically to her loved one! Cadogon had said she must let go and he was right, confound him! He'd said that Patrick would soon tire of living to excess and it seemed he might be right about that, too. Not that Patrick was a reformed character, exactly; she knew he still crept out as before, but not so often, and she had Joshua's emphatic assurances that he was never more than pleasantly merry.

The rattle of Madame de Tourne's fan as the japanned spines snapped open checked her wandering thoughts.

"You are not attending me, Miss Brady," said the peevish voice. "I repeat, I do not know where is your aunt. I had expected her to bear me company. There was a matter of the gravest importance upon which I wished to address myself to her." The fan wafted deliberately.

Not if I can prevent you, thought Clementina. Aloud she said, "I believe I saw her with Prince Metlin. I know he wished to make her known to Count Pozzo di Borgo. The Prince is such a charming man and has shown Aunt Seraphina the most extraordinary kindness."

There was an uncomfortable moment of silence; the Comtesse stiffened, her rigidly confined bosom straining against its bondage. "Your family ingratiates itself all round, mademoiselle. I feel it my duty to point out to you, however, that in Paris you cannot behave as you please! Flout our conventions and you will quickly find that even your crude attempts to interest the Duc de Berry will not save you from the consequences."

"Oh? Do you think not?" Clementina saw that Madame Grover was visibly quaking and felt for her. Drat Henri for placing her in such a position! She made a determined effort to be pleasant. "Well, of course, I should be sorry indeed to forfeit so much good will, but whilst I have every respect for the customs of your country, I really cannot consider myself irrevocably bound by them, you know; any more than I can honestly believe that society will shun me simply because my notions of propriety are not yours." She sought desperately to change the subject. "Oh, do tell me, madame, is that not the prettiest dress that Princess Galitzin is wearing this evening? Silver gauze and all those little rosebuds. It is exactly right for her!"

But the dowager was not to be so easily turned from her

purpose. Clementina's obvious lightness of mind was but further proof to her, if proof were needed, of her total unworthiness; had she troubled to look into her adversary's eyes, her error must have been apparent, but the maternal fires burning deep in Madame's soul were already being fanned to a consuming blaze by her fear of this foreigner, this interloper, who was bidding to alienate her from her son. Her voice was a low, venomous hiss.

"You are not what I hoped for! I make no secret of my disapproval. But, since Henri will not be guided by me in this, I must do all that I am able to ensure that you do not entirely disgrace him as well as yourself, as you are like to do if certain scandalous stories are true . . ."

"Madame, do not I beg of you proceed further!" Clementina urged, her patience almost at an end. "I am in general the most biddable of creatures, but I do have a quite irrational dislike of people who intrude themselves unwarrantably into my affairs. I tell you plainly, I will not answer for my conduct an' you make a scene!"

The Comtesse's thin nose quivered; the muscles in her scrawny neck were working in a most alarmingly jerky fashion, so that Clementina prayed she had not gone too far. Heads turned; the Comtesse's mouth opened and at first nothing came out. Then: "I do not make scenes!" she gasped.

It seemed that a clash was inevitable. Oh, why couldn't she have held her tongue!

"Miss Brady! *There* you are!" A familiar, unctuous voice, sounding slightly aggrieved, broke in upon them. Both women looked up with a sense of shock to behold Monsieur Guillard's plump, unsuitably bedecked figure bearing down on them rather like a ship in full sail.

In Clementina he induced a sudden inclination to dissolve into hysterical laughter, which she mastered valiantly, seeing in this fat, complacent man with his fat, complacent manners her savior; he was far too insensitive to realize how he intruded, but his timing was perfect.

"Monsieur!" she exclaimed, looking, she hoped, suitably penitent. "Our dance! I was having such an absorbing discussion with Madame de Tourne, it quite slipped my mind." She extended her hand. "Do say that you forgive me?"

He became incoherent in his anxiety to reassure her, bowing over her hand, which all but vanished beneath the great froth of lace ruffles falling from his cuff. He bowed also to the Comtesse, who did not invite him to sit, but rather attempted to glare him out of countenance. In this she so nearly succeeded that Clementina, determined not to be left alone again with the old harridan, made shameless use of him.

She stood up, laid a hand lightly on the sleeve of his mulberry velvet coat and said, smiling brilliantly at him, "Monsieur, you come most opportunely. I was about to go in search of my aunt. She's been gone quite a while and I am growing a little concerned about her. May I prevail upon you to escort me?"

He puffed and preened, uttering little cries of delight that seemed to indicate that he was hers to command. He bowed yet again to the Comtesse, who drew in her breath through pinched nostrils with such malevolence that he blinked in a rather startled fashion. Clementina she completely ignored. And so they made their adieux, leaving poor Madame Grover to bear the brunt of her mistress's wrath.

Clementina very quickly came to regret her impulsiveness, however. Monsieur Guillard talked nonstop, of the weather; of the honor Miss Brady was doing him in soliciting his aid; of his recent visit to Versailles—had Miss Brady visited Versailles as yet? She would find it a most moving experience, so many ghosts from the recent past! The Duc de Berry might perhaps invite her since she had been honored by his patronage—a note of peevishness here. And on—and on!

The contra-danse had ended and several times people stopped to speak, but Monsieur was not to be shifted from her side. There was no sign of Aunt Seraphina or Alexei, so Clementina sighed and resigned herself to making appropriate noises now and again, her thoughts elsewhere. She ought not to have spoken so to Henri's mother—it was unmannerly, disrespectful and downright impolite—but such interference was surely not to be borne?

"It occurs to me—" Monsieur Guillard's voice intruded once more upon her thoughts "—that since your good lady aunt seems nowhere to be found, I might remedy our earlier disappointment by soliciting the honor of your hand for the next dance—a quadrille, I believe?"

Staring blankly at him, Clementina noticed the moist pink eagerness of his face, the beads of perspiration standing out on his upper lip, and all her sensibilities shrank from any further intimacy of contact. But how was she to extricate herself without giving offence? The quadrille, she knew, was promised to Henri, but he should not have it after the way he had behaved! If only Alexei would materialize—or Patrick, even . . .

"I regret I must disappoint you yet again, Monsieur," she improvised hastily, her eyes scanning the room in desperation. "Such a pity, but I am already promised to . . ." She saw a couple strolling toward her. ". . . to my cousin Lord Cadogon," she finished triumphantly, stepping forward to grasp Cadogon's hand, pressing it with some urgency lest he betray her, her eyes imploring his support. "I vow, you must have quite given me up, Dominic! I did promise you the quadrille, did I not?"

For once she blessed his impassive countenance. He bowed assent, directed a brief glance at Monsieur Guillard who was looking crestfallen, and drawled, "You did, my dear Clementina. But, knowing the unpredictability of your memory, I was on my way to find you. You have not met Madame Robart as yet, I think? Elyse, may I introduce Miss Brady, my cousin from Baltimore."

Clementina saw at once how wildly inaccurate had been her preconceptions, for in place of the mousy nonentity of her imaginings was a serene vision with smooth black hair, skin like magnolia petals, and enormous dark eyes that smiled shyly at her in greeting. Why, she is a beauty! The thought came unbidden, disconcerting her.

Monsieur Guillard, who had stood a little aside during their introduction, coughed delicately. Clementina belatedly drew him into the conversation until the couples began to move toward the dance floor, when he bowed reluctantly and, on the point of withdrawing, said, "If I should encounter your aunt, Miss Brady, what would you have me tell her?"

Clementina, being thus made aware of the shabby way she had used him, had the grace to blush. She found it hard to meet his reproachful gaze with equanimity and once more she was indebted to Cadogon, who informed them blandly that her aunt was safe in the Duc de Menton's very capable charge.

Monsieur still hovered, his attention coming to rest upon Madame Robart. Hope flared; he wondered if she was engaged for the quadrille? She was momentarily disconcerted.

"I, that is . . . no." Her soft, husky voice expressed a regret that gave every appearance of being genuine. "But I have promised most faithfully to bear Madame Corbonne company for a while. See. She is beckoning to me."

Monsieur observed a fat old lady in puce gesturing wildly

with her fan. *"Eh bien. Tant pis!"* His shoulders lifted in resignation. His bow accommodated them all, and at last he strutted away.

"And what was all that about, cousin?"

Clementina explained, biting her lip on a rueful laugh. "Oh dear! Do you suppose I have wounded his sensibilities irrevocably?"

"I doubt it—the man is a pretentious bore!" said Cadogon with a conspicuous want of feeling.

Elyse Robart gently remonstrated with him, laying a hand on his sleeve, and Clementina was quick to note the exchanged smile, the way her hand was immediately covered with his own long, slim fingers. The quiet intimacy of the gesture was very revealing.

"I must go now to Madame Corbonne," she said. "Miss Brady, I am so pleased to have met you. Dominic must bring you to visit me."

"Thank you. I should like that." Conventional words, yet Clementina was surprised to find she meant them. She hadn't expected to like Elyse Robart at all. She watched Cadogon raise the imprisoned hand, his lips brushing the young woman's fingers. There was a closeness in the look they exchanged, and his eyes followed her progress across the room with such tenderness that Clementina felt a twinge of something remarkably akin to envy; to be loved like that must be quite something! Elyse had reached the irascible old lady now and was leaning forward with an air of absorbed interest to listen to her complaints.

"Are you ready to take to the floor, cousin?"

Clementina found that the Marquis was regarding her sardonically.

"The sets are forming," he prompted.

"Oh, gracious!" she cried, half-embarrassed. "You don't really have to dance with me, you know."

"There I can't agree." He grasped her arm and led her inexorably toward the other dancers. "You may play fast and loose with lesser men, but not with me. A promise is a promise. I can't abide people who try to wriggle out of their obligations."

"But I *didn't* promise . . ." she protested weakly.

At the very edge of the ballroom floor he stopped. *"I* know you didn't and *you* know you didn't, and I strongly suspect that Monsieur Guillard knows it, too. Will you have me call him back and confess that it's all a mistake?"

"You wouldn't?" Alarm and indignation met with blandness. She dissolved unexpectedly into giggles. "I really believe you might!"

"That's better!" And, seeing her puzzlement, "Your feathers were distinctly ruffled a little earlier and not, I think, wholly on account of the tiresome Monsieur Guillard. All right," he held up a placating hand as she stiffened. "You've had enough attention drawn to you for one evening! I have no wish to provoke you further."

"Good!" she said. "For there is nothing more tedious than to be trying to conduct an argument when half of one's mind is given over to following the intricacies of the dance. And besides, I am vastly indebted to you for not giving me away to that wretched man!"

"It was rather noble of me, was it not? I'll own I was taken aback to find myself accosted with such desperation. You are, after all, *so well* able to take care of yourself!"

Clementina chuckled appreciatively. "It's no use, cousin. I shan't rise to your sarcasm."

"Very strong-minded! Then, shall we dance?"

She capitulated. His hand on her back was pleasantly firm. As they made their way on to the floor she stole a glance at him from under her lashes. He was looking rather splendid this evening, dressed very much á là Français in black inexpressibles, a beautifully cut black swallow-tailed coat and snowy waistcoat, his cravat as ever impeccably arranged.

Her glance, continuing upward, encountered considering blue-gray eyes similarly engaged. One eyebrow lifted.

"Well, cousin Clementina, are you enjoying your first Royal Ball?"

She looked away from him and saw Henri threading his way through a press of people toward them, his face stiff with annoyance. A sudden stab of apprehension gave a defiant thrust to her chin. The Marquis turned to discover the cause of her discomfort. Again his brow quirked slightly, but to her surprise he offered no comment and in a moment the set was coming together, the music beginning.

Alexei was in their set with Katinka Galitzin for partner.

"Have you seen your aunt recently?" he murmured as they met briefly during the chaine Anglais.

"No. Why?"

He bestowed upon her an infuriatingly cryptic smile. "You will see."

She could not be expected to let the matter rest there and

presently demanded enlightenment of her cousin, who proved
totally unhelpful.

"I have no idea! Alexei delights in being enigmatic occasionally." He took her hands and together they executed a
graceful *tours-de-mains*. He really was a most elegant dancer!
She wondered why the fact should surprise her.

"I like your Madame Robart. Alexei wasn't in the least
enigmatic about *her*. He made me quite long to meet her."

"You should know by now not to believe all Alexei tells
you."

Cadogon was politely uncooperative, which made Clementina more curious than ever. However, he had already
switched deftly to quizzing her about her protégée and she
was obliged to let the matter drop.

Clementina told him quite truthfully that Clothilde was
making excellent progress under Justine's expert tuition, displaying, according to the voluble Justine, who was quick to
praise where praise was due, not only an astonishing quickness of mind, but a great natural aptitude for needlecraft, especially the trimming of a bonnet, knowing precisely where
to place a knot of ribbons for the greatest effect. There
seemed little point in dwelling upon the use to which
Clothilde put her skills with regard to her own appearance;
how the demurely coiled fair hair and neat gray dress—which
looked so proper whilst displaying with every subtle movement the graceful lines of the figure beneath its folds—drew
every male eye in the house; how often she incurred a rebuke
for just happening to be passing, oh so unobtrusively, along
the upper gallery when morning callers were leaving; and
how, if Joshua's sighing vapors were indicative of the behavior of the other male servants, it would be necessary to *do
something* about Clothilde before she created havoc belowstairs! Which was exactly what Dominic had predicted.

It was perhaps fortunate that the movements of the dance
made any continuous conversation impossible, and afterward
they were never again alone. Aunt Seraphina had reappeared
accompanied by the Duc de Menton, and they were soon
joined by Count Pozzo di Borgo and Madame Patterson
Bonaparte, who was on a brief visit from Rome. Madame
was eager for news of Baltimore and of her father, and she
and Aunt Seraphina were soon deep in reminiscence. Clementina watched her aunt with some curiosity, remembering
Alexei's mischievous comment, but apart from an unusual
degree of animation—a sparkle in the eye, occasioned no

doubt by finding someone with whom she could speak of home—there seemed to be nothing worthy of comment.

She was swept off to supper in the midst of this group and afterward six dancers from the Opera performed a most elegantly measured pavane and a turning waltz, composed specially for the occasion, so that by the time she and Henri met in the doorway to the ballroom much later her anger against him had all but evaporated. To her dismay, however, the same could not be said for him. His face was flushed and she suspected that he had drunk rather more than he should. Her way was barred.

"Ha! This time you cannot escape me," he glowered over her shoulder, "and there is no cousin to spirit you away, I think? I wish to talk with you." His finger closed around her wrist.

"Henri, please release me at once!" Clementina kept her voice low but firm, not wishing to precipitate trouble. "Now is not the time. If you want words with me, let it wait until morning and you may have as many as you like."

"No! Now." Henri's fingers tightened with unpleasant force.

This was a side of him that was new to her, but rather than draw unwelcome attention, she permitted herself to be propelled into a high, narrow anteroom embellished from floor to ornate rococo ceiling entirely with frescoes a la Grecque, its only furniture a bureau mounted with exotic bronze figures depicting Apollo's pursuit of Daphne, the latter suitably entwined in laurel leaves, and a *marquise* sofa too exquisite to be sat upon. But Clementina had no desire to sit. The moment the door closed behind them she turned on him, anger asserting itself.

"How *dare* you use me in this way, Henri! Release me at once!"

"You speak of being used. Ha! What of me? Do you seek to make me a laughing stock, here of all places?"

"You are being ridiculous!"

"Am I?" His eyes had narrowed to wild slits. "Everyone knows how it has been between us—do you think your behavior this evening has escaped them? How you avoid me and flaunt yourself with other men? Has royalty so quickly turned your head that you are lost to all sense of propriety, *hein?*"

"You sound exactly like your mother, Henri!" Clementina's

rebuke was truly wrathful. "I wouldn't take criticism from her, and I won't take it from you."

"Maman was acting from the best of motives." His voice had thickened slightly. "You will have need of her advice when we are married, for to be the Comtesse de Tourne requires qualities other than those which may suffice a mere Miss Brady from Baltimore!"

She could scarcely contain herself! Drunk he might well be, but if this was an example of Henri in his cups . . . ? He still held her wrist prisoner, and as she struggled to free it, she raged at him. "Qualities such as arrogance and presumption and plain bad manners, I suppose! Dear God! You are insolent beyond belief! We are not going to be married—not now, not ever, do you understand me? And now, let me go!"

To her dismay he began to laugh softly and far from releasing her, attempted to draw her close.

"I have never seen you roused to passion until now . . . it is more than I had hoped for! You are magnificent!" His arm tightened. "Of course we shall be married. In fact, when better than this evening to seal our betrothal—announce it to the world."

Clementina had always regarded herself as being reasonably strong, but she was no match for Henri. A little frightened now, she began to wonder how far he might go in his present mood. The possibility of being compromised, perhaps even ravished, within hailing distance of the cream of Paris society, lent a sharp urgency to her command that he end his foolishness and release her at once. "At once, Henri! If you don't, I shall scream so loudly that the reverberations will create a scandal from which your precious mama will never recover!"

For the first time he looked uncertain, but only for a moment. Then, "Enough of this foolishness, *cherie* . . . the time has come to submit . . ."

Managing to free one hand, she struck him a stinging blow, and at the same moment Alexei's voice broke in, sounding quite untypically severe.

"Monsieur le Comte, be good enough to remove your hands from Miss Brady's person or you will oblige me to knock you down!"

Henri swung round, his expression contemptuous. "Keep out of this, Metlin. Our business is private and in no way concerns you."

Alexei encountered a pleading glance from Clementina

that he found hard to interpret, but, rising nobly to the occasion, he declared with magnificent aplomb, "You are wrong, monsieur, for Miss Brady has this very evening consented to become my wife!"

"Your . . . I don't believe it!" Henri's face lost all color; his fingers bit painfully into Clementina's arm. "Is this true?"

She was almost as taken aback as he, but anger and astonishment made her slow to answer. Alexei had presented her with an ideal means of escape from an impossible situation yet, much as she was tempted, she knew almost at once that she could not take advantage of his generosity. She opened her mouth to say so, but Henri was already construing her silence as assent. He swore and released her with an abruptness that sent her staggering. It was only as he strode unsteadily from the room that she noticed the open door and a flutter of puce-striped draperies drifting aside to let him pass.

"Oh, no! What a coil!" She was aware of a sudden trembling in her legs and sank onto the sofa. She smiled helplessly at Alexei, seeing his face through a faint blur. "You dear, crazy, impulsive man! Why could you not have closed the door as you came in? If I am not mistaken, Madame de Duras has been hovering out there like a carrion crow devouring every word! By now, she will be distributing the choicest morsels among her cronies!"

"Well, then? Why disappoint them?" Alexei sat down close beside her on the little sofa and grasped her hand resolutely. "Clementina—*dushka*—it would make me the happiest man on earth," he declared, striving to sound as though he meant every word, "if you would but entertain my proposal!"

"No, it wouldn't. You would hate the whole thing quite dreadfully," she said on the ghost of a laugh. And then, lest she offend his feelings, "Oh, my *dear* friend, I am deeply moved by your offer, but I could never accept such a sacrifice! Besides, it isn't at all necessary. If we treat the story as a joke, it will soon die the death."

"You think so?" He met her amused eyes and grinned sheepishly in his relief. "You are sure this is what you wish, *dushka*?"

"Quite sure." Clementina withdrew her hand and stood up. "Come along, before the word has time to spread."

Alexei detained her a moment longer, his face filled with a sudden brooding seriousness. "Clementina Brady, you are a very remarkable young lady, and I am undoubtedly a fool, for I think I am more than a little in love with you!" His crooked grin flashed forth. "Were I not so sure that you would get a bad bargain for a husband, I would marry you tomorrow!" He tipped her chin and kissed her lightly on the mouth.

"Very affecting!" said Cadogon. His shadow filled the doorway and then he was inside and shutting the door. "Have you both taken leave of your senses, or do you not care that your names are being bandied about the ballroom in the most scurrilous fashion?"

"Oh, that!" said Clementina. "It's all a silly mistake."

"I am relieved to hear you say so," he said in his most cutting way. "It will, of course, make everything all right! Good God, Alexei! I don't expect much of Clementina, but I had thought you would use more discretion!"

Alexei gave a wry shrug, but Clementina was incensed on his behalf. "Don't be so stuffy!" she exclaimed. "Alexei behaved with great chivalry and I am very grateful to him. And anyway, you haven't exactly helped matters by following him in here and playing the outraged cousin!"

"My apologies," he said stiffly. "I shall know better another time."

"Good."

Alexei looked from one to the other. "Do you two never meet but you come to blows?"

Clementina swept to the door. "I'm sure I have no wish to quarrel with anyone, but I do get awfully tired of being told what I ought and ought not to do, when I am perfectly capable of deciding for myself!"

❦CHAPTER 12❦

Clementina was obliged to endure a fair amount of teasing as a result of the evening's happenings. As they left the Elysée Palace the Duc de Berry had commented with a twinkle, "You have had an eventful evening, mademoiselle!"

"It was but a series of misunderstandings, Your Highness," she pleaded ruefully.

"Quite so," he said. "However, I trust you have found your visit enjoyable. For my part, I look forward to our further acquaintance with interest."

On the following morning there were many more callers than usual in the Rue de Varenne, all with excellent reasons for calling and all eaten up with curiosity. The first to arrive, however, could not be accused of such meretriousness; his objective was immediately obvious. He came when Clementina was alone in the Grand Salon, a room that stretched almost the entire length of the house and that, when they had first moved in, Clementina had found as grand as its name implied. But in a very short space of time the whole family had so impressed their personality upon it that in defiance of the combined attentions of Maurice and his minions, they had achieved the seemingly impossible feat of making the grandeur seem comfortable. On this particular morning the salon was filled with pale winter sunshine as she took the card Maurice held out to her.

"Oh, how nice! Do show him up at once, and Maurice—" her eyes twinkled, "—be so good as to inform my aunt that the Duc de Menton is come to call."

"Assuredly, mademoiselle." Was this, then, the reason why Madame Westbury had risen so much earlier than her accustomed hour, and was looking so remarkably bright-eyed? Oh, la. Who would have thought it?

Clementina greeted the Duc with unconcealed pleasure.

"I am not too early?"

"No, indeed. I was riding at seven."

"Such energy." He sighed and glanced farther into the room with a seeming casualness, his disappointment imperfectly concealed. "Your good aunt is still abed, I suppose?"

"No, monsieur, she will be here directly."

Always an elegant figure of a man, the Duc had taken extra pains with his dress this morning. He sat when Clementina bade him, but she couldn't help noticing how his fingers played nervously with one of the glittering fobs on the chain adorning his waistcoat as he talked.

And then her aunt came in, a little out of breath as though she had been hurrying. The Duc rose smartly to his feet, his shoulders clad in a beautifully cut mulberry coat, straightening up with military precision. Aunt Seraphina greeted him with just the right blend of charm and propriety, but Clementina, standing a little apart, knew that she had not imagined the look that passed between them.

Heavens! But before she could give the matter any proper thought, more visitors arrived in the shape of the Courtney family, minus papa. They were closely followed by Mrs. Bennett, who had come, she said, especially to beg a copy of Aunt Seraphina's special recipe for plum pudding, which sounded so delicious that she had decided that her chef should make them one also for Christmas.

"Well, you shall have it, of course," said Mrs. Westbury doubtfully, "but I do hope your chef is more agreeable than our Monsieur Clichet, who all but threatened to give notice only because I wished to supervise the preparation. And naturally we all wanted to stir the mixture. We have always stirred our puddings for luck! But from his attitude you would have supposed we had taken leave of our senses."

Clementina caught sight of Madame Recamier, who had also called upon the flimsiest of pretexts and had been intrigued to find that all was as though nothing had happened. Her face was a study in disbelief at all this talk of plum puddings! How could they speak of puddings when she was far more interested in finding out why Alexei was present while Henri wasn't! As it became clear that no one was disposed to enlighten her, she was about to order her carriage when Maurice admitted a lackey bearing the most enormous basket filled with pink roses.

"Oh!" Aunt Seraphina sighed. "Roses, in November!" Clementina immediately supposed they were from Henri, an apology, but the card bore a royal signature and was accompanied by a charming note from the Duchesse de Berry inviting Miss Brady to the Palace on Thursday next at three in the afternoon.

"Well!" said Madame Recamier, for once deprived of words.

"Oh, gracious!" exclaimed Clementina inadequately, not knowing where to look, and meeting Alexei's eye was treated to a wildly quizzical arch of the eyebrow.

The flowers proved an acute embarrassment to Clementina, who had, overnight, firmly resolved to give up all pretensions to becoming a society butterfly. Flirtation, as had become painfully clear, was not her forte and led only to complications when there were many other, more beneficial ways she might pass her time. But her resolution was less than easy to implement, for it seemed that she was more in demand than ever, and without appearing rude she could not refuse the many invitations that came her way.

Henri had left Paris. Clementina didn't miss him as much as she had thought. When he made no attempt to seek her out she was sorry, for he could not still be under the impression that she was going to marry Alexei, and thought he had behaved very badly. But the blame wasn't wholly his, and the way his so-called friends behaved distressed her even more. Some said he had gone to Vienna to be consoled by his mistress; others, less kindly, said he had gone to escape his more pressing creditors. Mrs. Bennett confided to Aunt Seraphina in shocked whispers that she had heard that he had been threatened by a moneylender! Clementina did what she could to squash any rumors, but soon there were other, newer scandals for society to dwell on and she had many things to occupy her mind, so Henri was forgotten.

The question of Clothilde's future had become a pressing problem, which she knew she must solve if her whole establishment was not to suffer. It did not need Maurice's diplomatically worded appeals or Madame Rubal's lowered brows and constant mutterings to tell her that Clothilde would have to go. But where? She couldn't just turn her out. It was her dtuy, having made Clothilde her responsibility, to at least ensure that she would not slip back into the squalor from which she had rescued her.

Matters came to a head—and were resolved in the end with surprising ease—one afternoon when Monsieur Guillard called. Monsieur had become something of a pest; having decided that Henri's disappearance from the scene must be his golden opportunity, he had taken to calling almost daily and, as must have been inevitable, it was not long before Clothilde came to his notice. When, for the third time, Clementina was moved to rebuke her severely for being where she had no business to be, Clothilde had endured the reprimand with abjectly lowered head, and when dismissed to her quarters had lifted her sweeping lashes to give Monsicur the full benefit of those beguiling violet eyes, big with sorrow, glistening with unshed tears. It would have taken a harder heart than Monsieur Guillard's to withstand such a *coup de foudre*. He was eager to know what Clementina could tell him of the girl's history. This Clementina related with a judicious juggling of the truth, which she felt exhibited a nice distinction between fact and fantasy. "Of course," she confided, "the child is not suited in the duties of a lady's maid. It has been in my mind for some time to set her up in some little business—a milliner's shop, perhaps. She has a definite gift that way, but you perceive my dilemma, monsieur—Clothilde is so young and inexperienced! Without the protection of a gentleman of honor, she would fall prey to the first smooth-spoken adventurer who came along."

She saw that Monsieur Guillard was highly impressed by her reasoning—such a generous and unselfish nature, he said, must command admiration! She demurred, but said no more. Surely he would take the bait!

The following afternoon he was back, and in a very short space of time all was arranged. Clothilde, summoned to the Petit Salon, accepted her good fortune with a proper gratitude modestly expressed, and a shrewd look behind the eyes that assured Clementina that her protégée would waste not one moment of this golden opportunity and that Monsieur, without ever knowing it, would be skillfully manipulated.

Clothilde's going threw the servants' quarters into gloom for a full week and Clementina might have despaired of poor Joshua, who dragged himself around at half-pace and could hardly be brought to utter more than a dispirited "Yes'm" or "No'm," had she not recently taken delivery of a dashing new carriage, not, regretfully, the high-perch phaeton that had so taken her eye—but that would have scared Aunt Seraphina silly to see her driving—but a very nice cabriolet that offered more in the way of protection against the elements with its folded silk back hood. Joshua was chivied into new livery of blue and yellow to exactly match the wheels and one way and another was kept so busy that he had very little time to moon over a pair of violet eyes.

Paris soon became accustomed to the sight of Miss Brady from Baltimore (so odd, these Americans!) taking the air on crisp winter mornings along the Champs Elysées and into the Bois, her young Black in his impeccable livery up behind her—sometimes with a friend, lady or gentleman at her side, but more often than not, quite alone.

Whatever the Comtesse de Tourne and her cronies thought about such a flagrant disregard of decorum they expressed prudently behind closed doors, for since the Royal Family, in the persons of the Duc and Duchesse de Berry, had begun to display a decided partiality for Miss Brady's company, it was not for them to cavil at her behavior.

It gradually began to dawn upon Clementina that she was not the only one with a full engagement book; quite often now, it seemed that she returned to the Rue de Varenne and enquired after her aunt to be informed by a bland-faced

Maurice that "Madame has gone driving with Monseigneur the Duc de Menton" or "Monseigneur le Duc has escorted Madame to view the Art Treasures in the Palace of the Louvre." And in the evening more often than not the Duc was among their party at the Opera or the particular ball or card party or musical soirée of their choosing.

Even Patrick, engrossed as he was for the most part in his own affairs, began to refer to the Duc with affectionate disrespect as "Auntie's Beau," a term guaranteed to put Mrs. Westbury to the blush when he used it in her hearing. "Try not to tease her to distraction, love," begged his sister on one of the rare occasions when they were alone together.

Patrick, very much engaged in the study of his reflection in a heavily gilded peer glass, one of several that ornamented the walls of the Grand Salon, was endeavoring to decide whether his shirt points were not just a touch too high. His attention distracted, he swung round, staring. "You don't really suppose it could be serious?"

Clementina found his youthful incredulity amusing, if a shade irritating. "My dear boy, you don't have a complete monopoly on romance! It may seem inconceivable to you, but people don't automatically become immune to love the moment they pass forty!"

"Well, no, of course not. I just never supposed . . . that is, I never really thought about it, but . . ."

"Quite!" she said dryly. "But now that you have, you will try to use a little more tact, won't you? I daresay being in love can make a person very vulnerable, you know. I'm sure you wouldn't care to have your own tender passions held up to ridicule, however amiable the intention!"

Patrick flushed, searched his sister's face, and wondered if her words had any special significance. Had she heard about Madame Davide? Surely not, or she must have said! The mere thought of Madame melted his bones—she was an angel, not like anyone he had ever known! That she should even look twice at him was in itself a miracle . . .

The door opened to admit Alfred Bennett, who had come to take him off to look at a hunter he was considering buying. Alfred surveyed his friend critically. Patrick awaited his verdict in some trepidation. "That's a new waistcoat—haven't seen it before!"

"No."

"Yellow stripes. I like it. Not sure about the shirt points, though . . ."

"I feared as much." Patrick sighed. "Too high."

"Not high enough, dear fellow."

"No, damnit! I can hardly move my head now!" He saw Alfred's grin. "You're roasting me!"

Clementina laughed and declared them to be a couple of dandies. As they took their leave of her, a square of lace-edged cambric fluttered from Patrick's pocket. He bent to retrieve it but she was before him, recognizing it instantly. "This is mine! So you are the culprit. Justine has been blaming one of the maids for the disappearance of my handkerchiefs. Wretched boy! Do you not have handkerchiefs enough of your own?"

Patrick looked sheepish, but Alfred was quite amazingly forthcoming. "Wouldn't do—has to be a lady's, d'you see, ma-am. Always carry one myself—put Patrick on to it sometime back. Deuced useful, always supposing you take a fancy to a pretty woman and have no one to do the necessary. Wait till she's passing, let it fall—then pick it up, present it. Say you believe she dropped it. Neatest little trick I ever knew of!"

"Why, I never heard of anything so . . . outrageous!" Clementina was torn between laughter and indignation. Laughter won as Patrick assured her with a grin: "Maybe, Clemmy. Works like a charm, just the same."

"Abominable creatures!" she called after them as they beat a strategic retreat.

She related the story later to Prince Metlin, who was riding with her cousin in the Bois.

"Only fancy! Such deviousness—in one's own brother!"

Alexei chuckled. "It makes one feel positively ancient, eh Dominic? Ah, I had forgotten! The uncertainties—the agony of planning to bring oneself to the notice of one's intended inamorata, and the ecstasy of succeeding!"

"I can't imagine you ever having had any trouble!" said Dominic dryly.

"That is because you did not know me when I was a sensitive adolescent! Now, of course, I have plenty of address!"

This drew a peal of laughter from Clementina and a sardonic smile from the Marquis. He had been casting an expert eye over her carriage and, catching Joshua's admiring eye, felt obliged to acknowledge him, receiving by return an ear-splitting grin. This put Clementina quite in charity with him.

"Do you approve my equipage, cousin?" she asked.

"Very dashing," he agreed. "Nice bay gelding, too. I'm told

it's often to be seen turning in at the gates of the Elysée. You are moving in exalted circles these days!"

He sounded disapproving, which made her lift her chin. The pale sunlight lancing through the near bare branches of the trees, touched into flame the bright curls escaping from Clementina's little brown toque trimmed with fur. "Yes. Only fancy—the Duchesse de Berry has taken me up! Am I not fortunate?" Her eyes dared him to quarrel with her.

"And the Duc?"

"Oh, the Duc means to make a proficient flautist of me. We practice almost daily. He assures me that regular practice is essential. What he really means, of course," she added, determined that he should know how well she understood what she was about, "is that teaching me the correct fingering entails a certain intimacy, which gives him the most delightful opportunity for dalliance!"

"Precisely!"

"You need have no fear, cousin. I am in no danger from the Duc, for the Duchesse is most careful never to leave us alone!"

"*Doucement*, my children!" pleaded Alexei indulgently. "In a moment you will be quarreling again."

"Nonsense!" said the Marquis. "If we were quarreling you would be in no doubt of it."

"But you will allow that you don't always deal together as you should."

"That's hardly surprising. Clementina is not a particularly conformable young woman!"

"When we first met," Clementina told Alexei, enjoying herself hugely, "my cousin was wildly prejudiced. He had me tied and tagged as a pushy young interloper come to threaten the even tenor of his life by attempting to foist upon him— no, worse still, upon society at his expense—an embarrassing, penniless array of dirty dishes!"

Cadogon's eyes glinted. "Clementina Brady, stop trying to provoke me! Any notions I may have entertained regarding yourself or your motives at our first encounter are private and will remain so; and if you wish to promote a state of amity between us I advise you to pursue a less tortuous conversational path!"

A gurgle of laughter escaped her. "Very well. I won't tease you anymore."

Alexei looked from one to the other with growing curiosity and finally shook his head, unable to fathom the relationship.

By way of changing the conversation he asked after Clothilde. It was extraordinary, but he supposed he had seen her that very morning entering a tiny establishment just off the Rue Madeleine. Only he must have been mistaken, for she was by far too finely dressed and was on the arm of Clementina's would-be-beau, Guillard!

"No, you weren't mistaken, Alexei. Our little friend Clothilde is now under Monsieur's patronage." She explained what had happened and they both looked at her in awe.

"You mean you actually cozened that egregious nodcock into taking the girl off your hands?" demanded Lord Cadogon.

"Well, I rather think that Monsieur is convinced that the idea was all his. And I could hardly stand in Clothilde's light when she was so clearly destined for higher things!" She leaned forward and lowered her voice. "Do you think we might change the subject? Joshua is still nursing a somewhat bruised heart."

"Ruthless, quite ruthless."

"Not at all. Monsieur is content, Clothilde is more than content, and I am rid of a dreadful bore!"

"Clementina Brady! As I live and breathe!"

The cry, delivered in strident tones, issued from an approaching barouche.

"Oh, no! I don't believe it!" Clementina groaned. "Emmelina Worthington!"

The barouche drew to a halt alongside Clementina's carriage. Two ladies leaned forward, the elder unbecomingly attired in puce velvet, a hat like a large squashed cushion nodding with plumes surmounting a face that could scarce be described by the most amiable of critics as anything other than plain. The young girl at her side seemed, by contrast, quite devastatingly pretty.

"I don't believe it!" echoed Mrs. Worthington, her darting eyes assessing Clementina's sable-trimmed redingote, her stylish carriage *and* her two escorts with disconcerting thoroughness. "Fancy us meeting like this, so far from Baltimore! And how well you're looking, my dear . . . you were just a bit peaky when you left us, I remember. Your aunt is with you, of course . . . and *dear Patrick—*" Clementina winced. "I must say you seem very much at home . . . I daresay you'll have made lots of friends . . . ?" She looked pointedly at Clementina's companions.

There was no way out of it; Clementina stifled a sigh.

"How very remiss of me. Mrs. Worthingon, Miss Alice Worthington, may I present to you Prince Alexei Metlin? And this is my cousin Lord Cadogon."

The gleam in the lady's eye grew distinctly predatory. "Delighted to make your acquaintance! I daresay," she added archly, "we shall be forever running into one another. Mr. Worthington is here on business that could take several months. We've hired a big old house in the Rue . . . Saint Honoré, is it? Of course, it's full of the most awful old furniture at present, but Mr. Worthington is seeing to all that. We shall soon have it twinkling like a new pin and then you must come and visit with us! My little Alice don't know a soul here, as yet!"

Alexei rose nobly to the occasion, assuring her that such an ommission must soon be rectified, at which little Alice dutifully lowered her eyes in blushing confusion.

"Don't, I beg of you, encourage that woman's pretensions, Alexei!" Clementina implored him as the barouche drove away. "She is quite the most awful creature of my acquaintance!"

He chuckled. "But I find her fascinating! How do you suppose they mean to rid themselves of all those priceless furnishings that so offend them?"

"I have no idea! Burn them, most likely."

"Rich?" hazarded the Marquis.

"Oh, as Croesus!" said Clementina. "We are as nothing to them, I assure you!"

✖CHAPTER 13✖

Madame Robart's house lay in a quiet, tree-lined boulevard set well back from the road. Clementina and her aunt were warmly welcomed, their outer layers of garments were removed and whisked away by a smiling maidservant, and they were led into a delightful salon, which even on so dark and dismal a day was bright with shades of golds and browns, a family room where books were scattered in comfortable disorder and sewing half-done lay on a small table beside the sofa.

Here they found Alexei, his legs stretched out before the fire with the easy familiarity of an old friend. "You see?" he said, coming to his feet to greet them with a twinkling eye. "I, also, am invited to take tea."

Mrs. Westbury sighed her pleasure aloud as she was encouraged to take a chair so perfectly placed that she could toast her toes without the least appearance of being thought ill-mannered. She had known, from the first moment of seeing the house through winter's intricate lacing of branches along the tree-lined drive, that this was not just any house, but a home—like her own dear home in Baltimore. She hadn't thought about it now for some little while, but one glimpse of the long, low house with its graceful lines had been sufficient to fill her with nostalgia.

Clementina was curious to discover whether her first instinctive liking for Elyse Robart would withstand further exploration, for they were not in the least alike, and was pleased to find that it did. Elyse was quiet, but it was the quietness of a serene spirit, and as her shyness melted in the warmth of Clementina's open friendliness, and as Prince Metlin made her laugh with outrageous compliments to all three ladies in turn, she was soon quite at ease. It had been clear from the beginning that Alexei was a fairly regular visitor, and before long he was demanding to know where was his little princess. With some diffidence Elyse wondered if the presence of a lively five-year-old would disturb her guests.

Clementina and her aunt looked equally astonished.

"My dear madame," said Mrs. Westbury happily. "I cannot offhand think of anything I should enjoy more."

The child who was presently ushered into the room by a nurse was as fair as her mother was dark. An enchanting, diminutive creature with eyes of deepest blue, she was on her very best behavior as she made her curtsies in turn to each of the ladies, spreading the skirts of her pretty sprig muslin dress with perfect composure.

When she reached Prince Metlin, the curtsy was just a fraction deeper, the cheeks a little pinker, and the eyes demurely lowered. But when Alexei said in rallying tones, *"Eh bien,* little Suzy, and how is my favorite princess today, heh?" she peeped up at him through long lashes and her mouth curved in a smile of pure coquetry that delighted Clementina.

"Bonjour, monsieur le Prince," she piped in a breathy

treble. "I am very well. I thank you and I am *very* pleased that you have come!"

"Well then, come and give me a kiss, *mon ange,* and we will be comfortable together."

Within a very short time she was sitting happily on his knee, her head resting against his shoulder while the amusing red-haired lady regaled her with stories of America, which was a long way away, so far that she had had to travel across the sea on a ship. She wondered why, sometimes, her stories should make the other lady look so sad.

"Don't let Suzy tire you with her questions, Miss Brady," said Elyse with a wry smile. "Her thirst for knowledge is insatiable." But it was proudly said.

"I don't mind in the least," Clementina insisted. "It is by far more enlivening than being obliged to bore on forever about the latest trend in bonnets!"

"But surely, Clementina, your social palate is not already becoming jaded?" Alexei murmured in mock dismay.

She grinned. "Not in the least, but an unrelieved diet of champagne can occasionally make one long for a nice, refreshing drink of water."

"You wish for a drink of water, madame?" Suzy sounded puzzled. "But I thought you had come to take tea?"

They all laughed. Elyse said, "Dominic should be here shortly . . . if you would not mind waiting a few moments longer . . ."

As Clementina reassured her, she happened to glance up. From where she was sitting the window gave her an excellent view of the front porch and at that precise moment she saw the Marquis emerge from its overhanging shelter with an older man whose neat, rather somber greatcoat gave him the look of a lawyer. The two men stood in the middle of the driveway for a few moments in earnest conversation and then Cadogon gestured imperatively and a groom came running with the visitor's horse.

It ought not to have surprised Clementina that her cousin had been in the house all along, yet it still came as something of a shock to find him so very much in command. She had little time in which to ponder the reason for her disturbance, however, for in a moment he was entering the room for all the world as though he had but that moment arrived, blandly as greetings were exchanged.

Without a word, Suzy slid from Alexei's knee and ran across to push her hand insistently into his. He looked down at her, his face softening perceptibly and, without a word, swung her up to sit on his shoulder, where her arm curled confidently round his neck.

"Well, my friend." Alexei grinned. "It is easy to tell who is the most favored one among us."

Dominic laughed, ruffling Suzy's golden curls. "Is your vanity wounded? Well, no matter. You must allow me the odd conquest, after all!"

The child put her mouth close to his ear and whispered something.

"What does your maman say?" he murmured in answer.

"Suzy!" cried her mother, half laughing. "It is about the skating, I suppose? You should not trouble Monsieur Dominic with such things just now." Her eyes lifted, vaguely troubled, to meet his. "Miss Brady has very kindly offered to teach Suzy to skate when the winter comes, but I am not sure . . ."

"I may, mayn't I, *cher Monsieur Dominic?*" Suzy crooned.

He looked quizzical. "That is for your maman to decide, little one."

"Mais oui, but she always does as you tell her!"

There was general laughter during which Elyse went pink with embarrassment and Alexei mopped his eyes and murmured, "Out of the mouths of babes!" Cadogon, looking imperturbable, called Suzy a baggage and lowered her to the ground.

"But I would very much like to skate for my birthday," she persisted.

"And when is that?" Clementina asked.

"The second day of February," came the prompt reply.

"Well, that is easily settled. If the weather obliges us, there is time enough to learn and if your maman will agree, we can hold a little birthday party on the lake!"

The child crowed with delight. "That might prove a little difficult to arrange," said Alexei. "At that time of the year the lake is almost invariably crowded."

"Then I shall reserve it for the day!"

"Just like that?" Cadogon said on the ghost of a laugh.

"Well, why not? I expect it can be arranged. Most things are possible if one only stirs oneself a little."

"If you have made up your mind, my dear cousin, the thing is as good as accomplished."

His words mocked her gently. As though making comparisons, his glance strayed to the sofa near the fire where Elyse leaned forward a little, her profile exquisitely etched by the leaping flames as she listened to Suzy's eager chatter, and just for an instant Clementina had the curious sensation of being shut out.

"Lord Cadogon appears to be very much at home in Madame Robart's house," Aunt Seraphina murmured within the close confines of the carriage as they rattled homeward. The heavy plush curtains pulled across the windows gave a feeling of snug intimacy, but one of them had been caught back a little, and in the darkness beyond the bobbing carriage lamps Clementina could just discern the figures of Prince Metlin and the Marquis riding abreast. "One cannot but be aware of the warmth with which the child regards him," Mrs. Westbury continued confidentially. "Almost as a father, wouldn't you say?"

"I believe Monsieur Robart and the Marquis were close friends." Clementina found herself less disposed than usual to gossip. "I have no doubt he feels a certain responsibility for Madame and Suzy."

"Well, yes, of course, dear . . . that would explain it, I suppose." But it was clear that such an interpretation did not satisfy Mrs. Westbury's more demanding romantic ideals. "It just seems strange, in the circumstances, that they have never married . . ."

Clementina recalled the intimacy between the two, the way Dominic obviously made free of Madame Robart's house. It was on the tip of her tongue to comment brusquely that Lord Cadogon appeared to be enjoying all the privileges of such a union without any need of matrimonial ties But her aunt would be shocked, and moreover it was a shabby thing to say of Elyse Robart, whom she truly liked.

Early in December Clementina received an invitation from a certain Marquis de Brissec to visit his chateau at Fontaine-bleau for two days. "There will be a small party of us, Miss Brady. Your brother will, I think, enjoy the fine hunting in the forest and you and your aunt, will, I trust, enjoy the company!" The Marquis had assured her cheerfully.

The invitation had surprised Clementina, for although she was acquainted with Monsieur de Brissec, she had not thought herself upon terms as would warrant such partiality. Alexei, when he heard, raised his comically expressive eyebrows, while her cousin, she thought, looked less than amused.

"But why are we invited?" She looked from one to the other. "Do you know something that I don't?"

"Nothing at all, *dushka*," said Alexei with a look of innocence. "I am sure that de Brissec wishes only to pursue your acquaintance a little further and it is pure coincidence that he also happens to be the very good friend of the Duc de Berry!"

"Oh, but . . ." She glanced at her cousin's rather tight-pursed mouth. "No. I won't believe *that!* The whole idea is totally absurd!" Cadogon said nothing, but gave her that look of polite disbelief she knew so well, and as always it put her on the defensive. "And even if it *were* true, I can't see that there is anything of significance in the invitation. The Duc has never attempted . . . we are not . . ." She caught Alexei's eye and exclaimed with a vexed laugh: "Oh, good God! If a man is planning a seduction, he does not invite the lady's aunt and brother along, surely?"

"No, but a weekend in the country does afford him an excellent opportunity to pursue a more intimate course of action away from the prying eyes of society," said Cadogon.

"Well, if that is all, I shall simply make sure that I always keep Aunt Seraphina close by me."

Patrick was in two minds about the invitation, torn between the exciting prospect of hunting wild boar in the forest—a new experience for him—and the unbearable wrench of leaving Madame Davide just when she seemed on the point of succumbing to his ardor. Clementina knew about Anys Davide, a young courtesan of quite exceptional talents. Alexei had pointed her out when they were driving in the Bois one day; she was afforded but a glimpse of guinea-gold curls, an exquisite profile, and heard the gay, tinkling laugh that wafted through the press of young gallants on horseback clustered about her carriage like bees about a honey jar. With a jolt of dismay, she had seen Patrick's figure amongst the courtesan's admirers.

"Be easy, *dushka*," Alexei advised. "Every young man must experience such a one as Anys Davide. Patrick will take no lasting harm." She hoped he might be right.

Dora Courtney was less optimistic; Patrick's latest infatuation had plunged her into the lowest of spirits. "Just when I was so sure that he had begun to like me! But how am I ever to compete with Madame Davide? Have you seen her, Miss Brady?"

"Yes, I have!" Clementina's sympathy was genuine, yet

notwithstanding her own concern, she could not but find Dora's air of tragedy a trifle comic. "She does seem to be quite distractingly lovely!"

"Oh, she is!" wailed Dora. "Exceedingly so! Every feature is perfection—her teeth are absolute pearls . . . every one!"

"I know what you mean. It has always seemed to me most unfair that one person should be so singularly blessed! But you are very pretty, too, you know, especially when your brow isn't furrowed with frowning!" The compliment fell on unreceptive ears. Clementina sighed and her tone grew more rallying. "Oh, come now, it isn't *so* bad! If I were you, I would flirt outrageously with someone else, but if you don't fancy doing so, you will have to wait until Patrick's passion cools, as it must before long."

"Do you think so?" Dora remained depressingly unconvinced.

"I am sure of it. I am becoming quite an expert at reading the signs. You must understand that a young man in the throes of infatuation is totally single-minded! However, the degree of concentration required is so intense that he cannot possibly sustain it for any length of time! So if you really care for my tiresome brother, and I'm sure he doesn't deserve that you should, then you will have to learn patience and be sure that you are around ready to pick up the pieces!"

Clementina smiled encouragement, but her words were bracing. "Meantime, we can't have you dwindling into a decline! Perhaps you would care to come out with me? I was on the point of driving to the Rue de la Paix; Madame Le Vestris has the most divine sable-trimmed cape, which I have quite nobly resisted buying for all of two weeks! Now, my resolve has suddenly melted away and I mean to have it this very morning! If your mama would spare you to me, we could go on a spending spree, for when one is a little cast down, you know . . ." Her smile widened to a grin. "I have found that nothing is so guaranteed to raise one's spirits as a wild burst of extravagance!"

The matter was thus settled and when, some little while later, the two young ladies emerged from the portals of Madame Le Vestris' salon, a frail little midinette trotting valiantly at their heels laden with packages, it was apparent that the expedition had been a huge success.

It was when the bandboxes had been safely stowed and Clementina was on the point of ordering Joshua to let go the horses' heads that she noticed a familiar, arrogant figure walking quickly down the steps of a nearby house, wearing an unaccustomed air of abstraction.

She hadn't known that Henri was back in town; having assured herself that Dora was by far too interested in her purchases to have seen him, Clementina sat quietly watching as he climbed into his curricle and drove away. It would have been so easy to attract his attention. She wondered why she had not done so—a fear of being rebuffed, perhaps? That wasn't like her. At any rate, the visit to Fontainebleau had come at exactly the right time to give her a respite in which to think.

Their departure was attended by a great deal of activity; from the amount of care lavished upon them by Maurice, one might have supposed they were journeying to the Polar regions instead of a mere thirty miles or so. He so packed the travelers about with furs and rugs, and with hot bricks wrapped in blankets, that they could scarcely move. In addition to a basket laden with food, he pressed into Clementina's hands at the last moment a generous flask of Armagnac, lest there should be any delay or trouble of any kind upon the road that might render his "ladies" exposed to the elements.

Joshua, sitting up beside the coachman, Pierre, clutched a firing piece to his bosom in a manner that afforded Clementina severe misgivings. She exchanged a speaking look with Patrick, who offered up a facetious prayer to the *Bon Dieu* that they might not fall prey to brigands, and thus earned a mild reproof from Aunt Seraphina.

Alexei arrived in time to bid them farewell, enveloped in a greatcoat whose enormous fur collar was turned up against a prevailing mist blown in little eddies by a chill easterly wind. He assured Clementina, his eyes brimming with wicked mirth, that he would be impatient for her return and she must be sure to give him a detailed account of their stay!

As might have been expected, his teasing aroused fresh misgivings about the purpose of the visit, but any nervousness she felt was soon dispelled by the warmth with which they were received. The Marquis de Brissec could not have been more welcoming, nor could his wife; and the comforting presence of at least a dozen other guests, most of whom she knew and all of whom were eminently respectable, convinced her that her cousin's forebodings had been quite without foundation and that Alexei had been roasting her.

The first evening passed very pleasantly with a superb dinner, a little music, and some stimulating conversation during which the Duc de Berry was not mentioned once; the ladies then retired to bed, well content, leaving the gentlemen to blow a cloud, play vingt-et-un and tell bawdy stories.

The following morning dawned crisp and bright after an early haze with a light frost riming hedgerows caught unawares, still drenched in the heavy mists of the previous day. The *chasse* was away into the forest before the sun had risen much beyond the topmost branches of the trees, tipping them with gold like lighted tapers in a cold, white world.

Clementina was on the steps of the chateau to watch the colorful party depart in all its splendor, smiling to see Patrick—pale with excitement and, she guessed, with not a thought in his head of Madame Davide—placed well to the fore. The huntsmen in full livery carried *cors de chasse*— huge circular horns upon which, she was told in all seriousness, they would play a merry tune each time a boar was killed!

Most of the ladies were still abed. Even the Marquise, who was a charming if rather indolent hostess, did not hold it to be within the bounds of her duties to rise much before noon, but Clementina didn't mind. She was more than content to wander alone, following the track a little way into the forest and, when all sounds of the hunt had faded, enjoying the absolute stillness of the morning.

Aunt Seraphina might take her ease today, but tomorrow would be a different matter. Clementina smiled, recalling the way the Duc de Menton had announced oh, so casually, that his own chateau lay not a few miles from where they were to stay and that he had been considering paying it a visit.

"If I were to come whilst you are staying with de Brissec, madame," he had suggested to her aunt, "perhaps you would care to see it?"

Aunt Seraphina had shyly agreed. Clementina wondered how long it would be before the Duc declared himself. She sighed, and chided herself for so doing. It would be churlish indeed to begrudge her aunt this joy, which was becoming more apparent with every day that passed, for no one deserved it more.

Those of the guests who had not gone with the hunt assembled in the chateau's vinery to partake of a light *dejeuner* served by an army of servants and thereafter repaired to Madame's favorite salon, where her personal musician played upon the spinet whilst the guests gossiped or fell once more into a doze. It was here that Madame's major-domo appeared presently, crossed to his mistress, and said something to her, soft-voiced. It was as though she had been expecting something of the kind; she rose at once and drifted across to where Clementina sat with her aunt.

"Miss Brady, I wonder if I might crave your indulgence for a short time? If you would come with me . . .?" Madame's soulful eyes were heavy with mystery and Clementina, feeling irked by so much inactivity and intrigued by her hostess's manner, went—all unsuspecting—along the mahogany-paneled portrait gallery and into a smaller salon. The door closed and she was alone.

But she was not alone, for a figure rose abruptly from a chair near the window.

"Henri!"

His appearance was so unexpected that she was bereft of words, her thoughts for once refusing to come to order as conflicting emotions surged through her. How was he here? Why had he come? And more important—she sat down rather suddenly as the scene in Madame's salon just now came so clearly back into her mind—had this whole visit been arranged for the sole purpose of affecting a reconciliation between herself and Henri . . .?

He was searching her face as though trying to gauge her reaction; Clementina saw that the handsome features showed signs of strain; she endeavored to be calm, to analyze her feelings—did her heart beat faster because of shock or because she was pleased to see him . . .

"Clementina, I have taken you by surprise, perhaps, but I had to come!" His words, jerky, betraying his unease, seemed to burst into the silence—and all at once she felt quite calm. "Do you have no word of greeting for me? *Ah, cherie,*—be kind! Tell me that you forgive me!"

She looked up at him consideringly. "You do feel, then, that you are in need of my forgiveness?"

"But yes! I behaved badly that night at the Elysée—stupidly, when I know well enough how Monsieur de Berry enjoys to flirt! Of course you were obliged to be pleasant to him. If matters had not already been a little strained between us, I would never have allowed myself to be so overcome with jealousy!"

Clementina clasped her hands tight in her lap. She wanted to cry out to him not to go on. It was all false, false, false— the man she knew him to be would never crawl to a woman, unless . . . but the words would not come.

"And you must admit that I was right about that little slut, for she has used you as I knew she would!" Ah, that was more in character, but almost at once his wayward pride was contained once more. "It was unforgivable of me, however, to leave you to face Maman alone. She does not mean——" He saw Clementina's straight black brows lift and he shrugged. *"Eh, bien,* you are right, of course. She is rude and patronizing and——yes, I admit it——insufferably arrogant, but she *is* my mother——" He stopped as though the words choked him, strode away, and almost at once returned to seize Clementina's hand in a bruising grip. "But you must believe me, I did not mean all those things I said! You *must know* that I desire more than anything in the world to make you my wife!"

So there it was——a declaration that should, surely, fill any right-thinking girl's heart with joy! If only he had sounded a little as though he meant it . . . if only he did not tug at his immaculate cravat as though it were too tight and constantly finger the diamond nestling in its folds, perhaps then she would not feel so empty of feeling.

Her lack of response filled him with a new urgency. *"Cherie,* you would not refuse me because of Maman?"

Clementina tried to free her hand and could not; she searched the handsome face and found there desperation, but not love. The discovery strengthened her resolve. She felt unexpectedly saddened as she rehearsed in her mind the conventional words of rejection——*sensible of the honor——affections not sufficiently engaged.* She knew part of the blame must be hers, for had she not encouraged his attentions, knowing in her heart that his motives were suspect, because just for a little while she had thought, had hoped——ah, well, whatever she had hoped, it was clear that he deserved more from her than the mere demands of convention.

Oh, lord! she sighed. Why can't I be a nice comfortable girl who will say "yes, please" nicely, and not ask awkward questions!

She stood up, forcing him to step backward. "Why do you want to marry me?" she asked, not unkindly.

"Why?" He dropped her hand as though it suddenly burned him, recovered himself, and said eagerly, but without quite meeting her eyes, "But——you know why! Because I adore you . . . I cannot live without you! Oh, *mon amour,* you know that from the very first you have had all my admiration . . ."

She remembered the way Cadogon had looked at Elyse Robart and felt a vague pricking behind her eyes.

"Admiration, perhaps, Henri—but not love, I think."

He gave a shrug of helpless irritation. "Always women must complicate matters with talk of love!" He crossed the space between them, pulled her into his arms, and kissed her with what, allowing for her woeful lack of practical experience, she deduced to be considerable expertise. It was, in fact, the first time she had been kissed in quite that way—for one could not count the furtive efforts of those daring young bloods of Baltimore society who had been smart enough to lure her into the shrubbery in her salad days; just for a moment, she allowed herself to respond to the not unpleasant sensations Henri's caresses aroused in her.

The Comte, excited by her apparent acquiescence and, sensing victory, shifted her slightly in his arms and grew more passionate. "Would such a marriage be *so* bad, *cherie?*" he murmured with all the old persuasiveness, just below her left ear. "You would have no cause for disappointment, I promise you!" His mouth sought hers with greater urgency.

"No, stop!" Reality asserted itself with horrifying suddenness; she pushed him away, acutely conscious of her discomposure, of the impression he must have gained of her. "Henri, when I talked of love, I did not mean . . ." She faltered, blushing furiously. "I did not mean *that!*"

"But you enjoyed it," he challenged triumphantly, attempting to draw her close again. "Come now, admit that you are no different from other women. You enjoy to be coerced a little."

"No!" Clementina resisted him, her hands crossed resolutely against the thudding of her heart, furious that she had so far lost command of herself as to give him cause to think . . . what he obviously *did* think! In an effort to regain some vestige of authority she said with cold formality, "I am not *other women,* Henri! If my momentary lapse induced you to think otherwise, then I can only offer you my deepest apologies."

His manner had changed. "Someone has been poisoning your mind—your cousin, perhaps, or Patrick?"

"Patrick? No, indeed. Why should he?" As her composure returned, she felt better able to cope. "No one has said anything to me, but—oh, don't you see, my dear Henri, I'm not awfully good at dissembling! If I were, perhaps I could swallow my natural inclinations and make a *mariage de con-*

venance." Her wry smile begged his understanding. "But I have always felt most strongly that I shall marry only when I can find someone who will be everything in the world to me and I to him!"

"Then you are destined to die unwed," he said harshly, "for such unions are rare!"

She flushed. "Perhaps. But since I am not yet grown to be an antidote, I believe I will pursue my foolishness a little longer." The look in his eye troubled her; she laid a tentative hand on his arm. "My dear, it wouldn't serve—your mother and I forever up in the boughs! But—" She hesitated, searching for the right words. "I hope we may remain friends, and if as a friend you would accept my help, then I would be happy to lend you sufficient monies to . . ."

His face was suffused with an ugly anger; not only was she rejecting him—a fact he found hard to accept—she had the effrontery to patronize him! "I, the Comte de Tourne, to borrow from a woman? *Dieu!* What sort of a man do you take me for?"

"I'm not sure, Henri," she said quietly. "Perhaps you will enlighten me." And when he did not answer immediately, "I don't understand men. You are insulted because I offer you a straighforward loan, yet I am expected to acquiese gratefully when you seek to marry me for my money. Well, I'm sorry, but I don't care to be used in that way!"

"You talk of being used? What of me? Oh, I was a fool to allow myself to be thus persuaded! The next time I do things *my* way."

She felt an unexpected frisson of fear, as though his words held a hidden threat to her. She didn't fully understand them.

"You were persuaded, you say—to offer for me? By whom?"

Henri's lip curled. "Your good friend and mine—de Berry. Who else? He has brought a party to the Palace for the hunting, but of course you will know that!"

"No, I didn't!"

"I had a particular favor to ask of him, which he was pleased to consider. He then turned the conversation to *our* estrangement, assured me that you had no thought of marrying Metlin, and suggested in an oblique fashion that it would please him very well for you to marry me."

Clementina was by now entirely mystified, and showed it. He laughed. "For an intelligent woman, my dear Clementina, you are still incredibly naive!" This time there was no mistak-

ing his meaning. She blushed. "Quite so. A married woman is
so much more . . . accessible!" Henri picked up his
greatcoat, which had been thrown across a chair, gave her a
mocking little bow, and strode to the door. "I advise you to
grow up, *cherie*—before it is too late! For now, I bid you
adieu."

When Henri had gone, Clementina sat on—for how long,
she wasn't sure. Finally, she went up to her room, alarming
Justine by her lack of response, donned a close-fitting pelisse
edged with chinchilla, tied the ribbons of a matching bonnet
firmly under her chin, and took a long walk in the gardens.
Not for anything could she have gone back into Madame's
salon to face the knowing looks, the unspoken questions; not
until she had come to terms with her outraged sensibilities
and stilled her quivering nerves.

How long she walked she wasn't sure, but when she returned to the front of the chateau the sun had attained a win-
try pallor and the air was growing chill. A racing curricle was
drawn up at the steps; it bore a royal crest and was accompanied by two captains of the King's Guard and a groom who
was coping competently at the heads of a pair of spirited
black horses.

On the chateau steps stood the Duc de Berry clad in a
flowing black cloak, richly embossed.

"Miss Brady." His face wore the look of hauteur she had
seen once before. She dipped the required curtsy with reluctance, her mood matching his.

"You will drive with me."

It was an order rather than a request. She gave him back
look for look.

"If your Highness will forgive me, I am a little tired."

"Nevertheless, you will drive with me." He stepped forward and extended his hand in a peremptory gesture; after a
moment's hesitation she allowed him to help her up into the
carriage.

"And you—" he addressed the outriders "—can go back to
the palace. I have no further need of you."

The two captains of the King's Guard moved uneasily in
their saddles.

"Your pardon, Highness," said the braver of the two. "But
we are under orders from His Majesty to accompany you at
all times."

"You will obey *my* orders!" The Duc flew into a rage,
cursing them with a lack of restraint that appalled Clemen-

tina, the blood surging into his face, distorting it, as he threatened to have them reduced to the ranks for insubordination. "Now go!" he thundered. "I am not a child to be wet-nursed at every turn because of some crazy, imagined threat to my life! *Merde!* Is a man allowed no privacy? *Allez-vous-en!* Go, go!"

They went, red faced.

In the silence that followed, the Duc ordered the groom to let go the horses' heads, and the man was left standing on the steps with orders to wait there for his return. The horses sprang forward, the wheels of the curricle bounced and churned up the neatly ordered gravel of the drive, and for the first few moments he was very much occupied in bringing his team under control. By the time they approached the perimeter of the forest at a brisk trot, the worst of his temper had been exorcised and he was made very much aware of Clementina sitting beside him, straight backed, severe, unyielding of profile. His tone was cool.

"I have shocked you yet again, Miss Brady."

"Yes, sir, indeed you have." No sign of relenting there.

"Because I lose my temper with fools?"

"Because you chose to berate, most unfairly—and in front of me, which I found most embarrassing—loyal officers who are simply doing their duty! If your uncle, the King, thinks sufficient of you to show concern for your safety, then I think it very churlish of you to reject his concern."

"Do you!" It was clear that no quarter was to be given. He sought refuge in rank. "Must I command you to be civil to me, mademoiselle?"

"You can't," she retorted swiftly. "Your Highness has no authority over me, and I thank God for it!"

He looked taken aback by her vehemence, met her fierce eyes and, much to her surprise, suddenly put back his head and laughed aloud.

"Ah, Miss Brady, I do so *like* you! Nobody ever takes me to task quite as you do!"

Unwillingly she smiled. "I'm sorry. I was impertinent."

"Yes, you were, exceedingly so. But no matter. Tell me, why did you send de Tourne off with his tail between his legs this afternoon? It was not kind of you."

"Sometimes," she said, giving him a very straight look, "people make it very difficult for one to be kind. Why did *you*, sir, encourage Henri to come here today?"

The Duc ventured a swift, appraising look, and shrugged.

"The de Tournes have always given loyal service to the Royal Family. Henri will never be the man his father was, of course—and the mother is insufferable—but nonetheless, one feels a certain obligation. Henri came to me recently with a problem—" another quick look "—He is in serious financial difficulties, did you know? Ah, yes, I thought you might! Well, I was able to aid him—not in a general way, you understand, we are not *so* benevolent!" dryly. "But in this one instance—a particularly troublesome creditor—I was able to be of some assistance.'

"And in return?" Clementina asked in rather a tight voice.

To her dismay, for they were by now deep in the forest, the Duc brought the curricle to a halt and turned to face her; the expression in his eyes warmed her cheeks in spite of the cold.

"In return, I suggested that he should swallow his pride, mend that silly quarrel, and make you his wife without further delay. For him, the benefits of such a union need hardly be stressed, and you, my dear—" his teeth flashed white in the gathering dusk "—you would make an enchanting comtesse. Are you sure you will not reconsider?"

"I won't marry a man I don't love and cannot respect, even to please you, sir!" And then, bitterly, "Especially when your own intentions are suspect."

She heard a little hiss of indrawn breath. "So young de Tourne's disappointment made him indiscreet. I must remember that! Still, it makes no matter." He slid one arm along the seat behind her.

Clementina was painfully unsure how to deal with him. Until this moment she had known only the best of him—the good-humored companion, gallant and charming—but she had heard much of that other self, hedonist, debaucher, dedicated to the ruthless pursuit of pleasure. And this very afternoon she had witnessed the terrible unpredictability of his temper.

"Sir, we should go back!" she pleaded. "It will soon be dark. My aunt . . ."

For answer, he possessed himself of one of her clasped hands, prising it free with inexorable determination. "Such a cold member . . . how it trembles!" Looking up, he said softly, "Are you *so* afraid to be alone with me?"

"In your present mood, yes I am," she replied on a caught breath. "For I cannot—I *cannot*—be what you want of me."

He regarded her hand intently, smoothing it with his thumb. "Are you quite sure, Miss Brady?"

"Quite, quite sure, sir!" And then helplessly, "Why me?"

The Duc looked up into her eyes and his own were oddly defenseless. "Because you are without doubt the most fascinating—the most challenging—woman I have ever known."

His words moved her more than she cared to admit, so that she took refuge in gentle raillery. "Oh come, Your Highness—my only novelty lies in the fact that I am, I suppose, virtuous! Horrid word! And for someone like you, that must always constitute a challenge!"

"You have a low opinion of me, Miss Brady," he said on the ghost of a laugh.

"No, indeed! But it is true just the same. Had I thrown myself at your head from the first, you would by now be finding me the most boringly prosaic of creatures."

"I refuse to admit of any such possibility."

A faint cracking of twigs, hardly discernible throughout their discourse, was now growing noticeably in volume. A horn was sounded fairly close and there were voices.

"It's the hunt! I had quite forgotten about it!" cried Clementina.

The relief in her voice did not escape the Duc. He lifted her hand to his lips and then returned it to its partner. "So you are saved!" he said dryly as the first of the horsemen broke cover. "But I refuse to give up hope!"

Threat or promise, Clementina heard the words with equanimity, for she felt now that they understood one another and that she had nothing to fear from him.

❧CHAPTER 14❧

"What do you think of it, dearest madame?" Etienne de Menton asked anxiously.

Seraphina Westbury gazed entranced from the carriage window at the many-turreted graystone building rising out of a backcloth of trees, its facade softened by red creeper, its windows winking in the afternoon sun.

"Oh!" She took off her spectacles, which appeared to have

misted over, and polished them in a dreamy way. "I was so afraid it would be very grand like Monsieur de Brissec's chateau, but it is really quite small and quite, quite delightful!"

The interior pleased her just as well, so far as she was permitted to view it, for, her cloak removed, she was led up a beautiful walnut staircase and into a small salon where all had been arranged for her comfort. Several restful-looking armchairs in soft crimson to match the hangings were grouped about a brightly burning fire and in one of these she settled with a little sigh of pleasure.

The Duc laughed at her innocent joy and picked up a footstool, kneeling to place it beneath her feet. Still kneeling, he looked up at her. The laughter faded. Leaping firelight sent unfamiliar shadows across his face to emphasize the rather hooked nose; they outlined the still firm jawline and made his eyes seem dark and a little fierce.

"Until you," he said deeply, "I had never believed that one could love on sight."

Her hands fluttered once and were still. No words would come.

Misinterpreting her silence, he asked anxiously, "Do I go too fast for you?"

"A little." The words were no more than a breath of sound.

"You even find me a little ridiculous, perhaps? For it is an absurd spectacle, is it not? A foolish old man down upon one knee apeing the young lover, and in a fever of anxiety lest his knees should lock when he attempts to rise!"

The dark eyes seemed to be imploring her understanding even as his mouth twisted in half-humorous self-denigration. She rushed impulsively into speech.

"No, no! Indeed, you must not say such unkind things of yourself! I do not think you in the least foolish and you are certainly not old! If I am slow to speak, it is because I . . . find myself . . . caught unawares, and so I am afraid . . . of being thought . . . transparent!"

It was a long speech for her, but in her desire to set his mind at ease she forgot her diffidence and treated him much as she would Patrick. Without conscious thought, she reached out swift fingers to smooth the lines that ran from mouth to jaw, found her hand imprisoned, and blushed rosily as it was kissed and held.

He looked into the gentle face; framed by her fair hair softly curling beneath a pretty lace cap, it held all the innocence of a child. He said with an air of wonder, "To think that such a short time ago I did not even know of your existence!"

"Oh, please, dear Duc . . ."

"Etienne," he corrected her.

". . . please, you must not kneel to me! Do get up and sit beside me. These really are *very* comfortable chairs." And when he was presently seated beside her, still with her hand clasped in his, "You will have to be patient with me," she said shyly. "I am not used . . . we lived very retired in Baltimore. I am slowly growing used to this world of yours, but . . ." She gestured uncertainly. ". . . it is still a bewildering place to me."

"And I confuse you further. Ah, *cherie*, it is your very unworldliness that so enchants me! I would not have you one whit different." The Duc's fingers tightened painfully on hers. "Whether I am worthy of you, however . . . no, no . . . it is important that you know. I can offer you little but an ancient and honorable name. I am not quite a pauper, but most of the estate is gone."

Mrs. Westbury made an urgent movement, and he said with a smile, "Yes, I know that will not weigh with you, but you shall know all. I was married when I was twenty-three years—a *mariage de convenance* arranged by my parents after the French custom." He smiled a little. "Louise was not demanding. I fathered a son in the approved fashion, and then a daughter, which was all she asked of me, and thereafter, I went very much my own way . . . taking my pleasure as it came, selfish as most men are selfish. Louise is now dead ten years and my children are grown and I was prepared to slide gracefully into old age . . ." The Duc looked into her eyes with a sudden intentness. "And then you came and I saw what I have been missing; for never, until now, has my heart been engaged! Ah, forgive me . . ." as she tugged a little at her hand. "If I rush my fences it is only that every moment has suddenly become precious. How can I pursue a leisurely courtship when time is so against me? I would have you my wife tomorrow."

"Duc, I . . ." She was halfway between laughter and tears.

"Etienne," he prompted again. "You *will* marry me?" He looked suddenly comically dismayed. "I have never asked, but . . . there is no Mr. Westbury?"

"No, no. There is no Mr. Westbury. Not for many, many years! But . . ." She made a last grasp for common sense.

"Oh, this is quite absurd! There are considerations . . . the children . . ." She put up a hand to cool her burning cheeks. "I cannot imagine what they will say!"

"I trust they will wish you happy," the Duc said.

"Yes, I am sure they will. But, you do see, don't you, how odd it must appear to them? I have never . . . that is to say, no gentleman has ever . . ."

"Then the men in Baltimore must be fools!" The Duc watched with delight the myriad expressions that chased across her face, betraying her more than she knew, as her confusion mounted. He said regretfully, "But I can see I must continue to court you in conventional fashion so that your niece and nephew may grow used to the idea?"

"Would you mind so very much?"

The unconscious pleading in her voice made him say warmly, *"Mignonne*—of course I will mind! But to please you, I will strive to be patient. Besides, I have every confidence in Miss Brady's good sense. If she has not already seen through the pair of us I shall own myself astonished."

"I am a little worried about Clemmy," she confessed. "I don't know if you are aware of it, but your nephew called upon her yesterday, they have been estranged you know . . . I don't perfectly understand it . . . but I so hoped that all would be well . . . only he went away again . . ." She sighed. "I have not liked to ask, and I must say she doesn't seem too much out of spirits . . . only with Clemmy one can't always tell, for she is not given to inflicting her troubles upon others!"

It was true that Clementina was making a determined effort not to be cast down by what had happened. In this she was aided unwittingly by the Duc de Berry who, far from exhibiting the least degree of disappointment over her rejection of his overtures, appeared to be in ebullient spirits, all of his energies being thrown into the organizing of his own hunting party to which he proposed to invite Monsieur de Brissec's guests also, coupled with the suggestion that any of the ladies not wishing to hunt, of which Clementina was one, might make themselves free of the Palace for as much of the day as they wished, and in the evening he would give an informal reception and banquet to which all were invited.

Of course, Clementina told herself, she must be gratified to discover how readily His Royal Highness's passion could be assuaged, though it came as a distinct blow to her pride upon reaching the royal chateau to find among the Duc's guests several ladies of the Court whose reputations more than qualified them to offer him consolation!

With an open invitation to wander wherever she wished, and with Aunt Seraphina carried off by the Duc de Menton and the rest of the ladies not disposed to stir themselves, Clementina spent a considerable time happily exploring the great rambling palace, which appeared more as a collection of double-storey buildings—a *rendez-vous de chateaux*, she had heard it called—than most people's conception of a palace. Indeed one's first sight of its plain stone facade in no way prepared one for so sumptuous an interior!

Each room was a revelation, from the enormous and magnificent *Salle de Bal*, to the delightful little boudoir that had been Marie Antoinette's, where Bartelemy's exquisitely painted ceiling depicting Aurora soared above her as she stood in wrapt contemplation before a Sevres biscuitware bust of the late queen, trying to equate the graven image with the flesh and blood reality.

A voice, making her jump, said conversationally, "One wonders, looking at that innocent profile, how she could ever have become the object of so much hatred."

"Cousin Dominic!" Clementina turned to find him in the doorway with quizzing glass raised, rather as she had first seen him, and looking very much at home. "Heavens, how you startled me! Whatever are you doing here?" And then, accusingly, answering her own question: "I just bet you came out of officiousness! You heard that the Duc de Berry was here and you thought me incapable of dealing with him!"

"After all the trimmings you have delivered on *that* subject? My dear girl, one would be flying in the face of Providence, indeed!"

"Oh, what a tarradiddle! As if that would weigh with you! But your journey is quite wasted, you know, which is no more than you deserve! I have already had it out with the Duc and now we both know exactly where we stand!"

Cadogan's mouth quirked. "And where, pray, is that?"

"Quite simply, I have convinced His Royal Highness that I . . . that under no circumstances would I . . ." She met his amused gaze and was confounded. "Oh, you know perfectly well! And so does he! As a result, we are now on the most amiable of terms."

"I am delighted to hear it!" The Marquis paused. "And Henri de Tourne?"

She nibbled furiously at her lip. "What an exasperating man you are! Is there nothing you don't know?"

"A great deal, I daresay." He grinned. "However, you needn't answer, for I'm confident that a young lady who has the temerity to repulse a royal prince would find no difficulty in sending a mere improvident Comte about his business! Now," He became brisk. "Have you had your fill of all this?" He waved a hand. "Because I had it in mind to show you grandeur of another kind. But you'll need to change out of that dress—" he put up his glass again "—becoming though it undoubtedly is . . ."

"A compliment! Milord!" She swept him an exaggerated curtsy.

"A warm, sensible riding habit and good stout footware will be more the thing for our expedition," he said repressively. "We are going to explore the forest."

"I had no idea it stretched so far or had so varied a landscape," she exlaimed some time later, as they tethered the horses they had borrowed from the royal stables on the fringe of a veritable wilderness and began to make their way over the rock-strewn heath on foot.

"This particular part is known as the *Gorges de Franchard*." Cadogon took her hand to assist her over the roughest parts. "But the forest abounds with many similar areas. Look out!" His fingers tightened in hers as the steep ascent ended in an abrupt drop to a raging torrent below.

With her skirt looped up over her free arm, she clung, laughing up at him as she gasped for breath. Her face glowed from the exercise, her brown eyes were polished to jewel brightness. He thought he had never seen her look so well— this was her *milieu*, away from all that artificiality. Her eyes, meeting his, widened into a question. "The open air suits you," he said.

"Oh, goodness! I haven't enjoyed myself so much in a long time, but I'm *so* out of practice! Still, I'm bound to say, dear cousin, that I'm very glad I came!"

By common consent they sat on a rock to rest, watching fast-moving shadows slide over the undulating landscape as clouds raced across the face of the sun.

"I wonder where the hunt is? I can't hear anything."

"Oh, they'll be miles away."

Without looking at him, she said, "You never did explain why you are here."

"No special reason, upon my honor. I ran into de Menton shortly before he was due to leave Paris and he suggested that I might care to join him here for a couple of days. Having nothing better to do, I accepted. As simple as that! As to this afternoon—" his grin was almost boyish "—your aunt was expected and I had no fancy to play gooseberry, so I decided to seek out my young cousin, to see how she was faring. And that is all." He spread his hand. "No ulterior motive, I promise you."

Watching the clear-cut features, the mobile mouth, she decided that he really could be quite nice when he tried!

The banquet that evening was a brilliant affair. The ladies, in a bid to outshine one another, were decked out in their finest jewels; the gentlemen wore orders and rivaled the ladies in magnificence. And the stars in the sky outshone them all as the whole company gathered on Fontainebleau's famous horseshoe staircase, its splendid proportions silvered by moonlight and further illuminated by flaming torches. They were assembled to attend the culmination of the day's hunting; in the courtyard below all the spoils of the chase were laid out for the *curee* whilst huntsmen in royal livery raised gilded *cors de chasse* to their lips and a solemn fanfare rang out over each head of game.

Clementina, wrapped in a cloak of white silk lined with ermine, was called upon to admire the fine boar that had fallen to Patrick, and of which he was inordinately proud.

"Poor piggy!" she said, teasing.

He protested that it was quite something to be so successful in almost one's first outing. "The Duc has presented me with the badge of the *Chasse!* I believe it's a very great honor not given to everyone."

Clementina declared that there would be no living with him, but she was very proud nonetheless.

"And what do you *really* think of it all?" Cadogon murmured in her ear as they turned to go back indoors.

She gave a gurgle of laughter. "It's just like a theatrical performance! I expected to see the curtain descend at any moment with cries of 'bravo.' "

"I thought you were looking a shade pensive during the ceremony?"

"Only because those poor creatures looked so bereft of their dignity laid out like that, especially the beautiful deer."

"Pure sentimentality!" He scoffed. "Do you forswear venison when it is presented to you at dinner?"

"No," she sighed. "And I am aware that my feelings are totally without logic, but then, feelings almost always are!"

The remainder of the visit passed without incident and was accounted a great success. Patrick was incredibly puffed up by his prowess in the hunting field. Aunt Seraphina looked blooming, and Clementina too, was surprised to discover how much she had enjoyed herself in the end. The Duc de Berry had parted with her on the most cordial terms. Finding her alone for a moment, he had expressed the hope that she would continue her visits to the Elysée as before— "For my wife sets great store by them—and I, too—" his eyes were gently mocking "—would be grieved if you felt unable to go on as before."

As they were all returning to Paris at the same time, Clementina suggested that her aunt should travel in the Duc de Menton's coach. Upon learning this, Dominic tactfully elected to ride with his cousins.

It was evening when they reached Paris, where a fine mizzle was descending, setting the pavement glistening under the street lamps. The coach had just passed the Luxembourg Gardens, when a figure ran into the road almost under the horses' hooves. The coachman bawled an oath and hauled back the reins. Patrick peered out as the carriage rocked and for an instant, as the figure—a young woman—scrambled to her feet, her face was clearly visible in the light of the carriage lamps, ravaged and twisted with pain, but unmistakably familiar.

"Stop!" He hauled down the window and yelled at Pierre and even as Clementina was demanding to know what he was about, he was already leaping down and running to the girl, lifting her. "Mademoiselle Rosa!" He peered into her face, much shocked by her appearance. "It is Mademoiselle Rosa? Whatever has happened to you? Are you ill?"

By this time the rest of the party had clambered out and were grouped about them, full of curiosity.

The girl stared around at them and then at Patrick, wild-eyed, trying to pull free. "Let me go, Monsieur. You do not know me! A-ah!" She put her foot to the ground and sobbed. "Ah! *Non! Non! Non!*"

"Patrick, do you know this—" Clementina hesitated, for even in the lamplight the raddled, painted face clearly portrayed her calling "—this girl?"

"Yes! Yes, of course I do!" Patrick was bewildered by Rosa's condition, but certain of her identity.

"No, madame, he does not know me. He is mistaken. *Ah, je vous prie!* Let me go!" She pulled away from Patrick and limped to the wall, where she leaned back with a sigh.

"You are hurt," said the Marquis, eyeing her keenly.

"My ankle, as I fell. It will be all right if I rest it a moment."

There came the sound of running feet and the girl shrank back, a moan torn from her. A man rounded the corner, saw the group, hesitated and came on, his manner suddenly obsequious. "Your pardon, ladies, gentlemen! I see you have found my . . . quarry. The wicked ingrate has not sought to molest you, I trust?" He turned on Rosa with a stream of invective that led the Marquis to intervene curtly.

"Monsieur, you are in the presence of a lady! Hold your tongue. I suggest you take your—the girl and leave!"

"No!" declared Patrick.

"One moment, cousin!" Clementina stepped forward so that the light fell on her face, framed as it was by an enchanting close-fitting bonnet. She looked the man over. "*I know you!* And I know your calling! You prey on young girls; you attempt to drag them down into your own vileness!"

"Clementina! For God's sake have a care!" Cadogon's voice was urgent in her ear.

"*You!*" The man spat the word at her. "*Merde!* Do you come from the Devil to plague me at every turn? Well, this time you can take yourself off! The girl belongs to me—I own her, body and soul. Ask her—go on, ask her if she does not work for me!"

The girl's head, sunk almost to her chest, portrayed her shame. Clementina felt a tremendous wave of rage well up in her. "People don't *own* people, monsieur! They own property and they own animals, but not *people!* And this girl shall not go with you unless it is of her own free will!"

The maquereau gave an abrupt laugh. "And who do you threaten me with this time, heh? Your Black? This pretty boy, here, who fancies my Rosa?" His malevolent glance, darting from one to the other, fixed on Cadogon. "Or the fine gentleman who advises caution? He knows the right of it well enough, I think!"

He stretched a hand to take the girl, Clementina cried out "Dominic, you can't let him do it!" and the man, goaded beyond endurance, called her a quite unforgivable name.

Cadogon's blow, unerringly delivered, caught him full on the point of the jaw, and he crumpled without a sound.

Into the silence, Clementina said with surprising composure, "Thank you, cousin! It is just what I would wish to have done myself!"

"By jove, yes!" Patrick was staring at the prone figure in awed admiration. "A flush hit! Best leveler I ever saw!"

"I suppose *that* must be your punishing left that so excites Mr. Jackson's admiration," Clementina observed judiciously. "It certainly is *most* effective!"

The Marquis, engaged in flexing his fingers, looked at her; in the dim light the classic features were etched as in marble, but there was an unholy glint in his eye.

"Clementina Brady, you are a menace! Isn't it enough for you that you display a singular talent for attracting trouble? Must you also embroil others in your causes?"

"That is really most unfair," she retorted equably. "And it isn't strictly true, either. I didn't ask you to hit that man, did I?"

He saw the futility of pointing out that it wouldn't have been necessary had she let matters take their course in the first place, and instead enquired with studied patience whether they were to stand in the rain all night.

"No, of course not. It is far too cold, and we are all getting decidedly wet."

"Clemmy?" Patrick sounded, for him, diffident. "What are we going to do . . . about Rosa?"

"Yes, Clementina," said the Marquis. "What *are* you going to do about Rosa?" He saw her bite her lip as she looked the girl over, and the smile of compassion as she stretched out a hand. "No, don't bother to tell me," he said. "You are taking her home!"

Rosa stood rigidly against the wall, not sure what was happening to her, not responding as Patrick tried to coax her into the carriage. Cadogon sighed, stepped across the still recumbent maquereau, and lifted the slight figure easily in his arms. "It's all right," he reassured her with surprising gentleness as he placed her in the corner seat of the carriage where she leaned back against the squab without a word. Patrick climbed in and sat beside her.

"Thank you, Dominic," Clementina said quietly.

"My dear girl, I never fight the inevitable. I only hope you know what you're doing!" He put out a hand to help her in, but she hesitated, looking down at the unmoving man.

"Oughtn't we to do something about him?"

"No," he said firmly.

She frowned. "You don't suppose you might have killed him?"

"I shouldn't think so," he said, uncaring. "But if I have, there will be one villain less in the world."

"What a shocking piece of indifference!" she protested, but he was urging her inexorably into the carriage. She went, but exclaimed, looking back, "Oh, good. See, he is beginning to stir!"

Dominic bundled her in the carriage, followed her, and shut the door.

During the short drive to the Rue de Varenne, most of Patrick's story came out, and Rosa, in halting accents, told how Monsieur de Tourne had wreaked his revenge upon her by taking her to a certain house in the Marias in which he had some interest, and where she was kept under close surveillance. From there, when she had proved uncooperative, she had been moved to another, less salubrious house, and it was from there that she had finally escaped.

Clementina was appalled—not only by Henri's inexcusable behavior, but that such things should be possible. "Oh, I know all about *that!*" she exclaimed as Cadogon pointed out as delicately as he could in the circumstances that Paris, like all cities, and perhaps more than most, abounded in brothels—from establishments of great splendor to the unbelievably squalid. "What I meant to say," she continued, "is that I didn't realize a girl could be confined in such a place totally against her will!"

Rosa said wearily, "When there is no alternative, madame, even the unacceptable becomes bearable eventually. But for me . . . I have a mother in Dijon if I can only reach her . . ."

"You aren't fit to go anywhere just now," declared Clementina. "But don't worry, as soon as you feel well enough, I shall see that you get safely to Dijon."

"This time old Rubal *will* give notice," said Patrick with a chuckle.

"No she won't." Clementina wasn't sure how much English Rosa understood, but she had no desire to hurt the girl's feeings by entering into an argument as to why her housekeeper might feel so outraged. She therefore contented herself with a confident: "This is not at all the same case as Clothilde!"

"That, my dear Clementina," said His Lordship on the ghost of a laugh, "is probably one of the most glaring understatements of all time!"

❧CHAPTER 15❧

The great Gothic nave of Notre Dame was in darkness except for a few dim lamps burning here and there. In the premidnight hush, the crowded cathedral seemed to hold its breath, quivering with expectancy. And then, onto the clear air of the December night the bell began tolling the hours, and on the twelfth stroke there came a tremendous burst of light. The choir shattered the stillness, the pure voices swelling in a great paean of joy and welcome. It was Christmas.

Clementina felt the shiver run up her spine to tingle in her back hairs. She had always loved Christmas, but never had it aroused such powerful emotions in her as now, in this most impressive of ceremonies—at Notre Dame with her family and friends around her. Her fingers found Patrick's and curled round them in an excess of pleasure. They exchanged a quick, happy grin. Her mind went back to past Christmases in Baltimore—the simple church ceremony, with Patrick's hand in hers as it was now, and Grandpa Brady resplendent in his flowered waistcoat and best coat that smelled faintly of the special snuff that he took only on highdays and holidays!

Impulsively Clementina turned to share the moment with Aunt Seraphina and found her standing very close to the Duc de Menton, her face lifted to him in wrapt absorption. She could not see the expression in her aunt's eyes; she did not need to, for it was faithfully mirrored in the Duc's own.

Clementina experienced a feeling similar to that which afflicted her when Dominic looked at Elyse Robart. The choir soared to new heights and she told herself stubbornly that it was the beauty of the moment that brought the tears pricking at the back of her eyes; absurd, after all, to admit that she, who had never been of a romantical turn of mind, could be envious of such a look!

She turned her mind resolutely to other things—the dinner, for instance, enjoyed earlier by family and close friends at which Monsieur Clichet had been persuaded to serve one of Aunt Seraphina's plum puddings, carried in ablaze with brandy. And after the midnight service the Christmas celebrations would begin in earnest when more than a hundred people were expected back in the Rue de Varennes.

For a while it had seemed that Patrick would not be among their number. He had broken the news to Clementina in the privacy of the Petit Salon not long before they were due to leave for church, and remained impervious to all her entreaties.

"I promised!" he had reiterated a little sulkily. "It is a *sauterie*—something special!"

It's that woman! she fumed inwardly. How dare Anys Davide spoil things! Since their return from Fontainbleau, she had monopolized him more than ever. "But, Patrick, it's Christmas! Can you not spare us this one evening? Everyone will think it so strange if you aren't there!"

"Fudge!" he scoffed. "As though anyone will miss me, when you'll have a regular bear garden of people filling the place!"

Clementina thought with compassion of poor Dora, who had been so pitifully overjoyed to know that Patrick would be free of *that woman* for one whole evening and was now about to have her Christmas ruined. At that moment she came nearer to hating Patrick than she would ever have thought possible.

"Damnation take Madame Davide!" she exclaimed in exasperation as her brother slipped from the room to escape further argument. "I hope her peal-white teeth rot and drop out one by one!"

"Dear me!" The door of the salon was pushed wider to reveal the Marquis. He looked quizzical, and then, eyeing her more closely, came in and closed the door. "You sounded decidedly vicious!" She bit her lip and dashed a tear angrily from her cheek. He regarded her with interest. "Am I intruding?"

"Yes!" she snapped, and then, "No—oh, what does it matter? You will have gathered that I have quarreled with Patrick—today of all days, when I would least wish to!"

"Over Madame Davide?"

She sighed and told him the whole; it seemed that she was destined to bring her worries about her brother to Cadogon's door. "I am profoundly thankful that I am not in love!" she exclaimed at the end of it all. "If you ask me, falling in love must be the very devil!"

Dominic uttered a short, derisive laugh and looked at her oddly. "My dear girl, Patrick's malady has little to do with love! It is compounded of blind idolatry mingled with a dash of good old-fashioned lust."

"Well, of course, I know that!" she declared, not in the least shocked by his outspokenness. "The poor boy is at a very impressionable age and I expect she is content to amuse herself with him for a little while, though I am surprised that anyone as gauche as Patrick would interest her."

Cadogon looked as though he was about to say something, stopped, and then said, "Do I take it that you have met the lady in question?"

"We have not met, precisely, but she has been pointed out to me on more than one occasion."

"And . . .?" he ventured with some curiosity.

"She is certainly *very* beautiful . . ." Clementina admitted, and then with a touch of obstinacy, "But she has hard eyes."

He lifted a laconic eyebrow. "I doubt if they appear so when they come to rest on Patrick . . . or whether he would notice if they did." He frowned. "I trust you were not so unwise as to mention to him this apparent flaw in the lady's charms?"

"Of course not!" she cried indignantly. "I am not stupid!" And then, meeting his eye, she grinned ruefully. "You think I'm being overprotective again, don't you? Well, I'm not, truly I'm not. I know perfectly well that he will outgrow her soon enough, if only she doesn't tire of him first. I wouldn't even have minded so much about tonight if it wasn't for poor Dora. I had hoped that just for once, he might be a little kind to her."

Dominic stood very close, looking down at her, his expression, as so often, unreadable. "What a funny girl you are," he said quietly. He flicked one of her red curls. Then he took her by the shoulders and turned her toward the door. "Go along. You are neglecting your guests."

She went reluctantly.

Just as they were on the point of leaving for church, Patrick had come up to her, his expression sheepish. "Clemmy, about tonight . . . I've changed my mind. You were quite right. It *is* Christmas, after all. I'll come back after Midnight

Mass, for a little while at least. I can perhaps slip away later when no one is looking."

She nodded wordlessly.

Still not wholly convinced of her approbation, he held out his hands. "Friends?" he coaxed with the smile that she could never withstand.

"Friends," she agreed, and wondered briefly what argument Dominic had used to bring about the change of heart. Whatever it was, it had more influence than hers—just one more break, in fact, in the bonds that had held them so close! Only this time the hurt was much less.

It took the better part of an hour for the immense crowds outside Notre Dame to disperse after the service, and the air was still echoing with "Bon Noel's" as the line of carriages finally traveled in somewhat halting procession to the Rue de Varenne. Once there, however, the guests spilled into the brilliantly lighted foyer, all laughing and talking at once, to find the cool black and white elegance of the hall transformed by an enormous Christmas tree lit with candles and laden down with presents, and everywhere festooned with evergreen. The Grand Salon, too, had taken on a festive air with yet another Christmas tree taking up one corner completely and huge log fires burning in the twin fireplaces. Soon the room had filled, every sofa and chair was occupied, and the fiddlers tuning up in the ballroom could scarcely be heard above the clamor of voices.

Clementina, ever sensitive to atmosphere, had been aware from the instant of crossing the threshold that something in her household was amiss, but the cause was not easy to pin down. Maurice, as imperturbable as ever, was handling his augmented battalion of lackeys with the consummate skill of a juggler, sending them scurrying here and there with laden trays. Yet something was missing—the bright, darting glances from those inquisitive black eyes, the air of ebullience that characterized his love of such occasions and that had certainly been in evidence earlier in the evening, had been replaced by a well-suppressed agitation.

When she could bear the suspense no longer, she drew him out into the gallery to demand an explanation of him. It was as though she had unstopped a dam.

"Ah, mademoiselle, if you did but know! Such a time as we have had! The kitchens in an uproar and Monsieur Clichet in a passion of hysteria, for never has such a thing happened to him before . . ." The major-domo's gestures were expressive but unhelpful. Clementina, making no immediate attempt to stem his flow, waited for enlightenment.

". . . one would not have troubled you at such a time, but it is like you to notice that all is not well! If that were not enough, we have the woman Rubal threatening to give notice if the girl is not instantly dismissed!" His eyes rolled heavenward. "Not that this would be any great loss! That woman, mademoiselle, lacks even the most infinitesimal drop of the milk of human kindness! I have always said as much . . . you will recall? But to be talking of turning that child onto the streets at this season of Noel . . . poor, foolish ingrate though she may be . . ."

"Maurice! Stop!" Clementina felt her senses spinning. The major-domo snapped instantly to attention. "Now, tell me slowly and clearly—who is to be turned out, and why?"

He looked surprised. "But did I not say? It is the kitchen maid, Lysette, mademoiselle—because of the baby, you understand . . ."

"Baby!"

Out of the corner of his eye, Maurice saw the ominously stiff figure of Madame Rubal approaching, her rustling black bombazine skirts expressing the full embodiment of her wrath. His voice quickened again with the urgent need to be first with the story.

"She is a plump girl, and so, voila! No one knew of it, no one even suspected! Of course, she was foolish to keep it from Monsieur Clichet, but she feared for her job, which is understandable. At such a time it is necessary to have compassion . . ."

"Compassion, bah!" Madame Rubal had arrived, her bosom swelling. The bristles sprouting from the mole on her chin quivered with the force of her indignation. "Lysette is a wicked, deceitful hussy! What would you, mademoiselle? If such behavior goes unpunished, where will it end?" Her arms flailed wildly. "There will be babies all over the place!"

Clementina began to appreciate Monsieur Clichet's unfortunate tendency to succumb to hysterics.

"I will come down to the servants' hall," she said. "Where is Lysette?"

"In one of the small pantries," Maurice explained eagerly. "There was no time to remove her elsewhere."

Clementina hurried back into the salon to explain her absence to her aunt; the word spread rapidly about the room, occasioning much amused comment.

"Quel horreur!"

"Is the child a boy or a girl?"

"I have no idea . . ."

"It will have to be named Noel, at all events . . ."

"You will turn the girl off, of course." This was Gaston Rivas, Patrick's friend.

She considered him, a slight frown between her brows. She had not liked the swarthy young man when Patrick had first known him—had been pleased when they began to see less of one another—and it now disturbed her vaguely to know that the friendship had flourished anew—and that he was superceding Alfred in Patrick's estimation. "Is that what you would do in my place?" she asked.

"Of course." He looked surprised. "Such behavior cannot be tolerated, surely?"

"Shame on you!" cried Alexei. "This is the season of good will. I vote that the girl be forgiven."

The argument was waging with good-humored intensity as Clementina left the room and made her way thoughtfully belowstairs to be greeted by a similar, but more excitable altercation.

The servants fell silent, however, as she approached, and her gown of white ruched mousseline de soie, trimmed with silver tissue, made faint whispers of sound as she stepped resolutely into the tiny pantry.

The miscreant lay upon an improvised bed, looking tearful and exhausted and pitifully young. Clementina squatted down beside her heedless of the housekeeper's protests that she would ruin her dress. A few gently probing questions elicited the information that the father of the child had been a footman at her last place of employment. Since she had come as part of Monsieur Clichet's entourage, the man would not be difficult to trace, but Lysette could offer no expectation that he would consent to marry her. The chef once more became excited, the girl's lips quivered, and fresh tears started as the vexed question of her future was broached. Clementina stood up.

"Lysette will remain here," she said quietly. And to the emotional Monsieur Clichet sternly, "And I suggest, monsieur, that in future you keep a better watch over the girls in your charge."

She knew that there would be a tussle with Madame Rubal over her decision to let the girl stay. The housekeeper had not yet forgiven her for bringing girls like Clothilde and Rosa into the house. She had already made it quite clear that she considered Lysette's fall from grace to be directly attributable to such evil influences, and Clementina didn't feel strong enough to embark upon an argument destined to convince her of the impossibility of this line of reasoning.

For her own part, Clementina had no regrets. Clothilde's little shop was flourishing quite splendidly, and as for young Rosa—when all the paint and powder was cleaned off and she was recovered from her ordeal, she proved to be such a bright, intelligent girl that Clementina was quite sorry to lose her and had promised to help her in any way she could if life in Dijon should prove too dull.

"What of the child, mademoiselle?" The housekeeper's voice came frigidly.

Clementina had forgotten about the baby. Now she saw it for the first time. Someone had wrapped it in clean linen from the kitchen and laid it in a drawer. It was tiny, incredibly tiny: Yet every fingernail was perfectly formed. And the face; such a face—as red and wizened as an old Indian warrior! Clementina was suddenly made aware of a terrible gap in her education. Ask her to balance a ledger, or run a household with efficiency, and she would be reasonably confident of her ability, but in the matter of babies she was woefully ignorant. She had very little recollection of Patrick as a baby, in her own childhood had never shown the least interest in dolls, and in later life, when friends back home had married and produced babies, she had left Aunt Seraphina to do the initial bedside visiting, being so much more interestingly occupied in helping Grandpa Brady with his empire building. As a result, she now felt totally inadequate, even a little shy, and to cover the moment, stretched out a hand to touch the child. Her finger was instantly seized and held in a grip of surprising strength.

She was quite astonished that anything so tiny could have so profound an effect upon her—a soft, melting sensation suffused her and she bent closer, the better to observe the small miracle.

"Is it a boy or a girl?" she asked huskily.

"A girl, if you please, ma'am."

"And how will you call her? Noelle, I suppose."

The girl's voice was a mixture of uncertainty and defiance. "I thought . . . Maria Angelina, ma'am?"

Such a large name for such a tiny scrap of humanity! Clementina suppressed a smile. "That is a lovely name. Well, tomorrow will be soon enough to talk about her future." She felt curiously reluctant to relinquish her contact with the baby and said on a sudden impulse, "Lysette, may I take your baby upstairs for my guests to admire? She is rather special, after all—a Christmas baby."

Without exception, the kitchen staff regarded her as though she had grown suddenly weak in the head; Madame Rubal almost growled her disapproval, but Clementina didn't care.

The child, hastily bundled into fresh linen, was so incredibly light that she had constantly to assure herself that her burden had not slipped away. As she approached the gallery the noise of the festivities grew progressively louder, and Clementina began to lose a little of her confidence. While she stood, hesitating, Maurice came from the salon. His astonishment on seeing her was comical to behold.

"Am I quite mad?" she appealed to him in a whisper.

A slow, delighted smile spread across his lugubrious features, lighting the black button eyes. "But, no, mademoiselle. Rather, I would call what you do a stroke of genius—*a nouveaute sans parielle!*"

"I hope my guests think so, too!" She nodded. "The door, if you please, Maurice."

"It is my pleasure, mademoiselle." With his most imposing flourish, he flung it wide.

Those nearest the door saw her first. Mouths fell open; word ran round the crowded room like a flame, consuming all conversation and expiring finally on a whispering gasp of surprise. Heads craned forward.

Clementina stood rooted in the doorway, feeling absurdly self-conscious.

"I thought you might all like to see the very latest addition to my household," she ventured a little breathlessly.

"How quaint," someone murmured uncertainly.

Then a high, tinkling laugh broke the spell and she was surrounded by friends, all talking at once.

"Such a novelty!"

". . . a capital notion!"

". . . a real Christmas baby . . ."

Alexei disturbed the bundle with a curious finger. "Such a face! She will not win prizes for beauty, that one . . ." There was fresh laughter.

"Hush!" Clementina implored them. "You will wake her."

She was aware of the various reactions; Aunt Seraphina was enchanted, Elyse amused in her gentle way, Cadogon frankly quizzical, the Duc indulgent. Even Patrick, who had been trying hard to appear as unconcerned as his friend Gaston—standing now a little apart, his smile looking as though it had been painted on—had been coaxed by Dora into the ranks of Maria Angelina's admirers.

Alexei was full of good humor. "You should marry and have lots of babies, Clementina," he teased. "It is a role that becomes you well!"

There were sly glances and Clementina's cheeks grew decidedly pink. She could think of nothing to say.

"And what is to be the fate of mother and child?" Cadogon's voice came smoothly to dispel her embarrassment.

She threw him a grateful look. "I haven't really decided," she confessed. "For the immediate future, I must see if the local convent will take them in. And later—well, Lysette will return to her place here. As for the child . . . I don't know."

She looked down to find that the wrinkles had rearranged themselves. Two of the bluest of blue eyes were staring up at her. Instinctively she cradled the infant closer.

"You will be courting folly if you countenance letting the girl keep it," Gaston said positively. As they all turned to look at him, he reddened a little and shrugged.

The bundle began to erupt disconcertingly. The blue eyes vanished; the wrinkles were turning bright red. Clementina's heart sank as the infant proceeded to demonstrate the prodigious power of its lungs.

"Oh, dear!" She looked imploringly at Elyse. "Am I doing something wrong?"

"I don't think so, my dear." Elyse smiled sympathetically. "But perhaps we are rather too many for her?"

"Yes, of course. She had better go back." Out of the corner of her eye, Clementina had noticed Joshua hovering; in a brand-new suit of livery he had been helping Maurice. She remembered his love of all small, living creatures. Summoning him to her side, she assigned to him the task of returning the baby to the kitchens.

He received his charge with infinite care. "Yes'm, Miss Clemmy." He beamed as the cries momentarily ceased. "Don't you worry none. This little old babe'll be just fine with Joshua."

Later, much later, when the party was at its height, she looked for Patrick and was told that he had left—with Gaston Rivas.

The rest of that week passed with scarcely a moment to think. The days were spent in the receiving and returning of visits, whilst every night saw them at some ball or soirée.

On New Year's Day the King held his usual Court Defile. Clementina had previously seen him only from a distance, so that at first his grossness repelled her. But he showed so much interest in her and conversed with such charm and generosity of manner when she made her curtsy that she was quite won over. The Comte d'Artois, she liked less; Monsieur was certainly better looking than his brother, being tall and slim by comparison, and he had good shoulders and, of course, the Bourbon nose. Having met Clementina previously at the Elysée on one of her visits there, he was pleased to single her out, yet as before she found his brand of charm slightly chilling—so different from his son!

Also very much in evidence, hovering around the King, was his chief minister, Monsieur Decazes—a dark, fine-featured Gascon. "Talleyrande has been heard to say," murmured Alexei irreverently, "that Monsieur Decazes resembles nothing so much as a moderately good-looking hairdresser's assistant! But it would be unwise, I think, to dismiss him so lightly! He has much influence with the King!"

It was as Clementina was about to seek out her aunt so that they might take their leave that she came face to face with Henri for the first time since her return from Fontainebleau. Madame, his mother, was with him. It was a delicate encounter, charged with hidden ferment though it lasted but a moment. Then Henri executed a curt formal bow, and Madame cut her completely.

❦CHAPTER 16❦

The baby's coming had a curious unsettling effect upon Clementina. It gave her life new purpose, yet her eager acceptance of responsibility for the baby's needs only served to highlight how little her own family now relied upon her. Patrick, going giddily from one infatuation to another, had long since ceased to regard her as his natural confidante and mentor, and Aunt Seraphina spent the hours when her beloved was not at her side gazing mistily into far distances.

Lying awake in those hours of early morning when the spirit is at its lowest ebb, she almost succumbed to the, for her, unforgivable sin of self-pity, which was in itself part of a wider dissatisfaction.

Being by nature a straight-thinking young woman, it irked her considerably that she was unable to attribute her low spirits to anything more concrete than a vague feeling of rejection, which was absurd when she considered how constantly she was in demand—no party was deemed complete without Miss Brady; royalty made a point of singling her out; and she could, if she wished, indulge in a mild flirtation with almost any gentleman of her choosing! Surely it was churlish of her to want more? She had always been proud to consider herself a truly liberated woman who was used to view falling in love as a poor substitute for a full and interesting life.

Yet here in Paris everyone, it seemed, was in love except her—and from being an interested spectator, the universal good companion, friend to all the world, she was astonished to find herself occasionally and quite illogically falling prey to the wildest unquenchable yearnings . . .

It was at this point that the irrepressible mixture of Brady and Durrell blood began to stir. She sat up in bed, dragging the recalcitrant blankets into a complex wig-wam of warmth around her, and drawing up her knees, made a comfortable resting place for her chin.

She was dwindling into melancholia. Could it be that she was growing bored with the endless round of pleasure seeking? To be sure, it had never suited her nature to be idle for any length of time; might it therefore follow that a surfeit of frivolity had put her in serious danger of losing touch with reality? Certainly her greatest satisfaction in recent weeks had derived from the challenge of rearranging the lives of Clothilde and Rosa to their mutual benefit and gratification. And now there was Lysette's baby. The poor little mite wouldn't be able to stay in the Convent forever. An idea began to stir and take shape at the back of her mind . . . Oh what a fool she had been, allowing herself to become so moped! The remedy was in her own hands—all that was needed was a little planning, a little imagination.

Clementina slid down among the tangle of blankets and curled up, one hand tucked comfortably beneath her cheek;

her last thought as she drifted into sleep was of Aunt Seraphina. It really was high time she married her Duc—she must be persuaded without further delay. If someone didn't make a push, she would wait until they were obliged to wheel her to the alter in a wheelchair.

She tackled her aunt the very next morning, walking in upon her while she was still at her dressing mirror. Misliking the light in her niece's eyes, Mrs. Westbury suddenly became extremely busy. But Clementina, with most of her plans now clear and sharp in her mind, waited patiently, and in some amusement, for Justine to finish dressing her aunt's hair. And when finally Mrs. Westbury could find no more for the maid to do, she was reluctantly dismissed.

Clementina came straight to the point.

Her aunt grew flustered, fidgeted with the trinkets upon the dressing table and finally, in a vain attempt to deflect Clementina's interest into less contentious paths, she launched upon a lengthy and somewhat incoherent account of the extremely boring card party she had attended at Mrs. Bennett's on the previous evening. At last, catching her niece's eye, she faltered and fell silent.

"It won't do, dearest." Clementina was gentle but firm. "Every time I try to speak of your attachment, you treat me to a chapter of evasions that I had not thought possible in you!" A sympathetic smile softened her words. "Well, you shall prevaricate no longer. I cannot and will not believe that the Duc is happy to be kept waiting for an indefinite period."

"Well, perhaps not happy, precisely . . . but we are quite agreed, Clemmy, I promise you . . ."

"No matter. The time has come to put an end to waiting. Don't you see? It is quite nonsensical for you to be hanging back when you might so easily be together!" Clementina leaned forward to still the fingers that were nervously twisting a ring round and round. In the mirror their two glances met. "And we both know why you will not set the day. It is because of me, is it not?"

Seraphina Westbury's pretty blue eyes held the sheen of tears. "Oh, my dear! I won't deny that I have entertained hopes . . . you are so very much in demand! I had thought that perhaps you and Monsieur de Tourne . . ." Clementina was silent, wishing neither to confirm nor confound her hopes. "Or the Prince, perhaps . . .?" Her aunt sighed. "Oh, well . . . I am sure I have no wish to press you, child . . ."

"But neither should you be obliged to wait upon my

pleasure!" Clementina declared passionately. "Aunt Seraphina, I love you dearly and shall miss you like the very devil, but I hope I am not such a monstrously selfish creature that I would ever stand in the way of your happiness! No, no, dear," as her aunt opened her mouth to remonstrate, "I am in earnest. I shall survive, you know! Why, I daresay I have only to stir myself, and I should find a most agreeable companion without the least trouble."

"Oh, no, Clemmy! I could never agree to such a thing!" Her aunt hesitated, then said, using the Duc's name with endearing shyness, "I have never quite liked to mention it, but . . . well, you know that Etienne would be very happy to open his home to you and Patrick . . ."

"And be obliged to suffer all our odd quirks!" Clementina's eyes twinkled suddenly. "No, dear Aunt, we will spare him that, I think! I have been my own mistress far too long. But I thank him for the thought."

"Then we will go on as we are for a little while longer." Mrs. Westbury did her best to convey that she was content, but she could not wholly disguise a certain wistfulness as she added, "Goodness me, it is not as though we were in the throes of our first youthful passion!"

She was at first relieved, then puzzled, then vaguely uneasy when Clementina made no further attempt to coerce her, but she was not, by nature, suspicious and when breakfast passed with nothing more taxing than a succession of cheerful anecdotes about this and that, it was clear that she must have made a better job of convincing her niece than she had supposed . . . and told herself stoically that she must be glad.

She would have been less easy had she seen Clementina not two hours later driving between a familiar pair of gates on the Rue St. Honoré to an inner courtyard and coming to a halt before the curving facade of a finely proportioned mansion.

The Duc de Menton was busy at a desk, set in the wide window embrasure of his library where it might best catch the morning sun. He rose as Miss Brady was announced and came forward to meet her.

"Miss Brady . . . Clementina! What an unlooked-for pleasure!" He looked suddenly alarmed. "Your aunt? Nothing is wrong?"

"No, indeed! I promise you."

"Then come along in and sit here by the fire. Will you not permit Gaston to remove your pelisse?"

"Thank you, no. I shall not stay above a few minutes." She glanced toward the desk. "I fear I am taking you from more pressing tasks?"

"Tradesmen's accounts," he said. "Very dull. It will give me much greater pleasure to entertain you. May I offer you some refreshment? Gaston, what do we have that we may offer a young lady?"

But Clementina declined again, smiling kindly at the elderly manservant. The Duc dismissed him with a nod and led Clementina forward to a large, comfortable leather armchair. She settled herself, stripped off her gloves, unfastened the neck of her pelisse, loosed the ribbons of her bonnet, and looked about her with interest. She had visited the house before, of course, but never this library, which, from the air of being lived in, was obviously his favorite room.

It was very much a man's room, lined with shelf upon shelf of books, the furnishings strictly functional, combining neatness with a somber elegance. A sudden mischievous smile curved her mouth.

The Duc raised a faintly interrogatory eyebrow.

"I was trying to visualize my aunt here. Shall you mind having her tatting left about the place, do you suppose, and your cushions scattered?"

The feathered white brows quivered very slightly.

"Does that sound shockingly presumptuous?" Clementina said ruefully. "I am frequently accused of being too direct. Would you prefer that we discuss the weather for a little while first?"

He threw back his head and laughed. "No, my dear Clementina, I would not! You must know that I also prefer the exact approach." He was still chuckling. "I told Seraphina that you would quickly penetrate our curious charade. Did it take you very long?"

"Good gracious, no! A matter of days, only." Clementina clasped her hands in a gesture of resolution and leaned forward confidingly. "Duc, will you do something for me?"

Much intrigued, he said, "My dear child, I am yours to command. You have but to ask."

"Good." She drew a quick breath. "Then will you please elope with Aunt Seraphina?"

The Duc looked dazed; his mouth opened and closed without sound. Clementina watched him anxiously. "That . . . is directness, indeed!" he ventured at last on a quick-drawn breath.

Could she have made a terrible error of judgment? She said with some urgency, "You do wish to marry Aunt Seraphina?"

"With all my heart," he assured her faintly. "But an elopement?" A look of distaste crossed the fine, aesthetic features. "I do not see the necessity. No, no, it is not to be thought of!"

"It's the only way you will get her to the altar," she said bluntly, and then, as the blood left his face and hurt flared in his eyes, "Oh, forgive me! Not for any lack of love, Duc! You must be aware that you have all her adoration!"

"Why, so I thought . . ."

"It is simply that Aunt Seraphina cherishes this absurd notion that we cannot go on without her. I have tried all I can to persuade her otherwise, but she will have none of it."

The Duc's face had grown hawklike and unapproachable.

"And this seems to you absurd? Then I must tell you, mademoiselle, that I honor your aunt the more for her sentiments, which seem to me most laudable."

The chill, undeserved note of censure stung her into passionate defense. "Of course her sentiments are laudable! They are also quite idiotic! Oh, believe me, I am not unmindful of my aunt's many truly good qualities, of the care she has lavished upon us most unstintingly all these years! And don't suppose for one moment that I shall not miss her quite dreadfully when she is gone, but . . ."

As she paused to draw breath he said slowly, "I am sorry, I was overhasty."

"No. It was I who did not explain myself very well. But you *do* see, don't you, why we must arrange matters for her? If Aunt Seraphina is permitted to wait for what she considers a propitious moment, she will wait forever."

"Yet I know," he said, "how deeply it concerns your aunt that her going would make problems for you."

"Oh stuff!" Clementina retorted lightly. "A terrible thing indeed that I should be put to a little trouble!"

"There is, however, a simple solution, which I have already broached with Seraphina." He made an expansive gesture. "My house, as you can see, is large, and I would be more than happy . . ."

". . . to open your doors to Patrick and me. Yes, I know, dear Duc, and I do thank you most kindly, but it wouldn't answer, truly it wouldn't. I am by far too independent and anyway, I doubt you would really care to have your lovely peaceful home cluttered up with your wife's relations!"

"My dear child, you must give me leave to decide for myself those with whom I would share my home!" He tempered the mild reproof with a quizzical lift of the feathered eyebrows. "May I ask what you *do* mean to do, since you have obviously given the matter considerable thought?"

Clementina sighed. "I should much prefer to go on as I am, but in the event I believe I must observe the proprieties." She brightened. "I shall, therefore, find myself some inoffensive little dab of a companion. I might even go home to Baltimore for a visit, but that rather depends on Patrick."

He appeared to hesitate. "Forgive an old man's impertinence, child, but . . . you have not considered marriage?"

For the first time Clementina's manner lacked certainty. She met his eyes, bit her lip pensively, and looked away again. She stood up and began to wander the room, mangling her gloves as she debated how much to tell him. His was a gentle inquisition, but an inquisition, nonetheless; he would not be fobbed off as easily as Aunt Seraphina.

"I have considered it, yes," she said at last. "But . . ."

"Henri?"

"He did ask me," she admitted, "but . . ."

"But you did not feel yourself able to accept? Oh, you need not fear to offend, me, my dear. Henri is my nephew, but this does not blind me to his many shortcomings." He gave a wry shrug. "Of course, my sister ruins him. She encourages him to live as befits a de Tourne, as though the past twenty years had never happened! I sometimes wonder if she even knows how close to the brink of disaster he strays at times with his gaming. At all events—" he smiled "—I am relieved to know that *you* will not become enmeshed in the messy business of saving Henri from his creditors . . . and more important perhaps, that you are not nursing a secret passion for him!"

She swung round, flinging her arms wide in a gesture that was half appeal, half rueful resignation. "Oh, dear sir! I look at you and Aunt Seraphina and I begin to wonder if I am even capable of such devotion!"

"Then you wrong yourself." He appeared to hesitate. "You know that Henri is back in town?"

"And flaunting his mistress?" she finished lightly. "Yes, I had heard, but it doesn't hurt me—except a little in my pride, perhaps! I know now that I grew out of Henri some time ago." Clementina's resolution reasserted itself. "So you see why I am so adamant that you should carry Aunt Seraphina off? She will otherwise feel herself obliged to succour me indefinitely!"

It was now his turn to betray unease. "Your reasoning may be admirable, my dear young lady, but your aunt will never agree to an elopement."

She frowned. "Perhaps you're right. Very well, then, don't tell her!"

"You mean . . .?" He gazed at her in awe. "Abduction! At my age!" His shoulders shook slightly. "No, no, mademoiselle. You cannot do this to me! I shall appear quite ridiculous and Seraphina will never speak to me again!"

"Stuff!" said Clementina bracingly. "She may be a little taken aback at first, but you will know exactly how to coax her round! In fact, I believe it is the very thing to appeal to her romantic soul."

The Duc sat down rather suddenly in his chair and put his head in his hands. Clementina came quickly to his side, eyeing him a little anxiously. "It is all very simple," she encouraged him. "You have but to make the necessary arrangements and I will pack a portmanteau and deliver it to you in advance of the appointed time. Then you simply call to invite Aunt Seraphina to take a drive with you and *voilà*—the rest is easy!"

He looked up at her then, and though he still appeared dazed, there was a hint of laughter lurking there, too. "You would not care to arrange the honeymoon for us, also?"

Clementina grinned. "No, dear sir. I leave that entirely to you!"

From the Duc's house, Clementina drove to the convent. Here she spent a most satisfactory couple of hours with the Reverend Mother, outlining her prospective plans and discussing how they might best be accomplished, by the end of which time that good lady was in much the same state as the Duc, unsure whether to call down blessings upon Miss Brady for her quite staggering generosity, or to go quietly off into a swoon at the prospect of so much upheaval!

Clementina, meantime, drove serenely home in time for dejeuner, her appetite nicely sharpened by the successful completion of her morning's work.

❦CHAPTER 17❦

The frost had come to stay; the whole of Paris, or so it seemed to Clementina, had taken on the aspect of a vast skating arena sparkling in the sunlight. The Petit Lac in the Bois de Boulogne was tested daily, and the moment it was pronounced fit for skating a large section of the fashionable world at once converged upon the lakeside, where Clementina was much entertained to observe that, with the comfort of several cheerfully blazing bonfires and a plentiful supply of hot punch and petit fours, an ability to skate came a long way down the list of prerequisites deemed necessary for the day's enjoyment.

She had not forgotten her promise to Suzy. Elyse had given her consent once she was satisfied that Clementina was not regretting her generosity. "Oh, my dear!" Clementina reassured her. "You cannot *imagine* how I shall enjoy it!" The skating lessons were to be a secret, to be revealed only upon Suzy's birthday when she would astonish everyone. Clementina entered enthusiastically into the compact and most mornings, before anyone else was astir, the two conspirators, together with Suzy's nurse who sat wrapped in rugs in the coach, a comfortable spectator, spent an hour and sometimes more at the lake. So eager was Suzy to learn—and so quick—that before long she had mastered all the basic skills and was pleading to be allowed to try something more adventurous. The most difficult part of all was keeping the secret; the little girl longed to show off. Could she not let Maman see how well she had come on? and perhaps her *cher Monsieur Dominic* who would be *so* proud of her! But Clementina was adamant. The best part of a surprise, she said encouragingly, was in the keeping of the secret—counting off the days until her birthday, by which time she would be even more proficient.

Clementina probably enjoyed this time of day best of all, for later the ice became crowded, often with too many sledges for comfort. As Alexei had foretold, very few French ladies skated, and since the pastime was forbidden to the *jeunes filles* by their mamas as being a quite improper manner of disporting themselves, her fellow skaters were for the most part gentlemen, together with the offspring of the more broad-minded Russian and Polish families and a few Americans.

The Worthingtons were very much in evidence, Mrs. Worthington's voice frequently being heard above all the rest and causing acute embarrassment to the other Americans present, as she sought to put her daughter forward. Alice didn't skate, but that didn't deter her mama, who had fixed on Alexei as a likely candidate for her daughter's hand.

His sledge was much in demand. As he had promised, it was magnificently fashioned in the guise of a leaping tiger, and there was much high-spirited vying for the privilege of riding among its tiger skin cushions, and in this Mrs. Worthington sought to ensure that her daughter was always to the fore.

Anys Davide's sledge created even more interest. Like a graceful swan, a day seldom passed when it was not to be seen skimming across the ice, propelled by an ever willing, ever growing band of admirers, her golden curls spilling against the brilliant rose-colored satin lining, her tinkling laugh echoing across the lake.

Patrick, of course, was never far away, though it seemed to Clementina that the courtesan's interest in him was beginning to wane. This should have pleased Clementina, for she hated to see her brother in so besotted a state, making a cake of himself for all the world to see. Yet, as new admirers were openly encouraged and Patrick grew more and more despairing, her reaction was more that of angry indignation.

"You should guard your expression more closely, my dear girl!" Cadogon, coming unexpectedly from behind, clasped her expertly about the waist and swept her off at great speed around the perimeter of the lake. "If your glances bore poisoned tips, the lady would by now be dead!"

"Lady!" she declared scornfully. "Oh, honestly! I had no idea that men could be such fools! To be so easily enslaved by a pretty face!"

"Tut, tut!" He chuckled, but his voice was gently chiding. "Do you know so little of the ways of men, even now, that you can suppose it is the prettiness of Madame's face that draws them! Anyway, I thought you would be pleased to see that Patrick is falling from favor."

"Yes, but I wanted him to tire of her first. This way, he's going to be horribly hurt!"

"We all have to get horribly hurt sometimes. It's part of a great refining process that goes on right through our lives and there's no way we can escape it or shield those we love from its toils." His gravity was dispelled with an ironic smile. "Dear me, we are in danger of becoming profound! I'll race you to that clump of reeds at the far end of the lake. The last one to arrive will be obliged to attend Madame Duvrais's next musical afternoon!"

"Oh, shame!" she cried, as he set off without waiting for her. She raced after him and they arrived almost at the same time and clung together, laughing, breathless. "Despicable man! You took an unfair advantage!" she accused. "I claim the victory!"

"We'll cry quits," he said, laughing down at her. His expression gradually altered and she began to feel self-conscious.

"Have I got a smut?" she enquired flippantly.

"No. As a matter of fact, you look—quite glowing!" He sounded surprised.

"It's the exercise," she said resolutely. And then, "I think we'd better go back."

Anys Davide finally cut Patrick at the Opera—in full view of everyone. Clementina wasn't present at the time but needless to say, word soon got back. She tried to talk to Patrick about it, but was cut short; and in a way that worried and distressed her, for this was a new Patrick, his fine, boy's face seeming suddenly much older, more withdrawn.

"Leave it, will you Clemmy?" he said. "I'm fine. I just don't want to talk about it. And for God's sake, don't set Aunt Seraphina on to me! That would be too much!" And then roughly, seeing her stricken look, "Oh, lord, don't look like *that!* I'm not going to do anything stupid, you know!"

But that didn't stop her from worrying. She soon guessed from Joshua's harassed manner that Patrick was staying out most of the night again, "though he ain't never come home like before, Miss Clemmy! He just ain't hisself—you know what I mean?"

Clementina did know. In desperation she appealed to Alfred, who was plainly ill at ease. "Fact is, Miss Brady, ma-am—Patrick and I, we're . . . well, not to put too fine a point on't, we ain't that close just at present . . ."

"Oh, but you have always been *such* friends! Don't tell me the wretched boy has fallen out with *you*, just because he's been crossed in love!"

Alfred's smile was meant to be reassuring. "Nothing so drastic, ma-am—more in the nature of a difference of opinion—bound to pass! Thing is, y'see, need plenty of the ready to go to places like Maison Joselyn—the play there's well above my touch! Silly fellow took umbrage when I wouldn't let him frank me. Deuced difficult situation."

"Are you saying that my brother is frequenting gambling hells? Oh, Alfred—he wouldn't, would he?"

The young man tugged uneasily at his cravat. "Emotions blighted—taken it hard! Deeply distressing, don't y'know. Fellow does the oddest things when he's blue-deviled! Daresay he'll come about before long, though," he offered hopefully.

The Marquis had much the same story from Alexei, though in rather more down-to-earth terms, as they rode in the Bois.

"I thought you would wish to know, my friend—since young Brady was introduced to Jocelyn's by Gaston Rivas, who *is* one of de Tourne's hangers-on. The play there is devilish steep—assuredly no place for the novice. Last night, with my own eyes, I saw Patrick signing vowels with a recklessness that bodes ill! I do not know what kind of an allowance is made to him, but I would hazard that it will not suffice; in his present mood he is like to find himself so deep in debt that he cannot extricate himself!"

"The Devil!" Cadogon muttered. "Chuckleheaded young fool! Why couldn't he go on the mop for a few days as he did before? Work that expensive bit of muslin out of his system in the prescribed fashion!" A touch of his heel set his young horse to a gallop. Over his shoulder he said, "I suppose I must save the young fool from himself!"

The Maison Jocelyn, though new, already had that aura of decadent opulence so typical of its kind. The furnishings were expensive and in the very best of taste; the Venetian chandeliers that lent brilliance to the grand salons and supper rooms giving place to discreet lighting above the tables in the gaming rooms. It was in the faro room that the Marquis found Patrick. From the curious blankness in his eyes and whitened knuckles of the hand lying clenched upon the table, it was apparent that he was badly dipped and plunging deeper. The sensible thing would be to haul him out, there and then, but his pride, already crushed, would hardly stand being mauled afresh. His Lordship sighed and prepared for a long and probably expensive night.

Patrick wasn't sure what to think when his cousin walked in. His first idea—that Clemmy had somehow got wind and had put him up to it—seemed unlikely since, beyond a cursory nod, Lord Cadogon showed little interest in his presence there. A place was made for him at the table and he sat down and was soon absorbed in the game.

The tiny leap of hope that perhaps his cousin had come to extricate him from a situation that was fast becoming not only intolerable, but a little frightening, and from which he hadn't the least idea how to extricate himself, died, and he played on with grim determination. Gaston's insistence that in pitting his wits against the cards he would discover an antidote for his misery had seemed at the first to be true. It was a world without women—no Clemmy or Aunt Seraphina to swamp him with their sympathy, no Dora with soulful eyes that followed him at every turn, and above all, no Anys. And it had been exciting at the beginning.

But the luck that had been with him at the start of the week had begun to desert him in the last two nights and he had been obliged to sign more I.O.U.'s than he ought, knowing full well that there was little in his bank account to back them up until his next quarter's allowance should fall due. His vowels had been accepted without question, coming as they did from the brother of the much-esteemed Miss Brady, and his heart sank at the thought of confessing to her how foolish he'd been. Any pleasure by now fled, he had decided upon one last night at the tables in an attempt to recoup what he had lost—surely the luck must change again, he decided stubbornly. Gaston had agreed and he had much the greater experience in such matters.

He could not have been more out, however, and at three in the morning when the game finally broke up, he attempted to tot up what he owed and was appalled by his findings. He watched, white faced and with clammy hands, as each of his fellow-gamesters settled their accounts with the Chevalier Giraud, who had held the bank for the evening, and when his own reckoning could no longer be avoided he haltingly enquired the extent of his losses. With the amount confirmed to him, he found his tongue cleaving to the roof of his mouth as he sought the words to explain his predicament. He sent Gaston a despairing, appealing glance and received an unhelpful shrug. The Chevalier waited, smiling, expectant—and then came Cadogon's voice, casual, so matter-of-fact, "No need for my cousin to be making out a draft on his bank. I believe I may have sufficient about me to settle his score . . . all in the family, after all!" There was some good-natured chiding at this—remarks about the generosity of some families—during which Patrick, bereft of speech, could only suppose his deliverance to be due directly to divine intervention!

Outside he felt the cold night air stinging his eyes. He wanted only to go home. Gaston was nowhere to be seen, but Lord Cadogon was at his elbow, one hand firmly grasping him. Without a word he walked him briskly along the boulevard and into a small, unfashionable café where a few young men still gathered in groups about ill-lit tables, arguing in a desultory manner.

The Marquis selected a table out of earshot, called for a bottle of cognac and two glasses, poured a generous measure into each, and pushed one toward Patrick.

"Drink it!" His voice brooked no argument.

Patrick did as he was bid in a rather sullen silence, grateful for the strong, burning liquid, hoping it would stiffen his courage. Guilt suffused him; a consciousness of the thanks due to his cousin warred with a general feeling of being ill-done-by and caused them to be uttered in a grudging fashion, followed by a defiant "I *mean* to pay you back, you know—every last sou."

"Of course. I intend to make sure that you do."

Shaken by the cold formality of Cadogon's reply, Patrick squared his shoulders in a manner curiously at odds with his deflated confidence. "Only—well, the thing is—I shan't be in funds again for another month."

The Marquis regarded him pensively, with that slight lift of the brow that could be so unnerving. Patrick flushed and gulped the remainder of his brandy in too much haste, choking as it went down.

"I know it *is* a great sum, Cousin Dominic, and if you can't wait so long, I'll . . . I'll just have to ask Clemmy to advance my allowance—it won't cover the whole, I know—but she's a tremendously generous creature, and with Christmas I'd say she'd be bound to come across with a bit extra, wouldn't you?"

"Knowing your sister as I do, *I'd say* she will be very curious to know *why* your pockets are so badly to let."

Patrick bit his lip, looking so ridiculously like Clementina that the Marquis smiled faintly. "My dear boy, don't be a gudgeon! I have just put myself to a great deal of trouble in order that Clementina should be saved from needless worry, so I'll thank you not to sabotage my efforts! I do, however," he added sternly, "require your assurances that you will *never* behave in such a skimble-brained fashion again—or at least," he amended dryly, "not until you come of age. After that you are free to choose your own road to perdition!"

Patrick's reaction was a mixture of relief and eagerness. "Oh, I shan't! You may depend upon it! To tell the truth," he confided, "I didn't enjoy it above half. I only went there in the first place because . . ."

"I know why you went," said the Marquis dampingly. "It's to be hoped you'll be a little less of a fool the next time! I know advice is odious, but for what it's worth I'd stick to friends like Bennett and young Gallatin in future. They may get up to some wild capers, but there's no real vice in them. As to money matters, you can hardly exist without funds," he pushed a small handful of coins across the table, retaining a hold on them as he quieted the boy's protests. "It can be added to the rest—a purely private business transaction between gentlemen—a loan, to be redeemed when you come of age."

"When I—? But, dash it, sir, that's very nearly two years!"

"I believe I shall survive," drawled His Lordship.

Patrick was overcome with gratitude, though troubled at the thought of deceiving Clemmy over such a matter. "She won't like it."

"It's a little late in the day for scruples, my boy. I am not, in general, an advocate of deception, but in this case you may console yourself that you will be saving your sister a great deal of heartache by remaining silent."

They had both, however, reckoned without Clementina. Her talk with Alfred had left her in a ferment of unease, which could only find relief in having the whole matter out with Patrick, and since he was no match for her when it came to the parry and thrust of one of her inquisitions, he was soon blurting out the whole sorry tale.

As a result, Clementina sought an interview with her cousin upon the following day. He arrived with admirable promptness and was admitted by Maurice, not without a certain degree of curiosity, to Clementina's own private sanctum—a small room paneled entirely in frescoes at the rear of the house where she might be reasonably certain of complete privacy.

He accepted her invitation to be seated with every appearance of composure, also a glass of her excellent Madeira, which she had instructed Maurice to set in readiness upon the nearby commode. Having exhausted the preliminary niceties, she plunged straight into the matter uppermost in her mind. With her usual forthrightness she told him how vastly obliged she was to him for his very generous intervention in Patrick's behalf last evening, the tactful way he had averted what might so easily have amounted to a devilishly awkward situation, and most of all, that he had accomplished the whole without setting Patrick's hackles up. "Indeed, he has done nothing but sing your praises, and though he didn't wish me to speak to you of it, I could hardly do otherwise!"

His Lordship crossed one elegantly booted leg over the other and examined the faultless gleam of his top-boot with every appearance of absorption.

"No, that would be too much to expect," he drawled. "Trust the young fool to blab!"

"Patrick didn't blab! It was Alfred who put me in the picture in the first instance; from there I simply had to ask Patrick and he told me the whole!"

"Of course! I should have known the lad'd be no match for you!"

His sarcasm touched her on the raw. "I had every right to know—and furthermore, I consider it downright shabby of you to be encouraging my brother to deceive me!" she retorted, and then, aware of how ungracious *that* must make her sound in the circumstances, added grudgingly, "However admirable the intention!"

"My dear girl," he said with maddening calm. "I thought you had managed to rid yourself of this notion that you are the only one capable of running Patrick's life."

"Oh, I am well aware that you consider your skills superior in that department."

"I was thinking of Patrick himself," he put in gently.

She flushed. "Patrick is still a minor," she said, "and I don't intend to abdicate my responsibilities nor, I hope, will I ever fail to show a proper concern when he is in trouble—and in this instance . . ."

"In this instance," Cadogon's voice had grown more

clipped, "he behaved stupidly and he knows it; I have his word that he will not gamble again, and I believe I know him well enough to be assured of his sincerity."

"He allowed you to pay his gambling debts—and give him money besides!"

"Correction. I paid the boy's shot because it was plain to anyone but a gibbering idiot that he was in a situation he was ill-equipped to deal with, and loaned him a little besides. I am satisfied that he has learned a hard, but valuable lesson that will sink home to far greater effect if he is obliged to pay the money back himself as he knows he must—at a time agreeable to both of us."

"That is all very fine, and generous of you, cousin, but it won't do." Clementina rose from her chair and crossed to a small secretaire that stood open beneath a charming fresco of entwined lovers. "It is quite nonsensical—and unnecessary— that you should be out of pocket on Patrick's account. I really can't permit such an arrangement." Clementina picked up a slip of paper and turned to find that the Marquis, too, had risen and was standing in front of the fire. "That is the amount, I believe—the full amount?" She held out the draft imperiously.

For a moment she thought he wouldn't take it; when at last he did, she felt the coldness of his anger like a chill draught of air. He glanced briefly at the paper.

"Quite correct," he said, tore it across again and again, and threw the pieces on the fire.

"Well, really!" she exclaimed. "Of all the idiotic things to do!"

His hand came out to restrain her as she half turned away. "Be thankful that is all I do! If you ever try anything like that with me again, I won't answer for the consequences! You may bear-lead everyone else, my dear Clementina, but you don't run my life—and you never will!"

With his other hand he took her chin between his fingers, forcing her to meet his eyes, which were narrowed to a strange, blazing intensity. "You know, if you ever stop being so busy, you might very well discover that once in a while it can be just as blessed to *receive* graciously as it is to give!"

❧CHAPTER 18❧

"Mr. Pengallan!" Clementina, driving along the Champs Elysées on a crisp, bright afternoon, was astonished to see Cadogon's friend riding toward her, his slim, elegant figure wrapped in the folds of a thick cloak, heavily braided and caped. "I had no idea! Lord Cadogon made no mention of your coming." She reflected that she hadn't seen the Marquis for several days.

"Didn't know . . . thought to surprise him, d'ye see? Intended coming sooner, but filial duty called . . ." Mr. Pengallan gave her one of his sleepy smiles. "Obliged to spend Christmas in the bosom of m'family. Thought I might try for New Year . . . always enjoy New Year in France, but dashed if the weather didn't hold me up!"

"It certainly has been very cold. You are just in time for the skating."

Mr. Pengallan looked vaguely alarmed. "Such an uncomfortable mode of exercise! And suppose one were to fall? One would be obliged to return home on the instant to change one's clothes!"

Clementina tried to look shocked at this palpable admission of foppishness, but was obliged to acknowledge that the spectacle of Mr. Pengallan indulging in anything as extrovert—and possibly undignified—as skating was unthinkable. She laughed. His eyes twinkled in return.

"No need to ask how *you* go on, Miss Brady. You are obviously in prime twig!"

"Thank you, sir! Yes, I am very well."

"Hadn't expected to find you here, but you are obviously at home to an inch . . . and setting Paris by the ears, I see." He cast an expert eye of approval over the cabriolet's gleaming paintwork. "In the habit of driving yourself, are you?"

"Oh, I have long since been accepted as an oddity. Perhaps I may take you up sometime, or would it offend the sensibilities of such an accomplished whip to be driven by a woman?"

"Nothing of the kind, ma'am," he declared gallantly. "I should account it an honor. Can't say I'd care for't in the general way mind . . . but I'm persuaded that you must always acquit yourself well."

She thanked him kindly for the compliment and asked where he was staying.

"I'm lodged with Stuart at the Embassy. Always stay there when I'm in Paris. Splendid fellow, Stuart . . . the Hotel Borghese, too . . . excellent place. Wellington bought it for the Government after the Revolution, y'know . . . from Bonaparte's sister Pauline . . . for a song, so they say! Superb gardens . . . but you'll know all that, of course . . ."

"Yes, indeed. I'm on my way to the Faubourg St. Honoré myself at this moment—to the Elysée Palace, having received a frantic message from the Duchesse de Berry's lady in waiting."

"You move in exalted circles, Miss Brady!" drawled Mr. Pengallan in his most languid fashion. "Then I mustn't keep you. Perhaps we shall meet again soon?" He smiled.

Clementina found Madame de Bethisy in a state of unease. "It is all on account of this Fête that His Royal Highness has arranged with his friends for tomorrow night . . ." There was disapproval in her voice.

Clementina had often wondered how much was known of the Duc's many infidelities. The Duchesse had never given any sign that she knew of his regular excursions into the "other world." She was such a strange, volatile creature, almost childishly possessive of her handsome husband. Yet, since they dealt well enough together, Clementina could only suppose that the Duc's undoubted charm got him out of trouble whenever her possessiveness threatened his pleasure!

It was ironical that on this occasion, Madame's spouse was involved in nothing more compromising than a spectacular and extremely public party—on ice!

"You are pleased to be amused, mademoiselle?" Madame Bethisy's tone had grown cool.

Clementina hastily composed her features. "No, madame. Forgive me. I was simply thinking about the Fête. I hear it is to be the most splendid affair, with fireworks and military bands playing and even a troupe of Swedish skaters who are to give an entertainment! And it *is* for one of the Duc's charities. Half of fashionable Paris is expected to attend."

"The Duchesse is not unaware of the event's many attractions," said Madame dryly. "Her fear is that the occasion will be used for an attempt on the Duc's life."

"Oh, but that is absurd!"

"Perhaps." Madame de Bethisy gave a little shrug. "I do not myself consider it likely, but one cannot deny that there have been rumors . . ."

"In Paris there are always rumors! Why, I declare I have never known such a place for idle speculation about plots and assassinations! If there were none, I believe someone would invent them! If it is not the King, then it is the Duc or Monsieur!"

"Nevertheless, mademoiselle, the Duc does have enemies, and with Madame unable to attend the Fête in her present delicate condition . . . well!" with a shrug. "You know that she miscarried last year? This time her physician is adamant that she must be kept calm during this most critical early stage. I have tried all I can," again the shrug, "but it avails little. It was thought that perhaps your common-sense approach might better allay Madame's fears."

Clementina grimaced slightly over this unflattering commendation and doubted her ability to do it justice; in the presence of hysteria she was inclined to favor the efficacy of a short sharp slap, but one could scarcely apply such a drastic remedy to a duchesse!

Still, one could not refuse to try. She found the Duchesse confined to bed in her luxurious apartments, swathed in clouds of exquisite lace, her blonde hair curling limply beneath an enormous frilled boudoir cap that made her face appear small and oddly defenseless, blotched as it was with the traces of recent tears.

Clementina's attempts at reassurance met with little success at first, but she held grimly to her good humor as she refuted the notion that anyone would wish the Duc harm.

"No, no, Miss Brady, you are wrong! There are men— Monsieur Decazes, for one! He hates my *cheri* . . . he thinks him frivolous and reactionary . . . and that is not all—I know that he carries lies about my husband to the King!"

"But murder, madame!" Clementina forced a coaxing note into her voice. "Come now. Surely it is inconceivable that the King's chief minister would be so stupid as to make an attempt upon the life of His Majesty's nephew!"

"That is just what he is, Miss Brady—stupid! And vain and pompous!" Her voice rose vindictively, and it took all of Clementina's skill and patience to wean her from these carefully nurtured convictions. At the end of a grueling hour, however, she was able to leave Madame, if not happy, at least much less fearful.

Clementina had scarcely quit Madame's boudoir when she encountered the Duc. His eyes warmed with something more than mere pleasure. She looked around for Madame de Bethisy, but she was nowhere to be seen.

"Miss Brady!" He bowed and came very close. "This is an unlooked-for pleasure. Madame de Bethisy informs me that you have been playing the good Samaritan to my poor Caro."

"The Duchesse is very disturbed, sir—I hope I may have eased her mind a little, but she is obviously frightened for you."

He shrugged his elegant shoulders. "You do not have to tell me, mademoiselle! But I am sure she is much improved as a result of your visit. My wife sets great store by your opinion." Clementina found her hand taken and held in his caressing clasp. "For this," he murmured, "I must everlastingly be in your debt!"

Envisioning only too well how he would best like to repay her kindness, Clementina withdrew her hand gently but firmly from his grasp and stepped back a pace, her cheeks tingling.

"You owe me nothing, Duc. Now, I must not keep you from your wife. You *were* on your way to visit her?"

He made her an exaggerated leg and smiled with droll good humor. "So it would seem, mademoiselle! You are quite sure there is no way in which I may demonstrate my appreciation?"

"Quite sure," she insisted. In the middle of her departing curtsy she was struck by a sudden thought. "Unless, that is . . ," she looked up at him pensively, "I suppose you would not consider foregoing your attendance at the Fête tomorrow night?"

"To please you, my dear Miss Brady?" He was all hope.

"To please your wife," she answered firmly.

"Ah!" he murmured, and raised her, blushing anew, to her feet. "But then, you see, I am so looking forward to my evening at the Petit Lac!"

"And if your going there places you in danger? Is it fair to put the burden of responsibility for Your Highness's safety upon your friends?"

The bright eyes under quirking brows were suddenly keen. "You are ever blunt. Miss Brady! Do my friends, then, find it so unconscionable a burden to protect me?"

"No, of course not, sir," she said in some confusion. "But you cannot expect them not to worry."

"No?" He appeared less than convinced. "And you really believe someone wishes to kill me? But who is to play the villain, eh? I have enemies enough, certainly." As he continued to regard her, seriousness gave place to a mischievous twinkle. "An avenging husband, perhaps?"

Alexei's words, almost to the letter! Except that he had added with a grin, "He's cuckolded enough of them in his time!" Remembering now, Clementina found it hard to meet the Duc's all-seeing eyes. But it seemed he could read her thoughts.

The twinkle turned to uproarious laughter. "I believe I will take my chance, Miss Brady. If I were to cower at home every time threats were made against me, I should be obliged to become a hermit! And that would not suit me at all!"

The Petit Lac in winter was a jewel set in a white fantasy world; on the night of the Fête it was a place of enchantment. From the Champs Elysées to the lakeside, soldiers stood sentinel, lighting the way with blazing torches. The lake itself was wreathed with lanterns, hundreds of them making everything seem as bright as day. More lanterns hung on the many sledges that had been decorated for the occasion; their constant swaying motion gave the scene an added magic. Fires burned at regular intervals, and at the near end a dais had been erected comprising several divans covered in the finest fur rugs, where the Duc's special guests were to sit.

Mr. Pengallan had been persuaded to attend, against his better judgment. He handed the ribbons reluctantly to his groom and stepped from an elegant little carriage, swathed from head to toe in astrakan. Clementina laughed at his expression of distaste, and drew him toward one of the fires, where most of their party was already gathered.

"I don't mean to stay," he informed them above the sound of a musical gallop being energetically rendered by one of the military bands. "Only came to refute Dominic's allegation that I was too chicken-hearted." He held his slim hands out to the blaze and said with his sleepy smile, "Matter of fact, I am to accompany Count Pozzo di Borgo later to some new gambling hell in the Palais Royale."

"Does the Count gamble?" asked Clementina, surprised.

"All Russians are gamblers, didn't you know?" said Cadogon with a pointed glance at Alexei, who was at that moment engaged in coaxing Dora to ride with Elyse in his sledge.

Alexei heard him and paused to take good-natured issue. "Why be so specific, my friend? Do we not all gamble at some time in our lives? Sometimes to live at all becomes a bizarre game of chance . . ."

His glance moved across to the dais where the Duc de Berry sat with some of his friends. Clementina had already noticed that he was never left alone for one moment, yet he appeared quite unconcerned.

"And there are those whose ventures take a more quixotic turn," Alexei continued. "As in the case of a certain young lady who played benefactress to the bastard child of her kitchenmaid!"

All eyes turned to Clementina. She was looking particularly well on this evening in a close-fitting redingote of thick ivory velvet, the neck closed very high and edged with swansdown; a neat little bonnet edged with more swansdown lent the contours of her face an endearing youthful innocence. Her eyes, like bright pools in the leaping lantern light, mirrored her good-natured acceptance of Alexei's teasing.

"Extraordinary coincidence!" Mr. Pengallan's words dropped ingenuously into the pregnant pause. "Didn't something of the sort happen to you, ma'am . . . around Christmastime?" His voice trailed away amid general laughter. Cadogon murmured something and he grinned sheepishly. "Ah . . . yes, I see . . ."

"Poor little Lysette!" Clementina defended herself. "Why, I declare, she is scarcely more than a baby herself, and not the brightest of girls!"

"You are fast becoming an expert on the youthful dross of Paris life!" Cadogon's voice was full of irony. "Pray, what does the future hold in store for this latest protégée of yours?"

Mistrusting the question, Clementina looked more closely at him and met only blandness. Did he know what she intended, or was he just guessing. She felt a momentary panic . . . this wasn't the way she wanted her plans exposed, with all eyes upon her! She had meant to choose her moment.

The music had changed to a slow, pulsating waltz and the ice began to fill up with gracefully moving figures. Clementina longed to be one of them, but everyone was now awaiting her answer. She sighed, thrust her hands deep into a huge sable muff, and clasped it resolutely against her.

"Well," she explained, choosing her words with care. "I have had a long talk with Lysette and we are both agreed that she cannot hope to cope with the baby and do her work, and so it is decided that little Marie Angelina will remain with the good sisters at the Convent and Lysette will be permitted to visit her whenever her duties allow."

Instead of satisfying their curiosity, she seemed to have aroused fresh interest. It was Alexei, however, who voiced the sentiments of the rest, saying with gentle irony, "But how very benevolent of the sisters, to do so much for a mere kitchenmaid!" He glanced at the Marquis. "Moreover, it leads one to suppose that virtue must bring its own reward, for only today we learned that the empty house adjoining the Convent has been mysteriously acquired and presented to the Reverend Mother. I understand it is to become a kind of creche."

"Oh, for heaven's sake! This is worse than the Spanish Inquisition!" declared Clementina between laughter and exasperation. "Why don't you just come right out with it and admit that you are aching with curiosity!"

"I should not tell them anything," said Elyse, though dancing eyes belied her primly pursed mouth. "It is none of their business, after all."

"No, it isn't, is it? But I am clearly to be given no peace until I have confessed!" Clementina put up her chin pugnaciously. "How did you find out about the house?"

Cadogon was at his most laconic. "My dear girl, how does one know anything in Paris? I daresay I could furnish you with a list of every visit you have made in this past week; you have been at least twice to your lawyer, Monsieur Marac, and several times to the convent, where I am reliably informed that on the last occasion Reverend Mother practically genuflected as you departed the premises! Shall I go on?"

"No, no, I beg of you!" she cried in vexation. "For shame, cousin! I had always thought that you, at least, were above such trivialities! Now I find that you have joined the sullied ranks of the tattle-mongers!"

"Can I help it if certain information comes my way quite gratuitously?"

"Not much escapes Dominic," Mr. Pengallan assured her.

"Why, so I am beginning to realize."

"A refuge for fallen girls and their little mistakes in the Rue de Varennes!" chuckled Alexei. "It is a prospect most enlivening, to say the very least! How will your neighbors react, I wonder? Do they even guess what comes to them?"

"Oh, but it won't be like that! Or, at least, only until we can organize something more permanent." Clementina had quite forgotten her initial reluctance to speak. "I am negotiating, through Monsieur Marac's good offices, for a house in a more suitable area, and Reverend Mother is to make arrangements for it to be properly staffed and run, though of course I intend to take a very personal interest in its progress."

It was only now that they realized how much she was in earnest, for enthusiasm brought to her eyes the shining zeal of the crusader; bright flags of color flew in her cheeks. It was this same driving enthusiasm that had first stunned and then inspired the good nun who had become her willing accomplice, as it very quickly became clear that Miss Brady had no intention of sitting back and awaiting events.

The effect on her present audience was rather one of awe, but she seemed unaware of it as she continued, "Lord Cadogon is pleased to jest about my 'experience,' but I believe I have learned a good deal in these past weeks—from Clothilde and more recently from Rosa—about the number of girls, not quite of their kind, for I hope I am not a prude and I do know that there are many who are happy enough to live under a man's protection, but girls like Lysette, little more than children, hopelessly naive and ripe to be used! Girls who end up in trouble, and who are then turned out onto the streets as some said I should have turned Lysette off, so that they are reduced in the end to selling the only commodity they have, and end up with procurers like that awful man whose schemes we thwarted! I simply want to give girls like that some kind of a choice."

A chuckle from Alexei broke the silence that had fallen. "*Mon Dieu!* We have been harboring a firebrand in our midst, my friends, and did not know it!"

"Do stop!" cried Elyse. "I think it is quite shameful of you to tease poor Clementina further. What she is contemplating doing is quite splendid!"

"Of course it is splendid," agreed Alexei with a broad grin. "I will go further and say stupendous! Magnificent!"

"No, it isn't!" They were all taken aback by the unaccustomed vehemence in her voice. Her eyes sought Cadogon. "My cousin will tell you it is pure self-indulgence on my part—and he is right! I have never been used to idleness, and I had grown bored with a surfeit of pleasure. Now I find I am enjoying myself enormously!"

It was Mr. Pengallan, unexpectedly, who voiced his thoughts. "Best reason I know of for doing anything," he offered gently.

Before more could be said, Alexei was summoned by the Duc de Berry. While they had been talking, a great number of people had arrived to swell an assembly of the most sumptuous elegance, swathed in rich fabrics, cocooned in furs of all shades and varieties, and looking absurdly out of place in such a setting, but drawn by the promise of novelty and spectacle, and for some, the irresistible possibility of witnessing an attempt upon the Duc's life. As more people joined the group by the fire and lackeys began to move among them with refreshments, Clementina seized the opportunity to slip away, skating with slow deliberation away from all the lights and excitement toward the far end of the lake.

The high, buoyant bubble of her elation had been pricked, leaving in its wake a curious feeling of deflation. It was small wonder they had all looked at her as though she had windmills in her head! Why was it that all the fine reasoning, which seemed so clear and right inside one's head, sounded unbearably smug the moment it was uttered?

The music was growing fainter. All the light, all the activity was concentrated in the area surrounding the Duc and his party. Clementina recalled Alexei explaining to her that this end of the lake was to be left in virtual darkness in order to create a more dramatic backcloth for the firework display, and for the procession of lanterns at the close of the evening.

It wasn't really dark, of course; the night had been specially chosen because the moon would be at its fullest. It hung now in the still, starry heavens like a huge luminous ball, flooding the cold white landscape with shimmering light. And through the trees, the prettily lighted pavilion built by the Duc de Berry's father for a bet years ago. She moved aimlessly across the ice, her cheeks soon cooling to a biting tingle in the frosty air, finding herself suddenly shy of returning to face her friends.

Her preoccupation almost led her into disaster. A bed of petrified reeds loomed in her path and what had been a gentle, aimless progression became an undignified swerving scramble followed by a scream of protest from her ill-used blades as she spun to a halt. A figure loomed up. It was one of the men preparing the fireworks. He asked gruffly if she was all right, and plainly thought her a little odd.

She gasped an incoherent reply and as the sharply drawn-in cold air stung her throat and brought tears to her eyes, she moved quickly away, feeling exceedingly foolish. With her vision still blurred, she didn't see the approaching figure until it was too late.

There was a muttered expletive, the white blue of a face beneath a curling hat brim, and a dark coat with wildly flapping capes that seemed about to envelop her. She swerved in a desperate attempt to avert the impact, but was caught, spun round, and with her skates taken from under her, went crashing down with her assailant on top of her and her cry lost in a soundless explosion of breath as she hit the ice.

✖CHAPTER 19✖

"Clementina!" The voice gradually penetrated the numbness in her brain, but she had no breath to answer. Hands, thorough but gentle, were moving over her, checking each limb methodically.

"Clementina! For God's sake, answer me!"

It was Cadogon, his voice sounding quite ragged with concern. She opened her eyes. She was lying flat on her back on the ice with his face, sharply etched in profile and looking strangely un-Cadogonlike, close above her. In spite of the cold, in spite of an uncomfortable restriction in her ability to breathe, a warm feeling began to grow inside her. With a faint smile she lifted a finger to touch that misplaced bone at the bridge of his nose. "It . . . really does make you look condescending!"

His eyes widened and she realized that she had spoken the words aloud. Covered with confusion, she snapped back into full consciousness and struggled to sit upright. Lord! Whatever must he be thinking of her!

"Easy!" His arm came round her. "I don't think you've broken anything, but you're bound to be stiff."

"Help me up!" she insisted.

The Marquis made disapproving noises, but did as she asked. "How do you feel?"

"Excessively ill-used!" Clementina gasped, stifling a groan. "Did you have to knock me down quite so roughly?"

"Considering the reckless pace at which you were traveling, you may think yourself lucky we didn't both go through the ice!" he retorted unsympathetically, but his eyes, raking her upturned face, were dark and seemed to betray a very different emotion. And he still held tightly to her.

Clementina was profoundly thankful for his support, for she rather thought that if he let go her legs would fold beneath her. It must be the fall, she decided, that had set her heart in such a tumult. She began to tremble.

At once Cadogon's expression changed. Moonlight planing the contours of his face made it an angry mask. "You *are* hurt!" he said.

"No, truly. I'm cramped and cold, and my wrist aches a little, but . . ."

"Damnit, girl!" he exploded. "Can't you, just for once, drop that mantle of composure to allow a little sympathy in? Or are you scared I might construe it as feminine weakness?"

"That's a terrible thing to say! I know you think me self-opinionated and meddlesome, but that's no reason to suppose that I'm totally devoid of sensitivity!" Oh, no—she was going to make a fool of herself! Why must he always be so critical? She sniffed.

It was an endearing sound—so full of woeful indignation that it made him draw in a sharp breath.

"Oh, Clemmy!"

He had never called her that before, though she knew well that note of half-amused exasperation. He cupped her face in his hands, lifting it to the light. She had to blink several times before his face became clear to her and then she couldn't read his expression.

"How can anyone so intelligent be so wrong?" he said. "You can't even begin to know what I think of you or you wouldn't be so full of muttonheaded notions! The plain fact is, my dear *incorrigible* cousin, I'm only just beginning to understand you, myself—really understand you, I mean. Everyone must be familiar with the ever popular Miss Brady who is equally gracious whether as hostess or guest, or friend to royalty and who is full of odd, amusing quirks about reclaiming erring girls and setting them back on the path of righteousness . . ."

She moved angrily to protest, but it ended in a squeak as he clamped a hand across her mouth and continued remorselessly, "But how many, I wonder, know that other young woman who has been *so* busy all her life trying to emulate a formidable grandsire that she has scorned the softer, more womanly qualities she undoubtedly possesses and who now finds herself struggling hopelessly with untried emotions . . ." His voice softened unexpectedly. "Sometimes, just recently, I have glimpsed that other Clemmy, who is desperately uncertain and vulnerable because she's finding there are some situations she can't control and she doesn't know how to relinquish the ribbons. Am I not right?"

It was so close to the truth that she stared up at him, bereft of words, terribly afraid she was going to cry. With a muttered exclamation, he swept her close, so close that she was crushed against him. She hadn't the strength to struggle, nor, she found to her surprise, did she have the least desire to do so. His mouth on hers was gentle at first, persuasive—but not like Henri; not like anything she had ever dreamed to be possible!

"You see? It isn't really so difficult!" His lips lingered, the words no more than a breath against her blissfully closed eyes; as she sighed, they came swiftly to claim her mouth again, no longer gentle.

At last he lifted his head, laughing softly as her langorous eyelids fluttered open and she tried unsuccessfully to make her quivering mouth behave.

"Well, now!" he said huskily. "That was remarkably revealing!"

Clementina didn't know what to say. She felt suddenly quite ridiculously shy. He peered closer.

"Why, I do believe I have discovered the way to silence you at last! I can't imagine why I never thought of it before!"

"You never had me at such a disadvantage before!" she retorted, showing a resilience of spirit that delighted him.

"Pardon . . . Madame . . . Monsieur?" It was the officer in charge of the fireworks, apologetic, embarrassed. "The display . . . it waits to begin."

Cadogon swung round, a rebuke already on his lips, but Clementina, fully herself again, laid a restraining hand on his arm. "Dearest cousin," she implored on a gurgle of laughter, "we are very much in the poor man's way; unless you wish to become part of the spectacle, we must leave and let him proceed!"

"Damn his eyes!" said the Marquis, but his answering grin gave him an absurdly boyish look. He rescued her muff from the ice and tucked her hands inside, noting as he did so that she winced slightly. "I'll do something about that wrist when we get back."

"No, really, it isn't anything . . ." she began, caught his eyes, laughed, and said, "Oh, well . . ." It was, after all, rather pleasant to be cossetted. "You think I'm quite mad wanting to start my home for unfortunate girls, don't you?" she ventured with unusual diffidence as they approached the crowded, brightly lit end of the lake once more.

"Yes. But I don't see any real hope of convincing you otherwise."

"There is a real *need* for such a place," she pleaded, wanting his approval.

"I don't doubt it, my dear. But I strongly suspect that, however pure your motives and Reverend Mother's may be, you are likely to be exploited."

"Oh, stuff!" She wrinkled her nose at him. "What a cynic you are!"

"No, my dear. I'm a realist." He grinned down at her. "Which is why I'm not even going to attempt to talk you out of it!"

Once back, they were soon swept up in the festivities again and eventually became separated. News of her latest venture had spread rapidly and she was quizzed on all sides, but in her lingering state of euphoria she took it all without a murmur. She saw Patrick among a group of young people looking quite his old self. He and Alfred had persuaded Dora to take to the ice and were struggling along supporting her on either side amidst gales of laughter; even the presence of Anys Davide did not appear to be causing him any noticeable anguish. Clementina was glad. She wanted everyone to be happy this evening. The fireworks passed in a dream. The Swedish skaters were superb, and when presently she found the Duc de Menton at her side she gave him a blissful smile.

"You were many miles away, I think," he said apologetically. "But perhaps that is not to be wondered at? I have been hearing the most extraordinary stories . . . are they true?"

She pulled herself together and made a little moue. "How can I say, Duc, for by now if Paris gossip is running true to form, I shall probably find myself being credited with some wildly ambitious scheme to open a series of brothels in order to play Madame to half the city's prostitutes!"

The Duc chuckled. "With the good sisters as your willing accomplices? Ah, well, *that* device has been used before now!"

Clementina chuckled appreciatively and, happening to look out across the ice, saw Dominic—and with him Elyse, very close, her arm through his, and even as Clementina watched, lifting an eager face to him. She saw rather than heard that soft laugh, saw his hand move to tuck in a straying lock of Elyse's hair, his eyes never leaving hers . . .

Dreams that had scarcely lived beyond the first joyful pangs of birth were already withering away into oblivion. Fool! To be so easily carried away that she could forget Elyse, who was her friend and whose claim to Dominic's affections went far beyond anything that she could hope to match! And what of Dominic? Had he, too, forgotten Elyse, or did a man have less of a conscience about such things?

". . . and so, knowing that your aunt was safely promised to Mrs. Bennett for this evening, it seemed the ideal opportunity to come and tell you that my arrangements are now complete." It was at this point that the Duc's words penetated her disordered thoughts. "It is for the day after tomorrow."

Clementina, dragging her mind away from her own problem, looked blank. "What is for tomorrow?" And then, as the fine, ascetic features, already a prey to embarrassment, registered dismay, "Oh, my dear sir, it is for you to forgive me! I was not fully attending! You must be thinking me quite scatterbrained . . ."

"I think something is troubling you. What is wrong, Clementina? Have you," he hesitated, "have you, perhaps, thought better of your advice to me?"

"Good gracious, no! Nothing of the kind, I promise you! I was just watching those men with lanterns forming up for the retreat and I believe the concentration of light must have dazzled me . . ." She was aware that edginess was making her gabble like an idiot. "The day after tomorrow, you said. That is indeed marvelous news!" He looked a little startled by her sudden changes of mood. Poor man! He must, by now, be seriously questioning her sanity.

"You don't think it too soon?" he ventured and couldn't quite keep the note of dismay from his voice.

"No, no! The sooner, the better!" she said decisively, and then, "Oh, dear, that did sound very much as though I cannot wait to be rid of you both, but I did not mean it so! I am so glad that you are now fully reconciled to the whole idea."

A look of pain disturbed his features briefly. "I have simply shut my mind to the impossibility of that which I attempt and pray for a miracle!"

"Oh, stuff!" She managed an affectionate, almost coy glance. "Am I to know your plans, or do you mean to keep them a deadly secret?"

"Hardly from you, my dear, since without you there would be no . . . er, plans. But they are very mundane, I fear." A wry smile hovered round his mouth. "I cannot hope to match you when it comes to flights of fancy! Also, the weather does not lend itself to a protracted journey. Therefore, I have decided to make use of my chateau at Fontainebleau. It has a small chapel, and there, unless Seraphina rejects me out of hand, the chaplain will perform the marriage ceremony. My only regret is that you will not be there to witness our union. You will not change your mind?"

"Oh, no. Much as it grieves me to miss an event that must be so dear to my heart, I don't want to give her the least excuse to wriggle out of it after we've been to so much trouble!"

"Your observations do not exactly bolster one's confidence, my dear, but I have no doubt you are right." He gave a rueful shrug. "At all events, allowing that all goes well, it is my hope that we shall return to Paris fairly soon to await the spring, when I mean to take Seraphina into Italy."

"Bravo! It will all answer splendidly! You have hit exactly the right note of simplicity. Aunt Seraphina cannot be other than enchanted."

Because she didn't want to be alone to think, she detained the Duc for as long as possible, making final arrangements, but the moment came when she could hold him no longer and she was left to her gloomy reflections. But not for long.

There was a cold hiss of blades on the ice and Alexei swept to her side. He had manifestly enjoyed himself and had reached a state of jovial intoxication. "I have scarcely seen you since the Fete's beginnings, *moya dorogoya!*" he cried, embracing her with unsteady enthusiasm and wreathing her in brandy fumes. "But my duty to our gracious Duc is now at an end and you behold me very much at your service. Will you make the final procession with me or are you promised elsewhere?"

She was on the point of refusing when she saw Dominic making his way purposefully toward her. "Yes," she said hastily. "I should very much like to!"

"Good. Then it is arranged. Come." Alexei still held her waist persuasively encircled. "We will collect our lanterns, yes?" He chuckled. "I must tell you—poor Alice! Her mama is furious that she will not attempt to skate and I had very astutely arranged for my sledge to be in use so that I could not offer it to her!"

Clementina roused herself to chide him.

"Yes, I know!" He sighed regretfully. "But she is like an exquisite doll, that one—beautifully packaged, but no conversation! No wit! And assuredly, no intellect!"

A voice hailed them. Clementina jumped nervily, but it was only the Duc de Berry. Alexei released her and murmured with a twinkle, "*I* will collect our lanterns. Five minutes—no more . . ." He kissed his hands to her and was gone.

"Mademoiselle Brady!" The Duc made her a leg, his bold features alight with merriment. "You behold me all in one piece to confound the pessimists!"

With an effort she met his mood, assuring him with a smile that she was every bit as thankful as the rest to find the rumors unfounded.

He glanced around. "You think these people all rejoice that I still live?" A thin vein of sarcasm ran beneath the good-humored quizzing. "You have not sensed the merest suggestion of an anticlimax, perhaps?" And then, relenting as he saw her discomforture, "Ah, well, you at least are sincere, my dear Miss Brady—and, who knows—" He shrugged. "Tomorrow is another day!" On which cryptic remark he observed that Alexei had returned and he bowed. "For now, I am required to lead this procession. Your servant, mademoiselle."

They moved into line not far behind the Duc. There was a roll on the drums and the ceremony began—several hundred people carrying lanterns of all colors going down the lake two by two into the darkness where they divided, sweeping round to form a great double circle. Clementina conceded that, yes, the spectacle was unbelievably beautiful, but in reality the lights were all blurred and there was an ache in her chest—a relic of her fall, no doubt. She wished only for the long, long evening to be at an end.

And then it *was* over. People began to stream away and she sat on the now almost deserted dais with Alexei, preparing to remove her skates. A shadow fell across her.

"I'll do that," said Cadogon, squatting at her feet.

Instinctively she withdrew them. "Don't bother. I can manage."

The brusqueness of her reply caused him to raise an interrogatory eyebrow, but he reclaimed her recalcitrant feet and resumed his task as calmly as though she had not spoken. The blood beat unsteadily in her veins.

"Where is Elyse?"

"She's gone on ahead to wait in the coach."

Divide and conquer. The words came unbidden into her mind. Wasn't that supposed to be a good old military maxim? And Dominic had been a good military man—well thought of by Wellington, no less. Suddenly and quite passionately she wanted to see his face, to know if she was misjudging him. But even when she leaned back, the brim of his hat obscured her view, and his voice gave nothing away.

"Perhaps you had better not keep her waiting," she said.

"She doesn't mind," he replied imperturbably. "I told her we had some unfinished business."

Alexei stood up and strolled past them, his skates slung across his shoulder. "Do not trouble yourselves, my friends." He beamed down on them. "It will give me the greatest pleasure to bear Elyse company until you come."

He was gone and they were alone except for the few who still lingered around the edges of the lake or strolled about, loath to quit the scene. It was astonishing how hundreds of people could so quickly melt away. Clementina tried to think of something to say, but her tongue would not obey her.

"There." Dominic patted her foot, stood up, and pulled her to her feet, smiling down into her eyes. Oh, treachery!

He took her hand and began to walk toward the trees. She resisted, gripped by sudden panic.

"Come," he insisted. "We can't talk here."

She allowed herself to be persuaded. It was quiet; the occasional twig snapping under their feet rang out like a pistol shot on the frosty air. They stopped at last where there would be little chance of being overheard.

"This is much better!" he murmured, attempting to draw her into his arms. "I have been impatient to get you to myself again. I had hoped we could make the last procession together."

Clementina resisted his soft words as she resisted his embrace. He tried to see her face.

"Clementina? You're in a very strange mood."

"I'm just tired."

"No, it's more than that." Again he attempted to take her in his arms, rallying her gently. "You were not so unkind earlier!"

She almost succumbed. Perhaps, she reasoned in her despair, if I allow him to kiss me just once more, I shall find the magic gone and everything will then be resolved. But no amount of reasoning could still the trembling within her. She collected the poor remnants of her common sense about her and drew back.

"Perhaps," she said steadily, "we would both do better to forget what happened earlier."

His reaction might have gratified her, had she not been so miserable. His grip was painful, his voice incredulous.

"You are joking?"

Clementina shook her head.

"Then I don't understand." He shook his head. "Did you imagine I was merely flirting with you? Have you forgotten so soon how it was between us, that you dismiss it so lightly?"

"No! I didn't . . . I haven't!" she cried and her throat ached abominably.

"Then, in God's name, why?"

Because however it may appear to you I am trying to do the right thing, she wanted to say. Because for once I am trying to be completely unselfish, to give up the thing I want, now—before it becomes too precious to me; because, though you may fancy yourself capable of being in love with two women at the same time, there is no way I can be a party to it . . . and still less can I contemplate depriving Elyse, who is my friend, of your love and protection, which she has come to value so highly!

Clementina was furious with him for not seeing for himself how impossible it was, but she would not risk saying so for fear of an argument that would serve no purpose other than perhaps to destroy the delicate fabric of Dominic's relationship with Elyse, and thus with little Suzy who looked upon her *cher Monsieur Dominic* as a father.

She must therefore convince him by other means. She

forced more lightness into her voice than she would have thought possible.

"It would be a pity, don't you think, to spoil the memory of such an idyllic interlude? It was quite the most romantic thing that has ever happened to me and I shall treasure it always." The words were rushing out, rasping a little in the cold air. "But, my dear cousin, we should never suit! We are far too much alike and should be at one another's throats in no time at all!"

He was so long in answering that her teeth began to chatter. The sound had a curious effect on him. He gave her a little shake, took her arm, and said with surprising gentleness, "Come on. Home. You've obviously got yourself into a state over something, and this is no place to resolve it."

Oh no! That wouldn't do at all. It must be finished now, here where the darkness would not give her away. He could read her face much too well! She heard herself say, "I have told you—there is nothing to resolve. It was a pleasant interlude. No more."

He swung her hard round, peering down. She steeled herself to meet his anger. "My God! I believe you are serious! A pleasant interlude!"

She laughed recklessly. "Oh, come now, cousin! A few moonlight kisses—a few declarations born of the moment? Do you imagine that you are the only man to have used me so?"

His breath was sharp drawn, his voice colder than the night around them. "Yes—like a fool, I rather thought I was." He gave a mirthless laugh. "Well! It seems nothing will be served by further argument!" He was taking her arm like a stranger, turning her in the direction of the waiting carriages. "Permit me to see you to your coach."

She offered no resistance. At least my purpose is achieved, she thought dully, for he now despises me so thoroughly that he will turn to Elyse with nothing but relief!

❦CHAPTER 20❦

Clementina had never been so wretched! She passed a sleepless night, and with Suzy's birthday on the following day and Aunt Seraphina's abduction planned for the day after, she was not even allowed a respite in which to indulge her misery, for if her aunt was vouchsafed the slightest suspicion that all was not well, nothing would induce her to leave Clementina's side.

The answer was to keep busy, so busy that there was no time to think. Suzy's party was to be in the afternoon, so in the morning she chivvied her aunt into visiting Madame Vestris's salon on the pretext of wishing for her advice upon the choice of a new gown.

"But you don't usually find it necessary to consult me, dear," said Mrs. Westbury. "And you always look very nice."

"Well, this time I *do* want you." Clementina searched for a reason. "Justine was saying only last evening that the flounce on my ivory silk was grown positively dingy and as that was ever your favorite dress, I want you to help me choose its replacement."

This explanation seemed to satisfy Mrs. Westbury, who dutifully donned her bonnet, though she had been half-expecting a visit from Etienne. In the modiste's elegant salon Clementina made a great show of choosing the new gown before observing quite casually that it was an age since her aunt had purchased so much as a spencer. A gently implanted suggestion that such skimping was all very well, but that the Duc might be pleaseed to behold her in ". . . say, this braided pelisse of soft gray velveteen?" was sufficient to rouse her interest.

"And by the greatest good fortune, dearest, I happen to know that Clothilde has just the hat to complement it, for I saw it not two days since—a neat little gray velour toque with three curling plumes of the palest pink! Really, the way that child has come on is quite astonishing! I have but to persuade the Duchesse de Berry to patronize her and she will be *made!* How Monsieur Guillard will preen! Now, what do you say to the pelisse, love?"

The matter was clinched, such an ensemble being much too pretty to be resisted; from there it was a relatively simple matter to persuade her aunt to add a gown of creamy lace— just perfect, had she but known it, for a wedding. Several other items joined these purchases, unnoticed by Mrs. Westbury, and Clementina returned home well pleased.

Suzy's birthday party, too, was a great success. Pale with excitement, the little girl performed her solo to music provided by the small band of players hired by Clementina for the occasion and was enthusiastically applauded by an admiring audience. Thereafter, she was partnered in turn by a succession of the most handsome gentlemen of her acquaintance, of whom her Monsieur Dominic held pride of place.

Halfway through the afternoon, Clementina's coach, which had departed unnoticed, returned, and out stepped Maurice followed by several of his minions bringing a birthday feast fit for a princess, which they proceeded to lay out at the lakeside with due solemnity. Last of all came Monsieur Clichet himself—a signal honor—bearing his piece de resistance, which he would entrust to no other; not a birthday cake, but rather a superbly castellated confection fashioned of nougat and fruits and cream, to delight any little girl's heart. It was greeted by a spontaneous outburst of cheering.

The seal was set upon a perfect birthday when, as often happened, the King's coach entered the Bois driven at its usual breakneck pace. At the Petit Lac it stopped to afford His Majesty a view of the festivities. A message was conveyed to the company requesting that they continue their celebrations without regard to his being there and when he heard of the birthday, commanded that Suzy should be brought to him. Clementina gave the hand nervously thrust into hers an encouraging squeeze and walked with her to the coach to present her to the immensely fat, jolly gentleman who chuckled heartily into his several chins at the awed child's deep curtsy, wished her *"bon anniversaire,"* and presented her with a tiny gold fob from the chain about his waistcoat.

And in all the afternoon's excitements, only Alexei, ever watchful, noticed how taut were the lines about his good friend Dominic's face; how Clementina laughed a great deal and was much too bright; and how, not once during the whole afternoon, did either address one word to the other.

He said nothing at the time, but the evening brought yet another ball and Clementina was there, her energies seemingly undiminished. She was like a firefly, he thought—never still; her red curls bobbing at the center of first one group and then another until it began to dawn upon him that she was quite probably avoiding him. So? There *was* something, and she did not wish him to probe, which meant that it was no light matter. Well, he would await his moment. It came at the end of an extremely energetic shottishe; she left the ballroom floor with her partner, still laughing and breathless, and walked straight into his arms. There was no escape.

"That was careless of you, *dushka!*" he said, and there was no mistaking his meaning. He took her arm so that she should not slip away. "You are ready for a few moments' respite, I think." He was edging her toward the door, making conversation.

"But I am promised to young James Gallatin for the next dance," she protested, hanging back. For so amiable a creature, he was for once surprisingly obdurate.

The color left her face, leaving it almost transparent. "Please Alexei!" she pleaded in a low voice. "Not now! I don't want to . . . to talk about anything tonight!"

They had reached a door leading to a conservatory. It was peaceful inside, a dim haven smelling of earth and greenery, and somewhere close by, water was playing.

"See—here is a bench." They sat in silence for some minutes, Clementina tense at his side. "Sometimes," he said, "it is better to talk than to churn oneself up inside."

She sighed. "You know, don't you?"

He shrugged. "I *know* nothing, *dushka*, but when two of my dearest friends do not speak to one another, it does not require genius to divine that all is not well."

Her bleak explanation revealed much that had puzzled him about her relationship with Dominic.

"You did not feel that you could speak to him of Elyse?"

"Oh, no!" She turned to him in alarm. "And I beg that you won't, either. I will *not* be the cause of an estrangement between them—for the child's sake as well as hers."

"But if Dominic is in love with you, surely a break is inevitable?"

"Not," she said steadily, "if he believes, as he does, that I am indifferent."

He looked thunderstruck. "But . . . you plainly are not indifferent to him! I am well versed in such matters and I *know* . . . I tell you . . . you cannot do this thing to Dominic!"

"Let me do it my way, Alexei—*please!*" This time her voice was less steady and the smile she gave him was charged with irony. "You see, unlike you, I doubt that my cousin's affections *are* irrevocably engaged, for he finds my character sadly flawed."

Alexei peered in distress at the hastily averted profile. "You are wrong to act this way, Clementina." The chin remained set. He shrugged. "But the decision is not for me. I will say nothing to Dominic if this is what you wish."

Alexei did not find this promise any strain, for Dominic was to leave Paris with Fabian Pengallan to visit friends near Orleans, and before he returned, much could happen. He had not, after all, given his word to not tell anyone else—and there was an idea he had in mind to try . . .

That same morning found the house in the Rue de Varenne buzzing with intrigue. Clementina was up betimes checking over with Justine the two portmanteaux that the maid had packed on the previous evening while her aunt was at the Opera; into the folds of the lace dress where her aunt would be sure to find it, she tucked the letter she had penned far into the night with much lip chewing in an effort to hold back tears that rendered more than one attempt useless. Such weakness annoyed her; she must—she *did*—wish her aunt happy with all her heart! It should not be cause for tears.

Maurice was by now in the conspiracy; it was for him to arrange that the portmanteaux were stowed away out of sight in the Duc's traveling coach when he arrived. The majordomo was highly entertained by this latest stroke of ingenuity on the part of his mistress and it being something that he could wholeheartedly approve, he threw himself into the deception with great enthusiasm.

Patrick came to breakfast in his dressing robe and yawned his way through several slices of ham in a manner that prompted a gentle reproach from his aunt that he had much better have stayed in bed.

"Don't tell me, Auntie. It's all Joshua's fault . . . the silly clunch shook me awake at an unconscionable hour! Dicked in the nob, I shouldn't wonder! All this jauntering around he's doing!"

Clementina in a bid to quell the argument said that she

had instructed Joshua to rouse him. "For you are becoming a dreadful sluggard, brother dear—out all night and asleep most of the day!"

The only reply to this being another gigantic yawn, she was left to hope that Joshua would get Patrick dressed and downstairs again before the Duc arrived.

Monsieur de Menton came at last, looking exceedingly smart, a trace of nerves visible to Clementina in the extra formality with which he doffed his curly-brimmed beaver hat to reveal his white hair immaculately groomed and pomaded to rival the mother of pearl buttons on his greatcoat.

"I thought, madame—a drive?" he ventured, clearing his throat and casting a glance of sheer panic at Clementina. "Though the day is cold, the sun is very pleasant."

"There!" cried Clementina, rising from her chair near the window and advancing upon her aunt. "I knew I was right to tempt you with that new pelisse yesterday. It is the very thing for you to wear!"

All unsuspecting, Mrs. Westbury donned the new outfit, blushed very prettily when everyone agreed that she looked most delightful, so complete in her own happiness that Justine's extra fussiness and Maurice's more than usual ebullience scarcely registered. Even Clemmy's sudden fierce embrace as she was leaving she attributed to spontaneous pleasure in her appearance, though to be sure, it did seem a trifle odd when a bewildered Patrick, appearing again at the last moment, was exorted by his sister to bid her goodbye.

It seemed deuced odd to Patrick, also. He hardly waited for the door to close on the couple before he was demanding to know "What, in the name of Jupiter, was all that about?" And when Clemmy, who never cried, suddenly burst into tears, he owned himself utterly astonished.

"Such an idiotic thing to do when one is happy!" She mopped her eyes.

"Well! I do think you might have let me in on the secret!" he exclaimed when all was revealed.

"I would have done so, love, had I been sure that you wouldn't give the game away."

"Oh, I say! As if I would!" Patrick could not, however, sustain his indignation, which turned quickly to amusement. "It's a bit of a facer, though, isn't it? Fancy the old fellow carrying Aunt Seraphina off like that, on the sly!"

That seemed to be the general consensus of thought on the

elopement; Mrs. Bennett was round the moment she heard the news.

"My dear! I was *never* so . . . surprised." Clementina thought she had been about to say "shocked" and quickly changed her mind. "Your aunt, of all people! Whoever would have thought it!"

"But so romantic, don't you agree?"

"Oh . . . why, yes, I suppose it is . . . only, one doesn't expect . . . at our age!" She laughed, still obviously a little ill at ease.

"Precisely," said Clementina firmly. "I've always thought it most unfair that the young should have all the fun!"

Alexei agreed with her. The news enchanted him. "But I see your hand behind it, my dear Clementina. The Duc would never have dared out of his own volition. Such an idea requires vision and daring of a special kind to give it birth."

"Oh, dear! Am I *so* transparent?"

"Only to those who know you," He grinned. "Is that not so, Elyse?"

Elyse agreed, but seemed a little abstracted. They had come together, bringing Suzy to make her thanks for her beautiful birthday party, which she would never forget, not ever so long as she lived! Clementina had laughed kindly and had summoned Joshua to take the little girl down to the kitchens that she might thank Monsieur Clichet also—and perhaps be treated to one of Monsieur's special petit fours.

"And now," said Alexei, rising from his chair, "I am going to leave you ladies to converse a little—all the knick-knack-eries of bridals that seem of such importance, eh? I shall return for you, Elyse, in about one hour."

It appeared to Clementina that the words—and the look that went with them—held a special meaning. When he had left, there was a small silence. Elyse got up and wandered about the room, asking halting and inconsequential questions about the elopement, until Clementina, unable to bear the sight of her friend so ill at ease, said abruptly, "You don't really want to talk bridals do you?"

With a look of relief, Elyse crossed the salon quickly and sat beside Clementina on the sofa. "No, my dear. I want to talk about Dominic."

Clementina felt anger coursing through her. "Alexei has told you. He had no right . . . he promised!"

"No, no." Elyse was soothing her. "He said he would not

speak to *Dominic*. But I am very glad that he came to me . . ."

"He shouldn't have! He knew it was the thing I most wanted to avoid . . . involving you!"

She laughed. It was so totally unexpected a sound that Clementina stared. "Yes—and I love you for it! But I already knew, you see. At least I knew that Dominic was in love with you."

"How?"

"On the night of the Fête. He was so obviously happy that I guessed and so he told me."

That must have been when she had seen them talking together. "And you don't mind?"

Elyse was busy arranging the pleating in her dress. "To say that I don't mind would be absurd. Dominic has been marvelous to me since Paul died; he has become a part of my life and I shall miss him dreadfully, but we have never been in love, you see—and it has always been implicit in our relationship that if either of us met someone else, we should be honest about it."

She lifted her eyes to Clementina's and they were overly bright. "Oh, my dear! I am not just saying this to ease your conscience. I would have come to you anyway had not Dominic told me later that you had repulsed him. It is why I am so pleased that Alexei confided in me."

There was no doubt that she was telling the truth. "Oh, lord!" said Clementina. "I've made a sad botch of the whole thing, haven't I? It seems I manage other people's affairs so much better than my own."

"It is not too late." She smiled. "When Dominic returns, all can be set straight." The smile broadened. "And then there will be another wedding in your family!"

Clementina's heart leapt at the thought. Oh, how Dominic would roast her! When he had forgiven her. It never occurred to her for one moment that he would not. There was a slight droop to Elyse's shoulders, which straightened directly Clementina asked, "And what of you? And Suzy? She will take it hard, I think."

"Suzy is young," said Elyse resolutely. "As for me . . ." A faint smile came into her eyes. "That was something else Alexei wished to discuss with me. He seems to feel that he is eminently suited to take Dominic's place."

Clementina gasped, laughed, and said wonderingly, "Are you quite sure? It's an idea, certainly, but . . ."

"Oh, I shan't expect him to be faithful." The smile didn't waver. "But, you see, we neither of us want a permanent relationship, so it will answer splendidly and at least Alexei will always treat us with great kindness."

Clementina, with a curious lump in her throat, felt that she would never understand this—to her—peculiarly Parisian attitude, but "Oh, yes!" she said warmly. "And he is so devoted to Suzy!"

❧CHAPTER 21❧

The time dragged interminably as Clementina waited for Cadogon's return. She hadn't realized until now how completely he had become the pivot of her existence; how often she was used to confide in him, to enjoy hearing his opinion—even when scathing—of her doings, his soft laughter when their humors were in accord.

She missed Aunt Seraphina, too, though a letter had arrived very promptly, carried by the Duc's messenger—a letter so full of incoherent expressions of love, astonishment, joy, and gentle censure in almost equal measure as to convince Clementina of her undoubted happiness.

No need now, at any rate, to be considering the taking of a companion; all such tedious decisions could be left until Dominic's return. Instead she would devote her energies to the finding of a property suitable to house her girls and to the settling of final details with Reverend Mother. When Monsieur Marac wrote to inform her that he had seen just such a property in the Rue St. Jacques, they all went to inspect it and decided that it would do very well; thus all was set in train.

The social life of Paris, meanwhile, continued unabated; if anything its pace increased. "It is always so at this time of year," sighed Mrs. Bennett as Clementina discovered her, very pink faced, seeking refuge in a quiet alcove during yet another *sauterie*. "One begins to long for Lent. That at least brings a measure of respite."

Clementina laughed. "I know what you mean! Why I have hardly seen Patrick at all these past few days, and when I have, it's all secrecy! Several times I've caught sight of him with Alfred and some of the others, giggling in corners like children. I can't imagine what they're plotting! Do you know?"

"My dear, don't even ask! It will be to do with the Carnival . . ."

"Carnival?"

Mrs. Bennett leaned closer. "They sit half the night in that disreputable Maison Doreé planning it. Of course, one pretends that one knows nothing . . . and Mr. Bennett assures me that it is all perfectly harmless. A kind of final fling before Lent." Her voice sank to a confidential whisper. "But I know it involves Opera Dancers! They and the boys dress up in the most extraordinary costumes—last year, I believe, it was fruit—each one different, and they parade through the streets on a series of elaborately decorated carts. Of course," she added hastily, "I have never actually seen them myself, you understand!"

Clementina hid a smile, but thought that it sounded like fun.

At that very moment, in fact, the fun had reached the heights of riotous good humor in which all serious discussion had been abandoned in favor of a very different kind of close cooperation with their pretty accomplices. Patrick was by now much less innocent and being also a very handsome young man, was much in demand. He had perfected the delicate art of balancing one girl on his knee while another hung about his neck murmuring wickedly seductive suggestions in his ear.

"D'you recall a time, young Gallatin," Alfred enunciated carefully, "when that boy there was so damnably shy, I had to coax him to shake hands with Celestine?"

"Now look at him!" James agreed. "Disgraceful!"

Eugene Courtney wagged a finger. "He don't even have the grace to blush!"

Patrick grinned. "You're all jealous because you don't have my panache!" To whoops of mirth, he leaned back a little in his chair to kiss the luscious red lips pouting their invitation just above him.

As the laughter died, a voice was heard to remark with amused cynicism, "But then we all know that—as with his sister—Patrick's favors are easily enjoyed!"

In the ensuing silence the blood left Patrick's face; slowly he put the girls from him and walked to the next table where Gaston sat drinking with two of his friends. After a brief disagreement, they had hardly exchanged a word since the debacle at the Maison Jocelyn.

"Easy, Patrick!" Alfred, shocked into sobriety, was at his elbow. "Cursed fellow's probably foxed."

"That don't excuse paltry manners." Patrick leaned across the table, dogged with determination. "I want a good loud retraction of that remark, Rivas, or I ram it down your throat!"

Gaston lounged easily in his chair looking up at him, a faint smile playing round his lips. "If that is what you wish, *mon cher?*" He spread his hands in an elegant gesture. "But an apology will not alter the truth of the statement!"

Someone laughed nervously, the sound broken off as Patrick's fist crashed into that supercilious face. Gaston's chair fell backward and he with it. "Oh, lor!" muttered Alfred as Patrick waited grimly for him to struggle to his feet.

"You'll answer to me for that."

"By all means." Patrick's voice was unfamiliarly curt. "Alfred? I can call upon you to act for me?"

"Yes, of course."

Gaston wiped a trickle of blood from his mouth with an elegant wisp of cambric, picked up his hat and his cloak and, followed by his companions, strolled to the door. "Then my man will call upon Monsieur Bennett tomorrow to discuss the terms."

It was hardly to be supposed that the duel would long remain a secret; by the time Alfred came to call on the following morning with the arrangements all made, Clementina already had Dora prostrate with hysteria upon the sofa in the Grand Salon, having had the news quite casually from her brother over breakfast. Clementina herself was pale, but composed, as reason superceded shock, for she hadn't the least intention of allowing the duel to take place. That she was balked at every turn simply made her the more determined. Patrick, taking the whole thing in his stride, seemed to have grown to manhood overnight. At any other time his coolness would have filled her with pride; now she saw it as mere obduracy. To all her arguments he returned the same answer, that she must not interfere, and finally, out of self-defense, kept to his room.

Her first thoughts flew to Dominic, but he was not there, so she must shift for herself. When Alfred came downstairs from seeing her brother, she was waiting for him, but primed no doubt by Patrick, he proved almost as unhelpful, his fresh young face puckered with eagerness as he sought to justify what had happened.

"Nothing *to* be done, ma-am . . . arrangements all in hand. Your brother behaved very properly . . . invited Rivas to retract statements that, well, no gentleman would stand to hear his sister spoken of in that way!"

"God in Heaven!" she cried. "Do you suppose I give a jot if some ill-natured creature takes my name in vain? If that is all!"

"Not quite all, ma-am. Rivas proved insolent . . . Patrick planted him a facer. Capital hit, too! Drew his cork!" Pride in his friend's achievement warmed Alfred's recollections until, seeing Clementina's set face, he ended lamely, "No going back, now. Matter of honor, d'ye see?"

"All I see is a lot of silly posturing that is like to get Patrick killed!"

"Oh, no, Miss Brady, that's not the way of it at all! It ain't a *killing* matter, you understand? Quite simply, the aim is to nick your opponent. Honor satisfied on both sides. Matter closed."

Clementina's choked laugh rose and was abruptly curtailed. "How very reassuring! And if your aim should be just a little out?"

Alfred, feeling more and more unequal to the task of dealing with this emotional female approach to such matters, edged toward the door. "No fear of that," he said bracingly. "Both good shots. No cause to worry."

To Clementina's disgust, Alexei could offer little more in the way of practical advice.

"Bennett is right, you know. Duels are not uncommon amongst hot-headed young men, but there is a strict unwritten code governing such things and Gaston would not be such a fool as to risk disgrace by flouting it. And Bennett will be there to see fair play. I, also, if you wish it."

"Alexei, don't insult my intelligence by feeding me platitudes!" she said angrily. "Are you saying, in fact, that there is nothing I can do?"

"Short of getting Joshua to sit on Patrick's head or tie him to the bedpost, my dear—no." He saw the light come into her eyes. "And I do not advise that if you value your brother's good opinion. A young man's pride is a delicate bloom—easily bruised!"

"Oh, stuff! Better to live with injured pride than to die, surely? Oh, if only Dominic were here! He'd find a way!" She saw Alexei's eyebrow quirk. "Oh, my dear friend—I am sorry! I don't mean to be critical of *you*, but—you have *no* idea when he is coming back?"

"None at all, I fear." Alexei took her hands and squeezed them. "Listen, I will speak with Rivas. Perhaps he can be persuaded to withdraw, or at any rate, to delope. If not," he sounded optimistic, "that brother of yours is good with a pistol. I have seen him." He did not destroy the illusion by adding that Gaston Rivas was better.

Men! fumed Clementina, driving home at a pace that had Joshua clinging perilously to his seat; like children with their pride and their codes of honor! And so complacent, as if it were that easy to just nick a man and not mortally wound him. Well, *she* wouldn't boggle at sinking her pride if it would save Patrick; or even—here she caught her breath—or even if she risked incurring his everlasting disgust of her!

She entered the house in sober mood and found that Patrick had foiled her as yet vague plans—perhaps had even anticipated them—by moving out in her absence.

"He has left a note, mademoiselle," said Maurice, taking her pelisse and ushering her into her sanctum. "Oh, and another note has come also; a groom delivered it about one hour since. I have laid both here on your secretaire." With infinite tact, he did not allude directly to what had passed, but his dark liquid eyes mirrored so much sympathy that her voice grew husky as she thanked him.

Patrick's letter was brief, almost formal. It expressed a desire not to inflict the added pain of his presence upon her until tomorrow was over; assured her that she should have no cause for agitation as he was fully confident of the outcome, but gave no indication of where he had gone. Just at the end, however, his composure had cracked sufficiently to add a scrawled: *"God bless you, Clemmy. I do"*—heavily underscored—*"love you!"*

The paper fluttered to the desk as she stared blindly at the wall. She must find him, of course. Only gradually did she become aware of the other letter. She picked it up and turned it over in her hands before breaking open the wafer. It was very brief, no more than a dozen words, but they leapt off the page at her.

"If your brother is to survive his duel, you will need my help. Henri."

Without conscious thought, she summoned her carriage again and drove to the de Tourne residence in the Faubourg St. Honoré. Monsieur was not at home, the black-garbed servant informed her with an air of disinterest. No, it was not known when Monsieur would return. And when pressed still further upon mention of the letter, her need to speak to the Comte—"Monsieur le Comte is promised to Madame Duvrais's for this evening. Madame will no doubt find him there."

She was beginning to feel that the whole affair was some macabre charade; looking back as she left the courtyard, she saw the curtain at the first-floor window move slightly, the pale outline of a face. The Comtesse, no doubt, checking up on visitors.

Clementina did not care for Madame Duvrais. From an admittedly brief acquaintance, she judged her to be vain, pretentious, and stupid. In general, though not for want of asking, she avoided Madame's musical afternoons and soirées, finding them rather a venue for the exchange of tittle-tattle than any gathering to encourage musical appreciation.

Now she was obliged to endure an embarrassingly effusive welcome before allowing herself to be drawn into Madame's opulent salon, resolved in the wake of a depressing and abortive attempt to find Patrick to stay not a moment longer than it took her to do what she had come to do. In an atmosphere oppressive with heat and an ill-assorted mingling of perfumes, the daughter of the house was demonstrating her prowess upon the harp against a constant murmur of conversation. Had her performance been less execrable, Clementina might have pitied her the more, but now, preoccupied with the need to find Henri, it simply made her impatient. She scanned the room in growing alarm; he was not here! Waiting only for the polite patter of applause to signal the end of Mademoiselle Duvrais's interminable recital, she made her way into the adjoining room and, bumping into her hostess again, was driven to ask for him. The coy look that accompanied the assurance that, yes, Monsieur le Comte was certainly expected, made her feel quite ill.

She returned to the main salon, obliged to endure a pair of singers, a long tiresome verse reading, and a solo upon the pianoforte, all of equal mediocrity, before he finally arrived

with his mistress on his arm. Clementina had seen them together several times in the past weeks, though they had never
been driven into close proximity. He made no attempt to approach Clementina now, though their eyes met in the first
few seconds. She recalled his appallingly unfeeling treatment
of Rosa; no doubt he wished to exact from her, now, the hu-
miliation of having to ask him for help. Well, for Patrick's
sake, she would not shirk, however much the words might
choke her.

She made her way round the room and had almost reached
him when a familiar voice cried, "Why, Clementina! I had no
idea you were to be here!" It was Mrs. Worthington. She extended her arms in a swirl of purple draperies and jangling
bracelets. "You are just in time to hear my Alice perform!
No doubt you will remember how prettily she sings?" She
peered around Clementina's shoulder. "I suppose Prince Metlin isn't with you? I told him we were to be here . . ." a simper. "He is quite taken with Alice, you know!" Clementina
kept her patience under severe restraint as she regretted
Alexei's absence, exchanged pleasantries, and finally excused
herself.

"I had your note, Henri," she said without any prelimi-
naries, upon reaching his side.

Henri took his time. He made her an exaggerated leg and
looked her over, openly appreciative of the embroidered
Chinese robe she was in the habit of wearing whenever a
little extra confidence was called for. Too late she remembered it had ever been a favorite with him. Oh, well, let him
think she had worn it for him, if it would aid her cause!

At last, with supreme arrogance, he drew ' is mistress forward. "I think you have not met Madame St. Denis? Desirée,
this is the incomparable Miss Brady."

Clementina swallowed her natural inclinations and nodded.
The beauty gave her an appraising smile.

"You will sit here and be entertained, *ma chere*," Henri
commanded. "Miss Brady and I have something of importance to discuss." Desirée pouted enchantingly, but obeyed.

"Somewhere a little more private, I think." He took Clementina's arm and a buzz of speculative comment followed
them from the room. In a small antechamber furnished in execrable taste, Henri closed the door and stood with his back
to it.

"I ever liked you in that shade of cerise, my dear Clementina," he mused. "So provocative against the flame of your

hair—and so right. In general you have excellent taste; it is one of the things I most admire in you."

Impatiently she swung round. "Henri, what did you mean—about helping Patrick?"

With a contemptuous lack of manners he sprawled in a chair, one hand drumming lightly on a table at his side. Watching him, Clementina noticed what one didn't observe at a casual glance, the slight spasmodic twitch at the corner of his mouth, the indefinable feeling that the elegant facade was being preserved with an effort.

"It is remarkably simple, *cherie*. Gaston is my very good friend. I have but to use my influence and he will withdraw his challenge. Even though it may require more finesse to achieve, he might apologize."

"You really think you might persuade him?" Hope leapt so strongly in her that it superseded any other instinct. "Oh, Henri, would you try? I know things have been strained between us of recent times, but I would be *so* grateful!"

"Would you!" He drawled the words in a calculating, sardonic fashion and at once she knew what a fool she had been. Her heart began to thud. "How grateful, I wonder. How much do you *really* value that brother of yours?" He smiled a little as he saw how well she understood him. "Enough to reconsider your aversion to marrying me, perhaps?"

"Wouldn't an unwilling bride prove rather unsatisfactory?"

Henri's eyes narrowed. "An unwilling *rich* bride," he corrected her. "You see my finances have once more reached a critical state. I do not scruple to speak bluntly to you, my dear, your grasp of such matters is prodigious, as we are all aware. As for your unwillingness," He spread white fingers, examined them, and finally lifted his eyes to look her over. "I have a fancy—nay, a positive obsession—to bend you to my will."

"It would take a better man than you, Henri!"

She saw the angry flush and knew she mustn't antagonize him further. What he was suggesting was, of course, impossible. She loved Dominic. But Dominic wasn't here and Patrick was due to meet Henri's friend tomorrow morning.

"Gaston can hit the center of a playing card at twenty meters, did you know? I have myself seen him do so." He smiled again.

"And you planned the duel with this end in mind." It was not even a question.

"How well we understand one another. I told you at our last unfortunate meeting that the next time I should do things *my* way."

She knew she had no choice. "Very well," she said, "withdraw your man and I will do as you wish.'

Lord Cadogon and Mr. Pengallan had not gone very far on their journey when the road before them became so treacherous with ice that the horses skidded, plunging their coach into a ditch and snapping one of the shafts. There was little to be done but to unhitch the horses and abandon the coach to seek shelter, which they found in the guise of a small nearby inn. The proprietor assured them that at first light a man would be summoned from the nearby village to put right the damage and in the meantime it would be his pleasure to make the gentlemen as comfortable as his limited means would permit. As this proved to be very comfortable indeed, it was no hardship to rack up there for a night.

On the following day it began to snow. The man from the village duly arrived and muttered and exclaimed over the coach for several minutes before announcing that yes, he could assuredly replace the shaft, but it would take, perhaps, two days? Dominic, wanting only to put as much room as possible between himself and Paris, was less than pleased, but Mr. Pengallan, having discovered in the cellars a considerable quantity of a most excellent burgundy, was in no hurry to quit so promising a hostelry.

"This port ain't half bad, either," he sighed, having done full justice to a brace of pheasant the innkeeper's wife just happened to have had hanging in her kitchen. "I doubt we'll get as soft a one where we're going."

"It's well enough." Cadogon knew he sounded churlish. "I'm sorry, Fabian." He gave an abrupt little laugh. "I fear I'm devilish poor company."

"Think nothing of it, dear boy. Didn't like to ask. And you needn't say a word if you don't care to . . . I shan't take it amiss, y'know."

"There isn't anything *to* say except that I've come as close to making a damn fool of myself as I wish to contemplate." His Lordship replenished his glass. "And it does not sit well with me."

It was clear that he did not wish to elaborate further and Mr. Pengallan didn't press him. Sounds from beyond the door indicated the arrival of another traveler. When the land-lord came in presently he confirmed the fact.

"Monsieur was traveling from Paris on horseback and did not fancy to continue his journey on such a night."

The Marquis ran into their fellow guest on the stairs a short time later and discovering that they were slightly ac-quainted, they exchanged the usual pleasantries. It was only as the man made to go that he said, "Bad business about that young cousin of yours . . . the whole thing damned smokey if you ask me—seems to be little doubt but he was provoked . . ."

Mr. Pengallan was more than a little astonished when Ca-dogon presently returned to their private parlour clad in greatcoat and top boots and pulling on a pair of gauntlets.

Cadogon gave him a brief account of what he had been told. "The innkeeper is having a horse saddled for me. Don't wait up, Fabian—I have no idea when I'll be back."

Mr. Pengallan rose resignedly from a comfortable settle beside the roaring fire. "But, damnit, man—you can't go charging off to Paris in this weather! Seems to me you've pulled that lad's chestnuts out of the fire more often than kin-ship demands already. Besides, you know what these affairs are like! All a bubble, take my word on't. Like as not *you'll* get bogged down in some deuced snowdrift and arrive there to find them all eating a hearty breakfast!"

"I hope you may be right, Fabian, but I don't like Rivas—and I don't trust him."

It was very late when his flagging horse finally rattled over the Pont-Neuf and made the spectacular swing under the im-pressive facade of the Louvre. Reaching his *pied a terre,* he startled the concierge out of an uneasy doze as he ran up the stairs and, a few moments later, ran down again.

Gaston Rivas' apartment was in darkness, but repeated knocking finally brought him to the door. "*Dieu,* but you are impatient." He lifted the candle and saw Cadogon's face. "What, in the name of . . .?" he stammered and tried to shut the door again, but not quickly enough.

"This is an intrusion, monsieur!" He protested angrily as his unwelcome guest prodded him with his riding crop along the passage to a lighted room at the rear. "I must insist that you leave. I was on the point of retiring!"

"So that you will be fresh for the morning?" suggested Dominic softly. "Well, I have come to save you that trouble."

The swarthy countenance showed a flicker of fear, quickly

replaced by a natural arrogance. "There is nothing you can
do."

"Oh, but there is!" Dominic laid the slim box he had been
carrying down on the table and raised the lid. A particularly
fine pair of dueling pistols nestled therein. "You insulted a
lady who is nearly related to me, I believe."

"You are mad, monsieur. My quarrel is not with you."

Dominic lifted a casual hand and whipped the back of it
across Gaston's face. "It is now. And I regret I cannot wait
for the morning. We will settle now." He indicated the pistols. "They are loaded. The choice is yours!"

Gaston was truly frightened now. "You *are* mad," he cried.
"We cannot fight here! The lack of space . . . the noise . . ."

Dominic looked around, then removed his greatcoat.
"Nonsense. You have a good long room, if we push this table
back—" he did so and measured the number of paces. "I
know you prefer to display your skill over a greater distance,
but it will suffice. Come, now, I am waiting. Choose!"

As though he were in some bad dream from which he
would soon wake, Gaston picked up the pistols in turn, balancing them, selecting one. He turned in despair. "You don't
understand, monsieur, none of this is necessary . . ."

"Are you telling me that you didn't insult my cousin?"

"No, but . . ."

"Then kindly stop wasting my time. I have had a very long
day. I grant the circumstances are a little unusual, but if we
take our places at each end of the room and fire on a count
of three?' The Marquis was already moving to take his stance.
"You may count if you wish."

The dream was not going to go away. The young man,
faced with the inevitable, shrugged, confident that his skill,
especially at such close quarters, must be unsurpassable. He
walked quickly to his place—and called!

The explosion shattered the room; pain filled his shoulder
and upper arm, and his smoking pistol clattered to the floor.
The air cleared and he was astonished to see the Marquis apparently unmarked coming quickly across the room. He
helped Gaston to a chair.

"I do not understand how I missed you," Gaston said
faintly.

"You didn't entirely." The Marquis lifted his arm to show
a rent in his sleeve, his voice rueful. "Ruined a good coat—I
must be more tired than I thought." And then, abruptly, "Do
you have brandy?"

"In the cupboard." Gaston half rose, indicated the direction, and sank back. He gulped the brandy gratefully and some color came back to his ashen face. Cadogon was examining his wound, cleaning it, binding it up.

"You'll live," he said succinctly. "But you won't use a pistol again for a while." Doors were opening, voices raised in querulous angry demands for explanations. The Marquis picked up his greatcoat and shrugged himself into it, replaced the pistols in their box, and turned a cold, implacable eye upon the young man. "As soon as you feel able, I advise you to leave Town for a while . . . preferably before tomorrow morning. Should word reach me of any further insult to my cousin, I shall return and put a bullet through the other shoulder!"

❊CHAPTER 22❊

A freezing February-gray dawn hung over the Bois, its opacity dulling even the sharp crystals of ice that encrusted the trees and bushes. Clementina felt the chill oozing into the closed coach where she sat waiting with Alexei. They had arrived some time ago, driven by Joshua, who would not be left behind; he had positioned the coach well back among the trees where it would not be seen.

"Better that Patrick should not know you are here," Alexei said when all his attempts to dissuade her had failed. He might have saved his breath, for how could she not be there—not know what was happening? No one had seen Patrick since the previous day; even Alfred had proved remarkably evasive. One part of her wished desperately that he might have run away, but *that* wasn't in his nature, nor would she be content to have her dilemma resolved at such a cost. No. Once Patrick was safe, she would find a way. One thing was certain—she had not the least intention of marrying Henri; but nor did she feel any shame in allowing him to think that she would. If he could stoop to such shabby scheming, then so could she! For the present all that mattered was this morning's piece of work and its outcome.

Carriage wheels crunched over the hard uneven ground and Clementina leaned forward, her face pressed to the window, one hand straying involuntarily toward the door. "Easy!" Alexei's touch on her arm stayed her. She watched, stony faced, as the carriage stopped and Alfred jumped down, closely followed by Patrick. He was wearing his new olive-green greatcoat and looked remarkably self-possessed— even cheerful—for a young man so close to staring death in the face. She was *so* proud of him in that instant that her throat hurt with it.

Alfred reached into the carriage for an oblong box, laid it lovingly on the ground, and opened it. Each withdrew a pistol, Alfred talking earnestly all the time. Then they began to pace out the distance, to take up the required positions with Alfred still holding forth, demonstrating the advantage of standing sideways on with his arm tucked in. It was like watching a macabre rehearsal of what was to come.

More carriage wheels; a small closed black gig bounced across the clearing, veered round, and pulled up. Clementina couldn't bear to watch, but was unable to tear her glance away. Henri hadn't said how or when he would stop Gaston. Suppose something had gone wrong . . . that he hadn't been able to contact him . . . ?

"It is but the doctor, *dushka*." Alexei meant the words as a reassurance, but seeing her look of alarm, "A precaution only! I am confident that he will not be needed, for although I could not persuade Rivas to withdraw, I gained the distinct impression that with his temper cooling this little charade will be but a gesture." She clung to his hand.

If only Alexei knew! But he mustn't know. If he got even a hint of Henri's duplicity he would want to go dashing off to *do* something about it—something brave and impulsive and utterly stupid. And she was determined that, since this was her coil, brought about largely by her own vanity and bad judgment, she must work it out for herself.

The doctor, finding his services not yet required, had retired again to the comparative comfort of his gig, and the two young men were stamping about swinging their arms energetically in an attempt to stave off the biting cold.

Alexei took out his watch and grunted in some surprise. "It wants but two minutes to the hour. Too soon as yet, perhaps, to hope," he added hastily, seeing the light flare in her eyes.

"Still, one does not expect a man of Rivas' experience to show such tardiness!"

The wait was interminable. A rider appeared; not Gaston Rivas, but another young man vaguely familiar to Clementina. He reined in, dismounted, bowed punctiliously, and spoke excitedly and with many gestures for several minutes . . . bowed again, and then was riding back the way he had come. The doctor, having leaned out from his gig to hear what was being said, nodded as though he had heard it all before, and also departed in the rider's wake. The two boys were cavorting about like children, laughing and hugging one another.

It was over.

Joshua, sitting huddled in rugs and mufflers upon the box, let out a shout of joy and Clementina, like a spring released, was out of the carriage and running, slipping and sliding over the uneven ground to fling her arms about Patrick, heedless of his good-natured protests, brushing aside his astonishment at seeing her.

"Well, but how could I stay away?"

"Is it not famous, ma-am?" crowed the jubilant Alfred. "Our man didn't even show! He's gone—fled the town after some kind of commotion at his apartment, so his second, Monsieur Chard informed us! He was disgusted, I can tell you!"

"Scared to face me, that's about the size of it!" said Patrick with the smug superiority of one who has achieved a bloodless coup.

"As *you* should be scared to face me, wicked unfeeling boy!" Clementina reproved, unable quite to keep the joy of her relief from showing. "I searched the town for you yesterday! Wherever have you been?"

"At Clothilde's."

"Clothilde's? Well, really!"

Patrick grinned sheepishly. "That girl's a regular trump! Said it was the least she could do for the brother of her benefactress. Treated me like a prince!"

"I can imagine!" said Clementina dryly.

Joshua had brought the coach up now, beaming from ear to ear, and Alexei was able to add his congratulations to the rest, chuckling as he was told about Clothilde.

In all the excitement, no one noticed a lone horseman who had watched motionless from a distance and who now turned and rode quietly away.

"Well," said Clementina, "I think we had all better go back home to breakfast before we freeze."

A look passed between the two young men. "The thing is, Clemmy . . . we have a sort of breakfast all arranged, a crowd of us, you know . . . a kind of celebration." Patrick met his sister's incredulous gaze with a shamefaced half grin.

"Were you *so* sure?"

"Not *sure,* exactly." The grin widened. "But if one can't be optimistic, one might as easily blow one's own brains out and have done with it! Still," he offered in a hasty attempt to forestall her indignation, "if you're set on it, I could come home with you first."

In this reluctant attempt to placate, Clementina glimpsed the child he had been so short a time ago, and she laughed. "Oh, go along!" she said. "I wouldn't dream of spoiling your party!"

"I do not think you need worry yourself any longer about *that one!*" Alexei chuckled as the two departed.

"No." She sighed.

He gave her a quick, comprehending look and said in rallying tones, "I hope you mean to invite me to partake of this breakfast you spoke of?"

"But of course!" She clasped his hands warmly. "And I do thank you, my dear friend, for being my support."

"It has been my pleasure," he said in his droll way. "I would that it had been more, but all has worked out in the end."

The next few hours passed in an agony of uncertainty as Clementina wondered what Henri's next move would be. She picked her way through a breakfast supervised by an ebullient Maurice in a mood of abstraction that Alexie attributed rightly, but for the wrong reasons, to an excess of nerves, and afterward—rather than be left alone to await a possible visitation—she accompanied him on a series of calls culminating with one to the Elysée Palace, where the Duc quizzed her about her brother's recent exploits and the Duchesse begged her company for a proposed visit to the Opera later in the week.

It was as they were leaving the Palace that they encountered Henri. Alexei would have passed him by with a curt nod; he looked surprised when Clementina not only returned his greeting, but accepted with composure Henri's expressions of regret that a friend of his should have been the cause of so much distress to her family. The Comte's manner, which had been guarded at first, grew more confident.

"One can only assume that Gaston was in his cups, though that excuses nothing."

"You are aware, Monsieur le Comte," said Alexei with some satisfaction, "that your friend slunk away rather than meet Miss Brady's brother?"

Henri flushed, but continued smoothly, "I find such an explanation hard to accept, Metlin; though he was in no doubt of my displeasure, I had not thought him a coward. There must, I think, have been more to it than is immediately obvious." He looked at Clementina as he spoke and there was a curious inflection in his voice.

"That was a little odd," observed Alexei when the Comte had taken his leave. "I had thought we were no longer to be accounted worthy of notice! Why is it, I wonder, that I trust Monsieur le Comte the least when he is being affable?"

Clementina murmured that he was probably moved by the wish to disassociate himself from his friend's behavior, and hoped that Alexei would not pursue the argument. That he did not was solely due to the fact that he perceived the Worthington barouche approaching. By the time they had taken evasive action, the danger was past.

She saw Henri again that same evening at a ball with his mistress. When their paths crossed, he acknowledged her with a gracious bow, but conversed little beyond a polite enquiry about Patrick. As the evening wore on and he made no attempt to solicit her for a dance, the suspense became almost unendurable, ruining any pleasure she might otherwise have enjoyed. Also, the duel was everywhere discussed and she grew quite weary of agreeing that yes, it had been very worrying at the time, and no, Patrick was none the worse for the experience and it was certainly extraordinary that Monsieur Rivas should run away! There had been talk of strange happenings at his apartments, explosions, even.

Clementina sustained a lively performance but did not deceive her friends. Elyse suggested that she ought to retire early, "for it would not surprise me to learn that you scarcely closed your eyes last night, my dear, though I know you like to consider yourself so much stronger than the rest of us!" It was said with affection, but the words jarred suddenly.

"You're right," said Clementina curtly, ignoring the way Elyse's face puckered with distress. "I can't think why I came in the first place. No, I don't want Alexei to come with me. I am perfectly capable of going home alone!"

It was only then, as she waited for her carriage, that Henri was at her shoulder, his voice soft. "It is my intention to call upon you tomorrow morning," he said. "Be in, cherie!"

The untimeliness of her arrival home together with the manner of it left Maurice's eyes big with unanswered questions and prompted Justine to enquire sharply if Madame was unwell. The reply being equally sharp, she attended to Clementina's requirements in a silence that was palpable with the force of her grievance; the effect, however, was lost upon her mistress, who waited only to be helped out of her gown and into her negligée before dismissing the maid, saying that she would sit up for a while.

Clementina remained rigidly erect until the door had closed behind Justine and then, as she curled up in the big chair before the fire's glowing coals, her shoulders drooped. For the first time in her life she doubted her ability to cope; it had all grown much too complicated. If only Cadogon might return so that she could lay it all before him and admit, as she had never done in her life before—"Look, I've got myself into the most awful mess and I don't know how to get out of it!"

He would settle it all in a trice, of that she had no doubt. But how? By confronting Henri—perhaps fighting him? No, she couldn't go through all that again! There must be a better way, a way that would put no one she loved at risk.

The firelight was making her sleepy . . . she snuggled deeper into the chair . . . Of course, the simplest means of achieving her objective would be to leave Paris very suddenly, taking Patrick with her. But where would they go, always supposing he could be persuaded? London was too close and besides, Henri had friends there. They could, however, go home! She sat up, her mind clearing as everything fell into place. If Henri could be fended off for a few days, long enough for arrangements to be made, she could then manufacture a note from Mr. Gourley telling of some dire crisis that would necessitate their instant return to Baltimore. They would be gone before he even knew of it!

It would mean not seeing Dominic for a while, but she could leave a letter with Elyse declaring her love—she blushed at the thought—and surely he would come after her? This house, everything here in Paris, in fact, could go on as usual, for once she and Dominic were married, Henri would have to seek a rich wife elsewhere, and they would be able to return. Oh, it was going to need a lot of planning, but it would serve splendidly.

When Henri arrived on the following morning he found Clementina remarkably cheerful. She was brisk with him as she had been in the past and he was obliged to keep reminding himself that he now held all the cards.

"But you *do* see, Henri," she reasoned, "we must allow time in which to effect a convincing reconciliation? A day or two, at least. Only think how odd it must appear if you suddenly announce our betrothal when everyone knows we have been estranged this two months past. That is, unless you wish them to learn how it was that Gaston did not keep his appointment with Patrick."

Henri's eyes narrowed. "What do you mean? How much can *you* possibly know of what happened?"

"Very little," she said innocently. "But you know how people talk. I can well imagine that someone might come to hear of your intervention and conclude that you had jettisoned your friend's reputation to serve your own ends!"

She thought he seemed relieved, but there was little evidence of it as he came very close, taking her chin uncomfortably between thumb and finger and forcing it upward. "I am not at all sure that I trust you, Clementina. I do hope that you do not think to cross me! We have an agreement, you and I. I should not be pleased an' you reneged!"

"My dear Henri," she said coldly, suppressing a shudder and crossing her fingers behind her back with a swift plea sent heavenward that Grandpa Brady would forgive her. "You have my word—and the word of a Brady, let me tell you, is every bit as honorable as a de Tourne's." Moreso, she added silently, salving her conscience with the recollection of Henri's many deceits.

"Very well." He bent to kiss her mouth lingeringly; Clementina emptied her mind and let him. He released her with an admonitory tap on the cheek. "Until the end of the week. Not one day more. I can stave off my creditors a little longer. But we shall not linger over the betrothal, I promise you."

There was not much time. She went straight to Monsieur Marac, her lawyer, who agreed to locate a ship with all speed and arrange passage for them; and all with the utmost discretion, he promised, assured that he would be entrusted with the sole handling of her affairs in Paris until her return.

Meanwhile her life had to go on as usual, but there was a

lightness in her step now as her natural buoyancy of spirit asserted itself. Elyse would not allow that any apology was
called for; Clementina had been abrupt because she was tired
and worried—it was perfectly understandable. So they were
all friends again. Patrick's carnival was a huge success and
they went in a group to cheer him, laughing to see the boys,
discreetly masked and bewigged, in the full glory of ballet
skirts! It set the mood splendidly for a *sauterie* that Count
Pozzo di Borgo was to give at the Russian Embassy on the
following evening.

"I tell you—it will be quite something!" said Alexei with
enthusiasm. "Just you wait and see!"

The next morning a bandbox was delivered to Clementina.
Justine unwrapped it, exclaiming as she drew out the most
enchanting Russian peasant costume, its headdress set with
tiny seed pearls and colored stones—a gift from the Count
with the request that she wear it to the *sauterie*.

She arrived to find Princess Galitzin and Dora—and
Dora's young sister Kate, who was not strictly "out," but had
been permitted to attend—together with all the other unmar-
ried young ladies, wearing similar costume. Only Elyse was
missing; she had slipped that very morning stepping down
from her carriage and had sprained her ankle. But Alexei was
in his element, very attentive to her in a determined effort to
keep Henri away and murmuring in his cryptic way of great
surprises to come.

As with all Russian parties, the hospitality was prodigious,
the entertainment lavish, the atmosphere soon lapsing into
unbridled gaiety as everyone drank too much Russian punch.
A mock archery contest was held in which a rope of fresh
flowers was stretched across the ballroom, behind which the
competitors were required to stand and amid enthusiastic
"huzzas" of encouragement throw silver arrows at the targets
beyond, with extravagant prizes for the successful contestants.

The happiness was infectious; even Henri's presence could
not dispel it as Clementina, rigorously coached by Alexei,
danced the mazurka, wearing wrist bands decorated with tiny
jingling bells. Only one person was missing to complete her
evening's delight and, as though the mere thought had conjured him up, he was suddenly there in the doorway—Cadogon, as elegant as any man present and a hundred times
more dear to her, his eyes searching the room until they
found hers, smiling at her! The joy of seeing him lit up her

face and Henri, seeing that joy, turned to discover what had prompted it.

Anger filled him, and with the anger came an acute sense of danger as he recognized in the Marquis not just an interfering busybody, but rather the ultimate threat to his ambition. He had been a fool not to see it sooner. In an instant he was at Clementina's side and before she realized his intention, had seized her hand and was propelling her up to the dais in front of the orchestra. He put up his hand for silence and announced with all the de Tourne arrogance the news he had, he said, long waited to impart to them—"for Mademoiselle Brady has, this very evening, consented to be my wife!"

In the commotion that followed there was little hope of denying it. Hemmed in by the tide of bodies that surged forward to congratulate them, Clementina was vividly aware of Alexei standing back, his nice, ugly face creased in a kind of puzzled disappointment, of Patrick's look of outrage. But most of all, above the flutter of hands reaching up to her, she was aware of Dominic, as he turned abruptly on his heel and left the room, and of Henri murmuring in her ear so that only she could hear, "You see, cherie, it has suddenly become very clear to me why you have sought to put me off!"

❧CHAPTER 23❧

Clementina finally broke free of Henri's retaining clasp and made her excuses to the laughing, teasing crowd of well-wishers as she pushed her way through their ranks, the smile stiff on her lips. She parried Alexei's kindly inquisition and shrugged off Patrick's furious demands to know how she could even contemplate marrying that loose fish, knowing all she did of him! With promises to explain later, she ran from the ballroom, heedless of the impression she must be creating, past dimly lit alcoves where whispered words and soft laughter betrayed the presence of shadowy figures, close-coupled, who were oblivious of the drama being enacted around them, her eyes searching for that one familiar figure.

But he was nowhere to be seen. On the stairway she encountered Mr. Pengallan making his unhurried way up. He greeted her with his usual charm, which she brushed aside.

"Have you seen Lord Cadogon?" she urged without preamble.

Mr. Pengallan's sleepy eyes opened a little wider. "Just got back—been away together, y'know. Bit concerned about him, to tell the truth. Never known him to be such poor company . . . not one to throw a damper as a rule . . . something on his mind, perhaps?" He looked hopeful, but Clementina had no time for idle conversation.

"He was here—oh, just a few moments since. He . . . he left in rather a hurry."

"Ah, that's it, then. Thought it was Dominic's rig! Took the gates at a wicked pace . . . not his style at all!" Mr. Pengallan sounded faintly aggrieved, remembering. "Almost had the paint off my wheel! In a miff, was he?"

Clementina uttered a choked little laugh. "Yes, you could say so!" She looked back the way she had come and said impulsively, "Mr. Pengallan, would you do me a very great favor?"

"Anything, dear lady."

"I'm going home. Would you, *please*, not tell anyone you've seen me?"

Mr. Pengallan's glance had grown uncommonly keen. "Do better than that, ma-am. Shouldn't go alone. It will give me great pleasure to escort you."

Coming from anyone else, the suggestion would have met with instant resistance, but she found his gentle, kindly concern uncommonly soothing and her own company was not *so* desirable just at present. Her wrap was brought and soon they were driving through the quiet streets, she wrapped in her own misery, he making no attempt to jolly her out of it.

Only when they reached the Rue de Varenne and she roused herself to thank him and to apologize for being such poor company, did he say with diffidence, "I'm not all that bright, but—well, it's clear to me, ma-am, you ain't yourself, either. Couldn't get much out of Dominic, but if you'd care to unburden yourself . . ." He coughed delicately. "You can tell me to mind m'own business, of course . . ."

"Oh, my dear sir!" Clementina turned to him with a shaky laugh. "I would indeed like to tell someone, and I can't think of anyone I would rather confide in, but it is grown so complicated, I shouldn't know where to begin!"

"Tell you what, ma-am—suppose we get your coachman to just tool around for a little, and you go right back to the beginning. Best way. I shan't interrupt."

And so she did. She spoke of her initial resentment of Dominic and her growing dependence on him; of how flattered she had been by Henri's attentions until she realized that as well as being a fortune hunter, which she had not resented so much, he was also proud, unreliable, and shockingly ruthless. It was only when she came to the way in which he had used Gaston to secure her promise to marry him that Mr. Pengallan uttered more than the odd grunt.

"Hah!" he exclaimed involuntarily. "So Dominic was right! He reckoned all along that de Tourne was like to endanger your brother's life! Almost always right, is Dominic."

"But how could he know?"

"Remember that nasty accident—in the park?" And as she sat up abruptly, he said, "It wasn't an accident—horse was nobbled!"

"Oh, no! Are you certain?"

"Certain as maybe," said Mr. Pengallan. "Animal showed every sign of being interfered with—no explanation for it."

Clementina was thoroughly shaken. "But . . . why did Dominic not tell me?"

Mr. Pengallan cleared his throat in an embarrassed manner. "He thought you wouldn't take it kindly. No lasting harm done. Decided to watch and wait, if you see what I mean."

"Oh, yes, I *do* see. It is just what Dominic would do! What he has been doing ever since, in fact. Every time Patrick's tumbled into the briars, he has been there to pull him out." Clementina could have wept for her own ignorance and stupidity. "If only I hadn't allowed him to go off thinking I didn't care for him, he would have been able to save Patrick from this latest scrape and I wouldn't have been obliged to suffer Henri's odious intimidation; as things are now, he must be disgusted . . ." For a moment she couldn't continue; when she did it was with a mixture of anger and despair. "Mr. Pengallan, I must see Dominic! Make him understand what a terrible mistake it all is . . . even if," again she faltered, "even if he now finds that he utterly despises me, he must know that I am not *so* fickle!"

Her distress was largely lost on her companion, however, who was still pondering her earlier words.

"Of course, it is no more than I deserve!" she continued, feeling that no answer was to be expected. "I should have been content with my lot instead of trying to flirt with society! Vanity, Mr. Pengallan, is a terrible sin and I have been more than guilty of it!"

"Miss Brady," he said, and there was bewilderment in his voice. "Dominic *was* here—the duel, y'know. It was Dominic who stopped Gaston Rivas. Did you not know?" He told her as much as he knew. "He was moodier than ever when he returned and at the finish the repairs took so long and he grew so deuced restless that we decided to abandon the journey to Orleans and return to Paris."

Clementina's astonishment had turned to angry indignation: "Well really! I knew Henri was perfidious, but to allow me to think that he . . . Oh! I remember now how strange he was when we met afterward. I thought he was being cryptic because Alexei was with me, but now I see—he wasn't sure how much I knew! When I think of the sleep I've lost over than man, the agonies I have endured! Why, I had even arranged to go home just to avoid having to marry him!" She outlined to him the plans she had laid. Mr. Pengallan was unstinting in his admiration of her resourcefulness, but gave it as his opinion that such drastic measures could no longer be necessary.

"Dominic'll soon send this de Tourne fellow to the right-about, m'dear. I'll lay a monkey it's got him rattled already, just knowing that Dominic's back in town! Why else would he go off at half-cock, announcing betrothals and the like?"

"Yes, but in so doing he has given Lord Cadogon quite the wrong impression," Clementina reasoned, "and now he may not give a fig if I marry Henri or not . . ."

"Miss Brady," said Mr. Pengallan reproachfully, "I always took you for a woman of sense."

She apologized meekly for the lapse.

"Well, and so I should think. Never seen a man so smitten! Ye don't suppose he'd be going around hauling that youngster out of scrapes from pure cousinly benevolence, do you? That ain't his style at all!"

By now Clementina was glad of the darkness to hide her blushes. "But what if he decides to call Henri out? I couldn't bear to go through all that again!"

"Shouldn't think for one moment it'll come to that," Mr.

Pengallan consoled her, quite ruining the effect by adding cheerfully, "More likely to give him a good thrashing!"

Clementina arrived home at last to find her major-domo hovering in the hall in a state of suppressed agitation. "Ah, mademoiselle!" he cried. "At last you are come! There is a visitor awaiting you in the Grand Salon since a long time."

She frowned. "At this hour? No, I'm sorry, Maurice, I can't possibly see anyone now." And then, as the thought came to her, "There is nothing wrong? My aunt . . ."

"No, no, mademoiselle!" He heaved a great sigh. "Only it is the Marquis, your cousin, and he will not go away until he has seen you!"

These last words were addressed to her back, for she was already running up the stairs, her wrap slipping unheeded from her shoulders; across the gallery she ran to fling open the salon door. Cadogon was standing before the nearer of the two fireplaces, his head bowed in contemplation of the flames.

He turned at the sound and his face was set in that inscrutable mask she now knew so well. With her back to the closed door and her heart beating right up in her throat, she stood like any tongue-tied schoolroom miss overcome with shyness.

"You are about to lose that delightful headdress," he observed in his soft, clipped way.

The sound of his voice released her. She straightened up, removed the headdress, tossed it onto a nearby chair, and ran fingers through her hair in a familiar gesture. He raised one quizzical eyebrow.

"I'm sorry," she said and there was an incongruous politeness in the words. "I hope you haven't been waiting too long."

"I have, but no matter. I have come, my dear Clementina, in order that you may tell me in your own words what the devil you are playing at!"

She opened her mouth to protest, acknowledged the futility of trying to explain, and said instead, "As a matter of fact, I have just been for a long drive with your nice Mr. Pengallan. We . . . we had a most interesting and fruitful talk!"

"The deuce you did! I make you my apologies, ma-am—I had supposed you had been celebrating your betrothal. Instead I find you adding yet another gentleman to your collection!" Clementina winced at the cutting sarcasm. "And what did *my nice Mr. Pengallan* have to say that was of such earth-shattering import that he must needs keep you out half the night?"

"Stop it! Stop being so damnably cynical!" Oh, this was awful! In a moment she would have lost all dignity and be screaming at him like a fishwife! She was doing her best to conciliate him and he wasn't helping her at all! She lifted her chin, biting her lip to stop it from trembling, and her bright brown eyes, still dilated from being so long in the darkness, shone fiercely black beneath their straight black brows. "He was obviously *quite* mistaken, for he seemed to hold the notion that you would be only too willing to straighten out my tangled affairs and . . . and deal with Henri . . . and indeed—" the words were beginning to choke her aching throat as she cast the last of her pride to the winds "—and indeed, *my dear cousin,* I would be more than happy if you will only consent to do so, for in truth they have grown so very involved and *I* am grown so tired of having to contrive . . ." His face was splintering into fragments of light, but not before she had seen the softening of his expression.

"Oh, good God!" he exclaimed with rough gentleness and stepped forward, holding out his arms. "Come here, my poor, dear, *idiotic* love!"

She went willingly and was folded in an embrace so all enveloping, so wholly satisfying, that she had no desire for it ever to end.

"If you hadn't been such a gudgeon," he murmured lovingly much later, "there would be nothing to untangle."

Her reply was hiccuped incoherently into the folds of his tear-drenched superfine lapels. He i d t ' ruin with equanimity and thrust a handkerchief into her groping hand.

"I never cry!" she asserted defiantly, blowing her nose with a prosaic thoroughness.

"I'm sure you don't," he agreed.

She looked up to meet his gently ironic smile and sighed. "I know you think me managing, but indeed, I did *mean* it all for the best!"

"I know. Elyse told me." He kissed her with satisfying thoroughness. "And *you* are the one who has so often taunted *me* with being noble!"

"That isn't the same thing at all!"

The door opened without ceremony and Patrick, still flushed with anger, strode in, checked upon seeing his cousin, and came forward saying, "Oh, are you back, sir?" and then, overcome by the full measure of his grievance, "I suppose you will not have heard my sister's latest news? I think she's gone queer in her attic! Honestly Clemmy, of all the clunch-headed pieces of work! I tell you now, you'd better not expect me to be civil to that fellow for it turns my bile just thinking of you with him after all he's done!"

"That will do, Patrick!" said the Marquis curtly, seeing his beloved's expression. "Your sister has been through a great deal on your account—at the very least you might show her a little consideration."

"Oh, no!" cried Clementina. "Patrick mustn't feel he owes me anything."

"Good. Because I don't see why I should, either!" retorted her aggrieved brother. "In fact, I'm getting a little tired of everyone trying to manage my life for me. I hope I've proved that I am quite well able to shift for myself," he flushed at the quizzically raised eyebrow, "and I certainly don't see how I can be held responsible for this engagement of Clemmy's . . ."

"What a monstrously ungrateful boy you are," said Cadogon mildly. "Also ill informed. Clementina hasn't the slightest intention of marrying Henri de Tourne, as I shall have the pleasure of informing him tomorrow."

"Well, that's more like it!" said Patrick, somewhat mollified. "I'd a mind to tell him so myself only he looked as mad as fire after Clemmy ran off. Anyway," he added with visible relief, "it'll come better from you, cousin Dominic. It's a jolly good thing you arrived home when you did!"

Clementina and Cadogon exchanged a speaking smile, but he could see that she was looking suddenly weary.

"Go to bed, now, both of you," he said. "The rest will wait until morning." He lifted her hand to his lips with so much warmth of regard that Patrick's attention was caught.

When the Marquis had gone, he grinned at his sister. "So that's to be the way of it!" he said.

She looked more flustered than he was wont to see her. "Shall you mind?"

"Not a bit of it!" He gave her a brotherly peck. "Splendid notion! Can't think what's taken you so long!"

Clementina slept dreamlessly and woke to a feeling of joy that she could not at first define. By the time Justine was bringing her hot chocolate, she was wide awake and quite unable to settle; and Justine, being cognizant, in that mysterious fashion known only to an exemplary lady's maid, of the exact state of her mistress's affairs, remained surprisingly placid when Clementina displayed an unusual degree of indecision in the matter of her toilette, changing her mind at least six times before choosing a favorite dress in amber twilled silk that had a matching cloak edged with chinchilla.

If she took an early breakfast there would just be time to visit Elyse before Dominic arrived. She had promised to go anyway, to tell her about the Count's party, but now more than ever she wanted to see her, to be the first to assure her that all was now well between herself and Dominic. The thought filled her with happiness. When a note arrived from Elyse begging her to be early, the matter was quite decided.

There was hardly a soul abroad as she drove along the Champs Elysées and into quieter streets with Joshua hunched into a heavy greatcoat, his hat pulled well down to meet his muffler so that only his eyes, large and round, peered out with disenchantment upon the cold white world touched magically to gold here and there by the rays of an orange sun.

Clementina took little notice of an advancing horseman until he rode deliberately across her path, forcing her to a halt. Joshua called out something she didn't hear, and at the same moment she recognized the maquereau of whom she had made such an enemy. A small frisson of fear moved up into her scalp, but her voice was calm as she called to Joshua. There was no answer.

The man was dismounting as two others rode from behind the carriage; they nodded. The one whom they called César smiled. "Your Black has met with a small accident, it seems!"

Clementina's concern at that moment was almost entirely for Joshua. Only as she attempted to step down did the full significance of her own position come home to her. César's horse was already being led away and he was pushing his way up to stand, legs astride, looming over her, still smiling unpleasantly.

"Get out!" she said and reached for the driving whip. He brushed her hand away and struck her, backhanded, across the face, the knotted hardness of a ring inside his leather gauntlet making grinding contact with her cheekbone. She gasped; her fingers probed the spot gingerly, showing a trace of blood on the ivory kid of her glove.

She looked full into the piggy eyes, pitiless in a florid, overindulged face, and her taut voice showed nothing of the very real terror she was feeling.

"Does hitting a lady make you feel a fine, strong fellow?"

He smirked. "When *you* are the lady, it gives to me a particular satisfaction. So, from this moment I advise extreme politeness!"

He could have no idea how wholeheartedly she endorsed his advice. He was sitting beside her now, smelling disagreeably of stale scent, taking up the reins, setting the cabriolet in motion. As he turned the equipage round she leaned forward to see Joshua in a frighteningly limp heap at the roadside.

Her breath caught and the man said unfeelingly, "It is no more than your fancy gallant did to me! I daresay that one will live—Negroes have hard heads, I'm told."

How long would it be, she wondered, before anyone became sufficiently concerned to raise the alarm. Too long to be of any help at all events, so there was little doubt in her mind that she was destined for the fate that had befallen Rosa. He had never given the impression of being a man who would be open to reasoned argument, but her position was already so hopeless that anything was worth a try.

"You are being very foolish, you know!" she said with as much calmness as she could muster. "You had much better release me now, before any real harm is done."

His laugh wasn't encouraging. "Afraid, are you? Well, I'll not deny I would enjoy to see you pleasured by certain of my clients, but I have no doubt you will be as well schooled where you are going!"

The streets were strange to her and soon it became clear that they were leaving the city altogether. A terrible suspicion began to grow in her mind.

"Where *are* we going?" she demanded.

"You will see."

There were trees now, a whole forest of them, and soon they were turning off the road, up a long, curving driveway and at the end of it, a small square-built house.

She was hustled down, the door opened and closed again behind her. Another door opened at the end of the hall and she had no difficulty at all in recognizing the man who stood with his back to the light.

"Henri!" she demanded furiously. "What is the meaning of this? Have you taken leave of your senses?"

🏵CHAPTER 24🏵

The Marquis, arriving on the stroke of eleven, was informed by Maurice that Miss Brady had gone to visit Madame Robart, but that he had been expecting her back any time this past half hour. As he had just come from seeing Elyse, who had been awaiting a visit from Clementina, he felt the first stirrings of unease. Further prompting brought mention of the note. It was searched for but could not be found.

"Did Miss Brady go alone?"

"No, monsieur." The major-domo's bright eyes were troubled. "The young black boy was with her. He would not permit anyone to harm her, I think." He hesitated. "Could they have met with an accident, perhaps?"

"I don't know. But I'm going straight back to Madame Robart's. If Miss Brady returns, send word to me there at once."

He found all in uproar at Elyse's. Alexei had arrived in his absence, followed shortly after by Joshua in a very distressed condition. The little he could tell them, though incoherent, was sufficient to fill them all with alarm. The doctor was sent for to attend to the massive lump on Joshua's head, but no amount of gentle reassurance from Elyse that he was in no way to blame for what had happened would console the boy, who sat rocking himself back and forth, muttering about his "Miss Clemmy"—and who was to care for him if she didn't come back!

"We'll get your Miss Clemmy back for you, Joshua," said Cadogon and sent him off with the maid to await the doctor.

"So how do we begin, my friend?" Alexei was grim. "Look for the pimp? He had grudge enough."

"I think not."

"You know where she is, Dominic?" Hope flickered in Elyse's eyes. It wasn't that certain, he said, and asked her about the note. She was most emphatic that she hadn't sent one. "There was no need. I was expecting Clementina anyway."

242

"She may have mentioned as much last night," said Alexei, looking from one to the other. "But someone wished to make sure—someone," he added and there was a quickening in his voice, "who was exceedingly angry when she ran from him last night!"

"Henri?" said Elyse doubtfully. "Oh, but he wouldn't, surely?"

"Oh, but he would!" said Cadogon.

In the Faubourg St. Honoré he met with the blank unhelpfulness of the servants.

The Comte was not home.

Then he would see the Comtesse.

Madame did not receive in the mornings.

"She will see me," said Cadogon in the tone that brooked no argument.

After an interminable wait, he was shown up to the dowager's apartments. She sat amidst the ornate trappings of a lost world, a black-clad figure, cold, unapproachable.

"You wish for my son. I cannot help you."

"Oh, I hope you can, madame—or I shall be obliged to broadcast to the world that Monsieur le Comte has caused Miss Brady to be abducted."

"That woman!" The Comtesse sat rigidly erect, drumming her fist upon the chair arm with every word. "She has caused nothing but trouble for my Henri!"

"The Comte makes his own troubles, madame."

She ignored him, speaking half to herself. "Miss Brady has flouted convention from the moment she arrived in Paris. If she now comes to her reckoning, it is no more than she deserves!"

"And if I do not find her, very quickly, your son will come to *his* reckoning and I shall make the name of de Tourne despised throughout the whole of Paris! Is that what you wish, madame?"

For the first time she hesitated, fingering the heavy gold locket lying ostentatiously at her breast. "Henri has a shooting lodge at St. Germain," she said, without meeting his eyes. "Of all places, it is the most likely."

As he was leaving, she said, the words almost torn from her, "Monsieur—I beg that you will not harm my son!"

Cadogon's voice was harsh. "That, madame, depends upon circumstance."

Alexei would not let him go alone—"for you do not know, my friend, what you must face!"

They found the lodge without much trouble, but at first glance it looked deserted. A persistent hammering on the door, however, brought the sound of feet. The door opened a crack and was instantly slammed back against the wall. César's protests died at the sight of Alexei's pistol aimed unwaveringly at his stomach.

"Which room?" barked Cadogon.

He shrugged and indicated.

Cadogon burst into the room, his usual calm deserting him. He stopped short. It was a gloomy room full of heavy dark furniture, but there was light enough to see Henri de Tourne lounging in a chair beside a sullenly flickering fire and Clementina's cloak discarded in a heap on the floor. Clementina herself, with her back to him and her skirt raised, seemed to be in the very act of disrobing. She looked round and saw him, and her face lit up.

"Dominic! You have found me! How very clever of you!" She let go her skirt, the petticoat dropped to the ground, and she stepped out of it and came toward him, her hands outstretched. "Oh, my dear love, you can have no idea how very pleased I am to see you! It was all becoming dreadfully difficult again!"

Only as he caught her to him did Cadogon see her face. "My God! Did he do that to you?" He put her from him and strode across the room, his mouth clamped tight with fury. "Get up, de Tourne!"

"No, no—it was César," she tried to explain, but he wasn't listening.

The Comte had made no attempt to move. "Get up," Cadogon repeated softly, advancing upon him. "Or, by God, I'll kill you where you sit!"

Clementina caught at his arm. "Dominic, do stop shouting at poor Henri! He isn't feeling at all the thing. And anyway, you can't possibly fight him now because . . ." she met the disbelieving eyes of her speechless love in rueful apology, "you see, I'm afraid I stabbed him—oh, not intentionally! In fact, it wouldn't have happened at all if he hadn't behaved so abominably! But the sight of blood makes Henri dreadfully queasy and although it's only a flesh wound, it is quite deep and I can't stop the bleeding."

Understandably, Cadogon was by now both speechless and bewildered. He saw upon looking closer that Henri was indeed very pale and that there was a dark stain spreading, even as he watched, across the elegant striped kerseymere waistcoat. He brushed it aside to take a look and then let it fall back.

Henri looked up at him, his eyes unnaturally bright. "Does the sight give you pleasure, monsieur?" he said gratingly.

"Of course it doesn't. Dominic isn't *so* unfeeling!" Clementina's tone was bracing. She picked up her petticoat and began to rip off the flounce. "I couldn't find anything else to use," she explained, coming to sit on the arm of Henri's chair, folding the material into a pad. "And I didn't want that awful creature out there to know what had happened. What have you done with him, by the way?"

"I sincerely trust that Alexei has dealt with him."

She looked up. "Oh, is Alexei here, too? Good—because I would really like some water—it should be washed, don't you think?" she said, moving aside the waistcoat and exposing the wound, which was a little above and to the side of the waist and oozing blood steadily. Henri winced as she laid the pad over it. "The dagger was a rather old, dirty one I took from the wall. And I'm sure he would be more comfortable if we got him out of his coat and laid him on that sofa."

"I'm damned if I'll lift a finger to help him!" exploded the Marquis.

"And I will be damned an' I permit you!" gasped the Comte.

"Oh, for heaven's sake!" declared Clementina. "This is no time to be striking attitudes!"

Cadogon gave his love a look of pure exasperation and, with another quick glance at the Comte, bowed to the inevitable. He strode to the door and called to Alexei to bring a bowl of water—for the Comte's wound.

Alexei came quickly. "You have dealt with him?"

"Not I!" Cadogon's extreme dryness caused Alexei's eyebrows to arch.

"Clementina?" he murmured, and grinned. "But of course! One should have guessed!"

Under protest Henri was stripped of his coat, moved to the sofa, bathed and bandaged. At the end of it all he was paler still and took without argument the brandy poured by Alexei from a bottle on the ancient oak dresser in the corner.

"I have the other one trussed like a chicken," said Alexei, who was beginning to find a certain drollness in the situation. "There are, otherwise, only two old retainers. So, what do we do now?"

"For myself," said Cadogon, "I feel we have already more than exceeded our obligation."

"You may all go away and leave my son to me." It was the cold voice of the Comtesse. She stood in the doorway and they all turned to watch as she walked stiffly to the sofa, her face expressionless as she looked down at Henri lying white-faced beneath a thick dark rug.

"He is not as bad as he looks, madame," Clementina said impulsively. "Only he has lost rather a lot of blood."

Still expressionless, the dowager's eyes lifted to the disfiguring stains on Clementina's stylish dress and further, to her bruised face. No trace of sympathy betrayed itself. "Go away," she said again. "You have done enough."

"Nom de Dieu!" said Alexei comically. "Were it not for Miss Brady's excellent ministrations, your precious son might well have bled to death!"

"Were it not for Miss Brady," said the cold, implacable voice, "my son would not have come to this."

"Madame, I protest—you are insolent!"

"Leave it, Alexei," said Cadogon.

"It's all right, Alexei." Clementina laid a hand on his arm. "The Comtesse is understandably upset."

He shrugged.

There were sounds of commotion from behind the door. A familiar voice was raised. The doorway suddenly filled with people.

"I say, have we missed all the excitement?" enquired Patrick, taking in the scene with considerable interest, relieved to find his sister in one piece. He was followed less exuberantly by Alfred, with Mr. Pengallan bringing up the rear in his calm, indolent fashion.

"Thought you might be glad of some assistance," he explained with a gentle, apologetic smile. "See it wasn't called for." And then, with concern, "That's a nasty contusion beneath your eye, Miss Brady. I trust it ain't too distressingly painful?"

She thanked him very kindly and said she was sure it must look worse than it was. Patrick, examining it with closer, more brotherly interest, agreed with Alfred that she'd have a regular shiner by the morrow, and hoped, with a facetiousness that hid his very real concern, that her opponent had worse to show!

There followed a lively and exceedingly complicated explanation of how they all came together, which appeared to begin when Patrick rushed round to Madame Robart's upon hearing from Maurice that his sister was missing, and found Mr. Pengallan visiting there; and there was news of Joshua too, whom Clementina was relieved to hear was fast recovering. From then on, the account became rather garbled and in the middle of Patrick's description of how they had had the great good fortune to spot the dowager's coach leaving, Cadogon picked up Clementina's cloak from the floor where it still reposed and draped it about her shoulders.

"My apologies," he said, as Patrick paused for breath. "We are vastly obliged to you all for coming, but Clementina has suffered a most trying experience and I must take her away now. I'm sure you will understand. Alexei—" There was a gleam in his eyes. "May I trouble you to bring my cousin's carriage back to town?"

"It will be my pleasure," he said with an answering grin. "*Bonne Chance,* both of you!"

Clementina paused by the sofa. "I am sorry, madame. Henri," she said, "I hope you are soon recovered."

His mother ignored the gesture and Henri, for answer, looked past her to Cadogon. "I wish you joy of her," he said harshly and shut his eyes.

Clementina sighed, but was not allowed to brood. Indeed she was scarcely permitted time to make her farewells before she was ruthlessly hustled from the room, and the door had closed behind them. In the dim hallway she held back, protesting, half laughing. "Dominic—we can't just walk out like this—leaving poor Madame de Tourne to cope!"

"*Poor Madame?* After the way she has treated you?" Cadogon pulled her close.

"Oh, well." She leaned back a little to look into his eyes. "It is clear that Henri is all the world to her—and in there just now she suddenly looked so lost . . . and old!"

He kissed her bruised cheek very gently and fastened the hood of her cloak close about her face. "You're a funny girl!" he said. "Come along."

He took her arm and she came obediently.

"Where are we going?"

"To the Rue de Varenne for tonight," he said, "and first thing tomorrow morning to your aunt at Fontainebleau."

She looked surprised but pleased. "Of course it will be lovely to see Aunt Seraphina, but . . ."

"No *buts,* Clementina. We are going to Fontainebleau, so that the priest who so obligingly performed the marriage ceremony for your aunt and the Duc can do the same for us at the first possible moment."

"Oh!" She went very pink and said in a meek voice, "I was only going to ask what we should do about Patrick."

"The Devil take Patrick!" he said softly. "We have both spent more time than enough worrying about Patrick—and for small thanks! Hereafter, he can fend for himself—stay with Alfred—go back to America—fly to the moon, for all I care!" He urged her up into the curricle, wrapping her round with rugs. One hand he kept tightly in his as he looked up at her. "Only one thing now concerns me. I am not letting you out of my sight again until we are man and wife!"

"Might not that prove a little awkward?" she said on a gurgle of laughter.

Cadogon grinned. "Baggage!"

He climbed up beside her and was about to give his horses the office to start when she exclaimed: "Dominic—I have just had the most splendid idea! I can't think why it never occurred to me before!"

He paused, ribbons in hand, eyeing her with foreboding.

"We could marry Henri off to Alice Worthington! She is quite pretty and excessively rich . . . and her mama could hardly cavil at a Comte from one of France's oldest families . . ."

"Clementina!" threatened Cadogon with ominous calm.

"But don't you see . . . it would answer perfectly! Alice is very young and *very* biddable! The Comtesse would be able to mould her to her exact requirements! And besides, only think . . ."

He silenced her in the only possible way.

About the Author

Sheila Walsh lives with her husband in Southport, Lancashire, England, and is the mother of two daughters. She began to think seriously about writing when a local writers' club was formed. After experimenting with short stories and plays, she completed her first Regency novel, THE GOLDEN SONGBIRD, which subsequently won her an award presented by the Romantic Novelists' Association in 1974. This title, as well as her other Regencies, MADALENA, THE SERGEANT MAJOR'S DAUGHTER, and LORD GILMORE'S BRIDE, are available in Signet editions.

Recommended Regency Romances from SIGNET

Big Bestsellers from SIGNET

* Price slightly higher in Canada

Buy them at your local
bookstore or use coupon
on next page for ordering.

Big Bestsellers from SIGNET

- [ ] HAGGARD by Christopher Nicole. (#E9340—$2.50)
- [ ] THE PASSIONATE SAVAGE by Constance Gluyas.
  (#E9195—$2.50)*
- [ ] THE HOUSE ON TWYFORD STREET by Constance Gluyas.
  (#E8924—$2.25)*
- [ ] FLAME OF THE SOUTH by Constance Gluyas.
  (#E8648—$2.50)
- [ ] WOMAN OF FURY by Constance Gluvas. (#E8075—$2.25)*
- [ ] ROGUE'S MISTRESS by Constance Gluyas. (#E9695—$2.50)
- [ ] SAVAGE EDEN by Constance Gluyas. (#E9285—$2.50)
- [ ] WINE OF THE DREAMERS by Susannah Leigh.
  (#E9157—$2.95)
- [ ] GLYNDA by Susannah Leigh. (#E8548—$2.50)*
- [ ] THE RAGING WINDS OF HEAVEN by June Lund Shiplett.
  (#E9439—$2.50)
- [ ] REAP THE BITTER WINDS by June Lund Shiplett.
  (#E9517—$2.50)
- [ ] THE WILD STORMS OF HEAVEN by June Lund Shiplett.
  (#E9063—$2.50)*
- [ ] DEFY THE SAVAGE WINDS by June Lund Shiplett.
  (#E9337—$2.50)*
- [ ] SO WONDROUS FREE by Maryhelen Clague.
  (#E9047—$2.25)*
- [ ] SWEETWATER SAGA by Roxanne Dent. (#E8850—$2.25)*

* Price slightly higher in Canada
* Not available in Canada

Buy them at your local bookstore or use this convenient coupon for ordering.

THE NEW AMERICAN LIBRARY, INC.,
P.O. Box 999, Bergenfield, New Jersey 07621

Please send me the SIGNET BOOKS I have checked above. I am enclosing
$_____ (please add 50¢ to this order to cover postage and handling).
Send check or money order—no cash or C.O.D.'s. Prices and numbers are
subject to change without notice.

Name _____

Address _____

City_____ State_____ Zip Code_____
Allow 4-6 weeks for delivery.
This offer is subject to withdrawal without notice.